FAREWELL TO AFGHANISTAN

JACK WINDRUSH BOOK 10

MALCOLM ARCHIBALD

Copyright (C) 2021 Malcolm Archibald

Layout design and Copyright (C) 2021 by Next Chapter

Published 2021 by Next Chapter

Edited by Graham (Fading Street Services)

Cover art by Cover Mint

This book is a work of fiction. Names, characters, places, and incidents are the product of the author's imagination or are used fictitiously. Any resemblance to actual events, locales, or persons, living or dead, is purely coincidental.

All rights reserved. No part of this book may be reproduced or transmitted in any form or by any means, electronic or mechanical, including photocopying, recording, or by any information storage and retrieval system, without the author's permission.

For Cathy

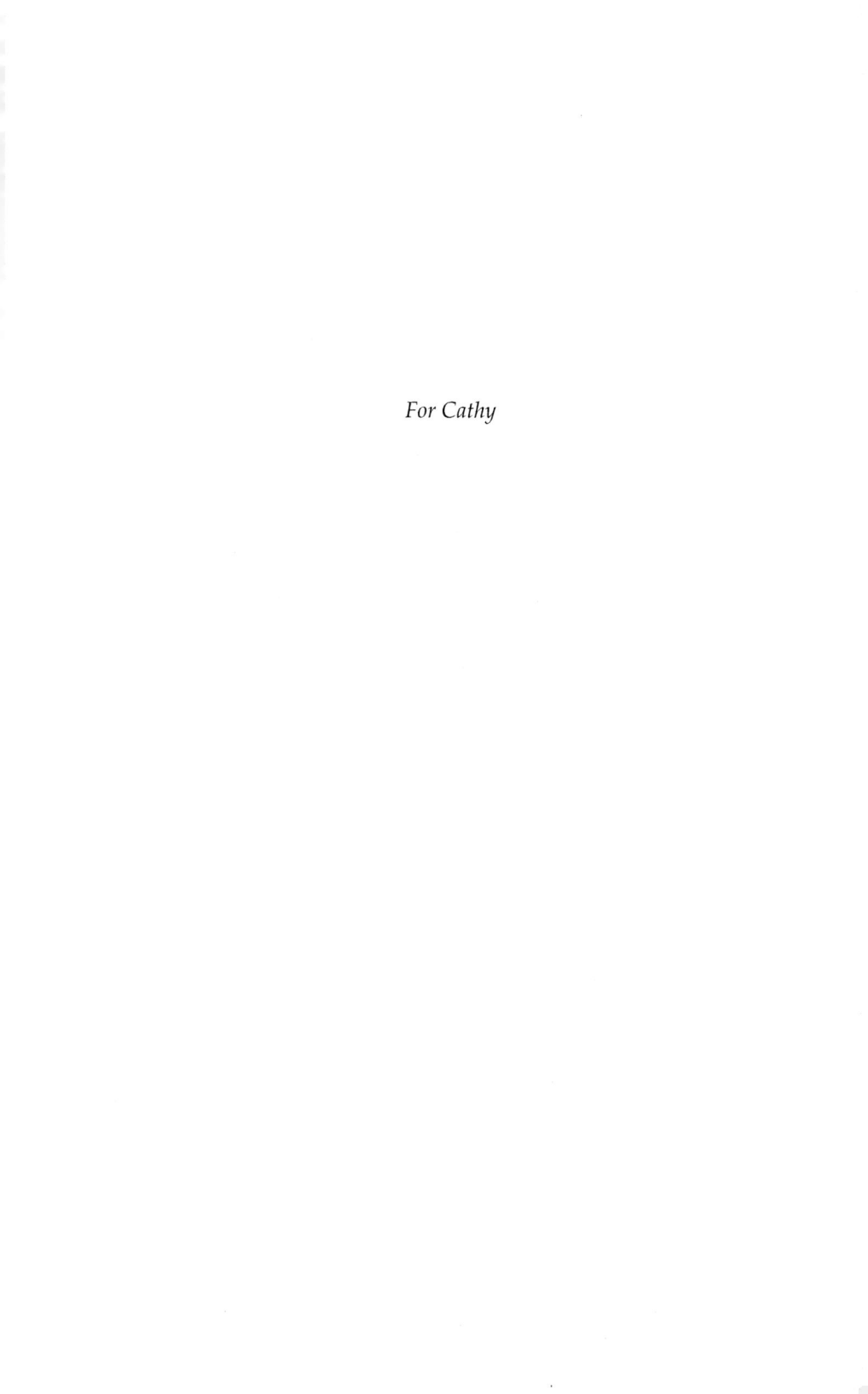

March, march, march away.
March for you'll be victorious.
Abul Fazl (1551-1602)
(Grand Vizier of the Mughal Emperor Akbar)

"What shall we do to save these?"
Second Lieutenant Honywood's last words as he held up the Queen's Colours of the 66th Foot, Battle of Maiwand, 27th July 1880.

CHAPTER ONE

Kandahar, Afghanistan, June 1880

"Everyone plays polo out here." Captain Inkerrow drew on his cheroot. "If you don't play, the Royal Malverns won't accept you."

"I'll bear that in mind," Major Jack Windrush of the 113th Foot said.

"The high season is in cold weather, of course," Inkerrow gave a well-bred laugh. "This hot weather polo is a low standard affair. One only plays to get exercise, with slow chukkas."

Jack nodded without listening. He was more interested in Inkerrow's attitude than his opinion.

"How many ponies do you have, Major?" Inkerrow raised his eyebrows as he asked the question.

"None," Jack said.

Inkerrow looked away in disdain. "I take it the 113th is not a polo regiment."

"No," Jack said. "The 113th is a fighting regiment." He paused for a moment. "And in the 113th, we address our senior officers as sir."

Inkerrow gave a short laugh. "Yes, sir."

Jack walked his horse away from Inkerrow in an attempt to find some shade. Sweat rolled from his forehead and trickled down his face. It formed a small globule on his chin before finally dripping to stain the hard leather pommel of his saddle. Jack blinked into the distance, hardly noticing the eight players engaged in the fourth chukka of the match. Around him, forming an armed escort for the polo game, a dozen mounted men slowly patrolled the outside edge of the dusty pitch. All the guards were soldiers of the Scinde Horse, the unit whose men made up one of the contending teams. The opposing team was formed of officers from the Royal Malverns, with Second Lieutenant William Windrush, known as Crimea, prominent. Crimea was the son of Colonel Windrush, Jack's half-brother. He rode easily as he swung his mallet to crack the ball forward to the Scinde's goalmouth.

"Good shot," Jack murmured as the ball hurtled towards its target. A Scinde rider intervened, using his mallet to deflect the ball.

Crimea jabbed in his spurs, trotting forward on the line of the ball, while two opposing players charged alongside, hoping to reach the ball first. As one of the Scinde players hooked Crimea's mallet to block the shot, the other leaned over from his saddle and passed the ball to a third Scinde rider. From that point, the Scinde horsemen cantered up the pitch, exchanging the ball in a series of short, accurate passes that the Malvern's team could not intercept.

Two of the Malvern riders galloped towards their own goal, shouting as they strove to prevent the Scinde men from scoring, with one fair-haired subaltern thrusting out his mallet to block the shot.

"That's the way, Walter!" Crimea encouraged, kicking in his spurs as his horse's hooves kicked up dust from the hard ground.

Second Lieutenant the Honourable Walter Sarsens laughed as the ball clicked against his mallet and fell crookedly to the ground. Pushing his horse into the Scinde trooper, Sarsens tapped the ball to Crimea, who trapped it forward expertly and passed it back to Sarsens.

"Pass!" Crimea yelled, pushing his horse to find a scoring position. "Pass, you Griffin, you blasted Johnny Raw!"

Instead of passing, Sarsens tried a long-range shot, with the ball trailing dust as it rose from the ground.

A Scinde rider intercepted the ball with a deft movement of his mallet, turned like a centaur and cracked the ball to a wiry team member.

"You should have passed!" Crimea criticised, spurring furiously in the direction of the ball.

Jack admired the wiry Scinde rider's skill as he lifted his mallet and hit the ball as it moved. The Malvern riders could only watch as they lost another goal.

"That's five goals to nothing," the umpire shouted, to the delight of the Scinde players and open dismay of the Royal Malverns.

"We've still got time to strike back!" Crimea said. "You should have passed, Sarsens.

"It was more fun trying the long shot," Sarsens said. "Calm yourself, Crimea. It's only a game!"

"We want to win!" Crimea roared. "For the honour of the Royals!"

Jack smiled. Eighteen months in Afghanistan had physically matured Crimea, adding width to his shoulders and firmness to his face, but he retained his spirit and regimental pride.

My brother William should be proud of his son.

"There might be trouble, Major Blackwood sahib!" The risaldar in charge of the escort galloped to the umpire. "Riders are approaching from the north. It may be Ayub Khan."

"Ayub Khan is supposed to be north of the Helmand River." Jack joined the umpire. Ghazi Mohammad Ayub Khan was a late Amir of Afghanistan, Governor of Herat Province and was now tilting for the throne. In the disturbed state of Afghanistan, any dust cloud could mean a lashkar- tribal army- or merely a trading caravan of camels.

"That's where he's supposed to be, Windrush." The umpire, Major Henry Blackwood of the Horse Artillery, scanned the landscape, narrowing his eyes against the sun's glare. "He may be anywhere from Herat to the outskirts of Kandahar. That's as much trust I place in our spies. They're all born liars." He studied the dust clouds to the north, a sure sign of somebody approaching the city. Although they were only a few hundred yards outside Kandahar's walls, the polo players and their escort were wary of an attack. "We'll call the match a win for the Scinde Horse," Blackwood decided. "Best not take chances."

"We can finish the game," Crimea said.

"Yes, sir," Sarsens urged the umpire. "We still have a chance to score for the honour of the regiment."

"Back inside," Blackwood repeated. "What do you think, Windrush?" He appealed to Jack for support.

Jack pushed his horse closer. "Major Blackwood is correct," he said. "We don't know who is under that cloud of dust." He raised his voice. "Players, change and head for the Shikapur Gate! Don't dally! Escort, you're the rearguard!" He waited until the polo players shrugged on their uniforms and headed back towards Kandahar before he joined the escort, nodding to the risaldar in charge. The sowars - Indian cavalry troopers - formed a loose screen, watching the approaching dust cloud while not appearing to retreat.

Jack rode forward, touching the butt of his revolver as he approached the dust. He sensed the sowar at his back and knew he might be putting the man in peril. Both men tried to see what the cloud concealed.

"What do you think, sowar?" Jack asked in Pashto, the local language.

"I think it could be dangerous to linger, sahib," the sowar said diplomatically.

"You could be right, sowar." Jack accepted the rebuke and pulled his horse away. "We'll get back to the barracks."

The polo players were safe, and the risaldar had lined his men outside the Shikapur Gate with their swords balanced on their right shoulders.

"Thank you, Risaldar," Jack said as he passed through the arched opening, and the risaldar followed them. The Royal Malvern sentinels at the gate and on the wall above hefted their Martini-henry rifles in expectation. If the officer in charge thought it prudent, he would close the gate; at present, it remained open for merchants and citizens.

"Keep alert, men," Jack advised.

The corporal in charge saluted. "Yes, sir."

Unlike most British regiments in Afghanistan, the Royals still wore their traditional scarlet, with gleaming white sun helmets decorated with the Royal Malvern's badge. They were red-faced and hot but as immaculate as if they guarded Buckingham Palace rather than a city in southern Afghanistan.

Once inside the city walls, Kandahar closed around them with its narrow streets, clamorous population, and myriad smells. Jack glanced over the polo players, frowning as he noted that one of the Royal Malverns rode without his sword.

Second lieutenant Sarsens newly joined from England. My brother will have to tighten up his discipline, Jack thought. *An unarmed British soldier in Afghanistan is only a target.*

The Kandahar people watched the horsemen ride past. One or two men muttered curses under their breath while one heavily veiled woman turned away as if scared the infidels might contaminate her. Her husband, a bearded Pashtun with a jezail slung across his back, glared at the horsemen.

"We're not wanted here, sir," Blackwood said.

"No, we're not." Jack shook his head. "I know the powers-that-be hope to extend the borders of British India to include Kandahar, but it will take some work to persuade the locals to accept us. This city is as different from India as India is from London."

They rode on, ignoring a gaggle of small boys who threw stones at them as they traversed the city to reach the citadel at the opposite side, beyond Topkhana Square and next to the Eedgah Gate. The sentries at the citadel gate slammed to attention once they recognised the ranks of the riders.

Dismounting at the stables, Jack threw the reins to a waiting servant, gave orders in fluent Pashtu, and walked straight to the officers' mess.

"How was the game, Windrush?" Major Baxter of the Royal Malverns asked, snapping his finger for a *khitmagar* – a waiter.

The man came at once, soft-footed, and efficient.

"Two brandy and sodas," Baxter ordered. *"Jildi!"*

"The Scinde Horse were far too strong for your boys," Jack accepted the brandy and sipped at his glass, "and the game was interrupted by a dust cloud. We weren't sure if it was a raiding lashkar or the viceroy come to visit."

"Better safe than sorry out here," Baxter said. "I heard that a young ghazi attacked two men of the 66th in the bazaar only last week. The ghazi was only about ten years old. He pulled a knife and ran at them from nowhere and stabbed one man in the forehead before the swaddies subdued him."

"We're certainly not popular in Kandahar," Jack agreed. "Was the soldier badly hurt?"

Baxter shook his head. "No. It was only a superficial cut."

"What happened to the youngster?"

"The provost marshal has him." Baxter finished his brandy and signalled for another. "I've no idea what will happen to the little reptile. We can't hang a child, although God knows he deserves it."

"I've only arrived in Kandahar recently," Jack said. "Are such attacks normal?"

Baxter nodded. "The Royals have been in garrison here for a month, as you know, Windrush. We don't know what's happening. One day the politicians say we'll evacuate Afghanistan, and the next, we're keeping Kandahar to ourselves." He sipped at his fresh brandy. "I'd say there has been one such incident every week, with ghazis attacking lone soldiers or unprotected servants. We're not under siege as such, but we're certainly not popular with the locals."

Jack looked around the officers' mess. As he would expect from the Royal Malverns, everything was in impeccable taste, with numerous *khitmagars* and the best selection of wines and spirits between Calcutta and Valetta.

"You're here for the durbar, I believe," Baxter said. "We're all hoping the local tribes will support Sher Ali," he raised his voice and glass. "Sher Ali Khan, Wali of Kandahar, God bless him!"

Two other officers joined in the toast, with Inkerrow downing a *chota peg* – a single whisky - in one swallow and demanding another from the *khitmagar*.

Jack smiled. "We'll see what happens."

Baxter leaned back in his chair. "We have a choice, Windrush. Either we reinforce the garrison in Kandahar and come down hard on the tribes and ghazis here, or we withdraw completely and hand the entire country over to Abdur Rahman Khan, the soon-to-be new Amir. Having Sher Ali in charge is inviting disaster."

Jack agreed but allowed Baxter to continue. "Do you think Sher Ali is that bad?"

Baxter smiled. "He is the veriest puppet that ever danced to political music, and I read that in *The Times of India*, so others share my opinion. If we leave Kandahar, Sher Ali won't last a day or half a day. He is a marionette, without power or influence. Rahman will be a martinet, of course, a despot of the worst kind, but he'll keep his house in order and not allow the Ruskis to intervene."

Jack nodded. The British in India had constant nightmares about a Russian presence in Afghanistan.

Baxter signalled for another drink. "You're new in Kandahar,

Windrush, so let me tell you the local news. Some ghazi fires at Captain Garrett and wounds him. Sher Ali makes big promises to find the assailant. Nothing happens."

Jack nodded.

"A well-known troublemaking mullah encourages a band of famous *badmashes* – evilly disposed fellows - to murder Major Wandby. Sher Ali fails to capture a single one but instead hangs three wretched brutes who were probably miles away at the time. Now, Windrush, how will such a man hold Kandahar if we return to India and the people rise against our placemen, as they will?"

"He won't," Jack said softly. "It takes a hard man to control this country."

"Exactly," Baxter agreed. "Sher Ali will either join Ayub Khan, flee, or somebody will find his body in a ditch, minus the head. Walis or Amirs here must rule by fear. The people are semi-human savages, and the British papers tell us they love us and welcome our presence." Baxter finished his brandy. "And by that principle of bunkum, the deluded British public believes we will hold Afghanistan."

Jack understood the bitterness.

"If we divide the country," Baxter said, "we'll invite a civil war, which seems the natural state in Afghanistan anyway." He eyed Jack shrewdly. "If I recall correctly, you're a friend of that Afridi fellow, Batoor Khan."

"That's correct," Jack agreed. "Batoor's taking a risk coming here, well out of his tribal territory."

Baxter grunted. "We all take a risk every time we step out of doors in this blasted country."

Jack finished his brandy and turned down another. "If you'll excuse me, I'd better get ready for the durbar. There's an informal gathering first, then the durbar in the evening."

"Good luck, Windrush," Baxter said, lifting his glass for another refill. He sighed as Sarsens and Crimea Windrush entered the mess. "That's an end to our peace and quiet. Sarsens arrived from England last week and thinks he's a veteran. He teamed up with the colonel's arrogant young pup, treats the natives like slaves and swaggers around as if he's a sixth form prefect." Baxter shook his head. "I don't know why young Crimea has latched into him. He should know better."

Jack nodded. "I know the type. A few weeks in Afghanistan will teach Sarsens manners. We all have to learn."

* * *

Jack stood erect as an efficient private of the Royal Malverns made the final adjustments to his dress uniform. Private Pawcett stepped back to inspect his handiwork, then took a small brush and removed a minuscule speck of dust from Jack's collar.

"There you are, sir," Pawcett said.

"Thank you, Pawcett." Uncomfortable in the tight scarlet, Jack turned to look at himself in the long, free-standing mirror.

The brilliant scarlet of the 113th full dress uniform showed his slim figure to perfection, while the array of medals on his left breast told the story of his experience.

"You're looking fine, sir," Pawcett said, applying his brush once more. "You look very impressive, if I may say so."

"You may not say so," Jack growled. He knew his comment was unfair to a man who could not retaliate, but he hated wearing full dress and wished that Donnelly, his long-time servant, was with him.

Pawcett retreated into silence.

Jack immediately apologised. "You've done a good job with most unprepossessing material," he said. "Thank you, Pawcett."

"Thank you, sir."

"What were you in civilian life, Pawcett?"

"I was a valet, sir."

"A very good one, I would imagine," Jack said, wondering why any man would throw up such an excellent position to enlist in the army. No doubt Pawcett had fiddled his master's books or got a servant girl pregnant. It was unlikely Pawcett had enlisted for any love of queen and country. Jack grunted; although the army was more selective than it used to be, a fair selection of ne'er-do-wells still joined the ranks.

"Thank you, sir." Reading his officer, Pawcett relapsed into silence and stepped back.

Both men looked around when the door opened, and Helen Windrush walked in. Jack sighed. Helen was the wife of William Windrush, Colonel of the Royal Malverns and Jack's half-brother.

"Good afternoon, Jack." Helen gave a mock curtsey.

"Good afternoon, Helen. Should you not be with your husband?" Jack replied. As usual, Helen was impeccably dressed. Her sweeping dark blue skirt nearly touched the floor while her light blue top opened at the neck to reveal a gold chain, from which hung a single emerald that reflected the light.

"Oh, William's too busy to talk to me." Helen perched herself elegantly on one of Jack's chairs and examined him. "Besides, you have more medals than he has."

Jack nodded. Knowledgeable people could read half a soldier's life by the medals he displayed. "Perhaps so, but he has a higher rank."

Helen smiled. "I always thought that was unfair. The army should have promoted you years ago. What are all these medals for?"

Jack glanced down at his chest and shrugged. "Twenty-odd years of undetected crime."

"What's this one? I don't think William has this one." Helen touched a dark blue and red ribbon.

"I'm sure he has. That's the Indian General Service medal," Jack said.

"You have two clasps." Helen was persistent, examining every detail. "Pegu 1852 and Umbeyla 1863."

"I know," Jack said. The Burmese War of 1851-2 had been his first campaign when he was a very raw subaltern, and the

Umbeyla campaign his first visit to the North-West Frontier between India and Afghanistan. "They were years ago."

"William has this one." Helen slid her finger along the row of ribbons.

Beside the Indian General Service lay the pale blue and yellow Crimean ribbon, with claps for Inkerman and Sebastopol. Jack's 113th Foot had found their soul at Inkerman, facing the massed Russian battalions. There was no clasp for the Redan, for that had been a defeat.

"I know William fought in the Crimea," Jack said. "I met you there, too."

Helen smiled. "These were stirring times, Jack. If things had been different, who knows what might have happened."

"Who knows indeed," Jack said. "But you married my half-brother, and I married Mary," he reminded her of their respective positions.

Helen looked away. "I'd have liked to be married to a good man," she said quietly.

Jack ignored her words. He and William were not close, but he refused to discuss his half-brother.

"I think William has this one, too." Helen realised she could not draw Jack.

Next to the Crimean ribbon was the scarlet and white Indian Mutiny medal, which Jack considered the most bitter war he fought. His two clasps for Lucknow and the Defence of Lucknow could not convey the savagery of the fighting or the sense of tragedy and loss when he fought British-trained Sepoys.

"That's where I first met Mary," Jack's eyes darkened with memory. "The only good thing to come out of that bloody war." He remembered the horror of the Mutineers' attack on Gondabad when the world turned upside-down, and certainties altered to betrayal and suspicion.

"Sorry, Jack." Helen realised she was stirring old feelings. "I don't know this one." Her finger rested on the yellow and black ribbon.

"Ashantiland," Jack told her. "My only campaign in Africa." The single clasp was for the capture of Kumasi, deep in the forest. Jack touched the coloured silk, remembering the blood, sweat, and horror of each campaign, as well as the courage and bravery of the British and Indian soldiers and their adversaries.

Helen appeared quite settled on Jack's chair, watching as Pawcett buckled on Jack's sword belt with the hilt of the Wilkinson's Sword blade appearing worn in comparison to the splendour of his uniform.

"It's time you got a new sword," Helen said.

"This one has served me well for years," Jack told her. "We are old friends, and I prefer a blade with which I am familiar."

"Maybe for fighting," Helen said. "You won't be fighting today. You should be wearing a sword of honour, complete with a gold hilt and scrollwork on the scabbard."

Jack grunted as Pawcett made minute adjustments to his belt. "We're in Afghanistan," he said. "We could be fighting at any time."

"We're in the citadel of Kandahar, surrounded by the British Army." Helen stood up and strolled to the window. "General Primrose knows what he's doing." She paused for a significant moment and glanced at Pawcett. "I hope."

"I would wish you were elsewhere." Jack had not been in Kandahar sufficiently long to comment on General Primrose.

"Oh, Jack." Helen faced him. "Don't you like me anymore?"

"Afghanistan is not safe for women."

"Afghanistan is not safe for men, either," Helen pointed out, "yet you are here."

"I must do my duty." Jack knew he sounded pompous.

"So must I," Helen said softly. "I am the Colonel's Lady, and I must look after my women and men."

Jack could not think of a suitable reply. "That's me set." He grasped the hilt of his sword. "I'd better attend this nonsense, and I'd advise you do likewise, Mrs Colonel's Lady."

"You wish I were elsewhere, Jack, and I wish you and

William were better friends. You've been in the Royals' barracks for two days, and you and he have not exchanged a word."

Jack nodded. The rift between the two Windrush half-brothers was nearly three decades old and showed no sign of easing. "If it keeps you happy, Helen, I will send him a note inviting him to visit my quarters."

"Would you, Jack?" Helen put a hand on Jack's sleeve. "Any sign of conciliation would help. I'd like my husband and my best friend to act as brothers again."

"I will," Jack promised, "although I doubt it will do any good."

Helen rubbed his arm. "You were watching Crimea play polo today, Jack. I saw you." She smiled. "He's a good boy."

"He's a promising young officer," Jack said and relented. "You've got a fine son there, Helen. I can see a lot of you in him."

Dropping into a curtsey, Helen smiled. "It was good to see you again, Jack." She left in a swirl of satin and silk, leaving a lingering scent of her perfume in the room.

"Will you require me again, sir?" Pawcett had been a mute observer to the meeting between Jack and Helen.

"No, thank you, Pawcett. You are dismissed." Jack watched as Pawcett withdrew. Within the hour, half the Royal Malverns would know every detail of his conversation with his sister-in-law. Garrison life was like living in a small village, with everybody aware of everybody else's business. It was tedious, and one had to be careful. Touching the hilt of his sword, Jack had a last glance in the mirror and left the room.

CHAPTER TWO

The first thing Jack noticed about Major-General James Maurice Primrose was his fashionable side-whiskers and neat hair. The second thing was his clear eyes and gentle face that did not sit well with his position as commander of Kandahar, a city in the south of Afghanistan and surrounded by some of the most intractable Pashtun tribes.

Are you the right man to command the garrison, General Primrose?

Britain's war in Afghanistan had started in 1878, two years previously, when perceived Russian interference in the country alarmed some British politicians. Jack and the 113th Foot had been part of General Roberts' force that had won a series of battles and occupied Kabul. Now, as Britain prepared to install a friendly Amir to rule Afghanistan, the military was slowly evacuating the country. However, politicians in Britain spoke of retaining Kandahar and the south as a buffer to protect British India.

What the devil am I doing in Kandahar? Jack tugged at his too-tight collar. *I should be with my regiment in Kabul, not here with the Royals.* He recalled the brief telegram that had summoned him to Kandahar.

Major Windrush. Accompany Royal Malverns to Kandahar. Persuade Batoor Khan of the Rahmut Khel to support the British. Hook.

Jack had sworn when he read the telegram. General Hook was head of British military intelligence and had known Jack for years, but although Jack regarded him as a friend, his messages usually presaged a dangerous mission. Jack preferred to work as a regimental officer rather than dabbling in politics.

The music started as Jack looked over the large, airy room in which General Primrose had gathered the British and Indian officers, close allies and Afghan maliks – tribal leaders - before the durbar. Tall, pointed windows allowed in light, while Persian script and abstract designs ornately decorated the walls. Every British officer wore their dress uniform while the guests, both Afghan and Indian, dressed in the clothes they thought best fitted the situation. Sher Ali Khan, the wali of Kandahar, was the guest of honour, a heavy-featured man with a shaggy beard and fine clothes.

Jack looked around the room but failed to see Batoor. *I hope you have come, Batoor, or I've wasted a long journey.*

General Primrose seemed perfectly at home amidst the glamour, talking easily to the Wali, Pashtun maliks, the Wali's officers, British officers, and women alike. Smooth and debonair, he smiled as his officers swirled around the floor. A staff officer and administrator rather than a fighting soldier, his diplomacy graced the room.

Standing with his back to the wall, Jack sipped an atrociously bad wine and watched everybody. He saw William Windrush, Colonel of the famous Royal Malverns and his half-brother, talking to Brigadier-General George Burrows and Colonel James Galbraith of the 66th Foot. They seemed animated, ignoring Helen, who drifted away, glass in hand, to seek more entertaining company. Jack watched her for a moment, then drew a deep breath when she stopped to talk to a group of Afghan maliks.

Batoor Khan stood in the centre of the group, as comfortable in the middle of the meeting as he was in battle or his own valley. With his *karakul* hat of Astrakhan fur and the ivory-and-silver-hilted pulwar- the curved Pashtun sword - at his waist, he looked as dignified as any of the guests. As Jack watched, Batoor laughed at something Helen said, leaning forward to touch her shoulder.

Thinking he had better pursue his duty, Jack stepped forward, sliding through the crowd.

"Ah, here you are, Jack," Helen said. "Batoor Khan here was regaling me of tales of Afghanistan."

"I'm sure he was," Jack said.

"Do you two know each other?" Helen asked.

"We've known each other for years," Jack said. "We fought side by side in the Mutiny and again in the Umbeyla campaign."

Batoor grinned, with his brown eyes alight. "And against the Russians," he said until Jack shook his head to silence him. He could not reveal his most recent campaign.

Helen glanced from one to the other. "You did not tell me you knew such a personable Pashtun malik, Jack," Helen said. By using the term malik, she was demonstrating her knowledge of the local culture.

Batoor bowed with as much aplomb as any Eton-educated British aristocrat. "Thank you, Lady Windrush," he replied.

"I do not have a title," Helen said.

"The British are at fault, then," Batoor said, "for by neglecting you, they are weakening their position."

Helen curtseyed in acknowledgement. "I will leave you men together," she said. "I'm sure you have much to discuss." She glided away to talk to Major Baxter.

"You were very gallant, Batoor," Jack said. "Where did you learn such manners?"

Batoor grinned. "You and I are similar, Jack. You are British and move among the Pashtun. I am Pashtun and move among the British." He touched his pearl earring. "You had better be careful with your sister-in-law. I am looking for a new wife, and a woman like that would make a splendid addition to my household."

Jack smiled, although he was unsure whether Batoor was joking. "Her husband would not appreciate that."

"Perhaps not," Batoor said. "I already have a younger woman in mind, but to marry a memsahib like that," he smiled. "Your brother is a fortunate man."

"He certainly chose a good woman," Jack agreed.

"You had also better be careful with these men." Batoor nodded to a small knot of maliks who stood at the edge of the room, watching everything through suspicious eyes.

"Who are they?" Jack asked. All three were large men with heavy beards and dark turbans, and all carried the ugly Khyber Knife at their waist.

"Babrakzai Khan, his cousin Zamar Khan and Hyder Ali." Even in Batoor's voice, the names sounded flat. "All from the Nazar Khel of the Zirak Durrani."

"Durrani? You are Durrani."

"I am." Batoor touched his pearl earring. "We are not friends. Babrakzai is my neighbour from the Bolak valley and constantly raids my herds. Zamar Khan and Hyder Ali are his cousins. Zamar belongs to this area and Hyder from Helmand."

"I think I'd better talk to these three gentlemen," Jack said. "Would you care to join me, Batoor?"

"Only if you wish me to kill all three," Batoor replied without a trace of humour.

"Not today." *Massacring our guests would not endear the British to the local Pashtun tribes.* "I'd best go alone."

With one hand on the hilt of his sword, Jack walked across to the three maliks. They eyed him from across the room and stood, unsmiling, until he arrived.

"I am Major Jack Windrush of the 113th Foot," Jack introduced himself.

The Pashtuns nodded briefly, with Zamar Khan's lip's curling into what he may have intended as a smile. "Where is General Primrose?" Zamar had a very steady gaze.

"He's over there." Jack saw Primrose in the centre of the room, talking to William and Galbraith. "I'll take you to him."

What the devil is Primrose thinking, inviting a trio of Pashtun maliks and not treating them as honoured guests? Is the man looking for trouble?

General Primrose smiled as Jack introduced the three Pashtun maliks. "Welcome to Kandahar," he said while Sher Ali Khan and the maliks exchanged wary looks.

Zamar Khan thanked Primrose with a nod, while Hyder and Babrakzai Khan stared at the general as if he did not exist.

Trouble. Jack thought. *These three will be carrying arms against us soon.*

Flanked by William Windrush and Colonel James Galbraith, General Primrose appeared the epitome of British military confidence, Smiling and urbane, he stood in the brilliant scarlet of his full-dress uniform with the light glittering on his gold braid and the row of medals on his chest. For a moment, Jack saw Primrose talking to the three Afghan leaders, a contrast between a general of the leading imperial power on Earth and men whose beliefs had scarcely changed in the last thousand years, and then a servant passed between them. When Jack looked again, the image had altered. Hyder had moved sideways, and William Windrush had shifted away.

Galbraith nodded to Jack. He was a distinguished-looking man, with bushy side-whiskers and slightly pouchy eyes under his balding head. He looked surprised when William Windrush spoke sharply to Jack.

"You may leave us, Major," William Windrush said. "This meeting is for senior officers."

"As you wish, sir," Jack bit back his angry retort. William was perfectly entitled to order a junior officer away. He was aware of the maliks watching as he withdrew.

"Your brother does not care for you," Batoor joined Jack.

"I know," Jack agreed.

"I had a brother like that, once." Batoor touched the silver hilt of his Khyber knife. "I killed him."

"We don't do that in our culture." Jack did not force his smile. "Sometimes, I think the Pashtun way is better."

"It is more honest," Batoor said. He met Jack's smile. "Why are you here, Windrush? Your regiment, the 113th Foot, is at Kabul."

"General Hook thought I might be useful," Jack said.

"General Hook thought you could persuade me to aid the British, support Sher Ali, and help Abdur Rahman Khan become Amir," Batoor said.

Jack nodded. He was not surprised that Batoor had worked out General Hook's reasoning. "Do I need to persuade you?"

Batoor touched his earring. "I will keep neutral," he said. "I've little time for Sher Ali, but the new Amir won't need my support. Once he's properly in power, Rahman Khan will rule Afghanistan with an iron fist."

"What's Rahman Khan like?"

Batoor angrily rebuffed a mess waiter who offered him a glass of wine. "I am Muhammadan!" and returned his attention to Jack. "Rahman Khan is about forty, not tall, overweight, courteous when he chooses and with a good brain. He'll match the British and Russian politicians for intelligence and outdo them for ruthlessness,"

Jack grunted. Batoor's assessment agreed with that of Major Baxter. "A weak man doesn't last in Afghanistan."

"That is so," Batoor agreed.

Both men looked up as Colonel Primrose gave an order, and everybody filed through to the durbar room.

The atmosphere altered in seconds. The room was smaller, with a raised dais on which Primrose and Sher Ali sat, with everybody else sitting on couches or chairs below. Jack moved to the rear of the room, with Batoor at his side and the three maliks remaining near the door. British and Afghan officers and officials of Sher Ali's court filled the remainder of the room.

"Welcome all," General Primrose spoke in Pashtu and English and began a long speech to inform everybody of the current situation in Afghanistan. Jack thought him a good speaker, if a little flowery. The British officers soon looked bored, while the Afghans listened with attention. Zamar and Babrakzai spoke quietly to each other, with Hyder looking around the room, taking note of everybody present.

These three are not here to discuss current affairs, Jack thought. *They are spying on us, checking our strengths and weaknesses.*

When General Primrose stopped talking, Sher Ali stood up. He raised his hands as if in prayer as he addressed the room, speaking in rapid Pashtu.

"Wait!" Primrose lifted a hand. "We'll need a translator." The job was evidently beneath the dignity of a general officer. "Major Windrush! Translate for the benefit of those who don't speak the language."

Jack mounted the dais and repeated Sher Ali's words. The Wali was extolling the benefits of a British alliance and telling everybody present of his power and control of the city and province of Kandahar. As he spoke, Jack saw the three maliks listening intently until Hyder Ali slipped away to talk to one of the Wali's officers.

Trouble.

When the Wali sat down, Jack expected General Primrose would ask for comments from his audience, but instead, he seemed content to finish the durbar. The officers left, some complaining that the whole thing had been a waste of time.

"Thank you, Major," Primrose said formally.

Batoor joined Jack in the outer chamber, where the informal gathering resumed.

"Where are the maliks?" Jack asked.

"They left immediately after the durbar finished," Batoor said.

"Are you staying?" Jack looked up as the door opened and a clutch of garrison wives entered, each one searching for her husband among the scarlet uniforms.

"I am not staying," Batoor said. "You may tell General Hook that your mission was a success, and Batoor Khan of the Rahmut Khel will support the new Amir and will not lead his men against the British." Batoor grinned. "Or not until it suits him."

Jack met Batoor's smile. "Thank you, Batoor." He watched as Batoor slipped out of the door.

Major Baxter approached with a glass in each hand. "Here you are, Windrush. I didn't know you were fluent in Pashtu."

"I've served in this area before," Jack said.

Baxter glanced at Jack's medals. "So I see, Major." The use of Jack's rank held an implied question. *Why have you not been promoted?* Baxter was asking.

"Do you know what my men are complaining about?" Baxter changed the subject to routine regimental matters.

"No," Jack said. As a guest officer from the 113th Foot, he had no contact with the rank and file of the Royal Malverns and missed the day-to-day conversation and worries of the men.

"There is a shortage of rum," Baxter said solemnly. "More is on the way, but at present, the men are forced to drink the local spirits." He grinned. "Forget the politics and whoever the Amir is this week; the Tommies have more immediate concerns."

Jack smiled. "The swaddies may have the right idea."

Baxter continued. "The Kandaharis, non-drinking Muslims to a man, make the local concoction from raisins, and it tastes foul. The Tommies call it Billy Stink, which it does, and choke it down with reluctant gusto."

Jack knew British soldiers well enough to know they would drink anything alcoholic. "If the lads are complaining about Billy Stink, it must be a truly vile mixture."

Baxter held up his glass for a refill. "That is one great advantage of a commissioned rank, my boy. We may have great responsibilities, but at least we can drink decent brandy. I intend to remain drunk until we leave this foul country."

"So I see, Baxter," Jack said.

"On to less immediate matters," Baxter said. "I heard there is more trouble up north. Ayub Khan has stirred things up in Herat direction and is heading south."

"There's always trouble in Afghanistan," Jack said. "Excuse me, Baxter, duty calls." He followed Batoor outside.

Morale in Kandahar was low, Jack saw, and despite the British garrison, the population was restless. As well as the constant threat of assassination from local ghazis – fanatics – there was a more distant danger in the north. Ayub Khan was the governor of Herat, Abdur Rahman's cousin and a claimant for the throne. If he stirred up the tribes, the British withdrawal from Afghanistan could be more difficult. Jack sighed, hitched up his sword and pushed the matter from his mind. Worrying about events could not change them. As he marched across the citadel, he noticed a Timuri merchant watching him behind a *kafilah*, a string of camels but walked on. Jack planned to compose a letter to Mary, his wife, that evening, so Ayub Khan and all of Afghanistan would have to wait.

When Jack reached his quarters, he saw the folded paper lying on his bed. He broke the simple seal and unfolded the paper. The message was brief, William's reply to Jack's attempt at reconciliation.

"My compliments, sir, and be damned."

Jack sighed and dropped the note into the wastepaper bin. He had expected nothing else.

CHAPTER THREE

Jack heard the noise before he realised the reason. William's voice was raised in anger.

What's annoyed my brother? I must find out.

Jack pushed William's door open with his foot and waited outside, peering through the crack. William stood behind his desk, shaking his fist at Second Lieutenant Sarsens.

"You're in Afghanistan, not bloody Aldershot!"

"Yes, sir," Sarsens said.

Colonel Windrush took a deep breath and increased the volume of his rebuke. "Have you read the standing orders? If you had, you'd be aware they state, and I quote, anywhere from Peshawar westward, British officers will not move without carrying arms."

"Yes, sir," Sarsens said again. "But we're inside a British garrison."

"You were outside the citadel and outside Kandahar, damnit!" William lifted his fist again so that Jack thought he might strike the young Second Lieutenant.

"We had an escort, sir," Sarsens said. "A dozen sowars of the Scinde Horse."

William lowered his fist and his voice. "I'll tell you what it is, young man. You may go without your breeches, but dammit, sir, you shall carry your sword!"

"Yes, sir," the subaltern said.

"You're now the duty officer, damn your impudence, and the first chance I get, I'll send you on active service to introduce you to the reality of life in Afghanistan. That's all. Dismissed!"

Jack moved away from the door before the subaltern escaped. For once, he agreed with William. Any British officer, and any British soldier, who took chances on the North-West Frontier or in Afghanistan, was seeking trouble. Of all the enemies Jack had faced, he considered the Pashtun warriors the most consistently dangerous. Courageous in attack, tenacious in defence, they had all the patience and skill of a hunting cat and more dexterity with sword and jezail than any warriors Jack had known. Young fools of subalterns, fresh from Sandhurst or Eton, were fair game for a Pashtun warrior.

Smiling as he remembered his impetuous youth, Jack walked on with his opinion of William heightened.

* * *

"I hear the ghazis were causing trouble again." Baxter sipped at his brandy and pointed to an article in the *Kandahar News*. "Four of them running amuck in the bazaar. They wounded General Tytler, no less, and a few rank and file."

"What happened to them?" Jack asked.

Baxter shrugged. "Some of the 66th got them with the bayonet. Neat work, but it's a bit worrying. One never knows who's going to turn ghazi next. One cannot trust anything these people say or do."

"They're not all like that," Jack said. "The Pashtun have a unique code, Pashtunwali, and they abide by it rigidly."

"Is that so?" Baxter said. "I heard that there is only one Afghan who never told a lie, and he was deaf and dumb from birth."

"Every Pashtun is a warrior, a theologian and a politician," Jack contended. "I think most have family feuds." He sipped at his whisky. "My wife, who knows such things, compares them to the Scottish Borderers as portrayed by Sir Walter Scott."

"I've read Scott," Baxter said. "*Lay of the Last Minstrel*. I can't remember him writing of ghazis, though, or of men running amuck."

"Nor can I," Jack agreed. "I think amuck is a Javanese word. It means to kill."

"Lovely people." Baxter waved his glass in the air. "It's time that Deen Mahomed took things in hand. He's the chief of police here. I heard he did catch a few thieves in the Sudder Bazaar, but I'd prefer him to stop the ghazis." He nodded to a large plate of apricots on the adjacent table. "Or stop the natives selling these damned things so cheaply. Half the men have diarrhoea."

"Better an upset stomach than the clap," Jack said. "It's more easily cured."

"Little chance of the clap here," Baxter said. "Touch one of the Kandahari women, and half the men will be her cousins and hunt you down with their dirty great pulwars." Both men looked up as the door opened, and two people stepped in.

"Guest in the mess!" Major Bryant, the regimental adjutant, was ten years younger than Jack and infinitely better connected. He spoke with the confidence of a man sure of his position in the world. *And why not?* Jack thought. Bryant was a senior officer in one of the best regiments in the British army, a scion of Eton and Sandhurst. Despite all Bryant's advantages, Jack could not dislike him. Bryant was a friendly, open-faced man, popular in the ranks.

Jack looked up as Helen walked in at Bryant's side. Elegant as always, she greeted the officers with a smile and accepted Bryant's invitation to a drink.

"The Malverns have long had a tradition of hospitality," Bryant explained. "We allow in female guests to the Mess, as long as they are announced, and insist that they do not part with a farthing."

Helen nodded solemnly. "That is a good tradition," she agreed. "I promise not to spend even an anna in your mess."

"And the colonel's lady is always welcome," Bryant continued.

Helen sat on one of the padded seats, keeping her back straight and her knees pressed together. Noticing Jack sitting alone at a table, she raised her glass in salute. Jack acknowledged and sat back, wondering when he could return to the 113th in Kabul.

This journey has been a waste of time and effort. Batoor will do as he pleases, whatever I said or didn't say.

"What the devil?" Major Bryant nearly dropped his glass as the mess door opened again, and Second Lieutenant Sarsens entered. He wore his undress tunic with a sword buckled around his waist, with no trousers, so he was naked down to his boots. A second later, the door opened again, and Crimea Windrush followed, similarly attired.

"Good God!" Baxter said, then smiled and looked away.

Jack half rose from his seat, then settled back down. He was not a member of the Royals' mess and had no right to interfere with what happened.

The two subalterns settled in a seat and ordered their morning drinks, seemingly oblivious to their state of half nudity. Helen glanced in their direction, let her eyes slowly drift over each man, smiled, raised her eyebrows to her son, and shifted her attention back to Bryant.

You did not turn a hair, Helen. Full marks to you.

The subalterns spoke together for half an hour before Sarsens broke into a popular song.

"We don't want to fight
But by Jingo, if we do,
We've got the ships,
We've got the men,
And got the money, too."

"Enough of that!" Major Baxter shouted with an apologetic glance at Helen. "This is the officer's mess, not a blasted infant's school. Get out and make yourselves decent!"

He glowered as the subalterns hurried away. Helen ignored them, lifted her eyebrows in Jack's direction, shook her head, and continued her conversation with Bryant.

"Major Windrush sahib?" A soft-footed Indian servant approached Jack.

"That's me," Jack confirmed.

"Brigadier General Burrows sends his compliments, Sahib, and requests your presence at your earliest convenience."

Jack nodded. "Thank you, please convey my regards to General Burrows sahib, and inform him, no, hang it." Jack stood up. "I'll come right away." Placing his empty glass on the table, Jack said his farewell to Baxter, lifted a hand to Helen, and left the mess.

I've never met General Burrows, but I'd better attend directly, although it will be some trivial detail, no doubt.

Burrows was in his quarters, issuing orders to senior officers. "Ah, Major Windrush!" He looked tired, a middle-aged soldier, more used to administrative posts than active command in the field.

"Yes, sir."

"Have you heard the latest news?"

"I've heard that Ayub Khan is causing trouble up by Herat, sir," Jack said.

"He *was* causing trouble up by Herat," Burrows said. "He has since marched south and is approaching the Helmand River."

"Are we doing anything about it, sir?"

"The Wali has ordered a mixed force of some twelve hundred men to Grishk," Burrows said, "and he's preparing a larger force of regulars, with artillery we handed to him."

Jack nodded. From what he had heard of the Wali, Sher Ali, he would need a great deal more than 1200 men to challenge Ayub Khan.

"If Ayub Khan crosses the Helmand," Burrows said shortly, "he'll be within a few days' march of Kandahar." He looked worried. "According to our spies, he has eleven regiments of infantry, thirty-six guns and a powerful cavalry force, plus a lashkar of unknown numbers of Durrani tribesmen."

Jack calculated figures. "Depending how many soldiers are in each regiment, that could be five thousand men or more, plus the lashkar."

Burrows gave a weak smile. "That was what I thought. A fellow named Luinob commands the advance force. I don't know much about him, but I'm told he was once Governor of Turkistan. Do you know him?"

Jack shook his head. "No. I've never heard of the man."

"A pity." Burrows sighed. "My people say that Ayub Khan is encouraging his warriors by telling them they can have all the loot and women in Kandahar once they have driven out the British." He shuffled some of the papers on his desk. "I know the Afghan mind, Windrush. Ayub won't trust his troops not to mutiny unless he keeps them occupied and attacking the infidels will be well received."

"That is so, sir," Jack agreed. He waited to see why Burrows wished to see him, although he already guessed the answer.

Burrows removed his revolver from its holster, checked the chambers and replaced it before he returned to the matter in hand. "The closer Ayub Khan comes to Kandahar, the more he'll unsettle the ghazis in the city and the tribesmen around."

Jack nodded. "That is true, sir."

"General Primrose has ordered me to take a brigade out to

teach Ayub Khan a lesson. As you have a great deal of experience fighting the Afghans, Windrush, I want you with us."

"Yes, sir. I don't have any men with me. I came with an escort of Guides for the Durbar, and my regiment is still in Kabul."

"I am well aware of that, Windrush," Burrows said. "Gather what you need and join my column."

"Yes, sir. When are we leaving?"

"General Primrose gave me my orders this morning, Windrush. I intend to march the day after tomorrow."

"Yes, sir." Jack stood up. He was too experienced in Afghan conditions to expect peace to last long. As soon as he had heard about Ayub Khan's advance from Herat, Jack guessed the British would have to fight him, for he had little faith in Sher Ali's ability to defeat Ayub Khan. "How large a force will you command, sir?"

"It's not fully decided yet, Windrush, but we'll advance in coordination with the Wali. Probably a battery of Horse Artillery, a couple of regiments of native cavalry and two regiments of native infantry, plus a British battalion."

Jack nodded. "About three thousand men, sir."

Burrows continued. "We'll march to Grishk, about sixty miles to the west, push Ayub Khan back to the Helmand River, and guard the fords. In the event Ayub has not yet reached the Helmand, we'll wait for him at the river."

Jack nodded. "Yes, sir. Ayub Khan will outnumber us, but if the men are steady, that should not be a problem."

I don't think any of the units in Kandahar have much recent experience of fighting. I hope Burrows is a better general than he appears.

"Dismissed, Windrush," Burrows said and returned to the paperwork on his desk.

The moment Jack left Burrows, he found himself struggling to picture the general's face. He was a man devoid of personality. Jack sighed. That was another lesson; a military leader needed to create an image, something distinctive for the men to follow.

Now I'm going back to the war. In Afghanistan, the war never seems to end. It alters its shape, and a friend today can be a foe tomorrow. It's like draining a swamp with a sieve.

Jack looked along the bleak stone corridor to the window at the far end and listened to the sounds of Kandahar.

We should never have entered Afghanistan, but now we are here, we'll have to show we are strong, or half the tribes on the Frontier will rise.

CHAPTER FOUR

Jack heard Helen's voice as he returned to his quarters.

"You displayed rather a lot of yourself in the mess today, Crimea." Helen sounded more amused than annoyed.

"I know, mother," Crimea replied. "Sarsens thought it would be a lark."

"Oh, Sarsens' idea, was it?" Helen asked. "He's the one with the elegant pair of legs, isn't he?"

"Mother!" Crimea rebuked.

"Long elegant legs, and I saw a hint of a shapely bottom as well," Helen continued, pressing her point home.

"Mother!" Crimea's voice was sharp. "A lady shouldn't notice such things."

"Indeed not," Helen was equally direct, "and a gentleman does not display such things in public. I expect better from you, Crimea. Your father was most annoyed!"

Jack withdrew into a recessed doorway as Crimea snorted and stormed away with the sound of his boots echoing in the stone passage. Helen followed a minute later. She gave Jack a mocking curtsey.

"Good evening, Jack. Did you hear that?"

"I heard some of it," Jack admitted.

"Well, you shouldn't listen in doorways, then," Helen told him. She favoured Jack with a smile. "As Crimea pointed out, a lady shouldn't notice such things as the shape of a man's legs, but a woman will." Helen ran her gaze down Jack's slim form from the crown of his head to his polished boots and back. "Such elegant legs," she said and walked on, leaving an intoxicating hint of perfume in her wake.

What the devil did that mean? You were always an unpredictable woman, Helen, and the years have not changed you.

* * *

Jack unfolded the map of Afghanistan on his desk, tracing Ayub Khan's possible routes with his finger. The best road from Herat to Kandahar ran a hundred and twenty miles south to Anantara before turning east for two hundred miles until he reached the Helmand River.

Jack studied the map through a brass magnifying glass, measuring distances with a wooden ruler and jotting down notes. If Burrows' spies were correct and Ayub Khan's army was at the Helmand, it was hundreds of miles from its base at Herat. In contrast, Burrows' allied force would be within three- or four-days march of Kandahar, and, therefore, much closer to supplies and reinforcements.

That is an advantage, Jack told himself. *With luck, Ayub Khan's men will disintegrate, tribe fighting tribe and province against province. If the Afghans ever pull together as a single people with a strong leader, they could be one of the strongest nations in central Asia. However, they are cursed by internal division and tribalism.*

Jack looked up as Pawcett entered his quarters. "Sorry to disturb you, sir," Pawcett said smoothly. "I've brought some extra ammunition for your revolver in case there's trouble. I've also packed two mules and checked all your kit, sir. There's a water *mussack* under the belly of each mule, sir, with two gallons of fresh water in each."

"Thank you, Pawcett." Jack knew the Scinde Horse and other Frontier units used such an arrangement. "It's been damned hot this last few weeks."

"It has, sir. That what's bringing the shepherds into the Kandahar Valley, sir. That was the dust cloud that interrupted the polo match, the other day, a shepherd driving his sheep to search for pasture."

Ayub Khan has not sent a raiding party to Kandahar yet, then.

"Thank you, Pawcett." Jack knew that Pawcett, in common with most officers' servants, would be privy to everything that happened in the regiment.

"There's a bazaar shave in the barracks, sir." Pawcett busied himself with packing Jack's last items of equipment. "The natives are greatly excited that Ayub Khan's men have cut up two companies of the 66th at Khelat-i-Gilzai."

"I hadn't heard that one," Jack paused for a moment. "Who started that shave?"

"Some fellow in curly shoes told us, sir," Pawcett said. "He's parked his camel in the citadel."

"A Timuri fellow with a yellow turban?" Jack asked. The Timuri people wore footwear such as Pawcett described. "I saw him the other day with his *kafilah*."

"I don't know what tribe he's from, sir. He's an ugly-looking brute, though."

"Thank you, Pawcett. I'll have a word with him." Although Jack did not believe the rumour, he wondered from where the Timuri had obtained his information. Leaving his quarters, he strode into the courtyard, acknowledged the salutes of the Royals' immaculate sentries, and saw the Timuri's tent beside his camels.

"*Salaam alaikum*," Jack said from outside the tent.

"*Wa-Alaikum-Salaam*," the Timuri responded, emerging into the darkness. He spoke in Pashtu, with a slight accent. "You are Major Jack Windrush."

"I am," Jack admitted. "And you are?"

"Armaghan," the man responded at once. "It means a gift of God."

Jack smiled. "What a gift God gave you, to see what happens in Khezat-i-Gilzai from many miles away."

Armaghan was smaller than Jack in height but broad in the shoulder and with bold, intelligent eyes above a thick, red-dyed beard.

"Allah grants his gifts as he thinks best." Armaghan held Jack's gaze.

"Tell me about the garrison at Khezat-i-Gilzai," Jack asked.

Armaghan lifted his eyes. "I did not see the place, Major Windrush. Others added that to my vision. I only saw the event."

"What did you see?" Jack asked.

"I saw scores of dead British soldiers within the mud walls of an Afghan compound," Armaghan said. "They were lying in heaps on the hot ground, with Pashtu and Durrani warriors of Zamindawar cleaning the blood from their swords. I saw ghazis celebrating. I saw a senior officer kneeling as he awaited death and a group of soldiers in khaki running forward into a mass of Pashtu tribesmen. I saw the figure sixty-six changing from white to red as a green flag covered the bodies, and I see a pile of bloodied khaki bodies leading to a cross."

Jack stepped back, disturbed by the clarity of Armaghan's vision. "It was a dream, then? A vision?"

"It was what I saw," Armaghan said.

Jack nodded and stepped away. "Peace go with you, Armaghan, and I hope your vision does not come to pass."

Armaghan bowed his head. "We cannot alter what will be, only what our actions may bring about."

Burrows' column was beginning to form, with sepoys and British soldiers exchanging banter.

"*Jildi*, you Berkshire boys! *Idder ow jildi!* – Get here quickly!" The NCOs of the 66th Foot chivvied their men onto the parade ground in the centre of the citadel. As Jack's mind moved on to the forthcoming expedition, Armaghan spoke again.

"Major Windrush!" Although Armaghan's voice was quiet, Jack could hear his words without effort. "Remember *zar, zan, zamin.*"

"What the devil do you mean, Armaghan?"

"*Zar, zan,* and *zamin,*" Armaghan repeated before he returned to his tent.

Zar, zan, and *zamin. Women, gold, and land.* Jack knew that these were the three things that mattered to the Pashtun. Next to Pashtunwali, the Pashtun code of behaviour, zar, zan, and zamin controlled their lives nearly as much as religion. *But what the hang has that to do with me?*

A sergeant's bellow disturbed Jack's train of thought. "Come on, you lucky lads! The Queen-Empress needs you! It's time to earn your generous pay!"

A few yards away, the native regiments filed from their barracks with the *naiks* – corporals – expressing similar sentiments in different languages.

Jack watched, wondering if Alexander the Great's Macedonians had acted the same way and decided they probably had. For a moment, he imagined the long trail of history, with NCOs from the Persians to the Romans, the Huns to Babur's Moghuls roasting their tired, grumbling men in the dawning before advancing on some mission of conquest. Soldiers were the same the world over, always had been and probably would never change.

"General Burrows!" Second Lieutenant Crimea Windrush was dressed in the scarlet of the Royals, with his sun helmet at a precise angle and his sword and pistol at his belt.

"Yes, Second Lieutenant," Burrows replied irritably.

"Colonel Windrush sends his regards, sir, and would deem it a favour if Second Lieutenant Sarsens and I join your column, in whatever position you wish." Crimea stood at attention, but Jack could see the sparkle in his eyes.

"Your colonel has already spoken to me," Burrows said wearily. "He wants you to temper your stupidity with a taste of action."

"Yes, sir," Crimea remained at attention. "Sarsens and I did not come to Afghanistan to moulder in a garrison, sir."

Burrows eyed Crimea up and down, shaking his head slowly. "Very good, Windrush. Report to Colonel Galbraith of the 66th. I am sure he can find a use for you. Sarsens," Burrows faced Sarsens, "you do the same. I'd send you to the Rifles if you had any notion of a native language. God help Galbraith with young fools like you under his command."

Jack watched the two subalterns saunter across to Colonel Galbraith, smiled and looked away. Every young officer in the British Army sought action, honour, and glory. They dreamed of defending the Colours in an advance against a ferocious enemy, so they gained renown and promotion. Jack knew that the reality was different: heat, thirst, discomfort, and hidden fear awaited any invader in Afghanistan or any other campaign on the fringes of the empire.

"Good luck, lads," Jack said softly. He watched Crimea salute Galbraith and shook his head. *You're my nephew and Helen's boy. You've got spirit, my lad, and that's a good start.*

* * *

Burrows' column left Kandahar before first light on the 4th of July 1880, with Jack riding slightly behind General Burrows. He patted his horse's neck, whispered in its ear, and looked around.

Major Blackwood's battery of Royal Horse Artillery, E Battery, B Brigade, rattled out of the Herat Gate, with a small crowd of Kandaharis watching. Some were expressionless, while one man spat his contempt. The artillerymen looked relaxed, confident, and supremely professional. Lieutenant MacLaine checked his men, patted his horse, and faced his front.

"The boys are keen as mustard!" Burrows sounded excited. "They can't wait to get at Ayub Khan's men."

Jack understood the tension behind Burrows' voice. A few months ago, he had been desk-bound as Deputy Quartermaster of the Bombay Army, and now he had his first brigade command in one of the most hostile environments on earth. Jack hoped Burrows listened to advice and didn't think he could fight the Afghans as if they were amateurs, or he was playing war games back in Aldershot.

Colonel Malcolmson's 3rd Scinde Horse rode out proudly, with their green uniforms nearly invisible in the dark and their turbans soft against the city walls. Jack had never campaigned with them before or with the 3rd Light Cavalry, Skinner's Horse, under Major Currie. General Nuttall commanded all three hundred sabres of the cavalry. Nuttall was an Aberdeenshire man of vast experience in India and had fought in the Mutiny and Afghanistan. Jack was glad to see him in the column.

The 66th Berkshire Regiment of Foot made up the British infantry section of the column. Jack thought the men looked handy enough as they marched solidly forward. After enduring garrison duty in Kandahar, with the constant threat of attacks by ghazis every time they left the barracks, the men were pleased to be outside the walls.

"Let's hope the Afghans fight," one stocky, tow-headed corporal said as he marched past Jack. "We'll give them what-for."

"I've had enough of skulking in barracks," his companion, a lanky, sunburned man, agreed. "If they want a fair fight, the Brave Boys of Berks will give them one!"

Jack watched the 66th march past, with Sarsens laughing with Crimea, who rode erect and tall. To Jack's knowledge, the Berkshire Regiment had seen no action since the Napoleonic Wars; they were as inexperienced as General Burrows.

After Galbraith's 66th in their faded khaki and sun helmets, Colonel Anderson's First Grenadiers looked lithe and agile. As their regimental number implied, they were the oldest of the sepoy units in the Indian Army, proud men, many of whom had followed their father and grandfather into the regiment. Jack thought the men looked very young, even boyish, with the officers, both Indian and British, also youthful.

Colonel Mainwairing's Jacob's Rifles were next, named after its founder, Major John Jacob. The regiment only dated from 1858, yet already had a formidable reputation earned in and around Sind, but with no recent experience in Afghanistan. Lastly, but certainly never least, was Surgeon-Major Edge's field hospital and a force of forty sappers.

Jack knew the popular misconception that soldiers sang as they marched. He looked at the column with its accompanying cloud of dust. Maybe soldiers sang in a balmy day in Herefordshire or Kent, but not in Afghanistan. Even talking was difficult.

"Well, Windrush," Burrows asked. "We're meeting the Wali and his forces at Grishk. He's on the Farah Road, I hear. By then, we'll know Ayub Khan's movements."

"Yes, sir. If he stands to fight, we can smash him." Jack said what the general would expect to hear.

Colonel St John, the political resident in Kandahar, joined them, with the Wali's representative, Nawab Hasan Ali Khan looking proud as he rode alongside.

"Our first stop is Kokeran," St John said.

"Will the Wali fight?" Burrows asked.

St John shrugged. "That depends on circumstances," he said. "If the Wali thinks we will win, he will prove loyal to his salt and fight like a tiger. On the other hand, if he thinks Ayub Khan will be victorious, he will negotiate with his enemy or simply join him and turn against us. The Afghans have a different philosophy of warfare than we do. If things aren't going well for us, we hang on or withdraw. The Afghans will change sides to fight for whoever they think is the stronger."

Jack grunted. "It's a matter of survival in this harsh land," he said. "Pragmatism wins over loyalty." He remembered the

Guides at Kabul when they died together, facing incredible odds. "But not always. The Pashtun are also capable of acts of amazing loyalty in the most unexpected circumstances."

St John glanced at Jack, frowning. "You're in the wrong position, Windrush. You should be in the Political Service."

Jack shook his head. "No, thank you, sir."

The men of the Horse Artillery rattled alongside. Major Blackwood lifted a hand to Jack while one group disregarded the dust and choked out a chant.

"We're the Horse Artillery,
The right of the line,
The pride of the British Army,
The ladies' delight when dismounted,
And the angels' pride when mounted."

Whatever happens on this campaign, the RHA will do their bit with professionalism and skill, as they always do. Ubique Quo Fas Et Gloria Ducun, lads. Everywhere with honour and glory.

The column marched on, with their boots thumping in unison and men already staggering in the punishing heat. Sarsens encouraged them with cheerful words, passing over a water bottle to a man who looked exhausted.

Well done, Sarsens, Jack thought.

"Keep going, lads!" Jack shouted. "We're nearly at Khezat-i-Gilzai!"

That's the scene of Armaghan's vision. Let's check its accuracy.

The small garrison at Khezat-i-Gilzai, a mixture of sepoys and a company of the 66th, greeted them with cheers.

"There's a rumour that the Afghans massacred you, lads," Jack told them.

The men of the 66th hefted their Martini-Henry's. "Here we are, sir," a red-headed sergeant said. "And not a single one of us massacred to date. Let Ayub Khan's men come! The Brave Boys of Berks will see to them!"

"Keep a watch out," Jack said, and the 66th laughed, confident in their ability to outfight any enemy.

Satisfied there had been no massacre, Burrows' column slogged out of Khezat-i-Gilzai to the village of Grishk, where it halted for the day.

"Make camp," the general ordered, and within twenty minutes, hundreds of tents rose in ordered rows, with the camp followers a confused mass outside the lines. The artillery and headquarters company, 66th Foot, camped in a graveyard, with the 66th posting a strong guard around the regimental Colours. Jack nodded his approval; soldiers regarded the Colours as sacred, the Holy Grail of the regiment. They embodied the battalion's spirit, a symbol of the brotherhood, comradeship and loyalty that held the men together through the chaos of battle.

Officers and men alike were prepared to die for the Colours. Jack recalled the story of Sir Robert Douglas, colonel of the Royal Scots, the 1st Foot at the Battle of Steinkirk in 1692. When the enemy captured the Regimental Colour, Douglas jumped over a hedge into the middle of the French, grabbed the Colour from the officer who held it and threw it to his men. Douglas knew he would sacrifice his life and accepted the price, dying under a score of bayonets.

Even when the Colours, shot-torn, weather scarred and often little more than discoloured rags, were no longer used, the regiment prized them. Old, retired Colours were carried to the regimental church to be hung on display, sanctified by human sacrifice.

Regimental pride is a strange concept when men will surrender their lives for a square of coloured silk. But for men who have never had a family, or a sense of belonging, the regiment is the only home they know.

As Jack ruminated, General Burrows threw out a screen of cavalry to watch for the enemy or Sher Ali's men. Skinner's 3rd Cavalry rode in small groups, seemingly casual despite the possibility of an attack.

While the infantry boiled meat and potatoes in their *deshkies*, the cooking pot the other ranks referred to as dixies, off-duty cavalrymen showed off their skills. Jack watched a group of Skinner's sowars place a bottle on the ground, gallop away, turn and gallop back to fire their Sniders, breaking the bottle's neck. Others planted a tent peg deep in the earth, rode in a circle and returned at speed to lift the peg on their lances as they passed.

"These boys are good," Sarsens enthused. "I'm glad they're on our side."

I won't tell him the Afghan cavalry is every bit as skilled.

When not tent-pegging, the sowars hung from the horse's mane at a gallop or swung underneath the animal. One man placed a brass *lotah,* a drinking vessel, on the ground, rode away and galloped back. He hung single-handed from his horse's neck, sliced the *lotah* in two with his tulwar, and returned to the saddle.

"How the deuce do they do that without falling off?" Sarsens asked.

"It's all in the saddle," Crimea spoke with the wisdom of eighteen months' experience out east. "Our saddles are slippery leather, but these Indian fellows put layers of cloth on top, so they don't slide off. Also, they use a different bit that can halt their horse even at full speed."

Jack nodded at Crimea's knowledge and noticed the raw Sarsens was suitably impressed.

Now that the march was over and the men fed, some British soldiers began to relax. Sergeant Kelly of the 66th fussed over his dog, a nondescript terrier named Bobbie, while the men played cards, swapped lies or sang.

Being typical British army songs, they alternated between the sickly sentimental and the bawdy music hall, often with added obscenities for colour. Jack smiled at *Little Nell* while the Irish soldiers sang *The Minstrel Boy*, with the English and Scots joining in without caring that they were the villains of the piece. After that came *Merrily goes the Mill, my Boys*, followed by *Sweet Evalina.*

"Dear Evelina, sweet Evelina,
My love for thee shall never, never die.
Dear Evelina, sweet Evelina,
My love for thee shall, never, never die."

Jack stepped away, satisfied that the British soldiers, at least, were content.

"The Wali should join us here," Burrows spoke with some confidence. "He is at Kadanak, a few miles ahead."

Jack lifted his head and frowned. "Something is happening," he said.

"What's that, Windrush?" Burrows wiped the sweat from his forehead.

"Something is wrong, sir," Jack said.

Burrows frowned. "What do you mean?"

"The atmosphere has changed." Jack looked around, loosening the sword in its scabbard. "I've been out here a long time, sir, and I know this territory. You can tell by the feel of the place when things change. I don't know what it is."

Burrows glanced at St John, who nodded. "Best warn the men, sir. Windrush knows Afghanistan as well as anybody."

"Scout ahead, Windrush," Burrows ordered. "See what you can find. Do you want any men with you?"

"A couple of the Scinde Horse, sir, if I may."

"Take my compliments to Colonel Malcolmson and ask to borrow two of his men. See what you can find."

Glad to be on an independent mission and away from the stifling confines of senior officers, Jack wheeled his horse. A sense of foreboding lay heavy on him.

* * *

The two troopers of the Scinde Horse rode happily beside Jack. Both were Baluchis who understood the area and kept a wary eye on their surroundings, watching the hills and dry ground with instinctive skill.

"I don't know what I'm looking for," Jack told them. "I only feel that something is wrong."

The troopers accepted his word without comment. They understood.

"Sahib. Over there." The leading man nodded ahead and to the right.

Jack saw the faint lift of dust drifting from a distant ridge. "Thank you. We'll meet it." He kicked in his heels and trotted towards the rising dust, aware it could be anything from an itinerant merchant with a camel to the outrider of Ayub Khan's army.

Jack crested a barren ridge and stopped. A lone rider was galloping towards them, with his head down, only part-seen through the curtain of dust. "We'll intercept him," he ordered and spread out his men before riding down towards the horseman. The man rode on, oblivious to everything except making distance.

"Hold there!" Jack stopped twenty yards in front of the man. "Where are you going in such a hurry?"

The rider reined in, reaching for the sword at his waist, but Jack's two Scinde Horsemen had already drawn their tulwars and approached him.

"Where are you going, my friend?" Jack asked. As the dust cleared, he saw the man wore the uniform of one of Sher Ali's regiments.

"Who are you?" the rider asked in Pashtu, with one hand on his sword hilt. He eyed Jack's dusty uniform and the two Scinde horsemen.

"Major Jack Windrush, with General Burrows' force. Who are you?"

The man lifted his hand from the hilt of his sword. "I have a message for General Burrows and nobody else."

"We'll take you to him," Jack said, turning his horse. The Scinde riders formed up behind the messenger, ensuring he did not change his mind and ride away.

Burrows looked up as Jack rode in with his prize. "What's all this?"

"A rider with a message, sir," Jack said.

"Fetch him some water," Burrows said, "and let him speak."

The rider drank thirstily, wiped his mouth, and spoke rapidly. "The Wali sends his greetings to General Burrows," he said, "and instructed me to convey a grievous message. I have to inform you, sahib, that the Wali is no longer in a position to support you against Ayub Khan."

Burrows took a deep breath. "Why is that, pray?"

"The Wali has instructed me to tell you that when he ordered his army to retire from the camp at Kadanak to join your Excellency's army at Grishk, his infantry deserted, taking with them their arms, ammunition and artillery."

While Burrows swore softly, Jack met St John's eyes. The political officer nodded slowly, keeping his face immobile.

The messenger continued. "The Wali also instructed me to tell you that all his officers have remained loyal, as have his cavalry, over one thousand men."

"So far," St John said, as Jack nodded. He had little confidence in the Wali's ability to retain the loyalty of any of his men.

Realising that General Burrows did not intend to execute him for bearing bad news, the messenger continued. "The Wali also wishes to tell you that the treasury is safe."

"Well, thank goodness for small mercies," St John said. "As long as the treasury is safe, there is hope for mankind."

General Burrows' mouth twisted into a sour grin. "We gave the Wali those guns recently, so it looks like we'll be fighting against our own artillery. We handed over six smooth-bore pieces, and we trained the Wali's men to use them."

"We'll only be fighting them if they escape, sir," Jack hinted. He addressed the messenger. "Where are the deserters now?"

"Across the Helmand River," the man said. "They were heading for the Zamindawar Valley."

St John looked away. "That's a good region for turncoats," he said quietly. "That's Alizai territory, one of the Durrani Pashtun tribes. The Nurzai, Barakzai and Alakozai Durrani tribes also live there."

"Zamindawar sounds like an amiable place," Jack murmured. "All they need is a few modern pieces of artillery and a thousand or two trained and fully armed men."

"It was warriors from Zamindawar who attacked Sir Donald Stewart at Ahmed Khel," St John said. "They are a truculent, dangerous breed."

"We can't let them get the guns," Burrows made his decision. "Damn it all. Wellington never lost a single gun in India, the Peninsula or Waterloo."

Jack glanced at St John and then Burrows. "What do you want us to do, sir?"

CHAPTER FIVE

"We'll go after them, by God," Burrows decided. "We can't let the deserters hand our guns to Ayub Khan." He shook his head. "They'll have Martini-Henry rifles as well as artillery. Imagine them in the hands of the Pashtun tribes."

"They have Sniders, sir, and Enfields," St John said. "We have a policy, ever since the Mutiny, not to arm the sepoys or our Afghan allies with our most modern weapons."

Burrows grunted, unhappy to be corrected. "All the same. I'll take the cavalry, horse artillery and four companies of the 66th and sepoys. Who leads the mutineers?"

"Mahomed Aslam Khan," St John replied at once. "He's an experienced man, sir, and no fool."

Jack grunted. "These Afghans are a formidable people. I don't know Mahomed Aslam. Is Ayub also a decent soldier?"

St John nodded. "I'd say he's one of their best. According to my people, Ayub's mentor was a Russian soldier named Medhi Ali, who pretended to be an Islamic convert."

"Pretended, sir?" Jack asked.

"He was a spy, working for the Csar, but he trained Ayub well in modern battle techniques, and Ayub's men love him."

Jack nodded. A Russian-trained Afghan commander would combine Afghan fire with modern knowledge.

"Get the men organised to cross the Helmand," Burrows interrupted the conversation. "Leave the remainder here in Grishk in a defensive position."

With the decision made, Burrows split his force to pursue the mutineers.

"3rd Lights, take the advanced guard," Burrows ordered.

Burrows rode erect as he followed the left bank of the Helmand River, with Jack joining the Third Lights. The infantry and Royal Horse Artillery followed in a column of drab khaki and steel.

"The river is low," a sowar pointed out. "Ayub Khan can cross nearly anywhere." He grinned, showing white teeth through his black beard. "And Mahomed Aslam can run faster when we chase him."

The mutineers had left an obvious trail on the dusty ground, so the sowars followed at a fast walk, barely stopping to check the route. Sohrab, the risaldar, posted three men a quarter of a mile in front to watch for ambushes, and two on the left flank, while the Helmand River flowed sluggishly on their right.

"Sahib." Sohrab indicated the ground. "They crossed the river here."

Jack nodded. The mutineers had not attempted to cover their tracks. "Send a sowar back to advise General Burrows sahib," he ordered. "We will follow Mahomed Aslan."

The Helmand River was fairly broad where the mutineers had crossed but too shallow to present any hindrance. The cavalry splashed across without difficulty, raising a curtain of muddy water that surged against both banks. The far side of the river felt like hostile territory, as though Jack was in a different country. He remembered a similar sensation when he had crossed the Pra River into Ashantiland.

We've entered Ayub Khan's world now. Maybe rivers are a mental as well as a geographical barrier, a frontier of the mind as much as of the body.

"Lead on, Risaldar," Jack said, following the mutineer's trail. "Send four men ahead now, and three on each flank," he glanced behind him where the tail of the cavalry was leaving the river. "I want a strong body in the rear as well, in case Ayub Khan's men try to cut us off."

"Yes, Sahib," the risaldar said. "I have already reinforced the front and flanks and sent six men as a rearguard."

Jack smiled. The risaldar knew his job and had politely rebuked him. "Good man, Sohrab."

They rode on, more slowly now, with the trail following the riverbank for a couple of miles. Jack looked up as a sowar of the advance guard galloped to the risaldar.

"The enemy is ahead, sahib," he reported.

"How many?" Jack asked.

"Mahomed Aslan's force, Sahib," the trooper reported, "a thousand infantry and six guns."

"Stand firm here," Jack ordered the risaldar, "and send a man to inform General Burrows." He waited until a sowar galloped back, raising a curtain of dust, and then moved cautiously ahead to view the enemy.

Jack saw a plume of dust first, gradually rising into the clear abyss of the sky, and then the twinkle of sunlight on equipment. He pushed on, reducing his horse's speed to a walk as he neared the enemy. The low walls of a village crouched ahead, with the rising towers of two small forts that the Afghans often doubled as homes and defences.

A field piece banged out, and then the rapid whoosh of a shot passed over Jack's head. The explosion came a second later, raising a fountain of dust twenty feet into the air.

Jack grunted, shifted his route slightly and approached the village again, moving at a canter and zigzagging to make himself a more difficult target.

The gun fired a second time, with the shot falling short.

I'm getting too close, Jack told himself. *Mahomed Aslan's warning me to keep clear.*

He shifted to the right and kicked in his spurs. Two guns fired that time, bracketing Jack's position without getting close. When he saw a plume of dust approaching him, he knew he'd better withdraw.

Mahomed Aslan has sent a patrol out. They might be horsemen, judging by the speed they're travelling.

Turning his horse, Jack cantered back to the cavalry, where Risaldar Sohrab was glad to see Jack back safely. "Burrows sahib would not be pleased if I lost one of his majors," he said.

Burrows brought up the remainder of his force within an hour and listened to Jack's report.

"Mahomed Aslan has sent his infantry ahead, and he's holding a position at a village ahead."

"Shoraki, sahib," Sohrab murmured. "The village is called Shoraki."

"Shoraki," Jack repeated. "Thank you, risaldar. Mohamed has sited his guns around the village, sir, and maybe has some horsemen, although I don't know whether they are regulars or merely villagers."

"Sher Ali's cavalry remained loyal," Burrows reminded testily. "We will advance towards this village of Shoraki."

With the cavalry as a screen and the infantry marching as a solid block in the middle, Burrows pushed forward until the mutineers' guns opened up in a controlled volley.

Jack saw Sarsens instinctively duck as a shell exploded fifty yards away.

"What the deuce?" Sarsens asked.

"That was the enemy's artillery," Jack explained.

Sarsens straightened up. "This is a lark," he said, grinning.

"No," Jack said. "This is in earnest. Men's limbs and lives are at stake here. You're no longer at Eton or whatever school you were at." He controlled his rising temper. "Stay under cover and don't do anything foolish."

Crimea fingered his sword, staring ahead. He was the last man to search for cover.

You're your mother's son, Crimea!

The Afghan artillery fired again, with all six shots crashing down thirty yards in front of the British positions. Fountains of dust rose, remained in the air for a few seconds and slowly drifted with the wind to settle across the plain.

"Good shooting," Jack said as the Horse Artillery unlimbered.

"Action front," Major Blackwood barked, "load with shrapnel!" He added rapid orders that saw the gunners hurry under the Afghan sun, and within three minutes, the guns were ready.

"Aim above the muzzle smoke," Blackwood said, waited for the gunners to obey, and ordered, "fire!"

All six horse artillery guns fired as one, with the powder smoke hanging in a grey-white cloud.

Jack saw the orange-yellow splashes of the explosions above the village walls and knew the artillery had shaken their target. He imagined the sharp shards of shrapnel cascading from above, slicing into heads, arms, and shoulders.

The Afghan guns fired again, with the horse artillery a few seconds later. As the Afghan's shells exploded around the British positions, the horse artillery fired a third time.

"We're getting off three shots to every two of theirs," Jack said.

Blackwood was too busy to reply, ensuring his guns fired as fast and accurately as possible. When the next Afghan salvo landed closer, he ordered half his battery to shift left and half right, then continued the attack.

The pause seemed to encourage the Afghans who fired faster with one shot landing among the British infantry. A man screamed, and a dooley bearer ran to help. Smoke hung heavy on the air, mingling with the dust.

"Can you see the target?" Blackwood asked.

The gunners nodded as a slight breeze blew away the smoke.

The Afghan gunners were visible through gaps in the wall, turbaned heads moving as they loaded their guns.

"Case shot," Blackwood ordered and watched the gunners load.

Case shot was similar to the blast of a shotgun, except many times more destructive. With the guns point-blank, without elevation, and each case holding one hundred and eight bullets that scattered like a fan, E Battery's next volley had a terrible effect on the village wall and the Afghan gunners. Jack saw a man's head rise in the air, trailing blood. The turban unravelled as the head descended.

"Sir," Jack hinted to General Burrows. "Our artillery is keeping the Afghan guns busy. Maybe if the cavalry outflanked them, you might gain a faster victory."

Burrows grunted. "I know how to fight a battle, Windrush."

"I don't doubt that, sir, but you asked me to accompany you because I have experience."

Burrows frowned and turned away.

The cavalry filed out a few moments later, with the Scinde Horse on the left and the 3rd Lights on the right. The Horse Artillery continued to pound the front of Shoraki village with case shot and common shell.

Before the cavalry arrived, the Afghan battery stopped firing, and Jack saw a score of riders fleeing from the rear of the village. The cavalry also noticed them and gave chase. What followed was more of a massacre than a fight as the Scinde Horse and 3rd Lights ripped into the retreating mutineers.

"You two," Burrows indicated Crimea and Sarsens. "Colonel Windrush said you wanted experience of battle. Find horses and join the Lights."

"Yes, sir!" Sarsens said at once. "Come along, Windrush!" Crimea was already moving, begging spare horses from the cavalry.

Throwing himself on a horse and drawing his sword in anticipation, Crimea bounded ahead with Sarsens seconds behind.

"Wait for me, Crimea!"

Both subalterns spurred forward, shouting as if they were at a game. Burrows watched them for a moment. "Young fools," he said. "But I think it's safe enough now, with the Afghans in retreat. Go with them, Windrush and try to keep them out of too much trouble."

"Yes, sir." Jack followed, wondering how to look after two high-spirited young men in a skirmish with the Afghans.

By the time Jack reached Shoraki, the last of the defenders were leaving. Mahomed Aslan's men dragged their dead away from the artillery and threw the bodies into a sluggish stream, which ran scarlet with Afghan blood.

"That's unusual," Jack said. "The Afghans usually carry away their dead."

"Look at that!" Sarsens pointed upwards, where a dozen women had mounted the flat roofs as the 66th advanced to take possession. They began to throw missiles and fire pistols at the British.

Glancing at Jack, Crimea slid his sabre into its scabbard and drew his pistol.

"They do say the women of the species are deadlier than the male," Sarsens said. "Bad form to shoot at a lady, though, Crimea, old boy."

"These ladies would cut you up slowly and laugh at your screams," Jack said grimly. "They are not your Hyde Park beauties, Second Lieutenant."

An Afghan man scrambled up a tree and opened fire with a long jezail, narrowly missing a corporal of the 66th, who lifted his Martini and replied at once. The corporal's shot hit the Afghan high in the chest, knocking him from his perch. Before the corporal had time to work the lever to open the breech to reload, a white-robed ghazi emerged from a ditch and charged forward, pulwar raised and with a small round shield protecting his head.

"*Allah Akbar! Din! Din!*"

Jack turned to help, but he was not needed. The corporal coolly waited for the swordsman to close, ducked beneath the shield, and rammed his bayonet into the ghazi's stomach. A cavalryman of the Lights ran up and finished the job with his sabre.

"Thanks, Johnny," the 66th private said, grinning.

By that time, the fighting was over. The Afghan gunners had fled, and the cavalry had cut down any who did not surrender. The prisoners were sitting in a group, some smiling in pretended friendship and others glowering at their captors. At the entrance to the village, men of the 66th helped drag away the captured guns with ropes.

"Major Blackwood," Burrows ordered. "Take care of the captured artillery. Cavalry, find the enemy infantry. 66th, march in pursuit. Scinde Rifles, remain here with the artillery."

The orders were simple, with the cavalry and 66th following the trail of Mohamed Aslan's mutineers. Jack rode beside the subalterns.

"You two stay with me! If you ride around Afghanistan alone, the Pashtuns will dice you into collops."

Crimea opened his mouth to retort, saw the expression on Jack's face and decided to remain quiet. They joined Currie's 3rd Lights, trotting forward on the enemy's trail.

As Burrows' cavalry advanced, the Wali's mutinous infantry disintegrated, with a few turning to fight but most running left or right. Burrows' cavalry hunted them down, killing any who showed signs of resistance. One stubborn group found shelter in a mud-walled enclosure and fired a ragged volley at the Lights.

"Leave them to the infantry!" Major Curry ordered. "That's their job. We'll harry the retreat until they've no cohesion left."

Pursuing ragged infantry was a job for which the Light Cavalry was admirably suited. The horsemen cantered ahead, superbly disciplined, as Jack called his subalterns together.

"We're infantrymen," he reminded. "You'll learn more about

your trade helping the 66th winkle out these mutineers than in watching the cavalry."

The subalterns nodded, reluctant to leave the chase. Crimea held Jack's gaze for a moment, then lowered his eyes.

"Come on, then, boys. Let's see how many mutineers are waiting." Jack leaned closer to Crimea. "Do as I order, and don't be stupid."

Jack led them towards the small group of houses, expecting the Snider's crack and the buzz of bullets around him. One shot came close, kicking up dust a few feet from the legs of his horse.

"Don't ride in a straight line," Jack advised, "and don't bunch. Spread out and weave, so the enemy can't guess where you are going next."

Jack rode at a fast walk, taking his own advice and dodging behind the occasional scrubby tree as he neared the enclosures. "Count the muzzle flashes," he said, "and let me know how many you see."

Jack had seen a hundred subalterns endure fire for the first time and placed them in three categories. Some men were openly afraid and would never make good officers. Other men hid their natural fear and showed potential, and a few were fearless. Jack remembered the young subalterns who charged forward into the ferocious Russian artillery and musketry at the Redan. Crimea was of the same stamp. He refused to flinch as the Afghan bullets whined and buzzed around them while Sarsens edged away, watched Jack, and pretended to be brave.

"Don't give the Afghans a target," Jack shouted.

"British officers don't bob!" Crimea said.

"British officers are no good when they're dead!" Jack said. "Keep moving."

He led them around the first enclosure, weaving from side to side as the subalterns raced beside him.

"How many flashes?" Jack ducked as a bullet whined past his head.

"I see ten," Crimea said.

"I only saw eight." Sarsens settled his horse as a bullet burrowed into the dust close by its front hooves.

"We'll call it ten," Jack decided. "Better to overestimate the enemy than underestimate, and only a fool underestimates the Afghans."

"How about the second enclosure?" Jack ducked as a bullet buzzed past his head. "I count nine."

Within a few moments, Jack decided on ten of the enemy for each enclosure. "That's long enough, lads."

The Afghans had their range now, with bullets coming uncomfortably close. Crimea fired his revolver at them with his face tense with concentration.

"That's the first shots I've fired since coming to Afghanistan," he said.

Why? How have the Royals avoided battle when every other regiment has been heavily involved?

"Time to withdraw, gentlemen," Jack said. "A messenger is only as good as his intelligence. Dead men can't convey anything."

"Yes, sir!" Crimea reloaded his revolver as he rode, controlling his horse with his knees. He ignored the Afghan bullets.

You'll go far, my boy, if you live. The men love an officer with character and courage.

✯ ✯ ✯

Currie had ordered a troop of his Lights to patrol around the enclosures, keeping the mutineers inside. Colonel Galbraith led the 66th as they arrived, with the infantry dusty and hot but efficient.

"The mutineers hold three enclosures, sir," Jack reported. "We calculate ten men in each."

"We'll soon winkle them out," Galbraith said. "Number One Company, form a defensive ring, facing outward a hundred yards from the enclosures. Don't let anybody enter. Number Two

Company, form a ring eighty yards from the enclosures, facing inwards. Prevent anybody from leaving." He waited until the men were in position.

"Number Three Company, remove the enemy."

"Watch and learn," Jack said as Sarsens dismounted. "Don't interfere when another regiment is busy unless they need help."

For a regiment that had not fought for decades, the 66th acted well. They spread out into open order and advanced with the bayonet, firing by sections to keep the defenders busy. The mutineers fired once, and then the 66th charged. The untried soldiers leapt over the mud walls and used their bayonets on anybody who retaliated. The skirmish was bloody but short. Within ten minutes, the 66th were in complete control of the enclosures.

"Nicely done," Jack said.

"Oh, my boys have been waiting a long time to show we're the best." Galbraith was unable to hide his pride.

As Number Three Company marched out of the enclosures with their prizes, a score of prisoners and thirty Snider rifles, the cavalry returned, looking equally triumphant.

"We scattered them across the countryside," Major Currie said, "and collected dozens of rifles."

"Bring in the prisoners and weapons," Burrows said. "We'll base ourselves at Kashk-e-Nokhowd."

"Not a bad result," St John said to Jack. "I'm not sure about the enemy dead. The cavalry tends to exaggerate their success, of course. They claim about two hundred killed, and all the other mutineers scattered. I'll report that to Simla, although I'd cut the figure by fifty percent at least. We lost one man of the 66th killed and a couple wounded, with a few horses."

"The 66th did well for an inexperienced regiment," Jack said.

"So did the sowars," St John added.

Jack nodded. "They're Indian cavalry. They know how to fight."

Kashk-e-Nokhowd was a small place, further from the Helmand River than Shoraki was, and only forty-five miles from

Kandahar. However, it was strategically positioned where several roads met, and the surrounding countryside was relatively fertile, with fodder for the horses and supplies for the men.

"We'll remain here," Burrows decided. "We can watch the roads from the Helmand and react if Ayub Khan moves to threaten Kandahar."

Jack looked around, felt the oppressive heat of summer, and wondered what Afghanistan held for them.

We've won one skirmish. We should push on now and hit Ayub Khan while we have the momentum. I wish we had Roberts in command or Havelock. Even old Colin Campbell would not sit tight and wait. Not in Afghanistan, where any delay allows the enemy time to gather the tribes.

CHAPTER SIX

While Burrows settled his infantry and artillery into Kashk-e-Nokhowd, he sent cavalry patrols to watch the local area. Standing and mobile pickets stopped any passing mutineers and relieved them of any weapons. After a while, the remains of the Wali's army camped nearby with the Wali's officers mingled with the British. The sowars joined Burrows cavalry in scouring the countryside for the enemy.

"We don't have much use around here," Jack told Crimea and Sarsens, "so we'll conduct our own patrols."

"Yes, sir."

Jack broke the subalterns in easily, first patrolling the immediate vicinity of the British tented camp and then moving further afield, allowing them to get a feel for the country. He showed them what to look for, how to find cover if the enemy attacked and taught them to look after themselves. He taught them to look for dead ground when approaching an enemy, how to keep a horse under cover and watch for any signs of movement.

"Don't ogle the local women," he said. "That's a sure way to invite trouble. Never go into a village alone, and always carry a weapon, as Colonel Windrush told you."

"The old man seemed quite upset." Crimea was beginning to relax with Jack.

"He's trying to save your life," Jack told him.

On the third day, the 19th of July 1880, Jack took them on a more extended patrol, heading towards the Helmand River. They rode along the south side of the still shallow water, baking in the sun, swatting flies, and eating dust when Jack nodded to a small settlement on the opposite bank.

"Did either of you lads see that?"

"I only saw a flash," Crimea told him.

"That was the sun reflecting on steel. It could be entirely innocent, or it could be a weapon. Dismount, lads," Jack said quietly. "Something is happening over there."

The subalterns had learned to obey.

"Pull your horses down as I showed you." Jack lay his mount down, making it less conspicuous. "Now, keep still and watch my horse while I scout ahead."

Pulling out his binoculars, Jack crawled closer to the river, sheltered in a hollow of dead ground and focussed on the settlement. As he had suspected, a group of horsemen had gathered in the village, talking to the local men. The horsemen were warriors, with long jezzails across their backs and pulwars or Khyber knives in their belts, but Jack expected that in Afghanistan.

"Sir." Sarsens slid up to him. "Dust, sir!" He gesticulated behind him. "Coming from the south."

Jack turned around without raising his head and lifted his binoculars again. "About a dozen riders, I think. Warn Crimea to keep still in case they pass this way."

"Yes, sir." Sarsens returned to Crimea.

The riders came closer, then altered direction and splashed over a ford of the Helmand River. Jack followed them with his binoculars, already guessing they were meeting the horsemen in the village. He wished he was close enough to listen but knew that the Afghans would see him if he approached. He watched as the two groups of riders greeted each other with great formality, and only when one man faced his direction did Jack grunt.

"Zamar Khan," Jack breathed. "What are you doing so far from Kandahar? And who are you meeting?" He lay under the sun as the day dragged on. The two groups of men disappeared into one of the flat-roofed houses, leaving only a few villagers to continue their routine work.

Jack returned to the subalterns. "You two get back to camp. I could be here some time."

"You might need us, sir," Sarsens protested.

"Go!" Jack hardened his tone. "Ride fast and inform General Burrows, with my compliments, that I am watching Zamar Khan."

"Yes, sir." Sarsens recoiled at Jack's expression. He fled, taking Crimea with him.

Another two hours passed before Zamar Khan emerged from the house, with his warriors around him. Jack did not recognise anybody in the other party. He watched both groups ride away in different directions and returned to his horse.

I know Zaman Khan. I don't know the others, so I'll follow them.

Allowing the riders ten minutes, Jack followed, following the trail, and riding slowly to ensure there was little dust to betray him. Jack's quarry headed north, deep into Helmand Province, then south again, recrossing the Helmand. Jack began to wonder if he would ride all night. He knew he was doing precisely what he warned the subalterns to avoid. He was putting himself at risk. If the Afghans captured him, his life would end in exquisitely painful torture.

As night fell, Jack found shelter in a clump of rocks and watched the twinkle of his quarry's campfire. He slept fitfully, woke before dawn, watered his horse from the *mussack* and headed for the direction where he had seen the campfire.

The Afghans were already away, and Jack followed the trail, keeping well back and constantly searching for cover. His main fear was Ayub Khan's men cutting him off from his line of retreat.

After an hour, Jack's quarry halted at a village, riding through the main gate as if they owned the place. Jack hurriedly consulted his map. *Sangbur,* he said. *They've taken a very circuitous route to get here. We must be about halfway between Kashk-e-Nokhowd and the Helmand River.*

Reining in behind one of the few trees, Jack focussed his binoculars, being careful to avoid the sun reflecting from the lenses. He grunted as he saw a larger company of horsemen and then a scatter of tents, with more in the distance. With the wind kicking up a screen of dust, Jack could not make out how many tents there were.

Ayub Khan, I believe, Jack said to himself. *Or part of his army, at least. I'd better get this intelligence to General Burrows.*

Sliding away from the tree, Jack turned his horse and headed back to Kashk-e-Nokhowd. After only a few minutes, he saw the cavalry approach and kicked in his spurs, knowing they would see his dust.

Come on then, boys!

The Afghans were superb riders, spreading out behind Jack to cut off any possibility of him veering left or right. One man fired from the saddle, but Jack knew the chance of a hit was remote, so he continued to ride in a straight line.

How many? Jack glanced over his shoulder. Six riders, wild-looking men with loose turbans and baggy clothes, complete with pulwars and rifles.

I might outride six, as long as their horses are not fresh.

A slight wind raised the dust, blowing it into Jack's face. He ducked his head, patted his horse's neck, and spurred again, relying on speed and power to escape his pursuers.

The Afghans were persistent, silent as they followed. Somebody fired again, with the bullet raising a fountain of dust ten yards to Jack's right. He rode on, swearing as he heard the drumbeat of hooves easing closer. One of the Afghans spurred ahead of the rest.

He'll ride his horse to death to break me, allowing the others to catch up. I can't fight five Afghan warriors.

Jack spurred desperately, feeling his horse surge forward and then slowly weaken as its strength failed. Jack knew he had to decide soon. Should he find somewhere to make a stand and take one or two of his pursuers with him? Or should he ride on until his horse fell and then fight, a mile or two closer to the British camp?

Jack looked up as he saw a second body of cavalry in front of him. They rode in a column of four, spreading into three lines when they saw Jack.

What the devil do I do now? My horse is about foundered. Fight, Jack. Find a suitable place and fight!

The landscape was bare, undulating, with a few heat-scorched trees. Jack rode to the nearest and pulled down his horse, intending to use it as a barrier. With the tree at his back and his horse in front, he might be able to hold off one assault and perhaps two.

Come on then, boys!

Strangely, Jack felt no fear as he pulled out his revolver, checked the chambers were loaded and lay behind his horse. He was a soldier, and death was part of the soldier's bargain.

I would have liked to see Mary again.

The trill of a bugle sounded as the approaching cavalry increased their speed to a canter.

The Afghan's don't use British bugle calls.

"3rd Lights!" Jack shouted. At that moment, the approach of Skinner's Horse was one of the most beautiful sights Jack had ever seen. He watched them break into a canter as the bugle sounded again, and then the sun glittered on steel as each rider drew his sabre.

As the Lights drew near, Jack's pursuers reined up and fled, with the subadar in charge of the Lights sending half a dozen men in pursuit. "Windrush sahib?"

"That's me." Jack reined in, panting and with sweat creating white grooves on his dusty face.

"General Burrows sent us out to find you." The subadar sounded disapproving. "This is not an area where British officers should ride out alone."

Jack accepted the rebuke. "You are correct, subadar. Thank you for rescuing me. Now, I have to see General Burrows. I'd avoid Sangbur if I were you. Ayub Khan's men are there."

"My orders were to find you, Sahib," the subadar said, "not to search for Ayub Khan."

* * *

Burrows raised his eyebrows as Jack told him about the proximity of the Afghan forces.

"So close!" Burrows said. "How many men, Windrush?"

"Not above a hundred at Sangbur," Jack said. "It looked like a small scouting force, but as they have tents, they might be planning to garrison the village or stay some time. I saw tents a bit further back. I could not see how many."

"I'll send a cavalry patrol out," Burrows said.

"I'd advise a strong one, sir," Jack said.

Burrows' face darkened at Jack's advice.

"Headquarters at Simla has sent a despatch," Burrows said. "The commander-in-chief wants us to attack Ayub Khan if we think we can beat him. It is considered of the greatest political importance that we should disperse Ayub's force to prevent it from advancing on Ghuznee."

Jack wondered if Burrows was asking his advice or scorning it. "Yes, sir. It seems crucial to find out how many men he has before you make any decision."

"Thank you, Windrush," Burrows said. "I had worked that

out myself. You'd better get some rest and find something to eat."

The 66th took Jack in as if he were one of his own, with Crimea and Sarsens included in their mess. They asked Jack what he had discovered and left him to recover, with one of the 66th grooms looking after his horse.

"I won't let any of these Indian fellows touch it, sir," the groom promised. "Don't you worry, now."

By that time, Jack's weariness had overtaken him, and he was glad to collapse inside a tent, uncaring of the heat, or even that he was unshaved. As he closed his eyes, he heard Sarsens' loud voice.

"What a lark, Crimea. This is better than Sandhurst, eh?"

* * *

As the British brigade baked in the heat at Kashk-e-Nokhowd, Burrows increased his patrolling. Over the following days, he sent cavalry squadrons to Sangbur and the surrounding area and collated the information they gathered. Jack continued to take Sarsens and Crimea out on patrol, trying to teach them to survive longer.

On the 26th of July, after more than a week sitting in the same village, Burrows gathered his senior officers together.

Jack sat on a camp chair at the back, with his sun helmet tipped at an angle against the heat.

"Gentlemen," Burrows said. "Our patrols have brought us news of Ayub Khan. His advance parties have reached Grishk, and he has units spread between Grishk and Hydrabad along the right bank of the Helmand River. Our patrols have found strong detachments of the enemy at Sangbur, and one troop of our Scinde Horse skirmished with the enemy on the plain below the Garmao Hills."

Jack formed a map in his head. All these places were north of

Burrows' brigade, with the Garmao Hills near the village of Maiwand.

"Ayub Khan is well aware of our presence," Burrows continued, "and his movements suggest he intends to turn our position by marching along the northern road to Maiwand. From there, he could debouch through the Maiwand Pass to Singiri, where he could block our passage to Kandahar."

Jack nodded. That was a sound strategy. He wondered why Burrows lingered so long at Kashk-e-Nokhowd, rather than moving to catch Ayub Khan's forces as they moved south. If Burrows had fought any part of Ayub's army, he could have scattered it and destroyed the rest piecemeal. With the British having a numerically weaker force, Jack considered it a better strategy to attack separate units of Ayub's army rather than allowing him to concentrate his forces. In Afghanistan, the tribes viewed inactivity as weakness, which only encouraged them to support the side they believed was stronger.

Jack traced his mental map. He would have gathered his men and marched through Maiwand and up the Khakrez Valley, striking at Ayub Khan's forces as he met them.

"Now," Burrows said, "our latest report from the Third Lights tell me that Ayub has two thousand cavalry. We also know that a body of ghazis has settled around Maiwand and Garmao, with Ayub and the bulk of his army marching to join them."

"Sir," Colonel St John interrupted the brigadier. "If I may?"

"Speak, Colonel," Burrows sounded irritated.

"My spies tell me that the bulk of Ayub's army has already arrived," St John said. "They estimate at least twelve thousand men at Sangbur."

"Your spies are exaggerating," Burrows said. "They are trying to appear more important than they are."

"They're good men," St John said. "I trust them."

"We can discount them on this occasion, I think," Burrows said. "We'll march for Maiwand tomorrow morning." He looked around the circle of officers as if expecting a round of applause. "We should arrive before Ayub's cavalry occupies Maiwand in force, and we'll chase away the enemy from Garmao."

The officers listened without enthusiasm. They knew that Ayub Khan outnumbered them and was a vastly experienced warrior.

"In addition, gentlemen," Burrows appeared not to notice the glum silence, "we get much of our grain from Maiwand. We'll take the village, and the supplies, before Ayub Khan arrives." He gave a small laugh, to which nobody responded. "We leave at half-past six tomorrow morning."

"Half-past six?" St John raised his eyebrows to Jack as the gathered officers departed to organise their men. "We should leave at half-past three at the latest, or we'll be marching through the heat of the day."

Jack took a deep breath. "I'd be happier with somebody else in command."

"Who? General Primrose?" St John shook his head. "He's another old woman, Windrush. A desk-bound warrior with no experience in the field. We can just hope Ayub Khan is not in great force, or his Herat and Kabul regiments squabble amongst themselves."

"Aye," Jack said. "We can hope." For some reason, he remembered Armaghan's story of massacred British soldiers. "Best keep your revolver handy, sir."

And may God be with us all.

CHAPTER SEVEN

At half-past six the following morning, the 27th of July 1880, Burrow's brigade struck camp. Jack watched as the usual organised confusion prevailed, the NCOs giving harassed orders, the recruits stumbling in the half-dark as they forgot items of kit, and the camels wandering in the wrong direction. A single camel could carry a day's supply for 160 sepoys, but even a brigade column also needed fodder and ammunition, water and tents, so there were hundreds of baggage animals. Eventually, after sergeants had roared themselves hoarse, all 2,600 fighting men were on the march, with the trail of camp followers wandering behind, all under the unforgiving sky of Helmand Province, Afghanistan.

"Well, Windrush." St John lit his first cheroot of the day, "here we go."

"Here we go, sir," Jack agreed.

"It's only twelve miles to Maiwand." St John wanted to talk that morning. "A single day's march, even with half of India in tow," he indicated the mob of camp followers that accompanied every army in India.

Jack nodded. For some reason, he remembered the march to the Alma in the Crimean War, when the British Army had set out in pomp and glory and left a trail of exhausted and diseased men before they reached halfway.

With the cavalry in front and on the flanks, the infantry marched steadily, soon sweltering under the sun. However, after only a couple of hours, Burrows ordered a halt.

"What the devil?" St John asked.

"We're allowing the baggage to catch up," Jack explained. "The Afghans love to swoop on baggage trains. They would massacre the camel drivers, grab the women and steal anything and everything before our rearguard even knew they had arrived."

"The general should have posted a strong baggage guard," St John said.

"We've only two and a half thousand men," Jack reminded. "And we don't know how large Ayub Khan's force is. I don't think the general can afford to weaken his column." He nodded upwards, where a pair of vultures circled the column. "These birds are hoping for food. They sense that something will happen today."

After half an hour, the column set off again. Jack noted that some of the infantry were already resorting to their water bottles.

"The men are feeling the heat, sir," he said.

St John grimaced. "It's going to be a long day."

As the sun rose and the heat increased, the march slowed and halted, waiting again for the baggage to catch up.

They marched in a fog of dust, with men choking, coughing, and recovering, spitting out dust, rubbing at irritated eyes and noses. Each infantryman could only see the back of the man in front, as his Martini, forty-nine inches long and nearly nine pounds in weight, seemed to grow heavier by the minute. The sun warmed the barrel and every metal part as the men stumbled on, cursing Afghanistan, cursing the army yet paradoxically hoping to meet and defeat Ayub Khan's men so they could return to India. Only Bobbie seemed unaffected as the dog barked and gambolled around the legs of Sergeant Kelly.

Jack glanced ahead, where the cavalry seemed to float on a sea of dust, with only their top halves visible. The landscape around was hazed, so the marching men saw everything through a yellow-brown film. The supply column followed behind the fighting men, with nearly two thousand camels, each with its little tinkling bell, plus ponies, lumbering bullocks, donkeys, mules, and horses. An army travelling through India or Afghanistan was slow-moving and encumbered, Jack thought.

"The advance guard won't see much in this stuff," St John said.

"Damned right they won't, and we're raising enough dust to alert anybody for ten miles." Jack touched the revolver in his holster.

Something doesn't feel right. I've been a soldier long enough to sense danger. I wish I had my 113th with me now. I'm cut off from these men, however good they are.

Burrows called another halt at Karezah, eight miles up the road and only four from Maiwand. Men lay on the ground, ignoring the dust that soon settled on them. The camp followers toiled up, humans and animals together.

A trio of cavalrymen galloped to Burrows while the dust began to settle. Jack removed his sun helmet, wiped the sweat from his forehead and raised his eyebrows to St John.

"Something is developing," he said.

"Come with me, Windrush," St John ordered. "I must know what's happening. I'm meant to be the intelligence officer, after all."

A jemadar was talking to Burrows when Jack approached.

"The spy told us that Ayub Khan is approaching, sahib," the jemadar said. "He is on the left front, thousands strong, and marching towards Maiwand."

"Nonsense!" Burrows said. "Ayub Khan is miles to the north. The spy is trying to lead us astray, jemadar. We've heard all these rumours before."

St John reined closer to the general. "This jemadar is a good man, sir, and he's familiar with the country. Maybe it's best to listen to his intelligence."

Burrows drew back slightly. "Thank you for your advice, Colonel, but I know these people. The Afghans are natural liars."

The column continued, slogging with heads down.

"Jemadar!" St John summoned the jemadar to him. "Did you see Ayub Khan's army yourself?"

"No, sahib." The jemadar was a man of about forty, with grey hair in his beard and wisdom in his brown eyes. "One of your spies told me."

"Very good, Jemadar. Take your men and patrol in the direction the spy indicated. See what you find and report back directly to me."

"Yes, sahib."

"And jemadar," St John called the man back. "Be careful. Don't get yourself killed."

"Yes, sahib." The jemadar kicked in his spurs and trotted to his men.

Jack stood in his stirrups to peer over the heads of the column. They marched on, deeper into Helmand with Burrows seemingly oblivious to the danger. Behind them, the supply column trudged through the dust in a motley collection of men and animals. Bare-footed bearers and servants mingled with the wagons and carts while the camel bells tinkled, less musical than tiresome.

The jemadar returned within twenty minutes, galloping past the marching men to find St John.

"Colonel Sahib!" He reined up in a cloud of dust. "Ayub Khan is here, sahib. I saw large bodies of cavalry on our left front, heading towards Maiwand."

"How many, Jemadar?"

The jemadar pondered for a moment. "I am not sure, sahib. The dust is thick."

"Make a guess, man!" St John ordered.

"Thousands, sahib," the jemadar said. "As many cavalry as we have men and more."

"Only cavalry?" Jack asked. "Or are they acting as a screen for infantry as well?"

Again, the jemadar considered his reply. "I don't know, sahib. The haze conceals the numbers."

St John spoke next. "Thank you, Jemadar. Watch them, would you? Keep me posted if there are any developments."

As the jemadar rode away, Jack took a deep breath. "I can't see Ayub Khan moving so many cavalry unless he also has infantry and possible artillery. I'd hazard that he has his entire army here."

"So would I, Windrush." St John sounded worried. "We'd better report to the general, although God knows what good that will do."

Burrows looked agitated when St John brought him the news. "Cavalry, you say?"

"Yes, sir. Thousands of horsemen, and maybe infantry as well."

Burrows pounced on the hesitation. "Maybe? Are you not certain?"

St John shook his head. "No, sir. Our cavalry patrol could not see through the haze. Between the heat and the dust, visibility is abysmal."

Burrows glanced at his watch. "It's nearly ten o'clock," he announced. "There's a village up ahead."

"Mundabad," St John murmured.

"Quite so. We'll halt there for a while and see how many of Ayub's force is ahead. I hope to prevent his main force from joining the cavalry."

"I believe Ayub Khan's whole army is waiting, sir," St John said.

Burrows frowned. "You're not sure. The cavalry patrols only guessed what was there."

As the British advanced guard occupied Mundabad, the rest

of Burrow's brigade, with its extended supply column, marched slowly forward. Once again, Jack checked his surroundings. The most noticeable feature was a deep gulley that ran north and south.

"Best watch that ravine," Jack said. "The Pashtuns would love to gather there and rush out in the dark."

On the far side of the gulley, the land stretched in a level plain, slowly rising to low hills. Fields of grain and fruit trees sagged sadly under the lash of the sun. Jack saw the haze in the east and lifted his binoculars.

"Dear God. Colonel!"

St John was already examining the plain. "I see them, Windrush. I wish I didn't, but I see them."

Even with binoculars, penetrating the haze was difficult, but Jack saw the twinkle of the sun on accoutrements and a host of disciplined men. They marched in rank after rank, their numbers impossible to judge but far exceeding the British brigade.

"Go and check," St John ordered. "Don't get close, but we need to know if that's only a part of Ayub Khan's army or if it's the whole thing."

Negotiating the gully took time, and Jack had to climb his horse up the far side and push it across the plain. He had only gone halfway when he saw a plume of dust advancing towards him.

They've seen me. How much further can I go?

Jack estimated he was eight hundred yards from Ayub Khan's army, and the cavalry patrol was only a hundred yards from the flank.

Another two minutes.

Jack spurred on, halted on a slight rise, and lifted the binoculars that hung around his neck. He focussed, trying to ignore the onrushing cavalry patrol.

Even at this distance, the haze shielded Ayub Khan's numbers, but Jack heard the rumble of wheels on the ground.

Transport wagon wheels? Or the wheels of artillery? I cannot tell. But this is a large army, not only the advance guard.

The Afghan cavalry was closer now and moving too fast for Jack's peace of mind. Dropping the binoculars, he turned around and spurred for the gulley.

I've left it too late. The Afghans' horses are fresher than mine, and they're gaining fast.

The Afghans were galloping, still riding in formation with the sun reflecting on swords and steel helmets. They covered five yards to every four of Jack's, with one man breaking formation to come at him in the flank. Jack cursed himself for being so foolhardy.

I should have turned back the instant I saw the Afghan patrol. I didn't learn anything worth knowing anyway.

The Afghan rider drew his sword and shouted something, with the words meaningless in the hammer of hooves on the hard ground. He snarled at Jack, with his teeth bared, drew close and slashed. Jack drew his sword and parried, feeling the jarring thrill of contact as the two blades met.

The Afghan drew away, turned his horse in a complete circle and attacked again with a sweeping overarm swing that would have parted Jack's head from his shoulders if it had connected.

Jack parried again, and this time he followed through, trying to slice at the Afghan's head. Jack swore as the point of his sabre tangled in his opponent's turban, and he only succeeded in raking the man's face. The glancing blow was sufficient to make the Afghan draw back, but he had slowed Jack down, and the other patrol members were nearly in touching distance.

How stupid it would be to die in a pointless skirmish in Afghanistan. For a second, Jack remembered his boyhood dreams of leading the Royal Malverns in a glorious attack on a French position, winning everlasting fame by planting the Colours in enemy positions in a Waterloo-style battle. The reality would be different, killed by half a dozen illiterate badmashes in central Asia.

"Come on, then!" Jack turned his horse towards the riders. *At least I'll die like a man, facing my enemy, not running away.* He flourished his sword, the old, familiar Wilkinson Sword blade he had carried as long as he could remember.

The Afghans galloped towards him, fierce men fighting for what they believed to be true, all determined to drive the feringhees and infidels out of their country.

Six of them. Six must be the standard size of Ayub Khan's patrols. I won't last a minute. Sorry, Mary, I'd like to see you one more time to say goodbye, but that's all part of the soldier's bargain. Arthur Elliot will take care of you. I hope David does well at Sandhurst.

The thoughts crowded through Jack's head without cohesion or sense as he instinctively slashed at the first man. And then the whoosh sounded, and the explosion as the shell landed a bare ten yards away, raising a fifteen-foot-high fountain of dirt and stones. A second explosion occurred moments later, and one of the Afghan riders fell back with his horse kicking and plunging on the ground.

What the devil?

Jack looked towards the British lines. Two of the Horse Artillery guns stood on his side of the gulley, with the gunners concentrating on what they saw as a body of Afghan cavalry.

Kicking in his spurs, Jack headed for the guns while the Afghans scattered across the plain.

"I'm British!" Jack shouted as he came close to the Horse Artillery. "Major Windrush of the 113th!" He knew that the dust would have covered his uniform, making him appear as wild and savage as any Afghan swordsman. "I'm British!"

"Well, damn me for a Frenchman!" one of the gunners shouted. "What the hang are you doing out here?"

CHAPTER EIGHT

Second Lieutenant Sarsens eyed the blood on Jack's sword and nudged Crimea. "What a lark."

"It's no lark," Jack said, cleaning his blade. "Where is Colonel St John?"

The brigade was readying for action, with infantrymen checking their rifles and cavalrymen their sabres, while officers stood in small groups, urgently listening to their superiors' orders.

"I'm here, Windrush. Glad to see you are all right."

"Yes, sir. I couldn't see much, but I heard wheels with Ayub's force, so I suspect he has artillery with him. I'd say that's his entire army."

"Whatever it is," St John said, "We seem to have begun a battle. Young Lieutenant Maclaine has taken over his guns to fire on them."

"Yes, sir. He probably saved my life."

St John grunted. "That wasn't his intention. He thought you were the enemy."

Both men looked around as the four remaining guns of the Horse Artillery battery struggled across the ravine, with the gunners hauling their pieces up the steep slopes.

"General Nuttall must have decided to support Maclaine," St John observed. "He'd be better to recall him until we ascertain the enemy's strength. There's no sense in taking a tiger by the tail."

The cavalry also began to cross the ravine, with the men riding or leading the horses by the head.

"What the devil is General Burrows playing at?" Jack knew it was bad form to criticise a senior officer openly, but he thought it foolish to attack an enemy of unknown but undoubtedly superior numbers. "Is he allowing one headstrong lieutenant to decide when we fight a battle?"

"Advance across the ravine!" General Burrows ordered. "We will fight the enemy on the plain and prevent his two forces merging."

"Tell him!" St John urged. He composed himself. "Windrush, give my compliments to General Burrows, and inform him that he's facing Ayub Khan's whole army!"

Jack galloped to the general with the information. "Sir! Colonel St John's compliments, and we are advancing against Ayub Khan's main force. I am sure he has infantry and artillery with him."

Burrows stared at Jack for a long minute. "Then we'll end his nonsense here and now. Join the 66th, Windrush. I am sure they could use an experienced officer. Take these eager young subalterns with you."

After nearly thirty years in the army, Jack could only obey orders. "Yes, sir."

Burrows' brigade crossed the ravine in a long khaki snake, with the men of the 66th marching grimly forward.

"Here we go, boys!" Lieutenant Chute encouraged his men. "It's time to show the world what the Brave Boys of Berks can do!"

"Come on, the Berkshires!" a sergeant shouted. "Keep in formation there!"

"Let's see the Colours, men," Colonel Galbraith ordered, and the two flags appeared, hanging limp in the sullen heat. The Queen's Colour and the Regimental Colour, symbols of honour and pride, thrusting high above the khaki sun helmets and ugly khaki uniforms on the dusty khaki plain.

Jack saw a small wood ahead, with the tops of the trees only visible above the dust haze, looking strangely disembodied, as if they were floating free.

Where are we going? Is the general going to form up on an open plain with our flanks exposed to a more numerous enemy with thousands of cavalry?

The Horse Artillery continued to fire, with the bright flashes of the explosions sometimes seen through the dust, sometimes hidden. The cavalry surged ahead, as much to find the enemy as to fight him, Jack thought.

"The enemy is over there!" the news spread around the brigade. "Thousands and thousands of them!"

Jack looked at the 66th. The men did not appear concerned. They were British infantry, men trained to fight the Queen's enemies wherever they may be. It was customary for British soldiers to face fearful odds, whether they were fighting on an Afghan plain, an African jungle or in the freezing winter of the Crimea.

"Thousands of them," Sarsens repeated with his eyes bright. "We'll see a battle, Crimea."

"You two," Jack said. "Report to Colonel Galbraith and ask where he wants you." He eyed them sourly. "Don't try any heroics, and for God's sake, don't lead the men into danger. Follow the advice of the senior officers."

Galbraith looked harassed as he pushed his men forward. "Inexperienced subalterns are not much use to me."

"They're keen men," Jack said.

"I can see that." Galbraith gave a brief smile. "All right, you, Crimea Windrush, go to Number Two Company with my compliments. Sarsens, go to Three Company." He waited until the subalterns hurried away. "Windrush, you've been in action before. Remain with me and help wherever you think best."

"Yes, sir."

A slight drift of wind cleared some of the haze, and for a moment, Jack saw Ayub Khan's army.

"Dear God!"

The spy's reports had underestimated Ayub Khan's numbers. The Afghans had dug in on a ridge of high ground, with the sun glittering on thousands of swords and the barrels of cannons.

"How many would you say, Windrush?" Galbraith asked.

Jack swept his binoculars across the plain, trying to estimate numbers. "At least twelve thousand, sir. Maybe fifteen thousand."

"Six or seven times our number, then."[1]

"Yes, sir."

Galbraith grunted and set his men in a double line, facing their front and with the officers patrolling the ranks. The plain sloped upward to low hills, still with the haze obscuring the Afghan army.

Burrows positioned the 66th on the extreme right, with the flank company dangerously exposed. Immediately to the left of the 66th were four companies of Jacob's Rifles, the 30th Native Infantry, then a company of sappers, steady men on whom Jack could rely.

The guns were in the centre, Blackwood's Horse artillery, still banging away at where they hoped the enemy stood. Beside them stood the Grenadiers, with their ranks slightly refused, to the rear of the artillery. Finally, the last two companies of Jacob's Rifles were on the extreme left. Jack scanned them with his binoculars, concerned at the preponderance of young faces in such a vulnerable position.

Burrows had placed the cavalry in the rear as a mobile strike force, ready to ride out if Ayub Khan attempted to circle the British. Further back and looking frighteningly vulnerable, the baggage train stood, suffering under the sun, with a few cavalry detachments as their only defence.

The brigade seems very small on the vastness of this plain. We are in the old chessboard pattern of Wellington's wars, or even Marlborough's, yet facing a very different kind of enemy.

After half an hour, the Afghan artillery replied. First, one gun roared, and then another until dozens of guns were firing at the static British brigade.

Galbraith grunted as the Afghan shells landed on the British position.

"Good shooting," he observed calmly.

The Horse Artillery brought forward the six guns captured from the mutineers and lined them up as E Battery continued the unequal contest. One Afghan shot smashed the rear wheel of a British gun, killing a gunner outright and wounding a lieutenant, while a shell landed on a limber box, blowing the head off the wheel horses, while the driver escaped unhurt.

"Bloody good shooting," a gunner said. "They must have Russian gunners working for them."

"Sir!" Major Blackwood approached Colonel Galbraith. "We have half a dozen smooth-bore guns but not sufficient men to fire them. May we borrow some of the 66th?"

"By all means," Galbraith said at once. "Major Windrush! You take command of a platoon of the Berks. You're a gunner now."

"Yes, sir." Pleased to be useful, Jack returned with the infantrymen. Blackwood organised them in minutes, placing the captured smooth-bore cannon behind the Horse Artillery guns.

"I'll lend you a sergeant as an instructor," Blackwood said and returned to his charges. He swore, pointing to one of the horses, which favoured its front left hoof. "Get a shoeing smith to attend to that beast. We may have to advance in a hurry."

The smith dismounted, swaying from the fever that pressed a film of sweat over his face. "I hope the first shot the Afghans fire will blow me to bits," he said.

A moment later, the Afghans fired again, and a shell burst right at the sergeant's side, killing him and two men of the Rifles.

"Where the devil did the Afghans get so many guns?" Jack asked.

St John produced a couple of cheroots, thrust one in his mouth, and passed the other to Jack. "They make their own, Windrush. We taught them well, didn't we? We introduced them to modern rifles and modern artillery and other benefits of western civilisation." He gave a twisted grin. "We showed one of the most warlike peoples on earth how to use the most deadly weapons and then march against them with a handful of men and expect to win."

"We must have the most stupid politicians in the world," Jack murmured. He scanned the plain with his binoculars. "The haze is clearing at last."

With visibility improved, Jack could see ahead. The ground was less level here, with more undulations than he had expected, and an irregular line of vegetation indicating a riverbed half a mile or so from the British positions. However, Jack was more interested in Ayub Khan's army that appeared before them.

"Plenty of them, eh?" St John murmured. He scanned the Afghan force through his binoculars. "I see seven infantry regiments, Windrush, with a couple of thousand cavalrymen on their right, a few hundred on their left and thousands of ghazis, with irregular infantry, tribal lashkars."

Jack had focussed his binoculars. "Agreed, sir. There are more in reserve, although I'm not sure how many."

The Afghan artillery fired again with the shells all landing short, raising large fountains of dirt. The Horse Artillery responded, aiming for the Afghan guns.

"How many guns?" Jack scanned the Afghan lines, searching for the gun flashes. They came again, spaced in batteries at regular intervals along the length of the Afghan army. "I'd say thirty."

"We'll soon have 'em out of action," one of Jack's gunners

said as the Afghans fired again. The rumble seemed louder this time, and the gun flashes more intense. The Afghan shot crashed into the British lines, killing and maiming men and horses. A man screamed from the Rifle's ranks, and two horses stampeded, with a transport follower panicking as he tried to control them.

"Get those horses under control!" Jack roared. "Keep the guns firing! Target one Afghan battery rather than spreading your shot!"

The artillery duel continued for about an hour, with the sun climbing to its zenith, pouring its heat onto the waiting British and Indian soldiers. By that time, the barrels of the guns were almost too hot to touch.

"Water!" Jack shouted. "Bring water to cool down the guns! *Pani! Jildi!*"

A *pani-wallah* – water-carrier – scurried up, naked except for a loincloth. He handed Jack a goatskin bag. "*Pani*, sahib," he said, then vanished as an Afghan shell exploded at his feet. Pieces of the man scattered in the air, covering Jack with blood and scorched flesh.

Wiping his face clean, Jack handed the goatskin to his gunners. "Cool the barrel," he said. "And maybe have a drink." That was the first water he had seen since early morning, and the men were parched and hungry.

Another Afghan shell exploded among the Horse Artillery, and Major Blackwood fell from his horse, holding his leg. He withdrew to the rear, losing a lot of blood.

"He'll be back," a gunner said. "He's made of tough stuff, the major!"

"Look!" Jack pointed to the centre of the Afghan lines, half-seen through the drifting artillery smoke. "Is that a scarlet umbrella?"

"You're damned right it is," St John replied. "That will be Ayub Khan himself."

The scarlet umbrella was square in the centre of the Afghan formation, with an infantry regiment standing on either side.

"That's the First Ardal Regiment," St John scrutinised the Afghans through his binoculars, "one of Ayub's favourites."

"The Ardul? They're the Herati men who helped murder Cavagnari and the Guides at Kabul!"

St John raised his eyebrows as Jack pointed out the scarlet umbrella to his gunners and the Horse Artillery. Two shells of the next volley exploded directly over the umbrella.

Jack saw a momentary swirl in the Afghan ranks, and the umbrella vanished, to reappear a moment later, although with a significant tear in the fabric. The shell fire must have stirred Ayub Khan into action, for despite his near three-to-one superiority in guns, he was losing more men than the British. The Afghans shifted forward towards the British lines, retaining their formation as well as any European army.

"These Afghan fellows are well trained," Jack said.

"Ayub Khan has them in hand," St John agreed.

"He's got Ruski gunners," a sweating private of the 66th said. "No bloody Afghan is that good."

Blackwood was back, with his trousers torn and a bloody bandage over his wound. "Fire on, boys!" he shouted as he remounted his horse. "*Ubique!*"

A gunner at Number Two gun reached for another cartridge when an Afghan six-pound shot screamed in and ricocheted from the gun wheel's iron tyre. The shot ripped open the sturdy iron and smashed into the gunner's left hand before fracturing the right arm of an officer at his side.

"Ruski or Afghan," a man said. "They're bloody good!"

When the Afghan army began an advance, General Burrows gave a general order. "The infantry may open fire when the enemy comes in range."

"Fire away, Royal Horse!" Blackwood rose in his stirrups to enable his men to see him better. "Never mind the shine!" He dismounted to help the men at the nearest gun. "Case shot, boys and blast them to hell!"

"You hear that, lads?" Jack lifted his voice to the gunners and the nearby 66th. "You have Martinis with a range of thirteen hundred yards. The enemy does not. Make every shot count."

The 66th responded with a will, opening a devastating fire on Ayub Khan's advancing army. However, the Afghan artillery also increased their fire, and then a massive force of ghazis, thousands strong, rose from the riverbed and charged the British flank.

"*Ya char yar!*" The chant rose from the entire Afghan army. "*Ya char yar!*"

"What are they saying, sir?" Sarsens had moved closer to Jack.

"It's the Afghan war cry." Jack had to shout above the sustained crackle of the Martinis and the yelling Afghans. "I think it says 'four friends' and refers to the first four Caliphs of their religion."

"Is that so?" Sarsens said and stepped beside the nearest section of the 66th. "Well, the 66th can shout as well. Who are we?"

"We're the Brave Boys of Berks!" a corporal replied.

"Come on, the Brave Boys!" Sarsens said, and his chant spread along the khaki-clad ranks.

"Brave Boys! Brave Boys of Berks!"

"Well said, Sarsens," Jack approved.

The ghazis were coming closer, thousands of white-clad fanatics wielding swords and with their heads bowed behind small round shields. Each ghazi man was willing to die for his faith as he firmly believed that he would go to Paradise for fighting the infidels.

"*Allah Akbar! Din! Din!*"

"Shoot them flat, 66th!" Jack shouted. He glanced along the line, where the Grenadiers and Jacobs Rifles were also firing into the flank of the charging mob, with their breech-loading rifles taking a terrible toll of the ghazis. Blackwood was encouraging the gunners, leaning to one side to favour his injured leg.

Crimea was standing in the front line of the 66th, firing his revolver like a veteran, shouting encouragement as he loaded, and firing again.

Helen would be proud of you, Crimea! I'll tell her you acted like a man! Damnit! You can tell her yourself.

The closer the enemy came, the more effective the British and Indian fire, until even the ghazis could not sustain their losses. One moment they were charging forward, and they turned and ran, with the Martinis of the 66th knocking them down by the dozen.

The surviving ghazis returned to the shelter of the riverbed, from where those who had firearms began a scattered fire on the British lines.

"Here, yarcharyars!" a 66th private shouted. "You couldn't face the Brave Boys, could yer?"

"Come again, yarcharyars! We're waiting for you!"

Between the artillery fire and musketry, Burrows' brigade was also taking casualties with British and Indian dead and wounded.

"Order the men to lie down." Burrows seemed quite confident of success despite the massive odds against him. "That should reduce the casualties."

The rank-and-file infantry did as ordered although many of the officers continued to stand, aware their actions would hearten the men. The cavalry was unable to comply, and their dead and wounded increased.

"Ayub's men are coming around the flanks," Jack warned Galbraith.

With his artillery keeping the British engaged, Ayub Khan pushed his men around both sides of Burrows' formation. The cavalry rode at extreme rifle range, waiting for their opportunity to charge.

Colonel Galbraith nodded. "Number Four Company will

move at right angles to the rest."

The company stood upright, shifted right to meet any Afghan flank attack and lay down again. By now, the Afghan artillery was concentrating on the British cavalry, so the terrible screams of wounded horses unnerved the men.

"We're getting slaughtered," Sarsens said. "Won't the general do something?"

Jack examined the 66th. They lay quietly under the bombardment, firing the occasional shot as an unwary Afghan cavalryman ventured in range. The gunners continued to fire, although few gun crews were complete. The officers pulled the casualties to one side for the medical staff to tend and gave quiet orders to the men. The sepoys were not so happy. Jack noted again that the Grenadiers and Jacob's Rifles were composed mainly of young men. The constant hammer of artillery, combined with the power of the sun and torment of the horses, was unsettling them.

"Something will have to give soon," Jack said. "These aren't the men of Waterloo to withstand hours of pounding."

St John gave a brief, worried nod. "Look at the left flank."

The young sepoys of Jacobs on the left looked shaken. The Afghan artillery had created casualties, and now their cavalry had formed up for a charge. Sounds of combat in the rear told Jack that Ayub Khan's horsemen were also attacking the baggage.

"We're nearing the crisis of the battle," Jack said. "Burrows will have to do something soon rather than leave the initiative to Ayub Khan."

The Afghans had moved around Burrow's brigade, surrounding them on three sides, so Ayub Khan's forces were in a horseshoe with the British in the middle.

"Stand fast!" Jack ordered.

There is no help here, nobody to depend on but ourselves. We fight and die here at Maiwand.

CHAPTER NINE

"Ammunition!" the gunnery sergeant with the 66th shouted. "Do we have any more ammunition for the smooth-bores?"

Jack passed the message onto Blackwood, who looked down from his horse with his face lined with pain. "No, Windrush," he said. "We only have what we captured from the mutineers."

Jack nodded. "The smooth-bores are running short, Blackwood."

"Fire what you have, then take the guns to the rear," Blackwood decided.

The loss of half their artillery seriously weakened the British defence. Ayub Khan immediately noticed the difference and ordered a general advance.

"You men of the 66th!" Jack shouted to Jack's gun crews. "Return to the firing line. The Brave Boys need you."

The Afghans retained their discipline as Ayub Khan pushed them forward, with their artillery to the fore, firing and moving closer to the British brigade before firing again. Their shells screamed into the British ranks, causing consternation among the young, already thirst-tortured sepoys, killing and maiming horses and men alike.

The Afghan cavalry was first to charge, yelling as they hit the left flank, where Jacob's Rifles tried to hold them with rifle fire. The crackle of musketry rose to a continual roar, with officers' orders hardly heard.

To the rear of Burrows' brigade, irregulars, tribesmen, and ghazis had blocked the British retreat, yelling their slogans as they brandished their bold green flags.

"We're surrounded," St John shouted.

"I noticed!" Jack borrowed a Snider from a wounded Rifleman and fired steadily into the advancing masses. The British rifles were causing massive damage, bringing down Afghans by the score, but there were always more Afghans to fill the gaps.

"We're not killing them fast enough!" a swarthy corporal yelled. "There are too many of them."

"Keep firing, lad!" Jack looked to the right and left. Sarsens was laughing, encouraging the men around him as he fired. Jack saw him take a blocked rifle from a frustrated private and grunted with recognition. The Martinis were fine weapons, with the revolutionary falling-block breech action and central firing pin and the seven-groove rifling perfected by the Edinburgh gun-maker, Alexander Henry. However, it had a tremendous kick and overheated quickly. Worst of all, the thin brass, bottle-neck Boxer cartridges often jammed in the breech.

Sarsens freed the cartridge with his pocketknife, handed the rifle back and shouted something with the words lost amid the general noise.

Another horde of ghazis erupted from the gulley that coiled around the British right flank.

"Volley fire!" Galbraith ordered, standing calmly in the middle of his regiment. "Officers to the front!"

Jack nodded. Galbraith knew his men. British soldiers liked to see their officers when they fought, and the NCOs had trained them to fire in volleys, which kept the men under control. Jack stepped forward, reloaded his Snider, and fired into the onrushing screaming mob.

"Allah Akbar! Din! Din!"

The words were familiar. Jack had heard them in a score of battles and skirmishes, from the old days of the Mutiny to the Umbeyla expedition and the recent encounters in Afghanistan. The ghazis were brave men, but the 66th met them with a steady stream of musketry that bowled them over by the score.

"Keep coming, you howling bastards!" the swarthy corporal yelled. "The Brave Boys are waiting for you."

An Afghan shell burst overhead, spreading deadly shards of shrapnel. The swarthy corporal stiffened and put a hand to his neck. Blood poured through his fingers and dripped down his uniform.

"Aye, would you? You dirty bastards! It'll take more than that to kill a Berkshire man!" Lifting his Martini, he jerked the lever, pressed home a cartridge, and fired with his blood sizzling on the overheated barrel.

A dozen yards away, Crimea was firing coolly into the charging mass, reloading with practised skill, and firing again.

"The Rifles are taking it hard!" St John said. "Look at the left wing!"

As the 66th repelled the ghazis, leaving the ground littered with white-clad bodies, Jack glanced to the left. The Afghan shellfire had pounded the two companies of Jacobs' Rifles, killing or wounding most of the officers, and the young soldiers were wavering. Another shell landed as Jack watched, shredding a British officer. A handful of the Rifles broke away from the ranks and ran to the Horse Artillery. Some sheltered under the limbers and gun carriages, cowering in fear. The gunners tried to eject them with boots and curses, slowing down their rate of fire.

"Windrush!" General Burrows noticed the confusion. "Take Sarsens and calm these men down!"

Before Jack moved, the Rifles collapsed. With a mixed force of cavalry and ghazis thrusting at them, their nerve broke, and they turned to flee. Their panic infected the Grenadiers, who until then had been standing firm, firing volley after volley at the oncoming Afghans. However, with hundreds of demoralised men pressing them and their left flank now exposed to the Afghan attack, the Grenadiers also broke. The whole mob, Grenadiers and Rifles mixed in a confused mass, ran from the screaming ghazis and triumphant cavalry, pushing onto Blackwood's toiling Horse Artillery.

Within moments, the British centre was a mass of ghazis and cavalry, hacking at the broken sepoys, who were too closely packed to resist.

"Fight them!" Blackwood roared. "Defend your guns, men!"

The artillerymen obeyed. Pushing aside the panicking sepoys, they fired another volley into the ghazis, then fought with handspikes and ramrods. The sappers, sturdy men with work-hardened muscles, joined the Horse Artillery in their stubborn defence. For a moment, Jack thought the British might hold the flank until the ghazis pushed forward in their hundreds.

Blackwood swore as the Afghans thundered against his artillery.

"What do you think, Windrush?"

"I think you'll lose the guns unless you move them," Jack replied. He had no more ammunition for the Snider but fired his revolver, felling three men without impacting the mass.

"Limber up and retire!" Blackwood ordered. "Save the guns!"

Jack understood. The guns were as crucial to the artillery as the Colours were to the infantry. Losing a gun to the enemy was considered a disgrace. There was a legend that Wellington had never lost a cannon in battle, and generals for the past sixty years had sought to emulate the Iron Duke.

Jack reloaded, ducked as a stray bullet whined past him and aimed at the ghazis. One wiry man with a huge beard ran straight at him, screaming, so Jack shot him in the forehead. The man's head snapped back, but his legs continued to move, carrying him forward another half dozen steps before he died.

"Limber up!" Blackwood repeated as some gun crews ignored his command.

Lieutenant Maclaine, hatless, wild-eyed and with sweat darkening his khaki uniform, shook his head. "Limber up be damned! Give them another round!"

A tall officer began to limber up, roaring orders to his men as Lieutenant Maclaine's two guns continued to fire canister into the screaming hordes. Maclaine's stand gave the remaining four guns sufficient time to withdraw, but he lingered a fraction too long as the ghazis poured over his position, hacking and stabbing.

With his wounded leg causing him intense pain, Blackwood tried to remount as the tribesmen and ghazis came again. Jack saw one of his gunners try to force through the Afghans to save the major, but without success. A knot of tribesmen surrounded Blackwood, swords flashing until one man sliced off the artillery major's head with a single stroke. The gunner was also wounded, with seven cuts that forced him back. Lieutenant Osborne also died as he fired his revolver into the screaming mob.

The ghazis employed a singularly unpleasant stroke with their Khyber knives, holding the weapon with the sharp edge upward and swinging backwards and up. As the retreating sepoys knew too well, one slash could split a man from the groin to the breastbone. The Afghans surged over Maclaine's two guns and charged onward, swords and knives ready to kill.

Swearing in frustration, Maclaine mounted his horse and galloped after the rest of the battery.

"You two guns!" Maclaine ordered the rearmost men. "Action rear!"

Two of the battery's four guns halted to face the advancing Afghans. Jack joined them, frantically trying to stem the tide of retreating sepoys. Panicking men surrounded him, young sepoys whose world had collapsed and whose officers lay dead on the blood-soaked ground.

The Afghans were a mixture of regulars, tribesmen and ghazis, with the green standards fluttering overhead. They bounded forward, their cries incoherent in the general noise, their swords raised to kill. Maclaine's guns fired two rounds of shrapnel, ripping through the enemy ranks, and one of case-shot.

Colonel Malcolmson appeared, shouting down from his horse. He had lost his sun helmet and sweat had furrowed through the powder smoke on his face.

"Retire! If you keep these two guns, you will lose them as you lost your own!"

Maclaine looked up with his mouth working, but he obeyed, limbering up and retiring. Jack withdrew to the nearest British formation, a double line of the 66th. He heard his breath gasping in his throat as he reloaded his revolver. He watched as his hand fumbled, and a brass cartridge dropped to the ground, seemingly in slow motion.

"It's just us now, lads," a sergeant said and thrust a stubby pipe in his mouth. "Load and present, boys, but don't fire until I give the order." He looked up as Jack slid into the ranks. "Afternoon, sir. Glad to see you."

Jack took a deep breath. "Good afternoon, Sergeant. It's a bit hectic today."

"Yes, indeed, sir. Now, if you'll excuse me, the 66th have a battle to win."

With two guns in Afghan hands and the other four running to the rear, the mingled mob of ghazis and fleeing sepoys smashed into the 66th ranks.

"Form a square!" Jack ordered. He holstered his revolver, lifted a discarded Martini, and fired. He saw his man fall and lifted a haversack, fumbling for a cartridge. "On me, the 66th!"

The haversack was empty. Jack held the rifle like a club, smashed it over the shield of the nearest ghazi and saw the man stumble for the swarthy corporal of the 66th to finish him with a thrust of the bayonet.

"One more for the Brave Boys of Berks!" the corporal shouted, twisted his bayonet, and withdrew. He stood there, panting, with his sun helmet at an angle and blood dripping from the eighteen-inch triangular bayonet onto the hard ground. He looked at the mass of ghazis approaching, swore, spat on the ground, and presented his bayonet.

"I'm not running from you bastards," the corporal said. "Come on, you serpents!"

"*Shabash*, Corporal." Jack drew his revolver as the corporal vanished amidst the mob.

The mixed rabble of ghazis and broken sepoys crashed into the 66th.

"Fire!" Jack ordered. "Shoot them flat!" But the men of the 66th were reluctant to fire into the sepoys, men with whom they had marched and campaigned. The regiment crumpled under the charge, with individuals and small knots of men fighting furiously. Jack saw some sepoys standing still, too petrified to resist as the ghazis slashed at them. Others, still in some formation, barely moved as the ghazis dragged them out of the ranks and butchered them.

"*Allah Akbar! Din! Din!*"

The shouts of triumph rose above the screams of horses and men. Jack grabbed a lone private of the 66th. "Stay with me, man!"

"Yes, sir!" The private looked more bewildered than scared. "What's to do, sir?"

"What's to do? I'll tell you what's to do!" Jack snarled. "We're getting out of here." He swore as a bullet, Afghan or British, he could not tell, hit his horse, which plunged and reared, throwing Jack to the ground. He swore again, rolled, and recovered, with the private helping him to his feet.

"Are you all right, sir?" the private asked. Another man joined them, and a third, looking nervous.

"Our cavalry is coming, sir!" the first private shouted.

Jack looked up, breathing heavily. "Thank the Lord for that," he said.

General Nuttall rode tall in the saddle as he formed up the

3rd Lights and the 3rd Scinde Horse. The cavalry had already taken many casualties from the Russian artillery, and some men were wounded as they took formation behind Nuttall. Jack saw one of the gunners join them, with blood on his uniform and a cavalry sabre in his fist.

"Come on, my men!" Nuttall shouted. "Recapture the guns!"

"With you, sir!" Sarsens pushed through the mass to form up beside Nuttall.

"Get back here, Sarsens!" Jack roared just as the bark of a cannon obscured his words.

Nuttall ordered a bugler to sound the charge and headed for the mass of Afghan infantry, with his officers and the lone gunner at his side.

The troopers followed for a couple of hundred yards, and then, because they misunderstood the orders or lacked the will to fight, they altered direction, leaving the British officers to charge alone. When Nuttall realised what had happened, he gave the order to return. Jack saw tears on his face as he walked his horse back to the crumbling British lines. Sarsens was at his side, yelling at the cavalry troopers, but Gunner Smith continued the charge, a solitary artilleryman on a horse until the Afghans killed him.

"It's no go," a private of the 66th said. "The cavalry has failed. The Afghans still have the guns."

Jack did not hear the order given, but Burrows' Brigade was in full retreat. The Horse Artillery crashed and jingled over the plain while the sepoys were a terrified mob. Only the 66th tried to keep in formation, with the officers and NCO's shouting orders. Every so often, the 66th halted and fired a volley at the ghazis, lashkars and Afghan regulars, slowing the pursuit.

Jack had gathered a dozen men and acted as a rearguard, withdrawing reluctantly before the Afghans. Although it was the 66th's first significant action, they acted like veterans, obeying Jack's orders, firing into the white-robed mob, and reloading with surprising calmness.

"Keep it up, lads!" Jack encouraged. "The general will order a stand soon."

Will he? I haven't heard anything from Burrows for some time.

"Sir!" Sarsens had rejoined Jack. He was bleeding from a slash across his left cheek, and his uniform was torn, but he still held his sword and kept his face to the enemy. He looked down from the back of his horse. "What can I do, sir?"

"Keep the men together, Second Lieutenant," Jack said. "And get as many out of this as possible. This battle is lost."

"Yes, sir." Sarsens had aged since Jack had last seen him earlier that day. "I'll do my best." He pulled on his reins and rode away, shouting to the infantry.

The ghazis tried another rush until the steady firing of Jack's men to halt them. "They're coming on the flanks, sir," a short private said. "They'll cut us off from the regiment if we're not careful."

"Thank you, private," Jack said. "Load, lads and shoot anything that gets in our way. Double, now!"

The men obeyed, pressing in the Boxer cartridges, forming a tight group, and moving quickly. An Afghan bullet claimed one, chopping him down, so he crumpled onto the ground. Jack hated to leave him behind, for the Afghans mutilated the dead and wounded, but there was no choice.

I didn't even know that lad's name.

Jack expected the general to organise a stand when they reached the ravine, but it was too late. The sepoys were too demoralised to fight. They crossed the gully in a mad rush, then fled eastward in a leaderless mob.

"Stop these men!" General Burrows shouted. "Halt there!"

Even the sepoys' officers failed to prevent the panicked flight, although a platoon of the grenadiers remained steady. They watched the retreat of their colleagues with looks of disdain.

"Jesus," a sergeant whispered. "I've never seen the like of that before."

"Neither have I," Jack admitted.

Without the sepoy regiments and only a remnant of the cavalry, what remained of the brigade limped away.

"Kandahar!" Somebody shouted. "We must get back to Kandahar!"

As the Afghan cavalry, infantry and ghazis attacked on all sides, with Ayub Khan's artillery still firing at any large group of the defeated survivors, the British formation crumbled further.

"There's a village ahead." Jack remembered passing it on the outward march. "We can make a stand there."

There was nothing much to Khig, an undistinguished village set within a baked mud wall. Colonel Galbraith, already wounded, looked around at the retreating remnant of the brigade.

"The 66th will halt here," he decided. "We'll hold back the Afghans and give the rest time to escape. Raise the colours!"

CHAPTER TEN

With the regimental and queen's Colours standing proud above the nondescript village, the 66th stood firm. A score of the sappers joined them and those of the grenadiers who had not fled. Jack led his handful of men into the mud enclosure and nodded to Crimea, who looked surprisingly calm.

"Not quite the glorious beginning to your career you had hoped, Second Lieutenant?"

Crimea gave a strained smile. "Oh, I don't know, sir. My father's first action was at the Redan. He nearly lost his life to a Russian shell, and now he's the colonel of the regiment. It's a family tradition, you see?"

"I see," Jack said. He remembered the carnage at the Redan, where the Russians had repelled a British attack with slaughter, and many young British soldiers had refused to fight. It was not a pleasant memory. He did not remember his brother taking part, but family tradition and the truth did not always coincide.

Jack had lost touch with Sarsens and St John in the confusion. He hoped both were alive and well on their way to Kandahar. He could not help them except to slow down Ayub Khan's advance.

Galbraith organised the defence, posting the men around the

walls as the Afghans approached. "Here they come, boys. Conserve your ammunition, fire when you have a target." His grin was pure Irish. "Open the lid of hell, boys!"

Oh, very colourful, Colonel.

Tall and distinguished, Galbraith stroked his whiskers while he waited under the limp Colours.

"Well, Windrush, what do you think of my 66th?" Galbraith's Irish accent was more pronounced than at any time since Jack had met him.

Jack smiled. "It's an honour to fight with them, sir. They are as good as any regiment I've ever seen."

"Quite right, Windrush." Galbraith pulled at his whiskers. "Let's see to these Afghan fellows, shall we?"

The Afghans came in a careless rush until the 66th met them with an aimed volley that knocked down scores.

"That's from the Brave Boys," somebody shouted as the ghazis raised their fringed green flags and charged again. The Berkshires responded with controlled volleys, cursing as some of the Martinis jammed through overheating.

"My ammo's running low!" a private complained.

"Don't waste your bullets," Jack shouted. "Pick your targets. If you can line up two men together, your bullet will go through the first and hit the second." He wiped the sweat from his face, wishing he had water with him. "After all, these bullets can penetrate a twelve-inch sandbag, so a human body is nothing."

"We've lost Captain Cullen," Galbraith said. "He was a Corry man from County Leitrim and the best of all men."

"We're losing a lot of good men today," Jack said.

"Captain Garratt's gone, too." Galbraith loaded his revolver, pushing home each brass cartridge with unnecessary force. "He's been with the regiment since '65. The Afghans shot him in the head."

"That's a clean death," Jack said. "A soldier's death."

"They're coming again!" Lieutenant Richard Chute shouted.

A mature twenty-four, he lifted a Martini and fired, bringing down a ghazi carrying a green flag.

"Good shooting, Chute!" Galbraith shouted, and then the Afghans charged, ghazis, tribesmen and regulars together.

Lifting an ammunition pouch from a wounded private, Jack worked his Martini's under-lever, pressed in a cartridge, and aimed. One broad-chested tribesman caught his eye. As the man was running at an angle, Jack took half a second, traversed his aim and fired. The Martini kicked at Jack's shoulder, and the tribesman leapt backwards as the huge bullet hit him in the chest.

Jack grunted with satisfaction. "Got you, you bastard!" and reloaded quickly. There were many more tribesmen attacking.

The 66th fired, reloaded, and fired again with the powder smoke adding to the men's thirst and the enemy dead piling up outside the walls. Lieutenant Chute of Chute Hall, County Kerry, died in that enclosure, facing the enemy, and encouraging his men to the end. Already wounded, Lieutenant Maurice Rayner, the twenty-three-year-old son of a Liverpool merchant, died with his revolver in his hand. Second Lieutenant Henry Barr died holding the colours. A Brighton man, he was not yet twenty years old when an Afghan marksman shot him.

The Afghans came again, and the defenders repelled them. Jack lost count of the number of assaults the tribesmen, regulars and ghazis made, with the 66th repelling each one, but every time the Afghans retreated, the defenders had fewer men and less ammunition.

Jack looked around the compound, with the trees dull under the sun and the smell of raw blood and powder smoke choking in the heat. Most of the 66th lay dead, and only a handful of grenadiers and sappers remained with the survivors. The casualties lay where they had fallen in crumpled heaps of blood-stained khaki.

Crimea pushed his final cartridges into his revolver. "Still here, sir," he said with a grin. "I must say, this is not the lark I expected."

"No." Jack cleared a jammed round from the breech of his Martini. The barrel was so hot he could hardly bear to hold it. "You're doing well, Crimea. Your mother would be proud of you."

"Thank you, sir," Crimea said. He opened his mouth to say more but closed it without another word.

"I've got the Colours!" Second Lieutenant Arthur Honywood shouted. Limping from a bullet in the leg, the nineteen-year-old had joined the 66th the previous year. As the Afghans advanced one more time, Honywood held the Queen's Colours above his head. "What shall we do to save these?"

"You're making yourself a target!" Jack said, just as Honywood staggered. The Afghan bullet caught him in the head, and he collapsed, after which another officer took hold of the bullet-scarred staff.

The Afghans came again, with the British, low on ammunition, meeting them with bayonet and rifle-butt. Jack saw Crimea throwing stones as if he were playing cricket. One moustached sergeant of the 66th seized a huge ghazi by the beard and hauled him onto a bayonet. Jack used his Martini like a club, firing his revolver with his left hand.

Not long to go now. We can't hold on much longer.

"Ammunition!" The cry came again. "I'm out of ammunition!"

One by one, the few survivors repeated the words. Jack saw them look at each other, knowing the end was near.

"We'll die together, boys," Jack said. He had long since fired off the last of his Martini ammunition and had only three revolver rounds remaining. He looked around for the colonel.

Kneeling, bleeding and still encouraging his men, Lieutenant-colonel James Galbraith of Clanabogan, Tyrone, and the 66th Foot, the Berkshire Regiment, died in that battered Afghanistan garden. Jack's last memory of him was with the regimental colour in one hand and the other on the hard ground, supporting himself.

"Windrush!" Galbraith croaked. "It's all done with us here. You're not of the 66th. Save yourself, man!"

"There are not many of us left," a whiskered lieutenant said.

"But what a lark!" Crimea gave a twisted grin. "I wouldn't have missed this for the world!"

Instead of a furious rush, the Afghans advanced in a disciplined formation, with their flags held high and each bearded, intense face focussed on the handful of British defenders.

"These are no ghazis," Jack said. "That's a regular regiment." He started at a sudden memory. "By God! That's the Ardul Regiment!"

Beside the Ardul Regiment came a lashkar with the familiar form of Zamar Khan in front, holding a bloody pulwar.

Chanting their warcry, the Heratis marched forward as ghazis formed on their left and the Nazar Khel on their right. When the Afghans stopped, Jack knew they were preparing for the final assault.

"Well, my lads," Jack said. "It's our time."

The soldiers of the 66th spat on their hands, stamped their feet, and checked their bayonets.

Jack searched the pouches of the dead for cartridges, handing a few to each man.

"Let's get this over with," one man said.

"We'll show them how the Brave Boys of Berks fight." Another thrust a short pipe in the corner of his mouth.

Jack drew his sabre, feeling the rugged ridges of the sharkskin hilt. "Follow me, lads. It's been an honour to fight alongside you all." He stepped outside the compound, fired his final three rounds, and threw his revolver at the Afghans.

Jack did not see the two cavalrymen until they came around the flank of the Ardul regiment. They charged at a gallop, skirted the edge of the enclosed garden, and smashed into him. He fell, gasping, and rolled in the dust. The leading rider slashed at him with his pulwar, missed and nearly overbalanced in his saddle. Jack rolled away, dodged the galloping hooves of the second horseman and thrust upward. The point of his sabre cut into the stirrup leather of the second horseman, who shouted something in Pashtu and swerved away.

The first horseman attacked again, leaning out of his saddle, pointing his sword towards Jack as he thrust in his spurs. Jack waited, holding his sabre. He felt the tension rise in his throat, wished he could have said goodbye to Mary before he died, and sprang aside as the horseman closed. The man swerved his horse like the expert he was, but Jack had expected the move and shifted back to his original position. When the horseman tried to compensate, Jack ducked back and hacked at the rider's leg. The sharp Wilkinson's Sword blade ripped through the rider's boot and deep into the muscle of his thigh.

The man yelled and inadvertently jerked sideways, blocking the second rider from attacking. Taking his opportunity, Jack lunged forward, thrusting the point of his sword deep into the second rider's side. The man tried to parry, missed completely, and his horse galloped away, with the rider dying in the saddle.

The first rider had dismounted and was lying on the ground. Jack finished him with a simple slice at the throat.

By that time, the 66th survivors had emerged from the compound. Jack's fight had carried him too far away to help, so he could only watch the drama unfold. The ten privates, two 66th officers and Crimea stood back-to-back, challenging the Afghans to fight. Every time the Afghans charged, the British fought them off until a burly Afghan stepped forward.[1]

"Zamar Khan." Jack recognised the man immediately.

Zamar Khan rapped an order, and a line of tribal riflemen appeared. They formed up in front of the defiant 66th and fired.

Jack watched, sick at heart as the Afghans poured in shot after shot. The British fell, shouting, swearing, and challenging. When Zamar Khan raised his hand, all the British were on the ground except one. Second Lieutenant Crimea Windrush half rose, lifted his sword, and limped towards the Afghans.

"Quarter, for the love of God," Jack said. "Grant the man quarter."

But Zamar Khan was not a merciful man. Taking a rifle from the nearest man, he loaded it slowly and stepped forward. As Crimea straightened up, Zamar Khan took careful aim and shot him between the eyes.

Crimea jerked back, with blood spurting from his head, and then he slowly crumpled to the ground.

Bobbie, the dog, eased free of the carnage, yapped at the Afghans, sniffed at one of the dead and slipped away, following in the survivor's path.[2]

For a moment, Jack was tempted to run forward and exact instant vengeance, but his pragmatic side took over.

Even if I mounted the dead Afghan's horse, I would not reach Zamar Khan before the Afghans killed me. Zamar Khan has hundreds of tribesmen behind him, as well as the Ardul regiment, and God only knows how many ghazis. My revenge will have to wait. I'll get you, Zamar Khan, if the Lord permits me to live, I will kill you.

As the Afghans began to mutilate the British and Indian dead, Jack mounted the loose Afghan horse and headed toward Burrows' retreating army. Their track was easy to follow, with a trail of dead and dying men, abandoned equipment and dead pack animals lying by the side of the waterless road. Many of the men seemed physically unhurt and had collapsed through thirst and heat.

Water. I must have water.

Jack's hopes that the previous rider of his horse had a water bottle proved futile. He kicked in his heels, feeling as if thirst had swollen his tongue to twice its normal size.

With his head pounding and every step the horse took jarring his spine, Jack continued.

Keep going, Jack. One step at a time.

After an hour, Jack saw the tail of the retreating army, a terrified gaggle of camp followers and straggling sepoys. He pushed through them, nearly falling from the saddle as he sought General Burrows or Nuttall.

Men begged him for water, and one threatened him with a bayonet. Jack ignored them all, staring ahead at the long column, the detritus of a defeated army.

"Move aside there! Move aside!" Jack ordered.

"Take me on your horse, sahib!"

"Stop, damn you! I want a ride! Bloody officers!"

After another half hour, Jack heard the distinct drumbeat of cavalry hooves behind him and the crackle of musketry.

The Afghans have found the tail of the column.

Jack kicked on until the horse staggered and fell, spilling him onto the ground for the second time that day. He stood up, shifted his sword from between his legs and walked on, pushing through the detritus, stumbling towards the head of the army.

"Major Windrush? Is that you?" Sarsens nursed a wounded arm, and his face was drawn with pain. Blood crusted on the sabre wound on his cheek.

"Sarsens?" Jack forced a smile. "I'm glad you're alive. Who's in charge of this shambles?"

"I don't think anybody is, sir." Sarsens was red-eyed, as though he had been crying. Jack understood without judging. War, horror, and fear could unman the bravest soldier, while true courage was to continue despite the terror and the tears.

"All right, Sarsens. Stay with me." Jack tried to order his thoughts. The retreating army didn't seem to have a rearguard, only a ragged mixture of exhausted, fearful men, many collapsing under the heat. "Find me some soldiers, men who have retained their weapons."

"Yes, sir." Sarsens replied at once, thankful for having somebody take control. "I think there's a gun up ahead, sir."

"Find it," Jack commanded. He saw a sepoy of Jacob's Rifles sitting on the road, hugging his Snider. "You, there!" Jack spoke in Urdu, then Pashtu. "Why are you resting?"

"I'm tired, sahib," the man said.

"We're all tired, man!" Jack fought to control the pounding in his head. "Get on your feet!"

The man obeyed. Jack saw that he was little more than a boy, a smooth-skinned youngster with terrified eyes.

"Have you cartridges for your rifle?"

"Yes, sahib."

"Have you two arms and two legs?"

The sepoy nodded, his face serious. "Yes, sahib."

"Then you can fight. Stay with me!" Jack winked and staggered on. He lifted a wounded naik of the Grenadiers next and a pair of stumbling sappers.

"March to attention!" Jack tried to install some military pride in his men. "We're going to act as the rearguard for this army."

A drunken private of the 66th stared at him.

"Get up!" Jack snarled. "Get on your feet, you disgrace of a soldier!"

The man pushed himself up, reaching for his rifle.

"Now join the rearguard," Jack ordered.

As Jack ushered his men on the hot trail to Kandahar, others joined him. Twice small bodies of Afghan cavalry approached, but when Jack had his men form a defensive circle, the Afghans withdrew to seek a less prickly target.

"Keep together!" Jack said.

"We need water," the naik complained.

Jack agreed. Most of the men they passed were unhurt. Heat and lack of water had defeated them rather than the Afghan army. "As soon as we find some, we'll fill our water bottles."

They moved on, picking up a man here and there. They added a dismounted cavalry trooper, stumbling with his sword between his legs, a man of the 66th, red-faced and swearing, two men of the Rifles, both wounded, yet refusing to give up.

"Sir!"

Jack had almost forgotten Sarsens.

"I've found the gunners, sir. They've halted a quarter of a mile ahead, with one gun, a limber and a wagon."

"Good man, Sarsens," Jack said. "We can use some artillery."

It was late afternoon now, and the sun was pouring its heat on them, adding to the dust that tortured the men.

The gunners looked efficient, despite their sweat-darkened uniforms and the battered condition of their equipment.

"Is there an officer with you?" Jack asked.

"No, sir," a serious-faced man replied. He nursed a badly injured arm. "Major Blackwood is dead, and Lieutenant Maclaine is missing. I think the Afghans captured him, sir."

Better dead than a prisoner of the Afghans.

"Very well," Jack said. "We're the rearguard of the army, and I'm taking you under my command."

"Very good, sir." The gunners accepted Jack's orders without question. "What do you want us to do, sir?"

"For a start, take the wounded men on your limber," Jack said, "and if we see any Afghans approach, blow the bastards to shreds."

The serious-faced man forced a grin. "That's the sort of order we like, sir."

Jack checked his men. He had thirty now, a mixed force from every unit in Burrows' brigade, limping on but with a new purpose in their eyes. "Sarsens!"

"Yes, sir!"

"Scout to the left. I'm not sure if that's a copse of trees or a troop of Afghan cavalry."

"Yes, sir." Sarsens had found a loose horse, a wild-looking Kabul pony with a native saddle and mobile eyes. He kicked in his heels, spoke to the animal in the accents of Eton and Sandhurst and guided it to the flank.

"Sir!" Sarsens was back in minutes. "They're Afghan cavalry, sir, and they have infantry as well."

"How many? Jack peered into the sun. The heat haze had

returned, obscuring visibility so ten men could be a hundred, and a group of trees might be an entire Herati regiment.

Sarsens shook his head. "I don't know, sir."

"Well, estimate, man! That's why I sent you out there!" Jack snapped the words.

"Maybe a hundred horsemen, sir," Sarsens said desperately, "and hundreds of infantry." The sword cut on his face had opened again, oozing blood down his face.

"Regulars or tribesmen?" Jack scanned the landscape, searching for a defensive position.

"Both, sir, I think."

Jack nodded. "Thank you, Second Lieutenant. We'll form up on that ridge." It was not a ridge, more like a slight rise, but the best place for a stand that Jack could see. He knew that a hundred Afghan cavalry could play merry hell with a retreating army, massacring the camp followers and leaderless infantry.

"We'll have to stop them, Sarsens."

"Yes, sir." Sarsens looked at Jack's ramshackle command and opened his mouth to talk.

"Speak, Second Lieutenant," Jack snarled.

"It's nothing, sir."

Jack had no idea where Burrows and the other officers were. He was only aware of the stragglers and unarmed camp followers in the rear, abandoned by the leadership.

"Gunners!" Jack said. "Place the gun in the centre, with the infantry in a square for all-round defence." He would have preferred a circle, but the army trained the men to fight in a square. Ever since the regimental squares had held off Bonaparte's army at Waterloo, the formation had been a stand-by for British infantry.

God knows what damage case-shot or one of these new Gatling guns could do to a regimental square. If the Pashtun ever get their hands on such a devilish device, we'll have to rethink our tactics.

Jack forced his wandering mind back to the present. He had

lost his binoculars somewhere and screwed up his eyes against the dust and haze to study the enemy.

"Gunners! Fire as soon as they're in range. We might scare them off with a warning shot or two."

"Very good, sir," a gunner replied calmly. "Action front, lads. Common shell."

The first shell exploded to the front of the advancing cavalry, who wavered, not expecting any resistance.

"Give them another," Jack ordered.

"We've only half a dozen rounds left," the gunner replied.

"That's six shells to fire, then," Jack said.

The infantry waited, hugging their rifles, willing to obey any orders that helped them escape this nightmare. The drunk man threw up, wiped his mouth, and began to sing until Jack snarled him to silence.

The Afghans were closer now, a hundred cavalry under green banners, with the infantry behind, outflanking Jack's tiny force.

"Fire," Jack ordered, and the gun barked again. The shell exploded amid the cavalry, sending a fountain of dust in the air, knocking down half a dozen horses. Jack fancied he saw a man sent flying through the air. The cavalry parted, then extended their formation to make them less vulnerable. They came on through a dusty miasma, horses and men dimly seen, misshapen, yet still hideously dangerous.

"Fire," Jack ordered again, counting the remaining shells in his head.

With the enemy lines extended, the shell was less effective, only downing a couple of men. The remainder increased their speed, with their chanting now audible.

"Get ready, riflemen!" Jack ordered. He lifted his Martini, worked the underlever, and aimed.

One of the Grenadiers fired, unable to withstand the tension of waiting.

"Wait for my order!" Jack snapped. "Don't waste ammunition!" He knew the defeat at Maiwand had shaken the men.

That was understandable, but an initial volley that felled a dozen men at once was more effective in checking an attack than a scattering of shots over a period of minutes. "Reload and wait!"

The infantry waited with the errant sepoy licking dry lips. Nobody spoke as they watched the Afghans approach, with a long line of infantry following the cavalry, who bunched as they neared Jack's men.

The gun fired again. The case shot created a massive hole in the charging cavalry, sending men and horses into kicking, screaming confusion a hundred yards in front of the silent khaki square.

"Good shooting," Sarsens approved.

"Right, lads," Jack said. "Pick your targets."

Thirty rifles rose, the Martini-Henry's of the British and Sniders of the sepoys. Thirty men took a deep breath. One man prayed, with his cracked lips moving silently. The drunk giggled and began to sing again.

"Fire," Jack shouted and squeezed the trigger of his Martini.

Half a dozen horsemen fell. The British reloaded, hands working the underlevers, nervous thumbs pushing in cartridges, one man invoking a Hindu god.

The gun fired again, and then again. Jack lost count of the number of remaining shells. *Is it one? Or two?*

"Independent firing!" Jack allowed the faster veterans to fire at their own pace without waiting for his orders.

Sarsens had found a Snider and fired slowly, aiming each shot, and giving a little grunt when he thought he hit his mark.

The constant crackling of rifles may have fooled the cavalry into believing that Jack commanded more than thirty men. They pulled away without completing their charge. Only the infantry marched on, ominously silent under an array of banners.

"We'll never defeat that lot," a sapper said.

Jack agreed. "Have you any ammunition left, gunners?"

"No, sir. We fired the last one."

Jack swore softly. "What's in the cart?" He nodded to the wagon parked beside the gun.

"That's the treasure chest, sir," the gunner said. "Lieutenant Maclaine gave me specific instructions to take care of it."

Zar, zan, and zamin. The words came into Jack's head unbidden, with Armaghan's eyes smiling at him. *Zan: gold.*

Treasure! Gold is one of the Pashtun's three vices, besides women and land. They would happily kill for gold.

"I'm countermanding Lieutenant Maclaine's orders, gunner," Jack said. "I order you to leave the treasure chest behind." He glanced over his shoulder. The Afghan cavalry had reformed on the flanks of the infantry, now only six hundred yards away. "Leave the chest in open view, take the weakest of the infantry and withdraw with the gun. We won't present Ayub Khan with any more of our artillery."[3]

"I won't leave the infantry here, sir."

"Move! Save the gun! That's an order." Jack nodded to Sarsens. "Go with them, Sarsens."

"I'm not leaving you, sir."

"I need an officer to take charge of the gun. That's you!" Jack forced a smile. "You did well, Sarsens, now save the gun."

Jack watched as the wounded and most exhausted of the infantry piled onto the artillery caisson, with the youngest sepoy straddling the barrel of the gun for a highly uncomfortable ride.

"Go," Jack ordered. He looked around the remaining men. His initial thirty had dropped to twenty. "Right, boys. We'd better get moving before Ayub Khan's men arrive. "He heard the whine of an incoming Afghan shell. "Get down!"

The explosion was close, with the ground erupting ten yards from where Jack stood. He threw himself to the ground as another shell landed, and then a third.

Ayub Khan must think that General Burrows has ordered a stand here.

The explosions continued, one after the other as the Afghans hammered the ridge. Jack felt something crash onto his head and tried to move. He could not. He swore, not feeling any pain but only a heavy weight pressing down on him. He tried again, swore, and fainted.

* * *

Jack opened his eyes. The Afghans were everywhere, regular infantrymen and tribesmen, with cavalry poking at British corpses with their swords. A large group were bickering over the treasure chest, coming to blows, Herati against Kabuli, tribesman against regular.

We slowed the Afghan pursuit, then.

Jack reached for his sword to find it missing. He saw a man examining the blade: Zamar Khan, grinning at his trophy of war. Jack closed his eyes again, knowing the Afghans would find him soon, and slice him into pieces.

CHAPTER ELEVEN

Jack was aware of a curious swaying sensation. It was not unpleasant, but he wondered what it was and where he was before the memory of the battle and retreat returned to him. He opened his eyes to see nothing but darkness, combined with a most curious yet strangely familiar smell.

I know that stench.

The swaying continued, dragging Jack from side to side, yet simultaneously up and down, as if he were within a tiny, dark, and stuffy boat.

"Halloa!" Jack tried to shout, but his throat was too dry to allow any sound. He attempted to move, only for something to constrict him, yet he knew he was not tied or gagged.

I'm inside something. A bag. Jack pushed outwards with his hand. *I'm inside a bag, and it's moving. That smell is a camel. I'm inside a camel pannier. Have the Afghans captured me?*

The only reason the Afghans took prisoners was to torture and then kill them. The thought brought a cold sweat to Jack's forehead. He struggled harder, pushing outward and then upward, to find a loose cover between him and the open air. Thrusting upwards, Jack breathed deeply of the crisp night air.

He was slung over the left side of a camel, in the type of

pannier the British army used to carry the sick and wounded. Another camel plodded behind him with the inexorable patience of the beasts, grunting with every few steps. Jack looked around. He could not see any Afghan soldiers or tribesmen, only the two camels and a solitary camel driver, hunched up in a poshteen.

"Halloa there," Jack said. "Who are you?"

When the man did not respond, Jack tried Pashtu. *"Salaam Alaikum."*

"Salaam Alaikum," the man responded without looking round.

"Who are you?" Jack asked.

"Who is anybody?" the man replied cryptically.

Jack tried to struggle free of the pannier. His head was thumping, and he had various aches and pains throughout his body, but as far as he could tell, he had broken no bones. "I know your voice," Jack said. "Where are you taking me?"

"To safety," the man replied.

"You're Armaghan," Jack said. "You are the Timuri!"

Armaghan twisted around to face Jack. "How are you, Major?"

"What happened?" Jack asked. "How did I get inside a camel pannier?"

"I put you there," Armaghan said.

"Why?" Unable to leave the pannier, Jack settled into the most comfortable position he could.

"I was saving you from Ayub Khan's army. If I had left you, they'd have killed you."

Jack remembered the explosions and the advance of the tribesmen. "What happened?"

"The Afghans shelled your position and killed some of your men. The remainder fled, and the Afghans took over." Armaghan spoke as the camels moved at a steady jog, eating up the miles. With the night overcast, Jack could not work out in which direction they were travelling. "They were squabbling over money when I arrived and never noticed me."

"*Zar, zan,* and *zamin.*" Jack thought of the artillery's treasure chest. "You told me to remember that."

"Did I?" Armaghan asked.

"You did. And you saw the massacre of the army too, except you got the location and the cross wrong."

"I saw the massacre," Armaghan said. "Others put in the location. The cross will come in time."

Jack grunted. He had been out East too long to ask questions. Strange things happened in India, things that people in comfortable British drawing rooms could never understand. It was better to accept them without question rather than seek an explanation.

"Are we going to Kandahar?" Jack tried to recognise his surroundings. "We should be close by now."

"No," Armaghan said. "Not Kandahar."

"Why not? That's the nearest British garrison. I'll ensure you are adequately rewarded for your help."

Armaghan gave a low chuckle. "I need no reward, yet perhaps you will help me later."

"You're talking in riddles, Armaghan."

They were silent for a while, with Jack aware they were passing between mountains yet unsure where they were. After a passage of time that Jack judged at half an hour, Armaghan passed a goatskin of water to him.

"Drink," he said.

Jack needed no second invitation. The water was warm and tasted of goat, but to Jack, it was as sweet as any he had drunk from a well in his native Malvern Hills.

"Is that better?" Armaghan asked.

"Much," Jack said. "Thank you. That is twice you have saved my life. Why?"

"Have you heard of *Pashtunwali*?"

"The way of the Pashtun?" Jack said. "Yes, I have."

"I am following the main commandments."

"But you're not a Pashtun," Jack said. "You're a Timuri."

Armaghan gave a brief nod. "Sone of my people have lived among the Pashtun for generations. We have adopted some of their ways. You know that the first commandment of Pashtunwali is *badal* – revenge."

"I do." Jack wondered what was coming next. He looked upward, where the sky was clearing to reveal the stars.

"*Badal* is a way of life to the Pashtun." Armaghan guided the camel over an area of rough ground. They were climbing, with a keen wind slicing through Jack's uniform. "The Pashtun do not count time when they apply *badal*. An individual or a clan or tribe can nurse a grievance for decades or longer."

"I believe that." Jack tried to work out their direction of travel by the stars. He thought they were heading westward, away from Kandahar, but with his pounding head and general weakness after the preceding few days, he was not sure.

Armaghan slowed his camels down and lifted his head, looking around him. "There is a Pashtun proverb that says, 'the Pashtun who took revenge after a hundred years said: I took it quickly.' Perhaps you understand that?"

Despite his situation, Jack managed a sour smile. "I can appreciate that. The Pashtun are a very patient people."

"And very vengeful," Armaghan said. He seemed satisfied the surroundings were safe and increased the camels' speed. "Yet even *badal* can be relaxed. If one clan feels it has lost and cannot continue the feud, it can approach the victorious *khel* and ask for mercy. The Pashtun call the process *nanawatai*. It is a terrible humiliation, but it exists."

Jack wondered where Armaghan was leading. "I have heard of *nanawatai*," he said.

Armaghan nodded, seemingly satisfied. "Do you know the second commandment of *Pashtunwali*?"

"*Melmastia*," Jack said. "The rule of hospitality."

Armaghan grinned over his shoulder. "You must have been studying the Pashtun. Yes, *melmastia*, which can sometimes be more important than *badal*. If somebody seeks refuge or sanctuary, it must be granted, whatever the circumstances. Honour demands that the person granting sanctuary must protect the seeker, whoever he is, and whoever his enemies are."

Jack nodded, still not clear why Armaghan was lecturing him on *Pashtunwali*.

"By rescuing you from Ayub Khan's men," Armaghan said, "I am following *Pashtunwali*."

Jack frowned. "I did not seek sanctuary with you."

"You needed it," Armaghan reminded. "If you had remained where you were, Ayub Khan's men would have killed you."

"That is true. I owe you my life."

Armaghan relapsed into silence to concentrate on riding his camel.

"Can you take me to Kandahar?" Jack asked. "I must join the garrison there."

"Why?" Armaghan asked. "Do you think they cannot do without you?"

"It is my duty," Jack said.

"Ayub Khan's army is between you and Kandahar," Armaghan told him. "He is besieging the city with twenty-five thousand men. Nobody can get in or out, not even the indispensable Major Jack Windrush."

"Where are you taking me?"

"To your friends," Armaghan said and prodded the camels to greater speed.

It was nearly dawn before Armaghan halted in a small valley. A collection of tents huddled beneath a high cliff, and the bleating of goats mingled with the tinkle of camel bells and the sound of women's voices.

"Welcome to my home." Armaghan dismounted like a youth, although Jack estimated him to be in his late fifties at least. "Come on, Major Windrush."

Jack found he was stiff after his journey and nearly fell from the camel. "Where is this place?"

"If I told you, Major, would you be any wiser?" Armaghan

asked. "It is a place you can rest and recover after your exertions and ready yourself for the next stage in your life."

Jack stumbled as he tried to walk. He straightened up, took a deep breath, and winced at the pain in his head. He touched the place, feeling matted blood in his hair. *Mary will laugh at me for having another scar.*

It was a long time since Jack had seen his wife, and he felt a surge of longing. *I wonder how she is and what she is doing. Yesterday, I thought I would die and never see her again.*

"This way, Major Windrush."

Jack realised that Armaghan was watching him, smiling slightly.

There were three tents, securely fastened and positioned above a small, fast-running mountain stream, with no sign of defence against raiders.

"Are you not afraid of *badmashes*?" Jack asked.

"Nobody will attack me," Armaghan said. "I am well known here, as was my father and his grandfather's grandfather."

"What do you do?" Jack asked. "Are you a trader?"

"I trade in carpets from Persia and other things," Armaghan replied vaguely. He held open the flap of the nearest tent. "Come in, Major Windrush."

The tent's interior was something like the Arabian Nights, with luxurious carpets on the ground and the walls, a perfumed atmosphere, and a tray of fruit laid out. All it needed was a sultry-eyed beauty, Jack thought and realised he was missing his wife again.

"Sleep," Armaghan ordered. "We'll travel once you've rested."

"I've slept enough," Jack began to protest, but suddenly the prospect of sleeping was overpowering.

* * *

"You'll need to lose your uniform," Armaghan said when Jack awoke some hours later. "I have clothes you can wear as we travel through Afghanistan."

"To where are we travelling?"

Armaghan lifted a bundle of clothing from a corner of the tent. "Wash first, Major, and put these on. Burn your uniform."

"Burn it?"

"If you wear it, the first man we meet will spread the news that a British soldier is loose. All the *badmashes* and *loosewallahs* for fifty miles around will hunt you down. If you bury it, the jackals will dig it up, with the same result."

Jack saw the logic. "You are right. Who are you, Armaghan and why are you helping me?"

"*Melmastia,*" Armaghan said. "And reciprocation."

Jack was pulling off his uniform, wincing at the renewed pain in his head. "Reciprocation? Is that part of the Pashtun culture as well?"

"No. Western philosophy." Armaghan grinned. "Did you think we are cut off from the outside world? I am a merchant, Major Windrush. I have to know how my customers think, whoever they are." He stepped closer and looked Jack directly in the eye. "I want you to make me a promise, Major Windrush."

"What's that, Armaghan?"

"Will you promise to abide by the Pashtun code of *melmastia*, Major, and offer hospitality to somebody, the next person who asks, whoever they are?"

Jack wondered what he was agreeing to as he assented. "I will do that," he said.

Armaghan smiled. "You must be part Pashtun, Major."

I may well be. I don't know my mother's antecedents.

Jack looked at the pile of Afghan clothes.

"You can wash in the stream," Armaghan said. "Get the blood and dust off you."

Jack nodded, lifted the Afghan clothing and walked to the river. He stripped off and stepped into the stream. Despite the summer sun, the water was barely above freezing, and Jack was about to retreat in haste when he realised he had an audience. Half a dozen children were watching him, with two women. Unlike the Pashtun women, neither wore a burka but instead sported colourful costumes, and the younger one was smiling at the sight of a naked man bathing.

Unsure of the correct procedure in such circumstances, Jack stepped into deeper water and smiled. "*Salaam Alaikum.*"

"*Salaam Alaikum,*" both women replied as the children began to laugh and point.

"Forgive them," the younger woman said. "You are a novelty to them. They haven't seen a feringhee before."

"Please assure them that I made the same way as an Afghan or a Timuri man," Jack said.

"We've already seen that," the older woman spoke for the first time. Turning around, she shooed the children away with soft words and waving hands.

The younger woman remained. "I am Durr," she said. "Armaghan's second wife."

"Should you not be chaperoned when there are men around?" Jack remained in deep water, feeling the cold begin to bite into him.

"I am not of the Islamic faith," Durr said.

Jack remained where he was.

"I follow the Zoroaster religion." Durr smiled at Jack's incomprehension. "We predate Islam and Christianity by thousands of years," she said. "Like you, we believe in one all-good God, a creator called Ahura Mazda, which means Wise Lord."

Jack listened for a few moments as Durr explained the fundamentals of Zoroasterism.

"People say that Christianity and Islam, and perhaps Judaism are based on our beliefs," Durr told him. "The idea of a single god and a constant battle between good and evil are common to all."

When Jack began to shiver, he lifted a hand. "Does your religion include torturing men by making them stand in freezing cold water?"

Durr shook her head, with her long black hair floating around her shoulders. "I am not stopping you from leaving the river. Or are you shy? Do you have something to hide?"

Taking a deep breath, Jack ducked under the water, emerged, and began to scrub himself with sand from the riverbed. He winced as he touched the raw wound in his head and fingered it gently. Even that pressure caused his head to thump again.

"Come out," Durr said. "I'll speak to you later." She favoured him with a final smile, turned and walked away. Her skirt swished above the ground, a swirl of colour against a drab landscape.

Remembering a similar incident in Crimea, where he had met Helen, Jack emerged from the river. For a moment, Afghanistan looked beautiful, with the sun dappling the tented encampment and the stream running clear blue. Jack wondered why some places seemed to attract violence and what this country would be like if peace descended for a length of time.

That's not my job. I'm a soldier, not a politician or a philosopher.

He listened as a child laughed, thought of his son, now a grown man, and shook his head. Considering himself sufficiently dry, Jack dressed, dragging on the *shalwar*, the traditional Pashtun baggy trousers and pulling the *partuggakh* drawstring tight. He lifted the knee-length shirt, the *kamitz*, and slipped it over his shoulders, smiling at the snug fit, and shrugged into the colourful *waskat*, the Pashtun waistcoat. With sandals on his feet and a *rakhchina* hat and turban on his head, Jack looked at his reflection in a quiet pool of the river.

"A Pashtun to the eyebrows," Armaghan said. He stepped back, examining Jack critically. "You even have a Pashtun face." He put his head to one side, eyes musing. "Your nose is prominent and slightly hooked, and you are darker-skinned than the average British soldier."

"My mother was Indian." Jack did not know why he admitted his parentage.

"That explains it," Armaghan said. "Perhaps you do have Pashtun blood in you, Major. You'd look more genuine with a beard, but our route will avoid most people. You'll have time to grow a beard before we arrive."

"Where the devil are we going?"

"I'm taking you somewhere safe," Armaghan said. "We'll be travelling hard and fast, so ensure you are well-rested." He threw over a long Khyber knife. "You'd better stick this under your belt. I dislike the things, but it will help you look the part."

Jack caught the knife. It was old and poorly cared for, with rust on the blade. He realised that Armaghan did not carry a weapon of any sort. "You're not armed," Jack said.

"No," Armaghan agreed. "I'm not." He grinned. "If we meet anybody, Major, your name is Bazgal, and you are my servant."

Jack nodded. "I'll clean this knife."

"We leave before dawn, Bazgal."

CHAPTER TWELVE

Leaving his family beside the river, Armaghan took Jack and two camels to the north. Although Armaghan did not appear to move quickly, he covered the ground at a steady pace with the camels long-striding at his side.

Jack walked with the second camel, trying to follow their route by the stars. Even when the light grew, he was not sufficiently familiar with this area of Afghanistan to identify the hills.

"You know Afghanistan well," Jack said after a long day of constant movement. They made camp a hundred yards from the banks of a furious stream, with a herd of markhor goats watching them, great horns twisted and shaggy coats looking uncomfortable. The hills frowned all around, stark in the dying light, yet with a rare beauty Jack had never appreciated before.

Armaghan gave a gentle smile. "I've spent all my life walking through this area, from Persia to Samarkand, Baghdad to Lahore, as did generations before me."

"Are you Afghan or Persian?" Jack asked.

Armaghan smiled again. "If I recognised any racial or national differences, I'd say I am a Timuri, as you already know," he said. "People say we are descended from the Timur Empire."

He looked away. "We may be, although my ancestors were here long before that."

"Do you consider yourself an Afghan?" Jack persisted.

"I don't consider myself as belonging to any nation or subject to any king, Amir or ruler," Armaghan said. "The Quran tells us that there is no deity except Allah, Lord of the Noble Throne. When kings enter a city, they ruin it and render the honoured of its people humbled."

Jack nodded. "There is a lot of truth in that," he said. "Kings, queens and whatnots seem to want to increase their power at the expense of others."

Armaghan smiled. "Maybe you'd best keep that opinion to yourself, Major Windrush. You have sworn an oath of loyalty to your queen-empress."

"The Bible says that people should render unto Caesar that which is Caesar's," Jack said. "In other words, obey our rulers. Does the Quran not say something similar?"

Armaghan lay on his back, watching the last of the light fade from the sky. "The Quran obliges Muslims to obey a ruler, even those who take power by force, to save bloodshed. The Quran disapproves of Muslims killing other Muslims."

Jack chewed on the cold leg of chicken that Durr had provided for them. "That sits badly with the Pashtun code of revenge for any insult."

"I think your old knights had a similar code," Armaghan said quietly. "During the ceremony of knighthood, a man struck them on the cheek, which was the only blow they were to take without striking back."

"Why are the Pashtuns so aggressive?" Jack resolved to milk Armaghan for as much information as he could.

"I think their environment shapes their culture," Armaghan replied, making a small fire. "They live in a land of harsh soil, rocky valleys and bare mountains. Life cannot get beyond subsistence unless they leave their homeland. For anything beyond survival, a horse, a rifle, even a wife, they must raid their neighbours or the richer lands of the Indian plains."

"Aggression seems to be part of their tradition," Jack said.

Armaghan put a handful of rice in a pot and placed it on top of the fire. "And the British tradition, too," he pointed out. "After all, you are a British soldier in their territory, yet I cannot think of a Pashtun warrior raiding in England's green and pleasant land."

Jack could not reply to that. He knew that the British had expanded their empire to every continent on the globe.

"Sleep, Major Windrush," Armaghan said. "We'll be up again soon. We have a long journey ahead of us."

Jack lost count of the days as Armaghan led them through the Afghan plains and across high passes where the wind plucked at them. They perched on precarious paths as eagles soared beneath them, and twice they saw the drift of campfire smoke.

"We won't go that way," Armaghan decided. "That's a raiding party."

Jack wondered what was happening in the outside world as they camped in the unfrequented places, avoiding human settlements.

"The world will be there when you return, Major Windrush," Armaghan told him. "The war will continue without you."

"Are you a philosopher, Armaghan?" Jack asked when they halted on the crest of a mountain pass. "You seem to know a lot about many things."

Armaghan patted the nearest camel. "Everybody knows a lot, but most people don't realise how much knowledge they have or how to use it."

"I notice that you don't carry a rifle or a sword." Jack tapped the hilt of his Khyber knife. "I think you're the only man I've ever met who travels unarmed in Afghanistan."

Armaghan smiled. "Even if I had a gun or a sword, Major

Bazgal, I'd never use it. I don't believe in violence. If somebody wants to kill me, then they'll kill me whether I'm armed or not."

"Surely you'd wish to defend yourself," Jack said. "Islam isn't a pacifist religion, is it?"

Armaghan began walking again, his strides long and confident as he negotiated the downward slope. "No. Islam allows justifiable wars, but although I can quote the Koran and the Bible, I am neither a follower of Muhamad nor Christ."

Jack had not expected to hear that. "My apologies, Armaghan. What are you?"

"The same as my younger wife. I follow the old religion."

"Zoroastrianism?"

"Among others." Armaghan looked sideways at Jack. "You will have heard of the three magi who travelled to see Christ?"

"Of course," Jack said.

They were silent for a few minutes as the camels padded down the narrow track, with the mountains silent on either side. Jack dislodged a loose stone and watched it fall down the praecipe to their left, tumbling over and over until it disappeared in the dark depths below. He did not hear its eventual landing.

"The word magician came from magi," Armaghan said at last, "and people from outside Persia believed we had the power to work magic."

Jack glanced sideways at Armaghan. "Are you telling me that you can work magic spells?"

"No," Armaghan said. "I do not believe in magic, or *djinns* or any other of the Arabian Nights tales. I am trying to educate you in this area. Our history goes back further than you imagine, Major Windrush. We are not only an area of warriors and fighting but of beliefs and philosophy."

Jack nodded. As a soldier, he had only met the aggressive side of Afghanistan and the people of the region. He knew something of the social side from Batoor but little of the spiritual.

Armaghan allowed Jack to ponder his words for the rest of

that day as they moved across a landscape of magnificent hills, interspersed with valleys so beautiful they took Jack's breath away. Villages nestled beside groves of fruit trees while flocks of sheep spread across the hill slopes, and the occasional landowner's house sat proudly behind enclosing walls. From above, Jack could see fountains of cool water amidst gardens that any British lord would envy.

"Afghanistan is a nation of great contrasts," Jack said as another day closed, and they settled down for some rest.

"Is Great Britain not the same?" Armaghan asked. "Terrible poverty beside luxury, the rich ignoring the poor and men scrabbling for increased wealth while people live on scraps from the street?"

Jack nodded. "It is," he agreed. "But we don't have tribes constantly killing and torturing each other."

"No," Armaghan said softly. "You send out your armed men to attack other countries instead."

Again, Jack could not argue with an uncomfortable truth.

Armaghan gave a small smile. "The world is travelling towards destruction and violence," he said. "Violence breeds hatred and fear among people of all religions and beliefs." He spoke quietly, as if to himself, yet Jack knew he intended his words to be heard. "I believe in nonviolence. I don't think we can solve the world's problems with the sword, be it Christian, Moslem or any other type of sword. I don't believe that we can achieve peace or tranquillity in the world until we embrace nonviolence. That is love."

"Christ said something similar," Jack agreed.

"Are you a Christian?" Armaghan asked.

"I try to be," Jack said.

"Then why do you carry a weapon?"

Jack had no ready answer. He was silent as he slogged over the majesty of Afghanistan. Armaghan walked easily in front of him, and the camels continued their remorseless, timeless stride along the secret paths.

* * *

"There, Bazgal," Armaghan pointed ahead. "You will recognise those hills."

Jack nodded. "We are south of Kabul."

"We'll be parting company tomorrow, Major Bazgal," Armaghan said.

Major Bazgal? That is correct, for I am a major in the British Army but the merest peasant in understanding this land and this man's philosophies. I have only scratched the surface of Afghanistan and the East.

"Who are you, Armaghan?" Jack asked. "What accident made you cross my path?"

"All is the will of Allah," Armaghan said.

"I thought you weren't a Muslim," Jack said.

"The will of God, then, if you prefer," Armaghan said. "You'll be arriving tomorrow."

"In Kabul?"

"I am not taking you to Kabul," Armaghan said.

Jack looked at Armaghan again. "You said you don't believe in magic, yet you've taken us across Afghanistan without meeting a single person. How have you managed that without magic?"

"By knowing the old roads that my people have travelled for generations, perhaps thousands of years," Armaghan said.

Jack nodded. He knew he would miss Armaghan and his quiet teachings, even the journeying, day after day, across the wild areas of Afghanistan with its rare beauty. If nothing else, the journey had allowed him to see the country through a different lens.

"Tomorrow, Major Bazgal, you will return to your world," Armaghan said.

For a moment, Jack felt a strange reluctance. He did not wish to leave Armaghan's quiet certainty and the lonely places of

Afghanistan for the fire and fury of the army, but he knew he must.

"How can I pay you back?" Jack asked. "I have money when things settle."

"*Zar, zan,* and *zamin*?" Armaghan said with his slow smile. "I crave neither, Major Bazgal. I don't believe that a man can own land. I have all the women I can handle and sufficient gold for my needs. I only ask that you consent when the next person requests *melmastia f*rom you."

Jack nodded, knowing that such an event was unlikely. "Reciprocation," he murmured.

"Indeed so, Major."

They moved before dawn the following morning, with the camels now familiar companions. Jack had become used to walking in sandals, so the track no longer felt rough under his feet, and the loose Pashtun clothes were more suited to the environment than any tight British uniform.

As the light increased, Jack recognised his surroundings. "We're above the Kabul to Kandahar road," he said.

"This is where I leave you," Armaghan said.

"Thank you." Jack held out his hand. "I'll make my way into Kabul from here. Thank you for guiding me here and for your wisdom. I will consider your words."

Armaghan's handshake was firm. He nodded, turned the camels around and walked away. Jack watched him go.

I'll never see you again, Armaghan, yet I know I'll never forget you, whoever you are.

Sighing, Jack resumed his journey, sliding down a steep hillside as he aimed for the road to Kabul. He became aware of the throbbing beneath his feet and instantly crouched down. Only a marching army created such a sensation, the regular thump of thousands of feet on the ground.

Has Ayub Khan marched on Kabul when I've been wandering the hills?

Jack ducked behind a rock with one hand on his Khyber

Knife. After days when he barely thought of a weapon, now he wished he had his revolver. He felt naked without it in the presence of armed men.

Knowing that any intelligence he gathered could be useful, Jack moved closer to the road, hoping to observe Ayub's army. He saw the dust rising in the distance and heard the thump of feet.

Many of them, thousands rather than hundreds. So much for Armaghan taking me somewhere safe!

Keeping under cover, Jack crawled closer, wondering if Armaghan had intended him to witness the Afghan army. After ten minutes, he had a clear view of the road and the men on it.

Dear God in heaven! They're British!

It was a British army marching on the road from Kabul. British and Indian regiments with rifles at the slope and a long baggage trail following behind. Jack felt an immediate surge of relief.

Armaghan was correct. He brought me to a safe place, but who the devil are they, and why are they marching out of Kabul? Have we finally abandoned the city? Are we leaving Afghanistan?

Rising to his feet, Jack raised a hand and hurried forward. "Halloa there! I'm a British officer!"

A group of cavalrymen lowered their lances and approached him at the trot. "Get the *badmash*! Kill the loosewallah bastard!"

Dear God! I've survived Afghanistan only to be skewered by a trooper of the 9th Lancers!

CHAPTER THIRTEEN

"I'm a British officer!" Jack roared as the first lancer thrust at him and missed by an inch.

"What's that he's saying?" The second lancer lifted his lance. "He speaks English, this one."

"A Paythan, what speaks English?" The lancers surrounded Jack, staring at him as though he were some freak from a circus sideshow. "He must be a spy!"

The first man shortened his lance and prodded Jack in the stomach. "Who are you, chum? And how come you speak English?"

Jack knew the lancers could kill him on a whim. British soldiers could be as dangerous as any Pashtun tribesmen if they took a dislike to somebody.

"I am Major Jack Windrush of the 113th Foot."

"He sez he's Major Windrush of the 113th," the first lancer said.

"That won't do, mate." The second lancer came closer, glaring at Jack. "Major Windrush is dead, see? Your mob killed him at Maiwand, see? You murdering Paythan blackguard. I say we run him through." He hefted his lance and backed off as though readying himself to lunge.

"And I say you don't," a familiar voice called. "Welcome back, sir. I didn't think the Afghans could kill you."

"Donnelly!" Jack said. Private Donnelly had been his soldier-servant for years.

"I saw the commotion, sir," Donnelly said, "and I guessed it was you."

Jack nodded. Donnelly had been born into the 113th and knew no other life but soldiering. In common with many long-serving soldiers, he had developed a sixth sense for danger, or when his officer was close.

"Is this Paythan fellow Major Windrush then?" The second lancer sounded disappointed he did not have the opportunity to run his lance through Jack.

"He is," Jack growled. "And I'd be obliged if you'd return to your patrol work, trooper."

"Very good, sir," the lancer replied, and the four troopers trotted away.

"Who's in command of this column, Donnelly? And what's happening?"

"General Roberts is in charge, sir, and we're marching to relieve Kandahar."

"Best take me to him," Jack said.

* * *

Major-general Frederick Sleigh Roberts rode near the head of the column. He tugged at his whiskers when Jack rode up and waved away the four men of his bodyguard, all Ninth Lancers.

"It's all right, damnit. A lone Afghan is hardly likely to attack me with half the British army present. Do you speak English, sir?" Roberts greeted Jack in Pashto and added, "Who are you, my friend?"

"Major Jack Windrush, sir, reporting for duty."

"Windrush?" Roberts looked closer. "Good God! So it is! Wherever did you spring from? And why are you dressed like a regular *badmash*? We heard that Ayub Khan had killed you at Maiwand."

"No, sir. I got away. What's happening, sir?"

Roberts tugged at his whiskers again. "Extraordinary. How did you manage to turn up here? Never mind, that's a story that can keep for another time. You want to know what's happening, do you? Well, General Primrose has got himself in a pickle, Windrush." Roberts lifted a hand and raised his voice. "Somebody find this fellow a horse, for God's sake. I can't talk to him like this."

Jack stepped aside, keeping pace with Roberts and his entourage until a harassed second lieutenant brought him a Kabul pony.

"He's all I could find, sir. He's not the best, but he's steady and sure-footed."

"He'll do admirably." Jack lifted himself astride the horse. "Thank you."

"Now, Windrush." Roberts was astride his Arab charger Vonolel, a horse little taller than a pony but suitable for the general, who stood five feet four. Roberts had bought the horse after his victorious Lushai expedition of 1871 and named it after the man he defeated. "Tell me your account of the unfortunate affair at Maiwand."

Jack did as ordered, being careful not to apportion blame to Burrows or Primrose but praising the Horse Artillery and the 66th.

Roberts listened, nodding gravely. "There was no fault with the men? How about the sepoys? I heard that they panicked and broke."

"They withstood hours of bombardment, sir," Jack said. "And lost most of their officers. They were young men, boys even, without experienced NCOs to steady them."

Jack knew that a veteran officer such as Roberts would understand as he explained the position. "There were two companies of Jacob's Rifles on the left flank, commanded by a twenty-one-year-old subaltern. The sepoys fought well, even though their Sniders were so hot they burned the men's hands. They only lost heart when an Afghan cannonball killed the officer."

Roberts glanced at the column that marched behind him. "Men need leaders."

"Yes, sir."

"I heard that Burrows lost nearly a thousand dead," Roberts mused, "and over a hundred and seventy wounded. How did you get here from Maiwand?"

"I picked up a knock at the battle, sir, and a Timuri rescued me. He told me Ayub Khan's army blocked our route to Kandahar, and nobody could get through, so he guided me here instead."

Roberts had been scrutinising Jack as he spoke. "Well, Windrush, now you're returning. We're marching from Kabul to Kandahar; we're going to raise the siege and smash Ayub Khan's army."

"Yes, sir." Jack had immense faith in Roberts' generalship.

"Are you aware of the current situation?"

"I've been in the wilds for days, sir. I don't even know what day it is."

"It's the eighth of August, Windrush. On the 22nd of July, Abdur Rahman became Amir of Afghanistan."

"Is that the third Amir in two years, sir?"

"I believe so, Windrush, although it's hard to keep count. If Ayub Khan gets his way, he'll be next on the throne, and we don't want that. An Amir who defeated a British army, however much the odds were in his favour, will weaken our position."

"I agree, sir. The Afghans will be cock-a-hoop. They'll think they drove us out of the country."

"Any hesitation on our part could be disastrous," Roberts said. "The last telegraph I heard, Primrose has expelled all the Pashtuns from Kandahar and is holding the walls against all of Ayub's army." He checked behind him again. "We're marching for Kandahar, Windrush, and next time I see you, I expect you to dress like a British officer, not some thug from the bazaar. Dismissed!"

"Yes, sir." Jack pulled his horse away, hiding his dismay.

How the devil am I to obtain a uniform out here?

Roberts' column was perhaps the leanest that Jack had ever seen in India. The cavalry brigade included the 9th Lancers and three Indian regiments, the 3rd Bengal Cavalry, 3rd Punjab Cavalry and the Central India Horse. Brigadier-general Sir Hugh Gough commanded the cavalry, with Brigadier-generals Herbert Macpherson, Thomas Baker and Charles MacGregor in charge of the infantry.

Jack had served with all four brigadiers in the earlier part of the war and knew them as experienced fighting officers. Neither man would be as hesitant as Burrows or as prone to make mistakes. He did not like MacGregor, a grim-faced man who often criticised and seldom praised, but he was a good soldier and courageous as anybody in the army.

The regiments were equally as good. Jack stood at one side, watching the column swing past. In the First Infantry Brigade marched the 92nd Gordon Highlanders, the 24th Punjab Infantry, the 23rd Pioneers and the 2nd Gurkhas. Even that single brigade held more experienced soldiers than Burrows had commanded. A combination of Gurkhas and Highlanders was enough to send a shiver up the spine of any enemy.

Baker's Second Infantry Brigade was equally formidable. The 72nd Seaforth Highlanders marched in the van, with the 2nd and 3rd Sikhs immediately following and the grinning, redoubtable, green-coated 5th Gurkhas nearly invisible behind a pall of dust.

Roberts is making sure this time. Ayub Khan can whistle for his kingdom with this lot on his tail.

Jack's spirits rose as MacGregor's 3rd Infantry Brigade stormed into view. The 60th Rifles marched in front with their distinctive swagger. Behind the Rifles, the 15th Sikhs, 25th

Punjab Infantry, and 4th Gurkhas formed as dangerous a combination as any army in the world.

Added to the striking power of the infantry were detachments of Royal Engineers. Jack frowned, looking for the Royal Artillery. For a moment, he thought that Roberts was daring a campaign without guns, and then he saw the Mountain Artillery with eighteen screw guns. These weapons were the most portable artillery the British possessed, carried in pieces on the back of mules and screwed together before action.

Finally, Jack saw the baggage train and camp followers. Even although there were less than usual, the mules, horses, and camels were present in vast numbers, with servants on foot and not a single wheeled vehicle in sight. A British regiment acted as rearguard, so dusty that Jack found it difficult to recognise them.

"Look! Donnelly wasn't pulling the longbow! It's Major Windrush looking like a Paythan!"

Jack felt a wave of elation as men looked at him with undisguised smiles. One or two even lifted a hand in acknowledgement until shocked sergeants bellowed them back.

The 113th Foot! My regiment!

Unable to stop himself, Jack threw a salute.

"We thought you were dead, sir!"

"Welcome, back, Major!"

"It's not been the same without you, sir!"

"Now, we'll set about the Afghans! Fighting Jack is back!"

Jack felt all the glow of homecoming as the men of his regiment welcomed him with comments and smiles. Although Jack had spent much of his career on intelligence work that had taken him on lone missions to diverse parts of the world, he was a regimental officer at heart. He had grown up expecting to join the family regiment, the Royal Malverns, but circumstances had forced him to join the 113th Foot instead. The 113th had been notorious as the worst regiment in the British army, and Jack had been ashamed of the association. After bitter fighting in the Crimea and the Mutiny, the 113th had redeemed its reputation. Now it could bear comparison with any regiment in the army.

Roberts called a halt soon after Jack arrived, and the column formed camp, with the cavalry on patrol outside the perimeter and each regiment providing pickets and patrols.

"Here we are, sir." Donnelly appeared at Jack's side. "I borrowed a tent, sir, and found some camp equipment for you."

Jack raised his eyebrows. "How the devil did you do that, Donnelly?"

"I called in a favour, sir, and it's amazing what you can find lying around when you put your mind to it."

Jack smiled. He knew that British soldiers would lift anything that wasn't nailed down, but he hadn't heard of a servant stealing a tent before. "You're a valuable man, Donnelly."

"Thank you, sir. I have a bit of a uniform as well. I'll have to make a few alterations to ensure it's suitable for your rank and our regiment, sir, but I think it will do." Donnelly revealed an officer's tunic and a pair of trousers.

Jack saw where the original badges of rank and regimental insignia had been removed and wondered which officer Donnelly had deprived of his second-best uniform.

"And boots, sir. They're slightly worn, but your size."

"Good God, man. You're a wonder."

"I couldn't get a revolver, sir, but I've got people on the lookout," Donnelly said. "I'm sorry, sir."

"Sorry?" Jack shook his head. "You're a marvel. What people do you have?"

"Some of the servants, sir, the *bhisties* and so forth." Donnelly sounded suddenly evasive, and Jack thought it best not to enquire too deeply. Donnelly evidently had a network of helpers working for him.

With his tent erected and the servants busily catering for the needs of officers and men, Jack reacquainted himself with the 113th.

Major Burridge had retained command of the regiment and

greeted Jack with a half guilty smile, for he knew Jack was the senior man. Captain Singer, once diffident, was now a confident officer. Jack could see a bright future for the tall man, while he had never got to like Lieutenant Trent.

"What happened in my absence?" Jack asked as the officers gathered in the large tent they used as the officers' mess.

Burridge answered for the rest. "Mainly routine garrison duty in Kabul, Windrush. Then we heard about the disaster at Maiwand. Your name was amongst the missing and the killed."

"I was certainly missing," Jack agreed. "I wasn't killed, though, thanks to a most unusual gentleman named Armaghan. He saved my life."

"A Paythan?"

"No, a Timuri, I think."

"I don't know the breed," Burridge said. "Once we heard about Maiwand, Kabul was in an uproar, and when he learned that Ayub Khan was besieging Kandahar, we were all ready for the Paythans to rise all along the frontier. We had visions of 1841 all over again." In 1841 the Afghans had destroyed a British army as it retreated from Kabul.

"We didn't have General Roberts in forty-one," Jack said softly. "I can't see any Afghan pulling the wool over his eyes."

"Nor can I," Burridge agreed.

"And we have some excellent regiments here. The pick of the army." For a second, Jack had a guilty wish that the Royal Malverns were in the column, but they were holding Kandahar against Ayub Khan's hordes. He thought of Helen and pushed the image away, thanking his God that Mary, at least, was safe in Gondabad.

"The general has been very strict," Captain Singer said mournfully. "Each British soldier is allowed only thirty pounds of baggage, including his kit, and camping equipment, with the poor sepoys restricted to twenty pounds. Even the officers have to struggle with only one mule apiece to carry everything and one mess mule between eight officers." He shook his head. "No carts or wagons as they'll slow us down, and only eight and a half thousand pack animals."

Jack knew Singer well from the earlier campaigns of this war. "That's terrible," he sympathised.

"He's nearly as bad as you were, sir, when we went after that Batoor fellow."

"More seriously," Burridge said. "We're on our own. With Kabul being evacuated, we've no base to fall back on. We stand or fall on our own resources."

Jack thought of the regiments he had seen marching past. "I wouldn't worry about that. Roberts has a fine army here." He made a quick calculation in his head. "About ten thousand fighting men?"

"Slightly under, with only a quarter of them British. We also have eight thousand dooley-bearers, servants, camel drivers, and other followers." Burridge glanced at his watch. "We rouse at 2:45 tomorrow morning, gentlemen, so I suggest we all turn in. We don't know what travail lies ahead of us."

Jack lay on the *charpoy* – a simple wooden framed bed - that Donnelly had managed to purloin and closed his eyes. The last thing he thought of was Armaghan, then he was asleep, dreaming of Zamar Khan shooting Crimea. The image ran through his mind a hundred times, from a hundred different angles, and always with the same result. Crimea fell dead, with his eyes wide open and his mouth forming the words, "What a lark."

CHAPTER FOURTEEN

Jack grinned as he heard the familiar roar. "Didn't you hear the reveille? You lazy sods! You sons of diseased hoors! By Queen Vicky's holy drawers, the sun's burning holes in your blankets. Rouse, you unwashed frequenters of the casual ward, you gutter rats and street Arabs. Bless my eyes if I have ever seen a lazier selection of scoundrels and sweepings!"

Sergeant Deblin was in fine form this morning.

Jack breathed deeply of the early morning air before walking through the ranked white tents of the 113th. He listened to the men's comments, dismissed the grumbles as ordinary soldiers' fare and gauged the regiment's morale. They seemed happy and eager to meet the Afghans.

Watch out, Yakub, Khan, the Kabul-Kandahar Field Force is coming for you.

After breakfast and the apparent confusion as the men struck the tents and packed the mules, the column set off at four in the morning. Two cavalry regiments formed the advance guard, with another on each flank and the first two infantry brigades next. The mountain battery's mules plodded behind the infantry, with the field hospital and the treasure following. Jack had heard of French and other armies who simply grabbed supplies from the countryside, but the British military preferred to pay for their provisions. In Afghanistan, where any man could be a warrior, it was more politic to appear friendly than to antagonise the natives by stealing their food.

Behind the treasure was the baggage and finally the Third Infantry Brigade, with two cavalry troops and the 113th Foot as rearguard.

Coughing in the eternal dust of the journey, Jack ran his gaze over the column that stretched for miles into the distance. The 113th marched with the grumbling patience of British soldiers, boots barely rising from the ground, Martini-Henrys at all angles over their shoulders, and sun helmets stained a dozen shades of khaki. In front shambled the camp followers, with the stately camels mumbling and spitting, natives fighting the donkeys and mules, shaggy-haired Kabul ponies and the pack horses with supplies, water, and ammunition.

"It's quite a sight," Jack observed.

Singer nodded. "We get used to it out East, sir, but if we ever get back to Britain, we'll look back on this with wonder." He grinned. "Thank goodness we have General Roberts in command."

Jack nodded. "Amen to that, Singer."

They halted for ten minutes every hour, with the rearguard rounding up the stragglers and pushing them into the column. Roberts had selected to travel by the Logar Valley, which was sufficiently fertile to help supply the men, and moved at a moderate pace to break the men in gradually. After months of garrison duty, the infantrymen were unused to long, brutal marches in rugged terrain.

That first full day, the column halted at two in the afternoon to escape the full heat of the sun, but it was another three hours before the rearguard ushered in the last of the baggage train.

"That's about twelve miles covered," Captain Singer said as he threw himself in a patch of shade. "How far is Kandahar?"

"About three hundred and twenty miles," Jack said,

comparing the steady lope of Armaghan's camels to the crawl of a military column.

"That's another thirty days," Singer said.

Jack nodded. "I think it's officially twenty-seven days if we're lucky and if the tribes don't attack us." He paused for a moment. "General Roberts wants to cover the ground in twenty-three days, including any rest days."

Singer produced two cheroots and offered one to Jack. "Do you think General Primrose will hold out in Kandahar, sir?"

"Thank you." Jack accepted the cheroot, lit it, and slowly inhaled the smoke. "I can't say, Singer. He has a couple of thousand good men, including the Royals and the remnants of the 66th, and Kandahar has stout walls. I believe he can hold until we arrive."

"I heard a shave that some people want Sir Garnet Wolseley to take over in Afghanistan." Singer leaned back in his chair. "You know Sir Garnet, sir. What do you think?"

Jack had fought in the Ashanti Campaign under Wolseley's command. "I think General Roberts is every bit as good a general as Sir Garnet," he said.

"We'll see," Singer said. "We're in a perilous position here, with no base to fall back on as we march through some of the most hostile territory in the world."

They looked up from the mess tent as Lieutenant Trent bustled in, red-faced.

"Damned natives," Trent complained. "I had to use the thunderbox, and there I was, with my trousers around my ankle, and some skinny brown arm reached under the tent and snatched my revolver. It was a brand-new Enfield 476, the best there is! That *loosewallah* rascal unfastened the belt cool as bedamned, and I couldn't do a thing." He threw himself into a chair. "By God, if I ever find him, I'll string him up."

"I'm sure you will," Jack said. "We have to be careful out East. The *loosewallahs* here would take the fillings from your teeth while you ate."

Trent swallowed his anger. "Yes, sir."

Jack finished his cheroot and retired to his tent, where Donnelly was waiting for him.

"That's excellent needlework, Donnelly." Jack examined his tunic. "I didn't know you were so skilled."

"It wasn't me, sir," Donnelly admitted. "I got one of the natives to help."

"Thank him for me, will you?" Jack said. "If I had some money, I'd pay him."

"Yes, sir," Donnelly said. "It's a her, sir, a woman."

"Even better, Donnelly," Jack approved.

"Oh, and sir," Donnelly said. "My friends came good for a pistol." He handed over a revolver.

"How did you come by this, Donnelly?" Jack asked.

Donnelly adopted the expressionless face of a ranker when being questioned by an officer. "I acquired it, sir."

Jack checked the chambers. The revolver was a .476 calibre Enfield, fully loaded. "Thank you, Donnelly. I hear that Lieutenant Trent lost his revolver earlier today."

"Did he, sir?" Donnelly looked utterly innocent. He handed over a leather holster. "Best ensure the gun fits in here, sir. They came from different sources."

"Did they, indeed?" Jack lifted the holster. Skilled hands had engraved the name Billings on the leather. "We'd best ensure that Captain Billings of the 4th Gurkhas doesn't see this, Donnelly, don't you think?"

"Yes, sir," Donnelly said. "It's a strange coincidence."

"It is indeed. The revolver fits like a glove."

Later that evening, Jack saw Donnelly talking to one of the camp followers, a bright-eyed woman shaped like a Greek goddess. He grinned and walked away. *Well done, Donnelly. You're helping improve Anglo-Indian relations.*

* * *

General Roberts tugged at his whiskers as he looked at Jack. "So, you're an Anglo-Indian, then? A country-born Eurasian, eh?"

Jack had heard all possible insults about his mixed blood. "Yes, sir. My mother was half Indian." He lifted his chin.

"I thought so, Windrush. Do you think that gives you a better insight into the country?"

Jack had not expected that question. "I don't know, sir. Perhaps it does."

"I think it does, Windrush. Think of some of our notable men. You'll have heard of Colonel Warburton at Peshawar; he's half Pashtun and a better man you could not meet. Or James Skinner of Skinner's Horse, or Sikandar Sahib, as he was known. Scottish father, Indian mother, and fluent in Persian."

"Yes, sir." Jack began to relax a little.

"And then there's me." Roberts fixed Jack with a penetrating stare. "I was born in Cawnpore, and my mother is half Rajput, although born in Edinburgh." He smiled. "My uncle John is Muslim, Chote Sahib."

"I didn't know that, sir," Jack admitted.

"Did you think I was pure Irish?" Roberts broke into fluent Hindustani. "Only by name, upbringing, and nature." He poured out two glasses of champagne and passed one to Jack. "I understand, you see," he said. "I understand."

"Yes, sir." Jack was unsure what message Roberts was communicating, but he recognised a hand held out in friendship. "Thank you, sir."

* * *

Jack heard the scratching at his tent flap through a blur of sleep. At first, he thought it was part of his dream and turned over on his side. However, the scratching continued.

Some damned jackal, Jack said to himself, reaching under his pillow for the revolver. He checked the chambers and rose groggily, still half asleep.

"Begone! Get out of it!" He opened the flap and thrust outside, gasping at the bite of the cold wind.

A man stood outside his tent, huddled into a dirty poshteen, the Afghan sheepskin coat and with a dull yellow turban on his head.

Jack kept his revolver handy. "Who are you, and what the devil do you want?"

The man said nothing but put forward a surprisingly slim hand with a scrap of paper on it.

Frowning, Jack took the note. Somebody had written two words on one side: *melmastia* and reciprocation.

Jack started. "Armaghan is at the back of this, isn't he?"

"Yes, he is." Armaghan appeared from the dark, smiling.

"Come in." Jack put his revolver away and opened the tent flap wider. Armaghan ushered the other man inside Jack's tent, where the three of them barely fitted. "What's the to-do, Armaghan?"

"*Melmastia*," Armaghan said. When Jack struck a Lucifer match and applied it to the wick of his lantern, a yellow circle of light illuminated them. The stranger stood in silence.

"*Melmastia*," Jack said. "The rule of hospitality." He tried to make out the features of Armaghan's companion. "Who is your friend?"

A jackal howled somewhere outside, and a sentry barked a hoarse challenge. The jackal howled again.

"Will you honour your promise to me?" Armaghan asked. The lamplight caught the intensity of his eyes.

"*Melmastia*," Jack repeated. "We are engaged in a war, Armaghan. It's not the best time to bring a guest."

"Will you honour your promise to me?" Armaghan repeated.

Jack raised the lantern high. Armaghan's companion was short for an Afghan, with his face so concealed that Jack could only see his eyes. *He must be a young man escaping from some blood feud.*

"Yes, I will," Jack could make no other reply.

"Then I will leave my friend in your care," Armaghan said. Before he stepped out of the tent, the flap flicked open, and Donnelly squeezed inside. Dressed in shirt sleeves and with his braces hanging loose, he pointed his Martini at Armaghan.

"Are you all right, sir?"

"Yes, thank you, Donnelly. This gentleman helped me escape from Ayub Khan."

Donnelly's rifle did not waver. "Is he causing you bother, sir? It's a strange time to visit."

"He's not causing any bother, Donnelly, thank you."

"How about the *khyfer*, the bint, sir?"

"The bint?" Trust Donnelly to ascertain that the second visitor was a woman.

"Yes, sir. Who is she if I may ask?" Donnelly prodded the woman with the muzzle of his rifle. "It's best not to have dealings with the local women, sir. They're trouble."

"The lady will be travelling with us for a while, Donnelly."

"Very good, sir." Donnelly shifted his rifle to cover Armaghan as the Timuri tried to edge to the flap. "Not so fast, you! We'd best search the woman for hidden weapons, sir. It wouldn't be the first time an Afghan bint has knifed a man as he slept."

Jack saw the logic. Despite the woman's connection with Armaghan, he did not trust her. "I can hardly search a woman, Donnelly."

"I can, sir, or I know a woman or two in the camp followers, sir," Donnelly offered.

"Tell your servant there is no need for suspicion," Armaghan said. "This woman will not attack you."

Jack held Armaghan's gaze for a moment before he nodded to Donnelly. "Thank you, Donnelly. I am in no danger, although I don't know where the woman will stay. She certainly won't be sharing a tent with me."

"I'll arrange something, sir," Donnelly said, "and if she gives any trouble, just let me know."

"I will," Jack promised. He waited until Donnelly left the tent. "Who is she, where is she going, and why can't you take her, as you took me, Armaghan?"

"The who, I cannot tell you," Armaghan said. "I want you to ensure she reaches Kandahar, which is why I can't take her." His smile was slightly wistful. "General Primrose is not welcoming Afghan guests at present. Ayub Khan has him under siege."

"How do you know what's happening? Kandahar is over three hundred miles away!"

"I have heard your name mentioned concerning the siege," Armaghan said. "But that is not your concern. Will you honour your pledge and take this lady to Kandahar?"

Jack grunted. "I said I would. I wish she would talk, though." He faced the woman. "Do you have a name?"

The woman remained silent beneath her poshteen.

"Why do you need my help?"

When the woman did not reply, Jack sighed. "Can you tell me more, Armaghan?" But Armaghan had left the tent. "Well, my lady, I'll leave you here until my servant can make alternative arrangements. You are welcome to sleep in my bed until rousing time."

Pulling on his uniform and revolver, Jack left the tent. The woman was an added complication; what else would Afghanistan throw at him?

* * *

The column woke at quarter to three the following morning, with the Third Infantry Brigade again in the rearguard. The bitter cold of the night soon altered to blistering heat as the column continued the march, boots churning up the dust and the men keeping their heads down.

"How much further, sir?" a bearded corporal asked as Jack rode past.

"Only about three hundred miles," Jack assured him.

"We'll be there by teatime, then, sir," the corporal replied and chivvied his section along. "Come on, lads, put some *jildi* in it. We're all sigarno with Bobs in command."

That was the first time Jack had heard the rankers' nickname for General Roberts, but by the end of the day, the name was on everybody's lips.

Private Todd, a square-featured, hard-eyed man with the reputation as a brawler, inserted the general's name into a short rhyme.

"Bobs is here; Bobs is there; General Bobs is everywhere."

Jack agreed. General Roberts was not a man to neglect his troops. His white Arab Vonolel became a well-known personality as Roberts rode him the length of the column, trotting up with his four lancers to encourage the men.

"We're all right, boys," men called, "here comes Bobs!"

Roberts' presence gave heart to the despondent and strength to the weak. Men marched faster, knowing Bobs was watching them, squared their shoulders and lifted their chins when he came close.

"Bobs is here; Bobs is there; General Bobs is everywhere!"

Jack had served with many commanders in his career, from the terminally stupid to the militarily brilliant, but none as universally loved as Roberts. In the early morning, Roberts galloped to the head of the column and led them straight ahead, down gulleys and up the other side, challenging the terrain as he defied the hostile tribes.

Unlike other British generals that marched through Afghanistan, Roberts had made arrangements with many of the maliks along the route. Even so, there was always a risk of rogue elements attacking the column, and a malik could alter his allegiance as quickly as he changed his mind. Amir Abdur Rahman had sent five hundred draft animals to help Roberts' column and persuaded a prominent mullah, Mushk-i-Alam, to assist. Mushk-i-Alam sent his son ahead of the column, together with a selection of tribal headmen, to arrange supplies and pacify any aggressive clans.

"Why has the Amir asked the chief to help us?" Singer asked.

"Because we are fighting his enemy, too," Jack explained. "If Ayub Khan gets too powerful, he will challenge Abdur Rahman for the throne, so if we defeat Ayub, we're doing Abdur a favour."

Singer shook his head. "I don't understand the politics of this place. Everybody is out to stab somebody in the back."

The column slogged on with the men alert for sudden ambushes, the cavalry guarding the flanks and the rearguard choking on dust and trying to ensure the stragglers rejoined the main force.

"If you fall behind!" Jack encouraged a *bheesti* – a native water carrier, "the Afghans will kill you."

"My feet are sore," the man wailed. "I have walked for days."

"We've all walked for days," Jack said.

"You have a horse," the *bheesti* pointed out.

"Oh, for God's sake!" Feeling like a school prefect rather than a British army officer, Jack held out his hand and pulled the man onto his horse. He carried the *bheesti* back to the camp followers and placed him gently on his feet.

"Keep walking," Jack said. "Better to have sore feet than an Afghan *choora* dagger across your throat."

"That's the way, Windrush!" Major Burridge called out. "Keep the water supply alive."

All the time Jack patrolled, he watched the rear and flanks, expecting a horde of ghazis to rush from a hidden gully to kill and maim. The supply wagons and camp followers were the weak points in any military column, and therefore the most susceptible to attack. He also wondered about the woman Armaghan had dumped on him, who she was, and what he would do with her. And whenever he paused for a rest, he saw Zamar Khan firing his rifle and Crimea falling slowly to the ground.

"I've found a space for your guest, sir," Donnelly said as they halted for the day. As in the previous night, Roberts had chosen well, with the camp beside fields of Indian corn and local farmers eager to sell their grain at high prices.

"Is she safe there," Jack asked.

"Yes, sir, unless you think she'd be safer sharing your tent."

That's very diplomatic, Donnelly, but no, I don't want an Afghan concubine, thank you.

"What arrangements have you made?"

"I've put her with a couple of servants I know, sir. The woman who did the stitching for me and her husband. He's with the mule train."

"Well done, Donnelly. I don't know what I'd do without you."

"Yes, sir," Donnelly accepted the praise without false modesty.

"I'll visit her later," Jack said.

Jack could not keep his guest a secret, and when he entered the mess tent that evening, a barrage of questions greeted him.

"Who's the black velvet, Windrush?"

"Did you pick her up on your travels, sir?"

"I hope your intentions are honourable, old boy!"

"This isn't the pre-Mutiny days when you could cohabit with these people. We've got to set them a higher example. We're British." Trent spoke in a murmur.

Jack listened to the comments, held his glass of brandy, and waited until the noise died down. "The woman is not for my personal use," he said quietly, "nor is she for any of you dirty-minded scoundrels."

Burridge looked up from behind a large whisky. "Then tell us the story, Windrush. Who is she, where did she spring from and why are you looking after her?"

Jack shook his head. "I don't know much more than you do." He explained his promise to Armaghan.

"So, you are abiding by some Paythan code of honour, sir?" Trent made *Pashtunwali* sound like an insult.

"I am," Jack agreed.

"Even to some Paythan woman you don't know."

"Even to some Pashtun woman I don't know," Jack said. "It's part of the Pashtun code to offer hospitality to strangers. Armaghan helped me, and I will help this woman."

"Well, that's a rum do," Singer said. "Are you turning into a Pashtun, sir?"

"I thought you were half Indian, anyway." Trent had been drinking more than he could handle.

"I am." Jack stared at Trent until the lieutenant dropped his gaze. He stood up. "My mother was Indian, and my wife is half-Indian."

"We know that, Windrush," Burridge said. "I know your wife well, and a finer woman never walked the earth."

Jack realised he was prepared to go on the defence against a non-existent attack. "I'd better check on this bloody woman," he said.

Donnelly had been as good as his word. The Afghan woman seemed quite comfortable with the two servants. She kept her face covered when Jack asked if she wanted anything, and the servants answered for her.

"We'll look after her, sahib."

"If you need anything, let Donnelly sahib know, and he'll tell me." Jack fished in his pocket for a few rupees and pressed them into the male servant's hand. "That might help."

"Yes, sahib."

Frustrated that he was kept in ignorance, Jack returned to his tent. The camp was already in darkness, except for the guards' perimeter lights, and he had sent Donnelly away.

The jackal was howling again, the noise hideous in the night, and Jack tried to close his eyes. The image of Zamar Khan firing his rifle returned to him, and the crack of the shot. Jack tried to lunge forward to stop him, but somebody was holding him back, the arm hard and sinewy across his throat.

"No!" Jack started up to see bright eyes in his tent and a shadowy figure against the perimeter lights. "What the hang?"

Then the arm around his throat tightened, and Jack was fighting for his life.

CHAPTER FIFTEEN

As soon as he felt the strength of the man, Jack knew he could not remove the arm that threatened to strangle him. Although his instincts told him to grab the constricting limb, Jack reached under the pillow for his revolver. He found it with his left hand, pressed it against the strangler's body and pressed the trigger.

The shot sounded loud in the silence of the night, and the strangler stiffened without releasing his grip. Jack fired again, aware that the second man had run to escape. He felt the strangler slump to the ground and followed the second man outside the tent.

"Sir!" Donnelly appeared in his trousers and shirt, with his rifle in his hand. "What's the shooting? Are you all right?"

"Get that man!" Jack shouted, pointing into the darkness.

Donnelly dashed away with his rifle at the high port while other soldiers emerged from tents, clutching their rifles. Trent, the duty lieutenant, trotted up with a corporal and ten men at his back.

"Somebody tried to kill me." Jack rubbed at his throat. "He went that way." He did not expect the guard to catch the second man, and after a few moments' fruitless search, everybody returned to bed. It was just another incident in Afghanistan.

Jack examined the body in his tent by the light of his lamp. "Pashtun," he said. He saw the pearl earring in the man's left ear. "Durrani. Why did he attack me? There are many far higher-ranking officers in the column."

Donnelly removed the Khyber knife from the man's belt and deftly searched him for valuables. "Only the knife and earring, sir. Nothing else. Do you wish to keep them?"

"No, you have them, Donnelly, if you want them." Jack knew the British soldiers' compulsion for collecting souvenirs.

"Thank you, sir. I know a woman who might like the pearl."

So might have Mary. Damn! Too late now.

"Maybe he wasn't after you, sir," Donnelly said.

"Do you think he chose the wrong tent?"

"No, sir. I think he was after the Afghan bint."

Jack swore. "That makes sense, Donnelly. I'm glad you put her somewhere safe. I'll speak to her tomorrow and try and get something out of her."

"Yes, sir. Do you want me to stand guard over her tonight?"

Jack thought for a moment. He could not think of anybody he would trust more than Donnelly. "No, thank you, Donnelly. An armed guard on a camp follower's tent would be like raising a flag saying "here she is" to whoever wants her dead. Best leave things as they are."

"As you wish, sir."

They dragged the dead Pashtun from Jack's tent and beyond the camp's perimeter for the jackals to dispose of, and then Jack returned to his *charpoy*. He tried to sleep, but his mind was busy wondering who the Afghan woman was. He had only got to sleep when a bugle blared, and Sergeant Deblin bellowed to wake the men.

"Rise and shine, children! The sun's burning a hole in your blanket, and we've a city to relieve!"

"Sir," Donnelly managed to look fully awake even at half-past two in the morning, "General Roberts is holding a meeting in fifteen minutes." He handed over a steaming mug. "Coffee, sir. Only goat's milk, I'm afraid."

"If ever you become an officer, Donnelly," Jack said. "You'll rise to general rank in weeks."

"Yes, sir," Donnelly said. "Your uniform is ready, sir."

"Our first major objective is Ghuznee." Roberts faced the circle of officers. "That's ninety-eight miles from Kabul. The Afghans might defend the town against us."

"Should we be ready to fight?" a red-faced colonel asked.

"We are always ready to fight," Roberts said.

The army marched on with the same routine, halting for ten minutes in the hour and the cavalry constantly patrolling the surrounding countryside. After the attack on Jack, the 113th Foot was angry.

"You men were meant to be on picket duty!" Sergeant Deblin roared. "Sentries? By the wrath of God, I've seen tin soldiers with more life than you!"

Jack knew that the Pashtun were among the best thieves in the world and did not blame the sentries. When Deblin had finished his ranting, he ordered that the pickets should be increased.

That means my men are more tired because of the blasted woman.

* * *

"Sir," a long-faced corporal approached Jack, "I thought I saw somebody on the skyline a moment ago."

Jack gave a weary nod. Every half-hour, somebody informed him they had seen somebody moving around the column. "Thank you, corporal." He lifted the binoculars he had borrowed from Singer and scanned the rocky ridge on their left. A cavalry patrol was passing beneath, kicking up dust, but Jack focussed on a group of trees, which would be a natural spot for anybody to watch the column.

As the dust subsided, Jack saw movement; although it could

have been an innocent shepherd, it might be an enemy. Pulling his horse away from the column, Jack focussed his binoculars until he made out a group of warriors.

The corporal was correct. These men are watching us.

Jack edged his horse closer, always ready to turn if a group of tribesmen or ghazis erupted from a hidden gulley. He saw four men beside the trees, undoubted warriors with modern rifles across their shoulders and swords at their waists.

You could be watching the column for Ayub Khan or waiting to pounce on that blasted woman.

That night, Jack doubled the guards and ordered them to stay in touch with each other. "There are some Pashtun warriors nearby, so if you see anything suspicious, don't challenge. Fire."

"Yes, sir," the sentries said. "What if it's a civilian?"

"Then it's my fault, not yours," Jack said. Out in Afghanistan, any hesitation could mean death.

When he had posted the sentries and organised the defence, Jack sought out the mysterious woman. Donnelly guided him through the followers' camp to the simple tent.

"I got them a slightly bigger tent, sir," Donnelly explained. "One that I could divide, what with the servants being Hindu and your woman, beg pardon, sir, the Afghan bint, probably being a Muslim, sir."

"You did well, Donnelly," Jack said.

The tent was of a British army pattern, with a regimental insignia half scrubbed off on one side of the flap. Jack did not look too closely to see which regiment had lost a tent. He mentally congratulated himself for choosing a servant who must have been one of the best scroungers in the army.

The servants scrambled away when Jack entered their tent, with the Afghan woman remaining in her half. A ragged blanket separated the two sides, with a rough charpoy on the ground and some army issue rations for food.

"All right, my lady," Jack spoke in Pashtu as he sat cross-legged on the ground. "You're causing me trouble, and I want some answers. Two men came to my tent last night, and they were not friendly. I think they were looking for you, so who are you and what's it all about? From who are you running?"

The woman had donned a black burka and sat erect on the ground, staring ahead. Jack leaned closer to her and tried again. "From who are you running? And to where are you running?"

"*Melmastia*," the woman said. "I claim *melmastia*."

"I have granted you *melmastia*." Jack kept his voice low. "Now, I want to know why and who you are. Two men came for you last night, and I don't know who they were."

The woman was quiet for a few moments. Jack listened to the noise of the camp outside and wondered if he should try more forceful methods.

No. I have granted melmastia, which does not have strings attached. This woman is my guest, and I will treat her as such to the best of my ability.

"What should I call you?" Jack adopted a gentler tone. "I cannot continue to call you that woman."

"Zufash," the woman replied. "My name is Zufash. It means a light that spreads over the world."

Jack smiled. "That's a lovely name," he said. "From whom are you running, Zufash?"

"From my husband," Zufash said. "My husband wishes to cut off my nose and lips, then probably kill me."

Jack nodded. He knew that Pashtun men had terrible power over their wives and could maim or kill them at any minor offence, real or imagined. "Why does he wish that, Zufash?"

"He thinks I have dishonoured his family."

"Have you?" Jack asked and shook his head. "You don't need to answer that, Zufash. I have granted *melmastia*, and I'll keep my word, whatever happens, and whatever you may, or may not, have done."

Zufash gave a slight nod. "I have not done anything to dishonour my husband or his family name." She hesitated for a moment. "There is another man I want, and I will have him."

"Very well. Where are you going? Where will you be safe?"

Again, Zufash gave the question a lot of consideration before she replied. "I am going back to my father's people before I claim my man. A woman cannot travel alone, so I need a chaperone."

Jack smiled. "Well, you have half the British army to chaperone you." He was unsure whether Zufash was smiling behind her burka. "Could Armaghan not take you to your father?"

"It has to be a British soldier."

"Why?"

"I don't know. Armaghan takes people across the country, but this time he said it had to be a British officer who escorted me."

Jack frowned. *What the devil is this all about?* "Well, Zufash, I'll deliver you to your father if you tell me who he is."

Zufash hesitated a little, then raised her head. "My father is Zamar Khan of the Nazar Khel."

Jack started at the name. He could see Zamar Khan lifting his rifle and firing. He could see the cruel twist to his lips as the bullet found its mark and Crimea crumpled to the ground. "Zamar Khan."

"Yes, Major Windrush. The Nazar Khel is of the Zirak Durrani, and father is with Ayub Khan's army at present."

Jack nodded as his mind raced. *What the devil do I do now?*

* * *

"She is who?" Major Burridge asked, with a cheroot halfway to his mouth. "She's Zamar Khan's daughter? By God, Windrush, the best thing you can do is turf her out of the camp right now! You're aiding and abetting the enemy!"

They sat on horseback as the column continued its steady progress toward Ghazni, with the fertile Logar valley around and the sun already clear of the horizon. The heat rose with the dust, and the men marched silently except for the rhythmic thump of boots.

"I gave my word," Jack said.

"You are putting Paythan honour before your duty," Burridge pointed out.

"Pashtun honour is similar to British honour in this respect," Jack said. "I gave my word to give hospitality to the first person to ask for it."

"That Timuri fellow used you," Burridge said. "He knew that woman, Zufash, needed help."

"That could be true," Jack agreed, "but Armaghan also saved my life. I owe him a debt."

"I wonder what he gets out of this," Burridge said, "or is that woman spying for Zamar Khan and Ayub Khan?"

Jack was silent for a moment as he pondered the question. "No. She won't see much with the camp followers. She'd see more standing on the heights with a pair of binoculars. I don't understand Armaghan's part, though."

"If you take my advice, Windrush, you'll get rid of her, or her husband will think she's run off with you." Burridge gave a wry smile. "You don't want a blood feud with a Pashtun khel."

"No, I don't," he said. "Nor do I want to be known as a man without honour, who broke his word."

Burridge looked around, checking his regiment. "You take things too seriously, Windrush. Nobody would think that of you."

"I gave my word and promised *melmastia*."

"You're not a Paythan."

Jack grunted. He knew that Burridge was a decent man, but he could not understand the Pashtun culture. *Perhaps it's because I'm part Indian that I see the cultures of Asia as equally relevant. We've been in India for nearly three hundred years, yet we still treat them as aliens. Surely, we've learned something after this length of time.*

"Think about what I said, Jack." Burridge looked worried. "I know that General Roberts gave me temporary command of the 113th, but you and I hold the same rank. I won't order you to kick the woman out, but I do advise you to lose her."

The march continued through the Logar valley, with Roberts leading them past cornfields and small villages whose inhabitants crowded to watch the British toil past. He led them past palm groves, where men longed to rest in the shade, and in the shadow of savage mountains, where groups of tribesmen waited on rocky knolls. Jack saw one old man sitting on a boulder, blowing on the match of his equally ancient jezail.

"They're watching us." Singer fingered his revolver.

"I see them," Jack acknowledged. "That's five days since we left Kabul, and not a single shot fired at us. The Amir's word has some potency behind it."

"It looks like there's a power struggle between Rahman Khan and Ayub Khan," Singer said. "Many of the maliks are waiting to see who's the stronger before they decide who to support."

"They'll see us as Rahman's ally," Jack said. "We're getting dragged into internal feuds here. The quicker we leave this damned country, the better."

As the 113th ushered the stragglers through the Sher-i-Dahan defile, Jack looked ahead. He could see the entire army in its seven-mile-long column, stretching forward, baggage, mules, guns, camels, proud cavalry, and slogging infantry.

What a sight! And what a tempting target for the Pashtun. Thank goodness that General Roberts made arrangements with Rahman in advance.

Once through the defile, Roberts reverted to his favoured formation. He organised the column to march on a broad front and rotated the brigades, so MacGregor's Third Infantry Brigade took the lead.

"Thank God for that," Singer said. "Others can taste our dust now, rather than us eating their's."

But I am further from Zufash. I can't protect her from miles away and with thousands of men between us.

"Sir!" Jack approached Roberts later that day. "I have a suggestion."

Roberts lifted his sun hat to fan his face. "What's that, Windrush?"

"The cavalry is hard-pressed, sir, riding up and down all day protecting the flanks and front. Last campaigning season, we trained Number One Company of the 113th as mounted infantry. I wondered if we could reconstitute them, sir, to ease some of the pressure on the cavalry."

"That may be useful, Windrush."

"The baggage train is especially vulnerable, sir," Jack said.

Roberts nodded. "It always is, Windrush." He mused for a moment. "We'd have to find more horses, Windrush."

"Yes, sir. As we consume food, some of the pack mules carry a lighter load. We can transfer supplies from the horses to the mules, and my men can requisition the horses."

Roberts pulled at his moustache. "All right then, Windrush. See what you can do." He gave Jack a searching look. "I'll station you permanently on the baggage train. That way, you can look after your Afghan girl, Zufash, isn't it, of the Nazar Khel?"

Jack nodded. He should have guessed that Roberts knew everything that happened in his column. "Thank you, sir."

Despite his best efforts, Jack could only raise twenty horses and chose twenty volunteers from the fifty men who raised their hands. All had been with him on his previous campaign and knew his methods well. Jack nodded his satisfaction. "We'll be apart from the regiment most of the time," he reminded.

"Yes, sir," a freckle-faced Irishman named Crozier said. "And away from that bastard Sergeant Deblin."

Jack pretended not to hear. Crozier might be disappointed when he found that Deblin was with the Mounted Infantry.

On the seventh day from Kabul, the column neared Ghazni, having marched 98 miles at an average of fourteen miles a day.

"Have the men load their rifles," Burridge ordered, "and double the flank guards."

Jack saw the lancers canter ahead to ensure no Afghan army held Ghazni, a city the British had to take by storm in 1839 during the First Afghan War.

The column held its collective breath as the lancers returned, but the news was good. Ayub Khan's men did not garrison Ghazni, but neither was there any information from Kandahar.

Roberts pulled on his whiskers. "I had hoped to hear something from Kandahar," he said, and Jack saw the worry behind his eyes. "March on."

Many of the men had hoped for a day's rest at Ghazni, but instead, Roberts pushed them on in a remorseless advance across increasingly difficult terrain. They had left the cornfields and ample supplies of the Logar valley and entered a land of heat and aridity.

The territory was akin to a desert, with loose stones sliding under the men's boots and the dust worse each day. The cavalry could not venture far from the flanks as mountains hemmed them in, and men staggered from the force of the sun. It was at this stage of the march that the camp followers began to suffer seriously.

"Pick these people up!" Jack ordered his Mounted Infantry as men and women lay under the pitiless sun, unable to continue the journey.

"How can we fight if we've somebody on the horse?" Private Todd asked.

"If the Afghans attack, we'll fight," Jack said. "I won't leave anybody behind if I can save them."

"We're soldiers, not dooley carriers," Todd grumbled, yet still managed to haul a skeleton-thin servant from the dust. "Up you get, chum. It's a free ride for you today."

By the end of that day, most of the Mounted Infantry carried a heat-stricken man as a passenger, and Jack ordered them to the hospital tent. He knew others had fallen unseen.

"Zufash?" Jack scratched on the wall of her tent before he

entered. Zufash looked exhausted. "Here." Jack passed over a goatskin of water. "Drink."

Zufash indicated her burka.

"I'll turn my back."

Jack gave her a good five minutes. "I'm turning around now." The goatskin was about a third empty, and Zufash had her burka back in place. "How are you managing?"

"I am all right," Zufash said calmly. "How far do we have to travel?"

"About two hundred miles yet," Jack told her. "Maybe fifteen or sixteen more days. Can you keep up?"

"I am a Pashtun," Zufash said. "I can keep up."

Jack smiled. "Well said. I have a Pashtun friend who would agree with that."

Zufash turned her head, saying nothing.

"Is Donnelly supplying you with sufficient food?" Jack saw the remains of army issue biscuits on the floor.

"Yes." Zufash was clearly not in the mood to talk.

"Rest, eat and drink," Jack said. "We'll have you back with your father before you know it."

After the friendly reception in the Logar valley, the next stage of the journey proved more trying. Bands of Afghan warriors followed the rearguard of the column, sometimes challenging the cavalry and mounted infantry without ever firing a shot, more often hovering within sight but out of range.

"The Afghans are getting bolder," Singer said. "Shall I take a section and chase them away, sir?"

"No." Jack shook his head. "There are always more Afghans. They'll lure you further from the column and then strike."

"Yes, sir." Singer did not hide his disappointment.

Thirst tortured every man and animal. During the early days, Jack dreamed of bottles of Herefordshire cider, clear and sharp. As the march wore on, his dreams altered, so he was once more on the verdant slopes of the Malvern Hills, slaking his thirst in one of the abundant wells, drinking pint after pint of pure water.

Nothing else mattered but the water and shade from the eternal sun.

"If anybody's got spare shade," Crozier gasped, "I'll give them my next month's pay for it."

"Next month? I'll give a year's pay for a shadow," Todd companion tilted his sun helmet and looked upward, where the pitiless sun poured down its heat.

"This hot wind's a bugger, sir," Singer said. "I feel like it's roasting the hair from my head."

"It's unpleasant," Jack agreed.

"It brings to mind Dore's pictures of the Infernal Regions," Singer said.

"Are you not meant to be guarding the left flank?" Jack reminded, and Singer pushed his horse away.

Although Jack tried to keep track of the days, the march seemed continuous. He could not remember which day the dust storm arrived, covering everything with fine grit. The wind blasted the dirt from the south, forcing men to walk with lowered faces and slitted eyes. Jack rode through a haze of dust, ate dust, drank foul, dusty water, and slept in loose dirt.

"Sir." Singer rode up again, with a length of cotton protecting his mouth and nose from the dust. "Did you know that every man eats a peck of dirt in his lifetime?"

"I've heard that said." Jack had to shout above the scream of the wind.

"Well, sir," Singer continued. "On this march, we've all eaten several bushels. Does that mean we won't have any more?"

"Very likely, Singer."

Laughing through his discomfort, Singer rode away to attempt his humour on somebody else.

On the days after they left Ghazni, the animals began to die in increasing numbers. Horses would collapse without warning, shedding their load onto the hot ground, so harassed servants redistributed the supplies, all the time watching all around in case the Afghans swooped.

Jack had grown up with horses, and each loss pained him, yet the death of a camel seemed worse. They died in harness, plodding on until they could no longer bear the burden of life. Then they dropped down and lay still, waiting for death. When their time came, they fell to one side, moaned, kicked their legs feebly and died without fuss.

The nights were the opposite of the days. When the temperatures plummeted with the setting of the sun, men who had cursed the heat shivered in their light khaki kit. The fortunate retained a greatcoat and blanket, which they huddled close to them as they longed for the torture of the sun. The generous loaned their blankets and made friends of the wretches that shivered through the night.

"How long will this march last?" Private Thomson asked Donnelly.

"Forever," Donnelly replied. "We're doomed to march forever, round and round in circles until the sun and cold send us doolally."

"Is that right?" Thomson asked.

"No, don't be stupid. Bobs knows what he's doing."

Rising before three and on the march by four, Jack checked on Zufash morning, noon, and night, ensuring she had food and water. Zufash had resumed her near silence, accepting Jack's offerings without gratitude and walking with the camp followers, head down against the dust.

The food grew less varied, with the British soldiers eating a slice of tinned bacon for breakfast, sandwiched between slices of Indian unleavened bread. They drank cold tea, nursed sore and swollen feet, swatted at the host of flies that tormented them and slogged on, often too tired to complain. Roberts had ensured there were supplies, with a tin of pea soup between two British soldiers, rum for the drinkers and meat for the others.

From the rear of the column, Jack used a heliograph to keep in touch with Robert's staff, seven miles in front.

"The camp followers are about done in," Jack reported to Dr

Hanbury, the chief medical officer. "We are carrying more of them each day."

Hanbury looked as tired as any of the men, for he had the medical care of thousands of men as his responsibility, working with minimal equipment in an unforgiving environment. "I'll arrange something," he said.

They slogged on, endlessly with Jack worrying about Zufash as the image of Zamar Khan returned to him, night after night. He saw Crimea fall in his dreams, and he saw him fall as he woke.

"Sir!" Donnelly pushed his horse to Jack as they prepared to stop for the day. "I can't find the Afghan bint, sir."

CHAPTER SIXTEEN

Jack swore. "When did you last see her, Donnelly?"

"A couple of hours ago, sir. I try to check her as much as possible."

"Thank you, Donnelly." Jack twisted in his saddle, staring at the rugged land behind the column. With the dust of their passage slowly falling, visibility was poor. "She can't have gone far in that time. I'll scout around for her."

"Yes, sir." Donnelly pulled his Martini from its bucket holster and checked the lock.

"I'll go alone," Jack said. "There's no need for you to come."

"No, sir, begging your pardon." Donnelly's ugly, squat face twisted in defiance. "The last thing Mrs Windrush said to me, sir, was to look after you. That means I must accompany you. I couldn't come when I caught the fever in Kabul, but I can now."

Jack sighed. Donnelly was an excellent soldier, but sometimes he displayed a stubborn streak that Jack could not shift. "Come on, then!"

They rode together, quartering the ground immediately behind the column with the rest of the Mounted Infantry following at a distance.

"What the devil are they doing?" Jack asked.

"Helping, sir," Donnelly said. "You know how quickly a shave spreads in the army."

As the dust settled, the light faded, and Jack noticed small groups of tribesmen drifting behind the column. They searched for anything Roberts' column had discarded and would happily knife any straggler they found.

"Keep your rifle ready, Donnelly." Jack loosened his revolver.

"I always do, sir," Donnelly replied.

The groups of tribesmen merged, then spread out to outflank the two British riders. Donnelly shifted his rifle, so he held it across the pommel. The previous year, Jack had equipped his mounted infantry with the shorter carbines, but now they had only standard-issue Martinis, more cumbersome to use when riding.

"I see ten men," Jack murmured.

"Me too, sir," Donnelly said. "Four on the left, two ahead and four on the right."

"If any point their firearm, shoot."

"Yes, sir."

With the dark concealing the remainder of the Mounted Infantry, the tribesmen grew bolder, advancing on Jack and Donnelly. When the men on the flanks closed in, Jack pulled his revolver.

"Time to dissuade these lads, Donnelly."

"Yes, sir." Donnelly raised his rifle. "Shall I fire?"

"Whenever you have a clear target."

Donnelly fired on Jack's last word, with the sound of the shot seemingly echoed as the Mounted Infantry behind them also fired. Not expecting resistance, the tribesmen turned and fled, leaving two men and one horse on the ground.

"That's the stuff to give them." Donnelly reloaded at once, peering around him. Powder smoke drifted, slowly dissipating.

"Are you all right, sir?" Sergeant Deblin called.

"Perfectly, thank you, sergeant. Keep looking."

The Mounted Infantry fanned out, keeping with sight of

one another as they searched the ground. Jack's heart lurched when he saw a body, but it was an unfortunate dooley bearer lying in a crumpled heap. The man must have lain down to die shortly before the tribesmen had found him, slit his throat, and robbed him of even his loincloth. He lay there, naked and abandoned.

"Poor bugger," Donnelly said. "What a terrible place to die."

They moved on, listening to the yipping of a pack of jackals somewhere in the dark.

"God help Zufash if she's out here," Donnelly said. "Between human and animal predators, she won't have much chance."

"We'd best find her, then," Jack said. He called her name, softly, then louder, with the Mounted Infantry joining in, bellowing across the dark.

"Quiet!" Jack shouted. "Halt and listen for her response!"

They stood still, with only a rising wind sending dust towards them and the constant yipping of jackals. When the wind shifted, it carried the sour smell of the British camp and the murmur of ten thousand men.

Jack peered into the dark, silently cursing. He had failed in his duty of hospitality.

"You lads go back to camp," Jack called. "You need your rest."

Not a man moved.

"That's an order!"

"Did anybody hear something?" Sergeant Deblin asked.

"Nothing, sergeant." Private Crozier grinned, so his freckles merged across his face.

"I think I did," Deblin said. "Over on the right."

Jack flicked his reins and walked his horse forward, listening intently. He heard a shuffling that could have been the wind and then a single long scream that raised the hairs on the back of his neck.

"Come on, Donnelly!"

Kicking in his spurs, Jack cantered in the direction of the

scream, holding his revolver in his right hand, and controlling the horse with his left.

"Sir!"

Donnelly shouted the warning. "Here she is, sir! She's not alone!" Donnelly dismounted with a curse, holding his rifle ready to fire.

Zufash was lying on her back in a shallow gulley, with a tribesman on top of her.

"Get off, you serpent!" Jack grabbed the tribesman, who lay supine. "Off!"

"He's dead, sir," Donnelly crouched at Jack's side, swivelling from side to side as he surveyed his surroundings.

"Zufash!" Jack lifted the tribesman away. Zufash lay on her back, wide-eyed, with her right hand holding a *pesh-kabz*, the long thrusting dagger of Afghanistan. She had stabbed the tribesman to death as he lay on top of her.

"You're all right, Zufash. He won't bother you again." As Zamar Khan's daughter, Jack guessed that Zufash had probably seen much worse things than a simple stabbing. However, witnessing violence, and killing somebody, were two different things.

Donnelly spoke over his shoulder. "Up you get, Miss. The Major's here for you."

There was little of the brash young woman as Donnelly lifted her to her feet. The heat and days of walking had worn Zufash down while stabbing the tribesman had finished the process. Jack helped her on his horse's crupper.

"Come on, Zufash. You're safe now."

"Leave me," Zufash pleaded. "I can't go on."

"Sir," Donnelly lifted his rifle. "Over there."

The mounted tribesmen had gathered again and converged on the tail of the column. Jack heard a low scream as a tribesman killed a camp follower.

"Dissuade them." Jack put an arm around Zufash.

Donnelly fired on Jack's word, reloaded, and fired again,

with the crash of the Martini attracting the other Mounted Infantrymen.

"What's happening, sir?" Sergeant Deblin asked.

"Another group of *badmashes*," Jack said. "See if you can scare them off, will you?"

"Very good, sir," Deblin peered into the gathering dark. "Three yards apart, boys, don't lose touch with one another. Walk forward and shoot anything that moves."

The Mounted Infantry obeyed, slowly vanishing into the dark and leaving Jack with Zufash.

"We'll stay here until the men return," Jack told her.

"Don't leave me." Zufash's stoicism had disappeared. She looked like the scared young woman that she was.

Jack heard the crackle of musketry and saw half a dozen muzzle flares, with no answering fire.

"They've gone," Deblin bellowed. "Back to the major."

Jack saw the figures emerge from the dark. "Well done, men. Who's on picket duty tonight?"

"We are, sir," Deblin said.

"Well, don't stray too far," Jack said. "The Afghans will be waiting."

"Come with me." Jack held Zufash tight as he returned to the column. Rather than put Zufash with the camp followers, he carried her to his tent. "Sleep," he said. "I'll find you some transport tomorrow, so you don't have to walk."

"I'll watch her, sir," Donnelly volunteered.

"We'll take it in turns," Jack said. "You need sleep too."

After that incident, Jack found a mule for Zufash, although he would have preferred to use the animal for a tired soldier or even a camp follower.

That blasted woman is taking over my life.

"Did you hear the news, Windrush?" Burridge asked. "No, you've been too busy with your little Afghan friend to pay attention. We've covered a hundred and thirty-three miles now, over a third of the way to Kandahar, but Ayub Khan is intensifying the siege."

"Is he?" Jack asked. "We'd better put some *jildi* in it, then, although I don't think we can march much faster."

"Bobs got the news from a spy," Burridge said. "There was more. The spy only gave brief details, but somebody called Windrush is acting the hero in Kandahar. Would that be your brother?"

Jack nodded. "I imagine so. Colonel William Windrush of the Royal Malverns."

As the column struggled with the appalling heat, the garrison at Khelat-i-Ghilzai managed to pass a heliograph message of another Afghan victory.

"What happened?" Jack asked.

"We're not sure," Burridge replied. "All we know is that the Kandahar garrison made a sortie, and Ayub Khan repelled it with terrible losses."

"Push on!" Jack said. He had little confidence in General Primrose commanding at Kandahar and did not voice his fears that Ayub Khan might capture the city before Bobs arrived. If that happened, the British column would be stranded in the middle of some of the most hostile country in the world, lacking food and water. They'd have to march to Quetta, another 125 miles.

That would be a march too far, Jack thought, looking at the men. *Primrose has to hold out at Kandahar, or we'll be the lost army.*

The column reached Khelat-i-Ghilzai on the 23rd of August. On the final days, Roberts encouraged the bands to play, entertaining any locals with music from the Highland bagpipes.

"The Khelat garrison might hear us coming," Singer said.

"That's probably Roberts' idea," Jack's eyes were never still, scanning the surroundings.

The Khelat-i-Ghilzai garrison had the Union flag flying and welcomed Roberts' column with fresh water and forage for the animals.

"Have you heard from Kandahar?" every officer and man asked, and the reply was reassuring.

"Kandahar's still holding out," the men of Khelat-i-Ghilzai replied. "They lost a lot of men in their last foray but inflicted casualties as well. Ayub Khan withdrew slightly, and he's not investing the town so closely."

The Khelat garrison looked strained. There were two companies of the 66th Foot, still numbed after the loss of so many of their comrades at Maiwand, a few hundred of the 2nd Baluchis and a hundred Scinde Horse.

Roberts allowed his men a full day's rest at Khelat-i-Ghilzai, and then evacuated the garrison and added them to his column. As they marched again, the Baluchis, part of Khelat's garrison, told Roberts' men they would all die.

"The enemy is countless," a Baluchi told a Gurkha. "Ayub Khan has raised all Afghanistan. They will kill us all."

The Gurkha laughed and told his friends what the Baluchi had said.

"He said the Afghans will kill us all."

The other Gurkhas joined in the laughter, and as the story spread, the entire Gurkha regiment was roaring at the joke.

"Kill us all!" a Gurkha said. "Doubtless, the Afghans think we are children to lie down before them."

"Hey, Johnnie!" a bearded Gordon Highlander asked. "What's the joke?"

The Gurkha explained in a mixture of Nepali, Urdu, and English, but the Highlander understood and passed on the information. Within minutes the Gordons increased their speed, and somebody asked the piper to strike up *Cock of the North*.

"Youse and us, Johnnie, eh?" the Gordon shouted. "We'll show the bloody Paythans, youse and us!"

The joke spread to the Sikhs, tall, solemn-faced men, who looked more angry than amused.

"I don't think Ayub Khan knows what's coming his way," Jack said.

Singer grinned. "I don't think he does," he said.

The news reached the 113th, with Private Todd lifting his head. "They're going to kill us all, are they? The Paythan barstids. They'll not kill the 113th so easily."

As they drew closer to Kandahar, the men became more alert, while Zufash was restless, looking around at a landscape that must have been familiar.

"We'll soon have you with your family," Jack told her.

"Yes." Zufash sat astride her mule, watching everything but saying little.

"Your little Paythan girl might be a spy," Singer mused.

"She's not," Jack said.

Knowing they were nearing the end of their epic forced march, the column completed seventeen miles on the 25th of August and camped at the village of Jaldak. The 113th's camp was in a level plain strewn with the skeletons of camels.

"What happened here? A camel massacre?" Singer asked.

"No," Jack said. "These poor beasts were part of General Stewart's force when he marched from Kandahar to Kabul earlier in the year."

"Afghanistan's a hard country," Singer said, "hard for animals and men."

On the 27th of August, Roberts sent forward Brigadier Gough with the Third Bengal and Third Punjab cavalry, two-thirds of his mounted force. "Advance to Robat," Roberts ordered, "and let me know what's happening. Take Captain Stratton with you."

"Bobs must be desperate for information," Burridge said. "Stratton is the leading signaller in the column."

Jack nodded. "Aye, the general is not confident that Primrose can hold out. If Kandahar has fallen, we'll be in a pickle." He watched the cavalry trot forward towards Robat, thirty-four miles closer to Kandahar and well within striking distance of Ayub Khan's army.

"We'll just have to wait," Burridge said. "It's all in Gough's hands now."

That evening, Jack saw the heliograph flashing from ahead as Stratton passed on his information.

"Ayub Khan has lifted the siege!" The news spread around the column, with men cheering and throwing their hats in the air. "He knows we're coming for him, and he's cut and run!"

Singer approached Jack with his hand held out. "We've done it, sir! We've forced Ayub Khan to lift the siege! Kandahar is safe."

"Don't cheer too soon, Singer," Jack said. "I wouldn't put it past Ayub Khan to attack us on the march. He'll be all cock-a-hoop with his victory of last month. Either that or he's withdrawn to a stronger position, for he must know that General Roberts has to defeat him to restore British prestige."

"General Roberts won't be fighting anybody," Burridge said soberly. "He's come down with a virulent fever. He can't even stand, let alone command an army."

CHAPTER SEVENTEEN

Jack felt his insides lurch. "Roberts is sick?"

"Sick as anybody can be," Burridge confirmed. "He's on his charpoy looking like death, sweating and shivering fit to shake the throne and with his Indian attendants flitting around in a state of near panic."

Jack took a deep breath. He thought of the brigadiers who were with the column. He knew that MacGregor, Macpherson, and Baker were experienced fighting soldiers who would give a good account of themselves and far better than Burrows. However, neither possessed the charisma of Bobs or the aura of invincibility that accompanied the little Irishman.

"What are we doing?"

Burridge lit two cheroots and passed one to Jack. "What would you do?"

"I'd carry on," Jack said at once. "Relieve Kandahar, smash Ayub Khan's army to show him he can't defeat a British force with impunity, then evacuate Afghanistan and never look back."

Burridge inhaled deeply. "That sounds good to me. Thrash the buggers to teach them no end of a lesson, and leave their damned country to its feuds, bloodletting, and hellish climate."

"What's the discussion?" the familiar voice broke in as

General Roberts appeared. A servant supported him on either arm; Roberts' face was drawn and white, his eyes bloodshot, but he was upright.

"We heard you were sick, sir," Burridge said.

"I am sick, dammit," Roberts said. "Laid low with some damned fever, but we're marching on. We have a city to relieve and Ayub Khan's army to defeat. Get your men ready to move."

"Yes, sir!" Burridge saluted.

The column marched again, with teams of dooley bearers carrying Roberts. At the first break, Roberts summoned Jack to his side. "It's a most ignominious mode of conveyance for a general on service, Windrush," Roberts said. "It's a damned nuisance, but there's no help for it. I can't sit on a horse, and better for the men to see their commander in a dooley than see him face down in the dirt, don't you think?"

"I do, sir." Jack felt tempted to tell Roberts that General Wolseley had been carried in a hammock during the Ashanti campaign but decided to refrain. Roberts might not wish a junior officer to remind him of his main rival at such a crucial time in the campaign.

"All right." Roberts lay back for a moment, with the sweat a dull sheen on his face. "Tell Badcock and Low, the quartermasters, to arrange provisions for the men. Order Major Leach to draw up a map of the country between Kandahar and Argandab, for that is where Ayub Khan is most likely to make his stand."

"Yes, sir." Jack hurried to obey.

The column moved forward again, inexorably heading towards Kandahar.

"We'll be there within a couple of days," Singer said. "Then we'll give old Ayub what for!"

Ayub's spies and scouts must have sent him very detail about the advancing British column, for he sent an emissary to Roberts under a flag of truce.

"Is Ayub surrendering?" Lieutenant Trent asked.

"No," Jack told him. "He's an Afghan. He's trying to gain

time to see how sick the general is, size us up and prepare his position to strike when we're unprepared."

Ayub Khan's emissaries stopped outside the British camp, with an escort of the 9th Lancers watching them. A dry wind played with the white-and-red pennons on the lances, whipping them this way and that as the Afghans awaited Roberts' reply.

Roberts lay back in his dooley, opened Ayub's letter and passed it to Jack. "Here, Windrush. You read Pashtu. Tell me what it says but paraphrase it. Leave out the flowery sentiments."

Jack scanned the letter. "Ayub Khan says that General Burrows forced him to fight, sir. May I quote a little?"

"If you must!" Roberts snapped.

"It says, "Early in the morning when my troops were marching to Maiwand, the British army came and began to fight."

"Did Burrows attack Ayub Khan?" Roberts proved that, however weak his body, his mind was as sharp as ever."

"I believe that Lieutenant Maclaine fired the first shot, sir."

Roberts coughed. "And now Maclaine's a prisoner of Ayub Khan. In your opinion, Windrush, would Ayub Khan have fought if Maclaine had not opened the ball?"

"Yes, sir," Jack said. "I think the battle was inevitable."

Roberts grunted. "All right. What else does Ayub Khan say?"

Jack returned to the letter. "What was preordained came to pass. I have given you the particulars, and this is the real truth."

"Enough of that." Roberts swore as one of the bearers slipped. "Change the dooley bearers, Windrush. These poor fellows are getting tired. What else does Ayub say?"

"He asks you to tell him what's the best course to pursue, sir, and I'll quote again. He asks that 'affairs might be settled in an amicable manner', sir."

"Does he indeed?" Roberts growled and raised his voice. "Fetch me pen and paper." He quickly scribbled a reply and read it to Jack. "I can only recommend you to send in the prisoners in your power to Kandahar and submit yourself unconditionally to the British government."

Jack carried the note to Ayub's emissaries, who accepted it with polite gestures and false smiles.

Politicians are the same worldwide. You can't trust a word they say or a gesture they make. This lot would slit my throat in an instant and smile as they gave condolences to my widow.

Before Jack returned to Roberts, a messenger brought a letter from General Phayre, who was leading a second relief column from Quetta to Kandahar. The letter said he had only marched as far as the Khojak Pass, fifty miles from Quetta.

"He won't reach us in time," Roberts said. "We're on our own, gentlemen. We've only twenty miles to cover, but I want my men to arrive in fighting trim. At present, we've too many men falling out with blistered feet and fever. We'll move in two marches and hope Ayub Khan stands to fight."

"Do you think he'll flee, sir?"

"He may retire towards Herat to regroup and try again," Roberts said. "Which strengthens my intention to attack without delay. If Ayub Khan slips away, we'll follow and bring him to battle."

The weeks of constant marching had divided Roberts' column into men who were disabled through heatstroke, weariness or blisters, and the majority, who appeared fit to march forever. The latter walked with a swing, and the pipers of the Highland regiments accompanied the steady rhythm of marching feet.

The column halted at Mohmand, ten miles from Kandahar, with the dooley bearers helping Roberts to his feet as the camp formed around them.

"Sir," Donnelly threw a smart salute, "There is a group of Paythans asking to see you."

Jack dismounted, stamped his feet, and brushed some of the dust from his uniform. "Where are they, Donnelly?"

"The Paythans got past the lancers' patrols, and Sergeant Deblin's picket stopped them, sir. They're under a flag of truce."

Jack checked his revolver was loaded as he remounted and rode to the perimeter of the column. A dozen Pashtun warriors stood twenty yards beyond Deblin's picket, with each side eyeing the other. Jack could taste the tension in the atmosphere and knew that any suspicious move on either side would bring violence.

"The big, bearded fellow shouted your name, sir," Sergeant Deblin said. "He was waving the white flag."

"Which big, bearded fellow?" Jack asked. The description could have applied to any of the warriors. They stood together, each man with a pulwar or Khyber knife at his belt and a rifle or jezail strapped to his back. Jack wondered how many Sniders and Martinis were locally made copies and how many were from the dead at Maiwand.

"*Salaam Alaikum!*" Jack approached the Pashtuns. "I am Major Jack Windrush. Who wishes to talk to me?"

The largest of the warriors stepped forward. Jack was always surprised at the size of these men. The average Pashtun dwarfed any British soldier. "*Salaam Alaikum,*" the Pashtun said, holding Jack's gaze.

Jack kept his hand close to the butt of his revolver, thankful that Sergeant Deblin was a veteran of half a dozen battles and skirmishes in the recent war.

"What do you want?" Jack asked.

"Zamar Khan of the Nazar Khel asks for the return of his daughter."

"Ah," Jack said. *How the devil do I know if these men are from the Nazar Khel?* "Which one?"

"Do you have more than one of Zamar Khan's daughters?" The big man assumed astonishment.

That was an attempt at humour. We seem to be teaching the Afghans something.

"I only have one under my protection," Jack said. "What is her name?"

"Zufash," the Pashtun seemed surprised Jack had asked him.

"Wait here," Jack said and raised his voice. "Sergeant Deblin, keep an eye on these men."

"Yes, sir," Deblin tapped his rifle.

When Jack returned with Zufash ten minutes later, the warriors had not moved.

"Toryal!" Zafush said immediately and began speaking so rapidly that Jack could not keep up with her. Toryal allowed her to talk for a moment.

"I am taking you back to Zamar Khan," Toryal said.

Without a word to Jack, Zafush stepped up to Toryal. The warriors closed ranks around her, and they walked away.

"Well, bless me with a feather," Deblin said. "Not a word of gratitude for all you've done for her, sir."

"No." Jack had not expected effusive gratitude from the daughter of a Pashtun malik, but he had hoped for some acknowledgement. He shrugged. "Well, lads, that's one worry less. We can get on with the war now."

On the 31st of August, the column marched the final ten miles to Kandahar, with Jack's Mounted Infantry in the van.

"There's no bloody flag flying!" Donnelly said. "Where's the flag? Has Ayub Khan captured the place after all?"

Jack frowned. Donnelly was correct. In his experience, the garrison of any besieged fortress would show their national flag to defy the enemy.

"There it is now!" Lieutenant Trent said. "About time. Are they scared to show the Afghans that they are British?"

The Union flag rose slowly, in little jerks, until it finally hung above Kandahar's walls. At the sight of the flag, General Roberts struggled from the dooley. "Get my horse! Where's Vonolel?"

Jack heard the commotion behind him, and when he looked around, Roberts was astride his Arab. The general sat as erect as any man in the column, although the fever sweat dripped from his face.

Jack saw Kandahar's Shikapur Gate open and an entourage of khaki and scarlet ride out to greet the relieving force, with General Primrose flanked by Generals Nuttall and Burrows. Even from a distance, Jack sensed something different about the gathering of officers. As he came closer, he worked out what it was.

Defeat.

The trio of generals looked defeated, which was something Jack had never felt before among British officers.

Roberts must have sensed the same thing, for he muttered under his breath when he approached.

"What the devil is this? No flag flying? And what hangdog expressions? Where is the British spirit in these men?"

"March to attention!" Jack returned to the 113th. *By God, I don't know what's happened here, but it won't affect my men.* "Straighten your backs! Heads up and march!"

"Old Jack's getting all regimental with us," an anonymous voice came from the ranks. "He must want to impress somebody important."

Not only the 113th, but all the regiments in Roberts' column straightened up as they approached. Rather than appearing as though they had marched over three hundred miles, they swung in like soldiers after a ten-mile route march on Salisbury Plain.

The Kandahar garrison poured out to greet them, with the cry "Kabul to Kandahar" shouted repeatedly. Indian sepoys and British Tommies shouted their welcomes in half a dozen languages and accents from Cornwall to Caithness, Kent to County Cork. Jack saw scarlet-uniformed men of the Royal Malverns among the crowd, but he could not see William.

Standing on top of Kandahar's wall, Helen was a lone figure. She had cut her hair short, and it hung loosely around her head, and she wore a simple skirt and a scarlet tunic, no different to that worn by the private soldiers in her regiment.

Helen! What must you have suffered? Jack remembered his early days with Helen, when he had first met her in the Crimea, and some of his old feelings resurfaced. *Do I feel affection? Or is it sympathy?*

"Glad you could come!" The garrison surrounded Roberts's column with outstretched hands and welcoming shouts.

"Aye, but you've been a long time coming!" somebody shouted. Jack remembered Highland pipers playing the tune at the relief of Lucknow and shook away his memories. Nostalgia was for old men, not serving officers in a war.

For a few minutes, the scene was no different to that Jack had experienced in the relief of other besieged towns, but it quickly developed into chaos. Possibly because the advance had slowed at the city gates, the baggage train caught up and then merged with the troops. Despite the hoarse shouts of red-faced NCOs and embarrassed officers, a horde of camels, mules, and horses surrounded the men.

"Get the sick inside Kandahar!" a beefy major roared, and the Baluchis from the Kalat-i-Ghilzai garrison pushed, shoved, and ushered the casualties through the Shikapur Gate. The exhausted and the fever-struck mingled with the merely blistered as they sat astride baggage animals or lay in dooleys.

As soon as the initial greetings subsided, the army surged inside Kandahar.

"Keep the men in hand!" Jack shouted. "We don't know when we'll be fighting again."

"Yes, sir," Captain Singer said.

Captain Inkerrow of the Royals stared at Jack as if he were a ghost. "Major Windrush." He looked shocked. His once immaculate uniform was stained, and his hair hung untidily over his ears.

"That's me," Jack said, suddenly irritated by the man's attitude. "Head up, man! You're a British officer, damn it!"

Inkerrow stiffened by instinct, although his lower lip seemed too loose for Jack's liking. "Up there." He pointed to the city walls, where Helen continued to stare outward. "That's Colonel Helen. Thank God for Colonel Helen Windrush."

"Where's the colonel?" Jack demanded. "Where's Colonel William Windrush?"

"He's no good," Inkerrow said. "His nerves have gone. Nervous exhaustion, don't you know?"

The garrison looked in poor shape but more mental than physical. "Their morale is broken," Roberts said. He pointed to the walls, thirty feet high and fifteen thick, with artillery embrasures at regular intervals. "I don't know why."

Jack agreed. He saw a sergeant of the Royal Malverns sitting in a corner, medal ribbons on his breast and his Martini in his hand, quietly sobbing.

"It's a disgrace!" Roberts said. "These men are demoralised. The officers I have spoken to consider themselves utterly defeated. If Ayub Khan had launched a proper attack, I doubt they could have offered more than minimal resistance."

"I've never seen the like," Jack agreed.

"Come with me, Windrush." Despite his fever, Roberts led Jack to the top of the city walls. Lifting their binoculars, they surveyed the surrounding countryside.

"Can you see Ayub Khan's army?" Roberts asked.

A range of hills ran north-east to south-west to the north-west of Kandahar. About two miles from the city, a kotal, a pass, divided the hills.

Jack concentrated on the kotal, focussing his binoculars until he saw the dark mass of men. "They're there, sir."

"That's what I thought." Roberts swayed slightly as his fever temporarily overcame his strength. "I'm all right, damn it!" He shook off Jack's supporting hand. He surveyed the heights, muttering to himself and holding onto the warm stonework of the parapet. "We must fight Ayub before he escapes."

Jack said nothing. He thought of the generals he had known. Raglan in the Crimea would have dithered for weeks, wondering what to do. Havelock would have thrown his men forward immediately, ignoring any odds. Colin Campbell would have grunted, made careful dispositions, and created a textbook battle.

"We'll camp outside the city," Roberts said. "General Primrose is an old woman, and I don't want the poor morale of the garrison to affect my men."

Jack said nothing. It was unusual for a general to criticise a senior officer to a junior, but Roberts was visibly angry at the state of the garrison and also suffering from fever.

"I want the troops camped near the old cantonments on the North-West of the walls," Roberts said, still holding onto the parapet for support. "I'm the senior general here, so I'll take charge of Primrose's army. By God, they need me."

"Yes, sir." Jack did not think it politic to say more, although he agreed. The garrison was as low in morale as any army he had seen.

Jack accompanied the column to its new campsite. The men barely noticed the short march and ignored the scatter of Ayub Khan's warriors who waited for them. The Afghans fired half a dozen shots from their jezails, and a few from Sniders, without causing any casualties.

"Ignore them," Jack ordered the 113th. "They won't stay long."

When Ayub Khan's warriors realised the newcomers were Roberts' men and not the demoralised garrison, they soon drifted away.

"Don't run too far, Paythans," Crozier jeered. "We're coming to get you!"

Todd watched Ayub Khan's men leave through narrowed eyes, hawked, and spat on the ground. "We're Bobs' boys, not some peacocks in fancy dress. We're the 113th!"

Jack hid his smile. He understood that Todd thought it strange that the Royal Malverns should continue to wear scarlet uniforms while the rest of the army adopted khaki.

The 113th remained with MacGregor's Third Brigade on the

left flank, camping among a collection of orchards and enclosures. Macpherson's Second Brigade was in the centre, with Baker's First Brigade on the right, on the rearmost slopes of a slight rise known as Piquet Hill.

Behind them all, the cavalry formed their lines, with the horses looking lean after their long journey.

"Well, here we are," Singer said. "It was a long march to see Ayub Khan tamely retreat."

"Here we are," Jack agreed. "But I reckon we'll be fighting Ayub as soon as Bobs is fit."

"He looked pretty bad, sir," Singer said. "I reckon it will be a long time before he's fit to fight."

Roberts is too stubborn to refuse a battle, but I'll have to find Helen. She looked terrible.

Major Burridge appeared, smoking a long cheroot. "Don't get too settled, Windrush. General Roberts wants to see you."

"Do you know why?"

Burridge shook his head. "I'm sure he'll tell you." He drew on his cheroot and studied the hills where Ayub Khan's army stood. "Bobs is sending Gough back out to probe Ayub Khan's position. Depending on what he finds, we'll fight Ayub tomorrow,"

Jack nodded. "I imagine so." *Roberts can hardly stand, let alone fight a battle! Are we heading for another Maiwand?*

CHAPTER EIGHTEEN

"Windrush!" Roberts coughed, dragged a damp handkerchief across his sweating brow and pointed a shaky finger. "Take a wing of the 113th and join Gough. I want an infantry officer's appraisal of Ayub Khan's positions as well as that of a cavalryman. I'll send the Sikhs, too; they're steady men, and the further away from Kandahar, the better."

"Yes, sir." Jack would rather accompany Gough than linger in Kandahar, with its atmosphere of defeat. *Sorry, Helen. You'll have to wait.*

"I'll have to speak to the Wali Ali Khan." Roberts leaned back, with his eyes seemingly sunk in his waxen face. "Is there anything you wish to tell me about Maiwand? I'll hear from Burrows today, but I'd like your opinion."

"The numbers were against General Burrows," Jack said.

"Would you have fought as he fought?" Roberts asked the direct question.

Jack took a deep breath. "It's not for me to comment on a senior officer's actions, sir."

"It's not for you to deny me an answer, Windrush. How would you have fought Maiwand?"

Jack replied at once. "I'd have taken a defensive position in the village, sir, rather than in the open where Ayub Khan could outflank me. And I'd have sent a message to Kandahar for reinforcements once I saw the size of Ayub's army. I'd also have posted more British officers with the sepoys; they were very young men and lacked the experience to remain steady under intense artillery fire."

"You have given it some consideration, then," Roberts said. "Good. We must all learn from mistakes, others as much as our own." He turned away. "Get about your duty, Windrush."

* * *

Gough nodded to Jack as he joined the other officers. "All right, gentlemen. We are embarking on a reconnaissance in force to discover the location and strength of Ayub Khan's army. We know he is a skilled commander, and we know he defeated us at Maiwand." Gough nodded again at Jack. "Major Windrush was present at that battle and can testify to Ayub's ability."

Jack expected the other officers to stare at him as though he were personally responsible for Burrows' defeat. He kept his face expressionless.

"We also know Ayub Khan defeated a powerful sortie from Kandahar. He will be quite confident in his ability to defeat another British army." Gough stopped there to allow his words to sink in. "Let's find out all we can about this fellow's dispositions so that we can smash him."

Jack studied the map Major Leach had created. Ayub Khan had camped his army at the village of Mazra in the Argandab Valley, which a hill spur separated from the Kandahar Plain. Two passes split the spur, allowing communication between the plain and the Argandab Valley. The Murcha Pass was more accessible but was further away and would necessitate a wide detour, presenting the flanks of the British army to an Afghan attack.

Nearer the point of the spur, the narrower, secondary pass of the Babawali Kotal was a spear stabbing at the valley. The

Afghans could also hold strong positions along the rugged summit of the hills, while Jack expected Ayub Khan to position his artillery on the individual heights.

Jack stabbed at the map with his finger. "I saw movement on the Babawali Kotal yesterday," he said. "That's the closest route to the Argandab Valley, and therefore Ayub Khan should have it well defended."

Gough nodded and touched his neat moustache. He was another Indian-born Irishman, a holder of the Victoria Cross and too experienced a soldier to ignore Jack's words. "We'll watch for that, Windrush."

Jack traced the spur with his finger. Beyond the kotal, the hills continued south-westerly, with a steep slope on the eastern face, until a mile later, it ended in a steep slope. The British called this final stage Pir Paimal Hill, named after the village of Pir Paimal at the edge.

"Are you ready, gentlemen?" Gough asked. He gave a faint smile. "Let's see this Afghan fellow."

The afternoon sun was hot as General Gough led his force towards the spur. The Sikhs marched vigorously beside Jack's wing of the 113th and the 3rd Bengal Cavalry with two guns rattling and bouncing in front.

The hill loomed up ahead of them, and despite the usual screen of dust from marching men and horses' hooves, Jack could plainly see the sun reflecting from artillery barrels on the rough slopes.

"Ayub is waiting for us," Singer said.

"He's a confident man." Jack thrust one of Burridge's cheroots in the corner of his mouth. "And so he should be. He's the only Afghan commander in the last thirty years to defeat a British Army."

As they approached the point of Pir Paimal Hill, the cavalry extended, and Jack saw a host of infantry at the village. A gun fired, the report echoing from the hill behind, and the smoke drifting slowly in the still air. The shell landed well in front, a warning rather than a danger.

"Missed," Todd muttered and added the expected, "You couldn't hit a bull's arse with a banjo."

"Here we go." Singer loosened his sword in its scabbard.

They marched on, with the 113th and Sikhs vying with each other to move closer to the enemy.

Jack knew his veterans would be loaded and ready. He glanced over them, saw the red-faced, determined faces and nodded his satisfaction. The 113th would not let anybody down.

Another Afghan gun fired, and then a third, with the explosions close to the 3rd Bengal Cavalry. One trooper fought to control his panicking horse as the advance continued. A risaldar barked an order, and the ranks extended further. Another order sounded, and the troopers drew their swords. Sunlight glittered on hundreds of sharp steel blades as a bugle blared out.

"Are the buggers going to charge the village, sir?" Singer asked.

"I hope not!" Jack replied and extended his men. The Sikhs were doing the same, and the infantry increased their pace to keep in touch with the cavalry, hundreds of khaki-clad men hurrying across the plain. Jack saw the turbans and sun helmets bobbing together. The artillery rattled onward, with men casually smoking pipes as they viewed Pir Paimal village.

The Afghan guns fired again, with tall columns of dirt and smoke rising among the extended cavalry. A horse fell, kicking and screaming as its intestines spilt onto the ground. The trooper hauled his leg free from his injured mount and limped away, still holding his sword and with the long scabbard trailing between his legs. The cavalry scouted around the village, provoking a response from the Afghan artillery, forcing the defenders to reveal their strength and positions.

Jack halted his men, raised his binoculars, and studied the village and the heights behind. The Sikh officers did the same, as the smoke and dust from the skirmish gradually drifted over them.

"Pir Paimal is well defended," Jack said. "Sangars, trenches and artillery."

"Lots of artillery," Singer agreed as another Afghan battery opened up, this time targeting the Sikhs.

"A formidable force of infantry as well." Jack saw the men massed behind the walls, with the white robes of ghazis mingling with the tribesmen and regulars. The sun reflected on sword blades and rifle barrels.

Gough's cavalry passed the village and eased toward the end of the spur, with the occasional shell burst following them, smoke mingling with the rising dust.

"Keep extended and move forward," Jack said. The 113th marched on, with men tipping their sun helmets back and looking around them. The Sikhs were to their right, hundreds of turbans bobbing across Afghanistan's plains, rifles at the slope and steady, bearded faces studying the terrain.

"Halt!" Jack ordered as the cavalry began to withdraw. Gough sent a galloper back to the infantry, the horse's hooves raising a plume of dust. The Afghans tried a couple of shots at him, with the shells exploding well behind the rider.

"General Gough sends his compliments," the rider was a smooth-faced jemadar with bright brown eyes, "and asks that you withdraw to the British camp. We have found out what is needed, sahib!"

"Thank you, Jemadar." Jack kept his eye on Pir Paimal, from where a column of mixed infantry and cavalry emerged. "Please convey my compliments to General Gough, sahib, and warn him that the enemy is coming in force."

"Yes, sahib!" the jemadar replied, wheeled his horse around and galloped back to the cavalry. Again, the Afghan artillery opened fire, with the jemadar wheeling around the explosions as though the war was only a game.

Oh, to be young again.

The Third Bengal Cavalry formed into troops and trotted past the village, ignoring the oncoming Afghans as they approached the British infantry. The British artillery covered them with a few rounds, distracting the Afghan guns until the cavalry passed through the infantry screen and headed towards Kandahar.

"Here they come," Jack warned. "Open up, boys, form a firing line with the Sikhs and watch the flanks."

Ayub Khan had unleashed a large part of his army as thousands of Afghan infantry, regulars and ghazis, advanced toward the British infantry. The British artillery fired another two volleys before limbering up to withdraw behind the infantry screen.

"We don't want another Maiwand," Jack said. "Ayub Khan's already taken a brace of our guns."

"They're getting no more." Singer sounded calm as he pulled out his revolver and checked the chambers.

The Afghan infantry advanced at speed, with the green banners held above them and the cries of *"Allah Akbar"* and *"Allah il Allah!"* high under the sun.

"Give them a volley!" Jack said. "Five hundred yards, try to dissuade them."

"You heard the officer, boys." Sergeant Deblin aimed his Martini. "Mark your target! Fire!"

The Sikhs did the same, so the rolling thunder of musketry crackled across the plain. In the dust, Jack could not see the result of the British gunfire but withdrew his men by sections, watching the flanks in case of a sudden rush by Afghan cavalry.

The Afghans did not falter, with the white-robed ghazis in the van, screaming their war cries as they came on, swords raised and bearded faces only a blur behind the dust and shields.

"Volley fire," Jack ordered, "fire and withdraw."

The Sikhs brought down a score of men with each controlled volley as they mounted an orderly withdrawal. With both companies of the 113th in action, Jack reclined the left flank as a company of Afghan regulars eased to their left.

"Take charge of the flank, Singer," Jack ordered, ducking as something whined over his head.

"The camp's awake, sir," Singer said and moved left, shouting orders.

The withdrawal had brought them close to Roberts' camp, and Jack heard the blare of a trumpet as "stand to" sounded. He imagined the organised confusion in the lines as men gathered their rifles and ran to their positions.

"Ayub Khan must believe he's pushed back a major attack rather than responding to a reconnaissance!" Sergeant Deblin said. "He'll add it to his litany of glorious Afghan victories over the kaffirs."

Jack gave a humourless smile. He could imagine an Afghan history book in years to come proclaiming Maiwand as a victory over equal odds and portraying this skirmish as a significant battle.

"They're coming closer, sir!" Deblin said.

Jack unholstered his revolver and took a deep breath. "Fire!" he shouted. "Reload and withdraw ten paces!"

Side by side, the 113th and the Sikhs gradually approached the British camp. A Sikh crumpled without a sound as an Afghan bullet found him, and another shouted the Sikh warcry, "*Bole So Nihal Sat Sri Akaal!*"

"Come on, you Paythan bastards!" a private of the 113th responded. "Cry Havelock!"

Jack started. The 113th had used that warcry during the Indian Mutiny, when General Henry Havelock led them in a series of victories over terrible odds. Jack had not heard it used in years.

The Afghans rushed again, ghazis in white and regulars who wore uniforms very similar to the sepoys. The Sikhs and 113th met them with controlled volleys that failed to stop the attack until Baker's First Infantry Brigade filed out of the camp, supported by MacGregor's Third.

The arrival of reinforcements ended the Afghans' attack, and they slowly returned to their positions, leaving their casualties on the field.

The Sikhs and 113th marched into camp, knowing the skirmish was only the beginning and wondering what the morning would bring. When Jack glanced over the plain, he saw the Afghans lifting their dead and wounded.

How many more men will this blasted war claim?

"Sir," Donnelly appeared at Jack's side, "a message for you, sir."

Jack unfolded the paper and read the carefully written note. It was crisp and to the point. "Attend meeting with senior officers tomorrow AM. Roberts."

The night was not quiet. As the British settled down and prepared for the following days' battle, an outbreak of firing sounded.

"Stand to, 113th!" Jack roared as he grabbed his revolver. Donnelly was already awake, waiting outside Jack's tent.

"It sounds like a raid on the pickets, sir," Donnelly said. "Nothing the lads can't handle."

"Rouse!" Jack ignored Donnelly's advice. In Afghanistan, it was always better to be safe, for the Pashtun warriors could make anybody sorry. "Get the men up and in firing positions!"

The other regiments in MacGregor's brigade also stood to arms, lining the rudimentary defences with rifles to hand and waiting for an attack by ghazis. When the firing died down, Jack kept every fourth man awake, resting them in turn. He paced the lines, realised that Sergeant Deblin was also checking the pickets and peered into the sinister darkness.

"You'd better get some sleep, Windrush," Burridge advised. "It will be a busy day tomorrow."

"I'll sleep later," Jack said, although he knew Burridge was correct. He thought of Crimea's death again and Helen's appearance.

Who the devil ever thought that war was glorious?

At six in the morning, the bugle drove the men to breakfast

with the old familiar call.

Come to the Cookhouse door, boys
Come to the Cookhouse door,
When you see the Sergeant Cook smile,
Come to the Cookhouse door.

"You'd better attend the general's parade," Burridge murmured as he watched the 113th fall in for breakfast.

Jack nodded, looked up at the dark, serrated ridge where Ayub Khan waited, and wondered what the day might bring.

* * *

"Where's Colonel Windrush of the Royals?" Roberts looked over the gathering of senior officers.

"Nobody's seen him for some time," St John said. "He's *charpoy* bashing. He took to his bed with fever after the death of his son."

"I want him here," Roberts demanded. "Windrush, he's your brother. Find him."

"Yes, sir," Jack said.

As Jack left the chamber in Kandahar's citadel, St John grabbed his arm. "We heard you were dead, Windrush."

"I'm still alive," Jack denied the charge.

"Glad to hear it, old man," St John said. "I must speak to you later."

Jack nodded and hurried away to William's quarters in the Royals' barracks, deep in Kandahar citadel. The room was empty, with the bed made and everything immaculate.

"You, there!" Jack pointed to an Indian servant. "Where is Colonel Windrush sahib?"

The servant looked startled. "I don't know, sahib."

"Where is the memsahib? Mrs Colonel Windrush sahib?"

"She's in her quarters, sahib."

"In her quarters? Doesn't she live with Windrush sahib?" Jack could not hide his surprise. "Never mind. Where are her quarters?"

The servant directed Jack to the opposite side of the barracks. After five minutes of frustration, Jack shouted, "Mrs Windrush! Where are you? Helen!"

"Here, Jack." Helen stood within a dark doorway. She stared at Jack through eyes like tunnels. "I thought the Afghans killed you, too."

"No." Jack touched her arm. "I'm sorry about Crimea."

Helen recoiled. "Are you, Jack?"

"I am, but I'm looking for William."

Helen stepped aside. "He's in here, for all the good he is."

William lay on Helen's double bed, staring at the ceiling. He barely moved when Jack entered the room.

"Get up, William," Jack ordered roughly. "General Roberts wants you."

William stared at Jack. "I can't," he said.

"Get up!" Jack shook him. "Roberts is holding a meeting, and he wants his senior officers. That means you."

As William continued to stare at Jack, Helen stepped inside the room. "You'd be as well to howl at the moon, Jack. He's been like this for weeks."

Jack swore.

"I've tried that," Helen said. "I've tried shouting, pulling, and being gentle with him. His mind's broken."

Jack swore again. "All right. I'll have to report to Roberts. Sorry, Helen, I've no time to talk." He hurried away and turned at the door. "I am sorry, Helen. Sorry about Crimea."

Helen held his gaze. "Did you see him?"

"I did," Jack said. "He died well, Helen. He was as brave as any man I've ever seen."

She nodded. "Thank you, Jack. Was it quick?"

"One bullet," Jack told her. "He didn't feel any pain."

Helen stiffened her back. "Thank you, Jack. Now go." She

pushed him away. "Please go."

* * *

Roberts sat on an armed chair, surrounded by his staff and with the other officers assembled before him. He grunted as Jack told him that William was unwell and unable to take command of his regiment.

"Sit down, Windrush."

Jack took a place at the back of the officers, near to St John.

"As I was saying," Roberts continued, "we will not attack the Babawali Kotal directly but will hammer the pass with artillery and demonstrate with the garrisons' cavalry and infantry to ensure Ayub Khan retains his men there."

Jack knew Roberts' methods of attack from previous experience. He threatened a frontal assault while hooking around the enemy's flank.

Roberts coughed, swayed, and continued. "Macpherson's and Baker's brigades will advance on Ayub's flank at the edge of Pir Paimal Hill, the village and eminence that General Gough reconnoitred yesterday. MacGregor's brigade will be in reserve, ready to reinforce whichever brigade needs their support."

The officers listened, with some scribbling notes that summarised their part in the forthcoming battle.

"When they have successfully turned Ayub Khan's flank, the First and Second brigades will force back the enemy's right. General Gough discovered that Ayub has a strong position between Pir Paimal Hill and an eminence called Kharoti. I anticipate some resistance there. We will overcome the Afghan defence and take in reverse the Babawali Kotal before pushing up the Argandab valley to Ayub's camp at Mazra."

Roberts coughed and dragged a damp cloth across his forehead. "With luck, we will catch Ayub Khan and show him the sharp edge of a sword or the benefits of British civilisation in India."

The officers gave their well-bred laughter at Roberts' joke. Jack watched the sheen of sweat on the general's face and wondered if he were fit to command an army.

Roberts continued. "The Bombay cavalry brigade will guard the roads over both the Murcha and Babawali kotals, backed by the infantry and guns from the Kabul garrison. Other regiments of General Primrose's command will remain to protect the city."

Jack nodded. Roberts entrusted the most dangerous and active part of the battle to the units he had led from Kabul while using Primrose's low-morale men as support and defence. It was a slap in the face for some of the regiments, including the Royal Malverns.

"While the infantry and guns defeat Ayub Khan's men in detail," Roberts continued, "General Gough will take his cavalry in a wide hook along the east bank of the Argandab River, then cut off the Afghan retreat. I want a comprehensive victory, gentlemen."

"Sir," Brigadier Macpherson asked. "How many men does Ayub Khan have?"

"We estimate his strength at four thousand eight hundred regulars with thirty-two pieces of artillery, plus eight to ten thousand tribesmen and ghazis."

"We have about ten thousand men," Macpherson said. "And the Afghans are well dug into secure defensive positions."

"That's correct," Roberts said. "St John, our political and intelligence man, assures me that Ayub Khan's men are the best that Afghanistan has to offer."

Macpherson sat down, looking pensive.

"My final point," Roberts said. "As Colonel William Windrush is unable to take command of his regiment, I have granted Major Jack Windrush command as a brevet Lieutenant-colonel until officialdom can confirm the promotion." He summoned up a grin that took years off his age. "Congratulations, Colonel Windrush."

CHAPTER NINETEEN

Jack heard the words without immediately understanding the meaning. He responded to the murmured congratulations with a lift of his hand as Roberts' statement sunk in.

Colonel of the Royal Malverns. I've made it. I have followed the Windrush tradition to command the family regiment, albeit temporarily until William recovers. What will Mary say?

"Colonel Windrush." Roberts stood beside him. "I thought you'd be eager to take over your regiment. It's not ideal taking command the day of a battle, but I am sure you're the man for the job."

"Thank you, sir." *Is that why you asked me about Burrow's tactics the other day? Were you checking my suitability for command? You're a devious man, Bobs.*

"I don't want you with the rest of Primrose's command," Roberts said. "I want you to bring the Royals to support Macpherson's brigade. I think they're still a fine regiment, despite their present despondency. If they see the Gordons and Gurkhas in action, they may remember how good they used to be."

"I'll do that, sir."

I've to take command of a broken battalion and bring it into action against a dangerous enemy without time even to assess their condition.

Major Baxter had the Malverns on the parade ground. "Good morning, Windrush."

"Good morning, Baxter. General Roberts had appointed me as brevet Colonel of the regiment." Jack decided to be militarily blunt rather than attempt diplomacy.

"Did he, by Jove?" Baxter raised his eyebrows. "Is that permanent, sir?"

"I don't know yet," Jack said. "We're marching to support Macpherson's brigade today."

Baxter looked surprised. "I thought we'd be defending the city, sir." He hesitated a little. "The battalion is not at its best."

"Are they ready to march?" Jack saw Sarsens, looking older now and failing to hide his nerves. The sabre slash on his cheek was partially healed into a livid white scar.

"Yes, sir."

"I'll address them," Jack said. He lowered his voice. "I'm glad you survived, Sarsens."

"Thank you, sir," Sarsens said. "Did I hear you had been promoted?"

"You did."

"Congratulations, sir!"

"Thank you, Sarsens. Now get on parade!"

Baxter had drawn the Royals up by company. After disease and skirmishes, 620 men stood on parade, looking shabbier than Jack expected yet still wearing the old-fashioned scarlet.

"Some of you may know me," Jack said. "Others may know of me. I am Jack Windrush, acting Colonel Jack Windrush, and as from today, I command the Royal Malverns."

If Jack had expected rousing cheers, he would have been disappointed. A few men looked at him while most stared stonily ahead.

What's happened to the regiment? They used to be amongst the best in the army!

"We're marching to dislodge and defeat Ayub Khan today," Jack told them. "We're in support of Number One brigade, so let's show the Sikhs, Gurkhas and Gordons how real soldiers fight."

Sarsens tried to raise a cheer, but few men responded.

"NCOs, ensure every man has seventy rounds of ammunition and a full water bottle." Jack waited until the NCOs checked their men. "Follow me!"

It felt strange to pass the 113th as Jack led the Royal Malverns out of Kandahar, past the British camp and towards the enemy.

"There go the peacocks, toy soldiers who avoid battle!" Jack recognised Private Todd's voice.

"Fighting Jack's with them," Crozier said. "Why's he with the peacocks?"

The sudden roar of heavy artillery broke the morning. Jack checked the now battered silver watch Mary had given him for their tenth wedding anniversary. "Five minutes past nine, and the battle has begun."

"What was that, sir?" Baxter asked.

"It's five past nine," Jack replied.

The gun fired again, joined by others. The British battery of forty-pounders on the right of Piquet Hill began their systematic bombardment of Babawali Kotal. The Afghans replied with their three-gun battery beside the pass, and the howl and crash of the shells soon dominated everything.

Jack saw Sarsens flinch as a shell burst close by, sending dirt and small stones into the air.

"It's all right, Sarsens." Jack leaned over to say. "Keep your head up, and don't let the men see you bob."

"Yes, sir," Sarsens replied. Jack saw the nervous sweat on his face and knew the experiences of Maiwand had affected the young man. *I can sympathise with that*, Jack thought. *I still have nightmares about the Mutiny over twenty years later.*

Jack led from the front, with Macpherson's brigade in column ahead and a cavalry screen on the flanks. Baker's brigade was parallel but a little behind, deeper into the plain to the left. Pir Paimal Hill rose five hundred feet above the plain on the opposite flank, crowded with tribesmen and decorated with standards, colourful under a bright sun.

The responsibility of commanding a regiment lay heavy on Jack's shoulders, despite his years of military experience, and he found himself repeating various scenarios in his mind.

"Sir! Colonel Windrush!" A galloper approached Jack tentatively, glancing at his badges of rank. "Sorry, sir, are you the colonel?"

"I am." Jack had forgotten to order Donnelly to change the insignia on his uniform. He would have to do that tonight, provided he survived the battle.

"General Roberts' respects, sir, and the Afghans have moved from their positions during the night. They have occupied the villages of Mulla Sahibdad and Gundigan."

"Thank you, lieutenant," Jack said.

That must be why Ayub Khan skirmished with our pickets. He was distracting us so he could advance his lines. That man is no mean tactician.

Mulla Sahibdad was opposite the British right, blocking Macpherson's advance, and Gundigan on the left, opposing Baker. The British would have to capture both villages before following their plan of attack. Jack examined the field through his binoculars, noting that Sahibdad seemed the more formidable of the two. Built on a steep hillock, the village's flat-roofed houses huddled together and rose to a crest, with tribesmen and regulars waiting under an array of flapping standards.

Roberts halted the columns as the cavalry cantered ahead to discover that Ayub Khan had fortified both villages, plus the adjacent gardens and enclosures. Regular Afghan regiments held the spaces in between, waiting to repel Roberts' attack.

"Ayub Khan's turned each village into a stronghold." Jack

scanned them through his binoculars. "He's loopholed the walls and added artillery."

"The cocky scoundrel!" Baxter said. "Coming out to challenge us like that!"

Jack grunted, looked over his shoulder to check the condition of his regiment and agreed. "Ayub Khan is probably the best Afghan commander we've met. He knows how to use his advantages."

With the British advance halted, Roberts ordered the horse artillery to concentrate on Sahibdad. The guns moved forward, the order, "action front!" roared out, and the British artillery began to pound the fortified village. The shells exploded over and around the walls, each explosion a deadly bright flower surrounded by smoke and flame.

The galloper approached Jack. "Brigadier Macpherson is going forward, sir, and requests that you advance the Royal Malverns in support."

"Thank you, lieutenant. You may tell the brigadier that the Royals will be there when required!"

Jack felt the old familiar surge of mixed excitement and fear as he gave the orders that brought the Royal Malverns forward. For a moment, he wished he had his 113th, but commanding the Royals was a privilege.

"The Royal Malverns will advance!" Jack shouted.

He kicked in his heels, not looking behind him, for British infantry resented constant supervision. He knew the Royals would follow.

With the shell fire forcing the defenders to keep under cover, Macpherson's infantry advanced without hindrance until they drew near Sahibdad. Only when the British artillery stopped firing for fear of hitting their own men did the Afghans rise from cover.

"For what we are about to receive," Major Bryant said as Ayub Khan's men opened fire.

With massed musketry augmenting their artillery, the Afghans greeted the British with a hell of fire.

Jack remembered the dust clouds at Maiwand, but today, the clear air allowed him to see every detail of the battle. The first volley felled several of the Gordons, but they gave a mighty cheer and charged forward with the bayonet. Major George White led them, sword in hand, and the Highlanders competed with each other to be first, racing ahead, roaring as they levelled their bayonets. Jack saw the Afghans waiting, firing from loopholes and crowded behind the walls, so the village was a black mass of warriors.

The Gurkhas advanced beside the Highlanders, little men in green uniforms yelling as they drew their kukris, the famous fighting knife of Nepal.

The Afghan artillery had been well-served at Maiwand against Burrows' static formation. Here, with the Gordons and Gurkhas moving at speed, most of the shells flew wide. In front, as relaxed as if he were attending a review, Brigadier Macpherson led by example.

Jack saw the kilted Highlanders and the dogged Gurkhas scramble over the defending wall. "Halt, Royals," he ordered. "If the Gordons and Gurkhas need us, we'll be here." He turned around to encourage his men.

"What the devil?"

About half the Royals were with him, with the remainder spread out over a quarter of a mile of the Afghan plain, their scarlet tunics like drops of blood against the dun landscape. Major Baxter was shouting himself hoarse, trying to round them up, helped by some NCOs and officers.

Jack stared, unable to believe what he was seeing. He remembered hearing about British soldiers refusing to advance against the Russians at the Redan, but this was a very different scenario. The Redan had seen very young men facing a hell of grapeshot and musketry; this was a mature regiment facing a few hundred tribesmen and ghazis.

"Royal Malverns!" Jack roared. "Get back here!" Kicking in his spurs, he galloped through his disintegrating regiment, swearing. "NCOs! Get these men back into line. Three lines deep, damn it, and shoulder to shoulder!"

It was not the best formation to fight the Afghans, but nervous soldiers needed the comfort of their comrades. "Major Baxter! What's all this? Inkerrow! Bryant! Sarsens! Control your men!"

Some of the Royals were drifting away, others lagging back, while about half were facing their front, ashamed at the antics of their colleagues. Jack dismounted and pushed men into place, shouting, swearing, and giving orders.

"Get in line there! You're soldiers, not blasted infants! We're a royal regiment, the best in the business! Move!"

Eventually, after much effort, the Royal Malverns began to appear like a regiment again. Jack formed them up in a tight formation, ordering the officers and NCOs to keep the men under control. The fight for the village continued, with the Highlanders and Gurkhas clearing the houses one by one as Afghan regulars and ghazis contested with jezail, rifle and sword.

The best thing for the Royals is to regain some pride. The Gordons and Gurkhas don't need help, but by God, they're going to get it!

"Follow me, Royals!" Jack climbed over Sahibdad's mud wall with the mangled body of an Afghan regular lying under his feet. Gunsmoke hung heavy between the internal compounds, with dead and wounded men on the narrow streets. Jack checked over his shoulder. The leading company of the Royals had followed, some men looking nervous, others resolute.

"Come on, lads! Clear the village! Junior officers and NCOs, look after your men!"

Jack stepped to a section that was hanging back, with a young subaltern biting his lips. "You're with me, men. Subaltern! What's your name?"

"Wilkins, sir," the youngster said.

"Is this your first time in action, Wilkins?" Jack refused to flinch as a jezail gave its distinctive heavy thump, and a ball crashed into the mud wall of a house at his side.

"Yes, sir."

"It's all right. You'll be fine. Take a deep breath, square your shoulders and shoot anything not British or sepoy." Jack forced a smile. "If you see anybody wearing a kilt or a green uniform, they're on our side."

"Yes, sir." Wilkins swallowed hard.

"On you go!" Jack pushed the subaltern forward.

The Royals were in the village now, with officers leading from the front and sergeants cajoling, encouraging, and controlling their men. The regiment had mastered its initial panic.

"Follow the Highlanders," Jack ordered, "and check each house for ghazis."

The Highlanders and Gurkhas would have killed or chased away most of the defenders, but Jack knew a potentially dangerous operation would help restore some pride to the Royals. Holding his revolver, Jack moved forward, allowing his men to experience the sights and sounds of battle.

A couple of casualties would help them, Jack thought, then hated himself for the idea. *I will not condemn my men to agony and death purely to help restore regimental morale.*

"Watch your backs, lads!" Jack shouted. "The Afghans have a habit of appearing in the most awkward places." He stepped over a group of bodies, teeth-baring ghazis holding swords and shields. The Gordons or Gurkhas had shot them and finished the job with bayonets.

"Keep moving." Jack walked backwards for a few steps, checking his men. They were slow, nervous, nothing like the soldiers he wanted.

Raw blood was slowly sinking into the dust, with flies buzzing at the feast. Jack estimated at least a hundred and fifty Afghans had died defending Sahibdad, and his Royals had not accounted for a single man.

The Gurkhas and Gordons assembled at the far end of the

village, shaking hands, sharing anecdotes, and passing around water bottles. They laughed together in that strange language that only Highlanders and Gurkhas understood, each talking in their native tongues yet in perfect coherence.

"Here come the Malverns," a Gordon sergeant said, grinning as he cleaned fresh blood from his bayonet. "I don't think we left any of Ayub's men for you."

"I don't think you did," Jack replied.

As the Gurkhas and Highlanders cleared Mulia Sahibdad, Baker advanced against Gundigan. The Afghans held a complex array of lanes and enclosures, each one of which Baker's brigade had to capture with rifle-butt and bayonet. When the Afghans, with white-robed ghazis in the van, counterattacked, Baker's men, the Seaforth Highlanders, 2nd Sikhs, and 5th Gurkhas stood shoulder to shoulder to repel them.

Jack saw the bursting shells and heard the hoarse cries of the fighting men. The Afghans resisted stubbornly, fighting with pulwar and rifle, but the British, Nepalese and Indians pushed them out. After an hour, the British had broken the Afghan's first line of defence.

"They fought well," Jack said. "The Afghans always fight well."

Macpherson walked his horse along the British front. "That's the first stage over," he said. "Now follow me, lads."

With the Gordons and 2nd Gurkhas pounding forward and Jack's ragged Malverns in support, Macpherson's brigade advanced towards the southwestern tip of Pir Paimal Hill.

The Afghan artillery waited until the brigade was clear of the village, then opened fire. The shells exploded in fire and fury around the British column, causing some casualties.

"Keep the men together!" Jack ordered. He knew that close ranks would make the Malverns a better target, but the men's morale would not allow for a more open formation.

I don't want any stragglers or panic. They'll damn well have to learn.

A crackle of musketry joined the artillery as the Afghans opened up from a dry watercourse. One of the Gurkhas fell, rolled, and got back to his feet as his comrades returned fire. Too far back to see details, Jack heard the shouts as the Gurkhas charged, cleared the watercourse, and marched on.

The advance was steady rather than spectacular, with small groups of Afghans shooting from walled orchards and mud-walled enclosures and the Afghan artillery firing from the spur of Pir Paimal Hill. The British moved forward, stopped to clear up any resistance, and advanced again. About an hour after they cleared Sahibdad, the leading company of the Gordons stopped. "Look, sir!" A bearded sergeant pointed ahead. "There's one of ours!"

The man wore the khaki uniform and sun helmet of a private of the 66th. He clambered over an orchard wall and ran towards the advancing British, shouting something incomprehensible.

"Ayub Khan must have captured him," the Gordons' sergeant said. "The poor bugger. Come on, son! You're safe now!"

The soldier staggered as he came closer, stumbling over the uneven ground. A private of the Gordons stepped forward to help, and the soldier stood upright, yelled *"Allah Akbar,"* and drew a pulwar from inside his tunic.

"Aye, you dirty bastard!" Half a dozen rifles cracked, with the force of the bullets sending the Afghan two feet into the air before he landed. The private who had moved to help stared at the Afghan's dead body with his mouth open.

"Get back in the ranks, Huntly!" the bearded sergeant ordered. "That man must have stripped one of our dead after Maiwand."

"Advance!" Major White ordered. "Forward the Gordons!"

The advance continued until a heavy fire on the left flank hammered into the 2nd Sikhs of Baker's brigade. The Afghans sheltered behind a loopholed wall, firing independently, and hitting both Sikhs and Highlanders.

Colonel Brownlow of the Seaforths dismounted and ran forward. He surveyed the situation, ordered his men to fix bayonets and gave the order "charge!"

As Brownlow spoke, an Afghan aimed and fired. The bullet caught Brownlow in the throat. He staggered back, one hand to his throat, then crumpled, mortally wounded.

"*Cabar Feidh gu brath!*" a red-haired sergeant shouted the regimental motto, Caber Feidh forever!" and led a ferocious bayonet charge that captured the position.

The advance continued, with Afghan artillery pounding the British when they reached open ground and Afghan infantry stubbornly defending any enclosures or watercourses.

As the two British brigades aligned, Afghan artillery on the slopes had a clear target and increased their rate of fire. The sound was a nearly continuous roar, with explosions raising dust and stones and the occasional shot causing casualties.

The Afghan guns made better practice at Maiwand. Jack thought. *They're not so good when their target is moving.*

A sudden rush of ghazis staggered the Sikhs, who stepped back a pace, recovered and held them until the Seaforths put in a roaring bayonet charge. For a moment, Sikhs, ghazis, and Highlanders exchanged blows, with tulwar and bayonets clashing, and then the ghazis reeled back, leaving sores of their number on the ground.

The British and Sikhs followed, chasing the thick column of fleeing men, firing, reloading, and firing again until the bugle sounded the recall. Both regiments returned together, Seaforth Highlander and Sikhs as comrades in arms.

Jack glanced at the Royals. Not a man had left the ranks. Even the young second lieutenants remained in place. Sarsens, who had been so keen to fight, had not requested permission to join the chase.

Have my men lost all their fire? I can see why Roberts did not promote Baxter to command. He shook his head. *I'm going to have a tough job reviving the Royals.*

"That's us cleared the flank of Pir Paimal Hill," Jack said. "We've chased Ayub Khan's men away and defeated every obstacle he put in our path." He looked up as General Macpherson called the senior officers together.

"I'd better listen to the general," Jack told Baxter. "Look after the men."

Don't lose control when I'm away.

CHAPTER TWENTY

"That's the first part of the battle complete," Macpherson nearly echoed Jack's thoughts. He sat astride his horse as he addressed his senior officers. "Now, my brigade will remain close to the face of the Pir Paimal Ridge and turn the Afghan flank. How is your regiment, Windrush?"

Jack glanced at the Royals. "A bit shaky, sir, but they'll get better."

Macpherson ducked as a shell exploded nearby, showering him with dirt. "Should I retire them to the rear?"

"No, sir!" The ignominy of leading his regiment away on his first day of command would have lived with Jack forever.

"All right." Macpherson gave Jack a stern look. "Keep your men in hand."

Macpherson flicked his reins and pushed in front, with his regiments following in a compact mass of khaki and steel with the scarlet coated Royals an anomaly. Once out of the line of Afghan fire, the Royals regained some confidence.

"Keep them together," Jack murmured to Baxter. "There is some stiff fighting ahead."

"Yes, sir," Baxter replied.

With the Highlanders and Gurkhas always leading and the

23rd Pioneers in close support, the Royals were in the rear, avoiding the most brutal fighting. Baker's brigade was to the left, guarding Macpherson's flank.

"The enemy's in strength here," Baxter murmured, stretching up from his saddle to peer over the heads of the regiments in front.

Jack raised his binoculars to study the terrain ahead. The Afghans had entrenched artillery and masses of infantry waiting southwest of the Babawali Kotal.

"Now the real fighting will begin," Jack said.

"Yes, sir," Baxter agreed.

"We might become involved." Jack halted the Royals. The men still looked nervous, some fidgeting and others looking around them at the heights.

"More Afghans are coming." Jack focussed his binoculars on the Afghan position. "Ayub Khan has sent reinforcements."

The Afghans moved in a disciplined column, regular troops hurrying from Ayub's standing camp at Mazra. Meanwhile, the Afghan gunners on the heights had shifted their artillery. The guns now pointed downward, enabling them to enfilade the British advance. Further Afghan batteries glowered in front, with thousands of Afghan infantry in disciplined formations on either side of the guns.

"If we break their line here," Jack said, "we'll win the battle."

"And if we don't?" Baxter asked.

Jack did not reply. *The crisis of the battle lies ahead. It all depends on the steadfastness of Roberts' infantry.*

The Afghans sat tight in an extended trench, with a small fort to the rear and a dominating knoll on the right. In the centre, the Afghans had cut loopholes in a steep mud-and-rock bank, behind which the barrels of captured Martinis and Sniders thrust out in chilling menace. As well as the steady regulars, ghazis waited to contest their position.

These Afghans lads know their job, Jack thought. *They're not just brave but as skilled as any European soldiers.* He looked at the

Royals, wondering if they would follow him in a bayonet charge.

Major George White of the Gordons had the same idea. He drew his claymore with a sinister slither and held it upright. Sunlight gleamed along the double-sided steel blade. "Ready, boys!"

The leading British units were in a watercourse, catching their breath, reloading, and ducking as Afghan shot and shell whistled and burst around them. Major White, prematurely balding and with a straggling moustache, did not look like a schoolboy's idea of a hero, but he stepped in front of the Gordons.

"Highlanders!" White said, "let us close the business!"

As a field battery covered them, the Gordon Highlanders presented their bayonets and surged forward, cheering. The high skirl of the pipes accompanied them as they spread across the plain and onto the rocky heights, kilts swirling beneath the khaki tunics. Once again, the Gurkhas came in support, their green uniforms matching the tartan of the Highlanders, as the 23rd Pioneers followed.

They charged over open ground, with the enemy firing from behind protective banks, while others from the slopes of Pir Paimal took the British in flank, adding musketry to the artillery. Major White led, long-striding towards the enemy, and his men followed, Highlanders, Gurkhas and Pioneers losing men as they advanced. White was first to reach the Afghan position, and Jack saw him wreathed in smoke, a commanding figure. As he plunged into the enemy, kilt swinging and his men at his heels, Jack thought he looked like a figure from the distant past, Ossian or Donald Dhu come to life.[1]

Mary would put that in more poetic terms, Jack thought. *If Walter Scott were still alive, he'd write an epic over Major White.*

As they reached the first Afghan gun, a Gurkha named Inderbir Lama slipped off his cap and stuffed it in the muzzle.

"This gun belongs to the Second Gurkhas – Prince of Wales!"

Inspired by that piece of daring, the Gurkhas competed with the Highlanders in pushing forward, while Macpherson continued the advance along the lower slopes of Pir Paimal hill. Despite their strong position, very few Afghans were foolish enough to face the combination of Gurkha kukris and Gordon bayonets. Those who did not flee died on that hill as the British, Indians, and Nepalese cleared the heights.

"Come on, Royals!" Jack urged his regiment forward, ignoring the occasional stray shot that whistled overhead. He felt frustrated that his men were not involved and hoped the 113th was giving a good account of themselves elsewhere.

To the left, Baker's men were clearing watercourses with the bayonet as the Sikhs, and 72nd Seaforth Highlanders destroyed everything that stood in their path. Baker's brigade commanded the dip between Pir Paimal Hill and the isolated Kharoti Hill. Once they reached their objective, they halted and waited for Macpherson's men to level the advance.

Seaforth Highlanders leaned on their rifles, lit their pipes, and watched Macpherson's brigade pushing the Afghans back.

Meanwhile, Baker sent half a battalion of Money's 3rd Sikhs to capture Kharoti Hill. Colonel Money led them in style, taking three Afghan guns as the Sikhs swept up and over their positions. With Kharoti Hill secured, the British could dominate the opening of the Argandab Valley.

As the Sikhs consolidated their position, Macpherson's First Brigade pushed the Afghans from the slopes of Pir Paimal Hill and again aligned with Baker's men.

"Right, lads!" Jack pushed forward, hoping for at least a taste of action to restore some confidence to the Royals. However, Macpherson's men had been thorough, and the only Afghans they met were dead or dying. A great mass of fugitives fled in the opposite direction.

Jack checked his watch. It was quarter past twelve. It had taken the British only three hours to smash through Ayub Khan's defences, turn his flank and capture many of his guns.

Looking behind him, Jack saw Macgregor's third brigade advancing in support and imagined the familiar faces of the 113th.

Jack lifted his binoculars and peered ahead, searching for the cavalry. Gough should be ready to pounce on the fleeing Afghans and turn a retreat into a rout. However, orchards, irrigation channels and walled gardens had slowed the cavalry's advance, and the Afghans fled without interruption.

Roberts noted Gough's inability to act and ordered the cavalry from the Kandahar garrison, survivors of Maiwand, to push through the Babawali Pass and chase Ayub Khan's army. As Baker and Macpherson's brigade's advanced, Primrose's cavalry erupted over the pass and fell on the remaining fragments of the Afghan army.

"Ayub Khan will make a stand at Mazra," Major Baxter said.

"Maybe." Jack was less sure. "I've never seen an Afghan army run like this before. They are not even stopping to pick up their dead."

General Ross, the infantry divisional commander under Roberts, halted Macpherson and Baker's brigade and ordered supply wagons to replenish their ammunition.

"We haven't played any part in the fighting, so we don't need to replenish," Jack reminded Macpherson. "With your permission, sir, I'll take the Royals forward and see what's happening."

Macpherson frowned. "Are they up to it, Windrush?"

"Yes, sir," Jack said with more conviction than he felt. "We'll see if Ayub has a trap waiting for us."

"All right," Macpherson agreed. "Don't do a Maiwand and barge into trouble."

"No, sir."

"And look for the prisoners," Macpherson reminded. "Ayub Khan still holds Lieutenant Maclaine."

"I will, sir." Jack pulled his horse back to the Royals.

"Right, lads, we're moving forward in a column of four. Number One company, supply an advance guard and flank guards, two hundred yards from the main body. Number Five company, you're the rearguard."

Jack watched as the officers gave clumsy commands and the men moved slowly, more like recruits than experienced soldiers. "Have you not practised these manoeuvres?" He asked Major Baxter.

"Not often, sir," Baxter said. "We were mainly involved in ceremonial guard duties, sir. Colonel Windrush, the previous colonel, sir, wanted us to be the first choice for that sort of thing."

Jack grunted. *I have a lot of training to do here. What's William done to this battalion?*

The Royals moved on, with Jack aware that the cream of the British army was watching them. After the morning's fighting, now the land was curiously quiet, with only the sound of marching boots and the distant drumbeat of horses' hooves breaking the silence.

Jack watched his men. They moved well enough, with arms swinging and rifles held at a precise angle, but their heads were down. They lacked something.

Spirit. Something's broken these men.

"Double!" Jack shouted and dismounted to lead by example. He saw Sarsens looking apprehensive at the head of his platoon. "Here, Sarsens, look after Tinker, my horse."

The regiment was watching him, not sure what to expect. After William's parade ground style, they were unused to a more flexible officer.

"Keep in formation," Jack ordered, "and keep up with me." He knew it was an unorthodox method of command, particularly with the enemy so close, but Jack needed to make an instant impression. Soldiers needed a character to follow, a leader with personality.

The Royals advanced at speed until they neared the Afghans camp at Mazra. "Halt!" Jack roared and reclaimed Tinker from

Sarsens. "Take command, Baxter," he said. "Extended order and move slowly with flank guards."

"Where are you going, sir?"

"With the advance guard," Jack said and kicked in his heels.

A nervous-eyed Captain Fladbury led Number One Company. He gave Jack a twisted grin. "I can't see any defenders, sir."

"Don't relax your concentration. The Pashtun can hide under a leaf and leap out to cut your throat."

However, Fladbury was correct. Ayub Khan had deserted his camp, leaving the tents standing and cooking fires still lit. Jack led the Royals in, allowing them to savour the fruits of a victory to which they had barely contributed.[2]

"Keep the men alert." Jack unfastened the catch that held his revolver. "Ayub is a tricky fellow. He could be drawing us into a trap." He looked around, waiting for a horde of ghazis to burst from cover.

There were none.

The Afghans had left meat cooking in bubbling pots, bread standing, half kneaded in earthen vessels, and even a bazaar still in place. Jack walked his horse around the camp, noting the range of foodstuffs on display, from dried fruits to flour.[3]

"This place could have come straight from the *Thousand and One Nights*," Sarsens said.

"It could," Jack said. "We're fighting a people with a culture and beliefs that have hardly altered in a thousand years. Only their weapons have developed."

The other British regiments joined the Royals, with Highlanders, Sikhs and Gurkhas checking the tents and searching for lurking warriors. Jack saw a huge marquee that only Ayub Khan could have occupied. When he peered inside, he saw splendid carpets lying on the floor, a hookah on its side and a tray of sweetmeats, abandoned in the rush to escape Roberts' advance.

"Sir!" Sarsens shouted. "Over here!"

Lieutenant Maclaine lay on his back a few yards from Ayub's tent, with his eyes wide open and his throat cut from ear to ear.

"And that's how Ayub Khan treats his prisoners," Sarsens said.[4]

"Windrush!" General Macpherson stared down at Maclaine's body. "Take your men a few miles down the valley and search for stragglers. I want to find out who murdered Maclaine."

* * *

The Royals marched out of Mazra and into the Argandab Valley, with Jack posting strong flank guards. They passed the bodies of some of Ayub's men that the cavalry had slain, but the villages they entered appeared friendly.

Men and women approached the Royals, smiling and offering melons and other fruit.

"What's happened to Ayub's warriors?" Baxter asked. "It's like they've turned into smoke and vanished."

"You're looking at them," Jack said. "It's a fine old Afghan tradition that men can try to shoot you in the morning and be your most trusted friend in the afternoon until they see another opportunity to stick a knife in your back. Many of these villagers would be fighting us a few hours ago. If we search the village, we'll find their rifles and probably some Martinis from Maiwand as well."

Baxter swore and loosened the revolver in his belt. "The previous colonel didn't prepare us for that sort of thing."

"Pass the message to the men," Jack ordered. "Keep alert, and if anybody shoots at them, fire back. Don't wait for orders."

Jack moved on, occasionally stopping to check on his men. He mounted a knoll to check ahead, lifting his binoculars. He could see the cavalry riding hard, occasionally stopping to engage in a skirmish and then pushing on.

"Do you think we should bring in a couple of the villagers,

sir? Hand them to General Macpherson to be interrogated?" Baxter asked.

"They'd deny everything," Jack said.

Even although he had been expecting it, the shot took Jack by surprise. It was the heavy thud of a jezail rather than the sharper crack of a rifle. He blinked as the bullet whined past his ear.

Baxter did not flinch. "Somebody's firing at us, sir."

Jack swivelled to scan for the smoke. A jezail was a long-barrelled weapon that took up to a minute to reload, so he was in no immediate danger. "Over there," he indicated a drift of smoke on the slope to the right. "Get me a Martini, Baxter." *The wind is steady from the north, so the marksman is on the left of the smoke. There is a group of rocks there. He'll use the low rock as a rest for the barrel.*

Jack lifted his watch and timed a slowly passing sixty seconds before kicking in his heels. As he had guessed, the marksman tried again, with the bullet passing with a vicious buzz.

"Closer," Jack said, hefting the Martini that Baxter brought. He adjusted the sights to four hundred yards, checked it was loaded and aimed. He took a deep breath, centred on the group of rocks, and squeezed the trigger.

Everything I do now is to create an impression on the Royals. I need them to follow me, so I must make them see me as a warrior and a leader.

Jack fancied he saw his bullet strike the rock. If so, the Afghan marksman would flinch as the bullet ricocheted past him, maybe showering him with savage splinters.

The Afghan fired again. As Jack stared directly at the man's refuge, he saw the muzzle flare and gush of smoke. He had no time to duck as the bullet zipped past his head. He handed the rifle back to Baxter. "Give that back to its owner."

"Yes, sir."

Jack raised his voice. "Number One Company! Form a defensive firing line. Number Two Company, follow me. Extended order!"

It was taking a sledgehammer to crack an egg using an entire company to hunt down a lone marksman, but Jack wanted to give the Royals some success in this battle. A regiment needed a tradition of victory to grow in confidence, and Jack was determined to regenerate the Royal Malverns.

Spurring forward, Jack put Tinker to the slope. On many occasions on the march from Kabul to Kandahar, he had wished for a longer-legged animal, but now he was glad he had a surefooted Kabul pony.

The slope was steep and undulating, with a hundred places where a man could hide. Jack held the reins in his left hand, guided Tinker with his knees and drew his revolver.

"Come on, One Company!" Jack rode straight up, ignoring the loose stones that rolled from under his horse's hooves. Looking to left and right, he saw the khaki figures clambering upwards, some with red faces, others looking scared or determined. One man dropped his rifle and stopped to retrieve it; another hesitated behind a sheltering rock until a corporal bawled him forward.

The group of rocks was only a hundred yards ahead, with a small thorn tree to one side. Jack saw the marksman, an elderly Pashtun with a henna-dyed beard and an ancient matchlock jezail. The man's turban was flapping loose, Jack noted, and his face was brown and wrinkled, with eyes that had seen three scores of summers and probably a few more.

Jack pushed Tinker on, hoping to get within revolver range before the marksman fired again. Number One Company stretched out, most of them behind him as the Pashtun levelled his jezail. Jack saw the utter fearlessness of the man. *He doesn't care if he lives or dies, so long as he kills a kaffir.*

For a moment, Jack was face to face with the Pashtun, reading the cold hatred in the man's eyes, and then he levelled his revolver and squeezed the trigger. Jack saw the Pashtun fire an instant later and instinctively ducked. His bullet smashed into the marksman's forehead, causing the Pashtun to jerk backwards and his shot to fly high.

As the marksman died, a yell arose from the hillside, and fifty Pashtuns rose from their hiding places.

"It's an ambush!" Sarsens shouted.

Jack saw the leader of the Pashtuns. Zamar Khan.

CHAPTER TWENTY-ONE

Zaman Khan! Is this how you thank me for saving your blasted daughter?

While half the Pashtuns slid behind rocks to fire on the British, the remainder charged the extreme tip of the extended line.

They're trying to outflank us.

"Stand firm!" Jack roared. "Shoot them flat!" He saw his men waver, and two turned to run.

"Stand, damn you, Royals! Fire!" Jack led by example, shooting at the Pashtuns as they bounded down the hillside. They were as fast as any ghazis and as deadly. Jack killed the leading man with a shot that entered his mouth, smashed his teeth, and blew away half his head. The rest came on, screaming their slogans.

"C section, guard the left flank!" Jack shouted. "E section, guard the right flank! The rest, face your front and fire!"

The Afghans were closer, thirty yards away and advancing at the run, leaping over loose rocks and careless of danger. Jack shot another, saw him stagger as the bullet caught him in the stomach, and heard an irregular spatter of musketry from his men.

More of the Afghans fell, while somebody screamed, long and loud, behind Jack. He saw Zaman Khan raising a sabre and swore, *that's my Wilkinson's Sword, damn it!* Jack fired again, missed as Zamar shifted left, and then the tribesmen reached the British line.

"Push them back, Royals!" Jack fired his last shot and used the pistol as a club as the nearest tribesmen leapt on him. The man was lithe but young, with white teeth in a gaping mouth and an immature beard. Jack wrestled him to the ground and pounded his head with the barrel of his revolver, gasping with effort. He saw one of his men lunge with the bayonet, saw another fall under the swing of a pulwar, and then somebody was shouting orders.

Jack heard the crash of a British volley, and the Afghans were retreating, diminished in numbers as they fled up the hillside.

"Another volley!" that voice sounded again, and Jack looked up. The young warrior who had attacked him was lying on the ground, his face and head battered to a pulp. Two of his men were dead and two wounded, with a scatter of tribesmen lying on the slope, and Second Lieutenant Sarsens stood panting at his side.

"I thought you needed a hand, sir," Sarsens said.

"You did well." Jack saw that Sarsens had brought up half a company in support. He wiped Afghan blood from his face.

"Here comes the cavalry." Sarsens pointed up the valley.

The British cavalry was returning, riding in column of four, with outriders on both flanks. They looked proud of their exploits in harrying Ayub Khan's defeated army.

"We'll return to camp," Jack said. "Baxter, collect our casualties." *The men looked nervous, even scared as if they expected me to lambast them.* He raised his voice. "Well done, Royals. We repelled an Afghan attack and inflicted casualties. We are already one of the smartest regiments in the army, and soon we'll be known as the best fighting regiment as well."

It's a start. I'll weed out the poor officers and NCOs and get the Royals into fighting trim.

With the battle of Kandahar won, the British returned to their tented camp. The men who had marched from Kabul were elated with their victory, while the Kandahar garrison had restored some pride with their part in the victory.

Roberts formed his Kabul men in their three brigades while Jack marched his Royals back to their quarters in Kandahar.

"Shoulders back, Royals!" Jack shouted. "You proved that you are still soldiers! There's hope for you, yet."

* * *

On the following day, Roberts had warm praise for each unit and especially the Gordons. "No other troops could have done it!" Roberts said. He toured his men, with each regiment, in turn, cheering him as the Royals listened. Jack knew his men were hurting and vowed to turn that pain to his advantage.[1]

Roberts had requested extra *batta* – field allowance – for his column and a special medal for the Kabul to Kandahar march. With low pay and often suffering the contempt of the civilian population in Britain, soldiers valued every penny they earned, while a medal allowed them an opportunity to show their courage. In Jack's opinion, a piece of metal and a coloured ribbon on the breast was a poor reward for the work soldiers did, while he knew the public was fickle. They would cheer a military victory to the echo and speak of their pride while shunning a private soldier in the street.

"Are you all right, sir?" Baxter asked. "You look preoccupied there."

"We have a lot to do, Baxter," Jack said.

"The previous colonel was more concerned with appearance, sir," Baxter said tactfully. "Every general used the Royals as guards at durbars and when we greeted dignitaries."

Jack listened. "I understand what happened," he said. "This

regiment has been out of action too long. The authorities used us as tin soldiers, known for our turnout rather than our fighting ability. Then the Royals were in Kandahar under a general without spirit and with a colonel with a nervous disability." He looked up. "Well, by God, I'll make the Royals a fighting regiment again!"

"Yes, sir," Baxter said. He hesitated a little. "The men would like that, sir."

Jack took a deep breath. "I have certain arrangements to make, Baxter, and people to meet. I want the men on parade at four tomorrow morning. All of them, cooks, sergeants, hooks, crooks and bottle-washers, without exception."

"Yes, sir."

"We're going on a route march, major," Jack said.

I'll build this regiment back up. By God, I will.

* * *

Jack heard the noise as if through a fog. He struggled through his nightmare when the Pandies were hunting down Mary in Gondabad, and he could not help.

"What's happening? What's happening?"

Reaching for the head of his bed, Jack unfastened his holster and grasped the butt of his revolver. The room was in near darkness, with only a sliver of light seeping through the shuttered window. He pushed aside the mosquito net and stood up, gasping as his bare feet made contact with the cold stone floor.

"Donnelly!"

"I hear it, sir." Donnelly arrived with a naked candle and Jack's uniform. "I don't know what it is."

Jack struggled to dress, buckling on his pistol belt, and lifting the Khyber knife Armaghan had given him and which he wore instead of a sword. "It's the Kandaharis," he mumbled, fighting off his recurring nightmares. "They've risen. It's the Mutiny all over again."

"No, sir," Donnelly dared to contradict his officer. "General Primrose expelled the civilian population from Kandahar, sir. There are none left to rise."

"You're right, damn it! Has Ayub Khan returned already?" Jack pulled on his boots and plunged out of the door. Donnelly followed in his shirtsleeves and with his rifle in his left hand.

Lanterns lit them through the stone corridors of the citadel, where bemused sentries crashed to attention.

"Can anybody tell me what's happening?" Jack demanded.

"Sir!" Sarsens was fully dressed and flustered. "There's a riot, sir."

"Who's rioting?"

"The regiment, sir, the Royals are brawling with the 113th!" Sarsens said. "I'm duty officer, sir."

"Show me," Jack demanded. He felt more frustration than anger. Inter-regimental brawls were fairly common but usually took place after a night's drinking, not on campaign.

Hundreds of soldiers had met on the maidan outside the citadel, with men of both regiments fighting each other with fists, boots, belts, and any other weapon on which they could lay their hands. As Jack watched, Private Todd of the 113th whirled his belt around his head and landed the heavy buckle on the face of Private Kerswell of the Royals.

"Yellow bastard!" Todd roared. "Bloody peacocks!"

Kerswell fell to rise again with blood streaming from a gash in his scalp. "Peacocks? You baby butchering bugger!"

People had insulted the 113th by naming them the Baby Butchers earlier in the century when their first operations had been against radical reformers in northern England. Jack had hoped the name died away when the regiment performed more heroic deeds. However, military memories were long where regimental insults were concerned.

Kerswell balled his fists and lunged at Todd.

Jack knew Todd well, a man allergic to any kind of discipline but the best soldier in the world when the enemy was close. He did not know Kerswell but imagined he was cut from the same cloth.

The scene was duplicated around the maidan as men brawled individually or in groups.

"NCOs!" Jack bawled.

"Shall I pull them apart, sir?" Sarsens asked. "I was quite the boxer at school."

"No," Jack said. "If any of these lads retaliates and strikes an officer, it's a far more serious case than merely punching a private. Fetch the NCOs. Get the Provost Sergeants. That their job."

Jack watched as Provost Sergeant of each regiment conferred, then led a team of twenty men armed with *lathis*, the long Indian police staff, to break up the riot.

These regiments are not the best of friends. How can they combine into a two-battalion unit? I've got my work before me, here.

The Provost Sergeants, selected for their brawn, dragged men aside and broke up fights with skill learned from years in the ranks. Within twenty minutes, they cleared the maidan.

"Shall I put them all in the cells, sir?" the Royals Provost Sergeant asked Jack.

"Would they all fit?"

"It would be a tight squeeze, sir."

"No. We don't want another Black Hole of Calcutta here. Send them back to barracks." Jack watched the procession of battered, bleeding men pass him, and, despite his concern, he felt a twinge of satisfaction. If the Royals could hold their own against the 113th, there was a hard core of fighters in the regiment. He could surely form them into something more than scarlet-coated peacocks.

* * *

Helen looked up from her chair when Jack knocked and entered her room. "I thought it was you," she said.

"How's the patient?" Jack tried to act buoyant. Helen looked terrible, with her face drawn and her eyes sunk into deep pits. She had always been proud of her appearance but now looked older than her years. Jack frowned when he saw the first tinge of grey in Helen's hair.

"Not good," Helen indicated the bed. William lay still, staring at the whitewashed ceiling, an old done man although he was two years younger than Jack.

"What does the doctor say?" Jack sat at William's side.

Helen shrugged. "What do doctors ever say? The patient is doing as well as can be expected. Nervous disabilities always take time to cure, but with rest and care, he will pull through." Helen rose and paced the room, pausing only to stare out the open window at the city of Kandahar spreading out below.

"I hate this place, Jack. I hate Kandahar and Afghanistan. I hate India and all it stands for. Why?"

"Why?" Jack repeated.

"Why do we have to go adventuring into these barbaric countries?" She dipped her head, still staring outside. "It's taken my son, Jack, and it's going to take my husband. Why? This whole continent is not worth their lives!"

Jack stepped closer and put a hand on her shoulder. "I don't know why Helen, but I guess the merchants make money and the nation gets prestige."

Helen shook Jack off and knelt at William's side. "He was an arrogant, self-opinionated man, but he had his good points, too."

"He's my brother," Jack said.

"Your half-brother," Helen corrected. She stood again and resumed her pacing. "Go, Jack. Don't you have a regiment to command?"

"I'm only a brevet colonel," Jack said. "When William is fit, he'll resume command."

Helen returned to the window. "I think we both know that won't happen, Jack. William will die here. He'll never command the Royals again." She did not turn around. "You always wanted the Royals, and now you have them over William's dead body."

Jack said nothing. He knew that Helen was hurting over Crimea's death and her husband's sickness. "I'll send up the army surgeon," he said. "I'll send up every medical man I can find. We'll cure him, Helen, I promise."

"You promise?" Helen's voice was low. "And can you cure Crimea as well? Raise him from his grave?" She waved a hand towards the window. "My son died out there, Jack. Out there in this barbaric, savage country."

"I know." Jack took another step forward.

"He came out full of pride and glory, a young man in his strength, and now he's gone. Go, Jack, leave me alone."

Unable to bear Helen's suffering, Jack withdrew, closing the door behind him. *Soldiers may gain the glory and see the horror, but women were often the forgotten casualties in war,* he thought. *What an evil thing war is. What an abomination to set men killing and maiming other men so that some merchants can increase their profits and kings, queens, Amirs and presidents can alter the colour of the map.*

Jack was in a foul mood when he returned to his quarters. He threw his tunic and pistol belt onto the floor and helped himself to a glass of William's brandy, tossing it back without taste. He was in the act of pouring himself another when he heard voices outside the room.

"Bugger off Pawcett! Fighting Jack's my officer. You go and attend to somebody else!"

"This is my duty, Private Donnelly," Pawcett answered in his cultured tones.

"Not anymore! Away and groom a horse. *Malum?*" Donnelly lowered his voice. "That means, do you understand, you peacocking bastard!"

Jack opened the door before the servants came to blows. "What's the to-do? Donnelly! Stop bullyragging that man and come in. Pawcett, I have reassigned you to Major Baxter."

Pawcett looked relieved at Jack's intervention. "Yes, sir." He marched away with his back straight as Donnelly entered Jack's quarters.

"The colonel of the Malverns does well for himself, I see." Donnelly took stock of his new working space. "I'll soon have this place up and running, sir. You'll need new uniforms with your new badges of rank and a sword. A colonel must have a decent sword and not that Khyber abomination, sir."

Jack grinned. It was good to have Donnelly back. "The regimental funds are in the strongbox, Donnelly, and I've drawn money from my account for my personal use. Take whatever you need." He hesitated for a moment. "I'm sorry to drag you away from the 113th."

"That's all right, sir." Donnelly was opening cupboards and drawers to check what he had. "I hear that Sergeant Deblin is also coming over."

"I've requested his expertise," Jack said. "We have to get this regiment in trim, Donnelly, before the Afridis rise, or the Russians invade, or whatever crisis next threatens the Empire."

"Yes, sir." Donnelly was checking the cupboards. "We'll have plenty of space here when we chuck out the last colonel's possessions, sir. He must have thought he was in Kensington rather than Kandahar."

* * *

The Royals looked sullen as Jack viewed them on the maidan. Some bore the marks of the previous night's brawl, with Kerswell sporting a purple bruise over his left eye. Two men had bandages across their knuckles. "We're going on a route march today," Jack said. "Ten miles around Kandahar. Every man with marching kit, rifle, full water bottle and forty rounds of ammunition in case the locals resent our presence."

Jack led them on a circuit of the city and then outside on a dusty march that tested the men's fitness. He watched their bearing and demeanour, listened to the comments as they grew tired and took notes. By the time he brought them back into Kandahar, Jack had a fair idea of the strengths and weaknesses of the regiment.

As the NCOs attended to the men, Jack interviewed the officers, one by one, starting with Baxter.

"How are the men?" Jack began with the same question, knowing that the best officers would know everything about the men under his command. If the officer did not know his men, Jack would post him elsewhere, whatever his connections and rank.

Baxter raised an eyebrow. "They're confused, sir. Your methods are very different to those employed by the previous Colonel Windrush."

"How much action have they seen?"

"None, sir, until you arrived. We missed all the battles in Afghanistan. The enemy seemed to let us pass in peace, and the last colonel was more interested in having us look smart."

"Thank you, Baxter. How is the RSM?"

Baxter shook his head. "We don't have one, sir. Only sergeants. The last colonel disagreed with raising a ranker to such a position of authority."

"Can you suggest a sergeant who could step up to be an RSM?"

When Baxter hesitated, Jack knew there were none.

"As you were, Baxter, I have a man for the job."

Major Bryant acted as the adjutant. Eton educated, he had no fighting experience but seemed popular with the men.

"I didn't care much for the previous colonel," he drawled. "He was not good with the men."

When Jack asked for details, Bryant refused to be drawn. "I can't speak ill of the dead," he said. "Particularly not when the late colonel was your brother."

The captains were a mixed crew, one or two only interested in their careers, but Jack believed that some others had potential.

Jack marked out Captain Inkerrow as a man who could be either a good or a bad influence, a man to watch.

The lieutenants were young, smart, and eager, with one exception, to whom Jack offered an immediate transfer.

The last officer Jack interviewed was Sarsens, who stood, shaking slightly, opposite Jack.

"Well, Sarsens." Jack leaned back in his chair, studying his man. "You're probably the junior officer who has seen the most action in this regiment."

"Am I, sir?"

"You've fought in two battles, Maiwand and Kandahar, and endured one siege, and you're not yet twenty years old. Not many men of your age can claim that." Jack saw the new lines around Sarsens' mouth and the shadows behind his eyes. "How do you see your career progressing, Sarsens?"

"I don't know, sir."

"Maiwand and the loss of your friends affected you," Jack told him. "That's natural. Our first action comes as a shock and remains with us when others fade away."

"Yes, sir."

Jack leaned forward. "Did you think of resigning your commission after Maiwand?"

Sarsens nodded. "Yes, sir."

"I hope you have reconsidered. The army needs officers like you, men with spirit who learn from experience." *God, I sound like an old man or a regimental colonel.* "You did well at that skirmish we had in the Argandab valley." Jack saw the surprise on Sarsens' face.

"Thank you, sir. Colonel Windrush, the last Colonel Windrush, would have bitten my head off for acting without orders."

Jack nodded; Sarsens' words told him a lot about the attitude of the regiment. "Have you reconsidered resigning your commission?"

"Yes, sir."

"Good. We have recently had a vacancy for a lieutenant. I want you to fill it."

"A vacancy, sir? I didn't know." Sarsens looked puzzled.

"Lieutenant Fairfax has transferred elsewhere. You'll hear about it in good time. Let me know your decision. Dismiss."

Jack watched Sarsens march away. *That's the first stage. Now I need to see how William has organised the regiment. I'll have to speak to Inkerrow again, though. I am unsure about that man.*

"Who are your signallers, Inkerrow? And where's the regimental surgeon and chaplain?"

"We don't have one, sir. Colonel Windrush disagreed with them." Inkerrow was sullen under questioning.

"Well, I do agree with them," Jack said softly. "I don't know how the regiment can work efficiently without signallers, a surgeon and a competent RSM." He smiled. "I'll see what I can do." *I'll borrow the surgeon of the 66th. He's a good man.*

When Jack toured the barracks, he found the atmosphere oppressive, with men leaping to attention when he appeared and some so nervous, they were nearly tongue-tied.

What the devil's happened to the regiment?

"Donnelly!"

"Sir!" Donnelly appeared immediately.

"There's something wrong in this regiment, Donnelly, and I don't know what."

"Yes, sir. I thought it was just because they weren't used to fighting, after being a ceremonial unit for so long, but the men are scared, sir."

"Scared of what? The Afghans?"

"No, sir. They're scared of the officers, sir, and the lash."

Jack started. "What?"

"Yes, sir. The last colonel, sir, he used the lash, sir, the cat-of-nine-tails."

Jack took a deep breath and lowered his voice. "Damn it, this is 1880, not 1780! Find the damned thing and bring it to me."

* * *

Jack knew how important intelligence gathering and communications were to the army, particularly when a regiment was detached from the main force. The British army had neglected the art of military signalling until recently, and Jack determined to make the Royals experts.

He asked the sergeants to choose the most intelligent men and selected half a dozen of the best to train as signallers. As they often worked independently from the regiment, signallers had to possess initiative. Jack sought fit, active men, good shots who were able to ride a horse and climb a mountain. He borrowed two experienced signallers from the Seaforth Highlanders to train his men.

"I want my men to be as good as anybody," Jack said.

The Seaforths eyed the potential signallers, sighed, shook their heads, said, "Aye," and got down to business.

"Let's be having you then, lads!"

The Seaforths started with the basics in map-reading and the prismatic compass and then moved onto semaphore and the heliograph.

"This machine," a laconic Seaforth named William Ray explained in a deadpan Inverness accent, "works by reflecting the sun's rays, so it's perfect out east and nae guid at all in Scotland." He waited for the laugh before he continued.

"I've heard that men can read the helio at over a hundred miles. The longest the Seaforths used it was seventy-two miles, between Darunta point outside Jellalabad, and Lataband, near Kabul." He gave a rare smile. "Most frequently, we used it at between ten and thirty miles. So will you."

The potential signallers listened, nodding at the right places as Ray explained that signal parties stood on hills and heliographed each other, enabling the army to pass a message hundreds of miles in less than an hour.

"What if it's cloudy or dark?" a man asked.

"Then we use limelight instead," Ray said.

Jack had seen the heliograph used but now understood the basics. *More modern technology in warfare. Things are constantly changing.*

Once Ray was satisfied that he had fully trained his men, they became regimental signallers and wore a badge of crossed flags above the elbow on their left sleeve.

That's another step forward.

* * *

"Well, Deblin," Jack said as Sergeant Deblin of the 113th slammed to attention before him. "How long have you been with the 113th?"

"Ten years, sir!" Deblin always spoke as if he were on parade.

"And before that?"

"I was ten years in the 3rd Foot, sir!"

"Why did you leave the Buffs? They're an elite regiment, and the 113th is not."

"I was bored, sir, marching around England. I wanted to see the world." Deblin remained at attention.

I doubt that. There will have been a woman involved, somewhere.

"Well, Deblin, I need a sergeant major to lick the men into shape. They're excellent parade ground soldiers, but I want fighting men as well. Are you interested?"

"Yes, sir. I grew up in Ledbury, so the Royals are my local regiment."

"Welcome aboard, RSM."

Jack knew that some of the Royal Malverns would be insulted by having a sergeant of the lowly 113th instruct them, but he did not care. RSM Deblin strode across the maidan as though born to it.

"Stand easy," he snapped at the Royals, then marched past them, shaking his head. "When you're resting, I'll tell you a little tale. When I was a young lad, I had a box of wooden soldiers, and I thought the world of them soldiers. Well, when we moved from barracks to barracks across the Empire, some thieving *badmash* swiped them, and it nearly broke my little heart."

Jack watched the company. The older soldiers had heard the tale, or something very similar, many times before, but some of the younger men appeared interested.

Deblin continued. "Well, my old mother said to me, 'Never mind, lad, you'll find your wooden soldiers again someday, and by all that's holy, here you are!'"

Some of the men laughed; others wondered if the new RSM was laying a trap. Jack watched, smiling. He had seen and heard it all before. He contrasted these short service soldiers with the men he knew in Burma and Crimea. Now most soldiers looked young, while back then, veterans had spent an adult lifetime following the colours. Jack had heard them termed as "elderly drunkards," which he thought a great injustice.

Jack looked up, hiding his smile as Donnelly approached, holding the cat-of-nine-tails. He had arranged this meeting to be as public as possible.

"What's that, Donnelly?"

"It's a whip, sir." Donnelly held it up for everybody to see. "You said I was to bring it to you as soon as I found it."

Jack held the cat, noting the dried blood on the thongs. Then, with the entire regiment watching, he produced a box of Lucifers from his pocket and set light to the stock. "We won't need that thing again in this regiment." He waited until the flames licked up to the thongs and dropped the whip on the ground. "Carry on, Sergeant Major."

Jack stepped back. He had demonstrated that the old times were in the past. RSM Deblin did not need his help, and he had other duties. With the Seaforths training the signallers and an RSM in position, Jack now wanted to raise a Mounted Infantry company and train the men in open manoeuvres rather than only drill. He hoped to hold joint exercises with the 113th and let the Malverns pit their skills against the veterans and learn by experience, trial, and error.

"Sir!

Jack became aware that Donnelly had more to say. "Yes, Donnelly?"

"There's a General Hook to see you, sir, with Colonel St John and an Afghan fellow. They're in your office, sir."

What now?

CHAPTER TWENTY-TWO

General Hook never seemed to age. He sat in Jack's seat, with Colonel St John at his left, yet it was the man at Hook's right that surprised Jack.

Armaghan gave a slight bow as Jack entered and did not hide his smile.

"Good afternoon, gentlemen," Jack said, trying not to stare at Armaghan. "To what do I owe the pleasure?"

Pleasure? General Hook has ordered me to some of the worst places in the world, while Armaghan is as enigmatic as ever.

General Hook poured himself some of William's brandy, offered the decanter to Jack, and leaned back in his seat. "You know Colonel St John, of course."

"I do, sir."

"And I believe you have met Armaghan."

"I have." Jack tried to read the Timuri's expression.

Hook sipped at the brandy. "Excellent brandy your brother has. I hope you appreciate it."

"I do," Jack said carefully.

"General Roberts appointed you as a brevet colonel," Hook said, then sighed. "Can't you find a seat, man?"

"Yes, sir." Jack turned away, just as Donnelly tapped on the door and entered. "A chair, sir. I brought it from Major Baxter's quarters. I also brought more glasses, as the previous colonel only had two."

"Thank you, Donnelly," Jack sat down gratefully, accepting the glass of brandy that Hook handed to him.

"Your brevet rank will be confirmed shortly," Hook said. "You'll hear about it when the administration catches up with the decision."

Jack did not ask how Hook knew. "Colonel William Windrush might yet recover, sir."

"He might," Hook said, "but he won't be able to command a regiment again. Big changes are coming for the Royals anyway. What do you know of the Childers Reforms?"

"I've never heard of them, sir," Jack admitted. He was still trying to accept that he would be colonel of the Royals.

"Hugh Childers is the new Secretary of State for War. You are aware of the previous secretary's reforms?"

"Yes, sir. Edward Cardwell pushed forward various acts to modernise the army."

Hook nodded. "Cardwell abolished the purchase system and adopted short service to create an army reserve; men now serve six years with the Colours and six with the reserve."

Jack nodded.

"And Cardwell linked the battalions of a regiment to create exchanges of officers and men between the home and overseas stations. He also linked each regiment with a specific county or an area in the case of Scottish regiments."

Jack nodded. "The Royals were not affected, sir. Nor were the 113th."

"They will be next year. Childers will alter the terms of enlistment to seven years with the regulars and five in reserve. He also plans to link single battalion regiments together and abolish the old numbers. The Royals and the 113th will become the first and second battalion of the Royal Malverns, with blue facings and regimental headquarters in Great Malvern."

Jack hid his surprise. "I see, sir."

"Many people will disagree, as the two regiments have little in common." Hook passed over the decanter. "Until now."

"Now, sir?" Jack realised that he was drinking heavily.

Hook looked grim. "You are the hinge, Windrush. Your family have had Royal Malvern associations since Marlborough's time, yet most of your career was in the 113th."

"That's correct, sir." Jack knew there was more to come. General Hook would not travel to Kandahar for such a trivial reason. *And what is Armaghan's connection with military reorganisation? Why is he here?*

"You are going to ensure the two battalions know each other well," Hook said, "for you're going on an expedition together." He put his glass down. "You will regard anything I say in the next half hour as top secret, and it will not leave this room."

"Of course, sir," Jack glanced at Armaghan.

Hook intercepted the look. "Armaghan has been my top agent in Afghanistan for upwards of a decade. What he doesn't know about the country is not worth knowing."

Top agent? Jack eyed Armaghan up and down. *Nothing in this damned country was simple. Friends one day were enemies the next, good regiments lost their morale, brave officers died, and nomadic Timuris with ancient religions were British agents.*

"I wondered what you were," Jack said to Armaghan.

"I didn't like to deceive you," Armaghan said, "but deception is my business."

"You do it very well." Jack gave a slight bow, not sure whether he was complimenting or not.

"Both battalions of the Royal Malverns will leave Kandahar," Hook interrupted the conversation. "You will march separately to Peshawar, where you will prepare for further service. Unfortunately, you can't meet Colonel Robert Warburton as he's on sick leave in England. Do you know Warburton, Windrush?"

"No, sir."

"He's a most interesting fellow. His mother was a niece of

Dost Mohammed, the late Amir of Afghanistan or one of the late Amirs. That makes Warburton related to the Durrani royal family, including the present Amir."

Jack nodded. "I'd like to have met him, sir."

"You might meet him later. As he's not available, we're going to rely on your reputation to pacify the tribes."

"My reputation, sir?"

"Earlier this year, Armaghan asked you to offer hospitality, *melmastia*, to a certain Afghan lady."

Jack nodded.

"Of course, you followed the honourable code and looked after her, although you knew her father was your enemy." Hook said. "We ensured that the news spread, and the Pashtun tribes, from the Yusufzai in Dir and Swat down to the Mahsuds in Waziristan know that major, now colonel, Jack Windrush follows the code of Pashtunwali." Hook held Jack's gaze. "They trust you, Windrush, and trust is an important commodity along such a volatile frontier."

"Was that deliberate, sir?" Jack asked. "Were you creating a reputation for future use?"

Hook sipped more of his brandy, taking his time as his gaze never left Jack's face. "You are part Indian, Windrush. I have long noted that you have an affinity with the Pashtun and other native peoples. General Roberts and I discussed you earlier in the year during that business with Batoor Khan."

"I didn't know that, sir."

"You didn't need to know. We wanted a colonelcy for you then but decided to wait until something suitable came up. As the colonel of the Royals, you'll be able to kill two birds with one stone. You'll cement together two diverse regiments, and you can help solve a very tricky question for us."

"What's that, sir?"

"As you know, we are evacuating Afghanistan but retaining control of certain enclaves."

Jack nodded.

"One of these is the Khyber Pass. I believe you've been there before."

"Yes, sir," Jack said. "I was there at the time of the Bunerwali expedition."

"You will be visiting again soon. In the meantime, I'd learn all I could about the area."

"Yes, sir," Jack said.

Hook glanced at St John, who had been a silent witness to everything that passed in the room. "You have something to add, St John?"

"Yes, sir," St John said. "You know Batoor Khan, Jack."

The use of his first name warned Jack that St John was about to impart bad news. "I know him well, sir."

"We knew that Batoor Khan intended to tilt for the throne of Afghanistan. I believe you helped persuade him otherwise."

"Batoor made that decision himself, sir," Jack said.

"We need a strong ally in Afghanistan," St John continued, "and Batoor may be that man. Your friendship, plus your known adherence to Pashtunwali, make you the ideal man to persuade him to hang his hat on our peg."

"Batoor is his own man, sir," Jack warned. "He might not wish to be tied to any side."

"Then it's up to you to persuade him," Hook said. "We've given you a strong platform from which to work. The rest is up to you." He leaned back, looking satisfied as if nothing more needed to be said.

Armaghan salaamed. "We know you have the ability, Colonel Windrush, sahib."

"Very well. I think we have given you sufficient to think about, Windrush." Hook rose from his seat and lifted his hat. "We'll leave you to command your regiment."

Jack stood as Hook left, exchanged a handshake with St John and Armaghan and finished his brandy. He needed the alcoholic stimulus.

The Khyber Pass. The main route from India to Kabul, where the

Afridis cause as much trouble as any two tribes. But I'm to be confirmed as colonel of the Royal Malverns.

The thoughts jumbled together in Jack's mind as he lay in bed that evening. On the one hand, he was pleased to be promoted. On the other, he had an unhappy regiment and what sounded like a dangerous expedition ahead. Jack had grown up expecting to command the Malverns someday, yet the reality brought only worries.

It's early days yet. Bring the regiment together, Jack, this is where you belong.

Jack heard the sharp crack of a revolver through his disturbed sleep and jerked awake. *Who the devil is firing at this time of night?* He scratched a Lucifer and checked the time. *It's two in the morning, for God's sake! Probably some irritated officer has shot a rat or a snake. I'll speak to them in the morning about firing discipline in the barracks.*

Lying back down, Jack tried to get to sleep, with the candle flickering in the dozen draughts and casting wavering shadows around the room. He sat up again when somebody tapped on the door.

"Sir! It's Donnelly, sir."

"What is it, Donnelly?" Jack knew that Donnelly would not disturb him without a good reason.

Donnelly opened the door. "There's been an accident, sir. You'd better come. Colonel Windrush, the other Colonel Windrush, has been shot."

CHAPTER TWENTY-THREE

"Shot?" Jack rose from the bed. "I heard the gun. Is he alive? Who shot him? Some *badmash*? A *loosewallah*? A stray thief?" He tried to collect his thoughts.

"I don't know, sir. Mrs Colonel Windrush told me to fetch you."

"Mary?" Jack's mood rose at the thought of his wife being present. "No, of course not. Mrs Helen Windrush."

"Yes, sir." Donnelly stood in the doorway in his uniform trousers and shirt sleeves. Even in the barracks, he wore a bayonet at his belt.

Slipping on his trousers, Jack grabbed his tunic and followed Donnelly through the barracks. A knot of officers and scared-looking servants stood outside William's room, talking in hushed tones.

"Clear the way for the colonel sahib!" Donnelly used his boot to remove a reluctant sweeper. "Excuse us, please, sirs," he said to the officers. "Colonel Windrush is here."

Jack pushed into the room. William lay sprawled across the bed, with a revolver in his right hand and half his head blown away.

"He's dead." Helen sat on a hard chair in the furthest corner of the room. Wearing her nightclothes and with her hair a tangled mess, she did not look like the sophisticated colonel's wife that Jack knew. Nor did she look like a distraught new widow.

Jack did not have to examine the body. "He's taken his own life."

Suicides were common in India. The heat and the stifling boredom of garrison life claimed many lives among British other ranks, who standing orders restricted from travelling far from their barracks. Suicide was less common among officers, who had more freedom and opportunities for sport and recreation. Jack could not think of another case when a senior officer had taken his life.

"The doctor said he was suffering from nervous exhaustion and a black depression," Helen sounded calm as she looked at the body of her husband.

"Come away, Helen." Jack put an arm around her shoulders. "Come away. I'll deal with William."

Donnelly stood guard at the door, barring entrance to the curious as Jack escorted Helen outside. "Fetch the surgeon, Donnelly."

"He's on his way, sir."

"Lieutenant Sarsens!" Jack shouted, "Keep this corridor clear. I want nobody here except the surgeon." He brought Helen to his office, ignoring the other officers' wives who appeared eager to help. "Sit down, Helen." He sat her at the desk and poured a brandy. "Drink this. It will help."

Helen drained the glass at a single draught. "I'm all right, Jack. Honestly, I am."

Jack sat down. "I don't know what to say."

Helen leaned back. "I should have known," she said. "He's been in a downward spiral for months, and the death of Crimea finished him."

Jack poured out more brandy.

"I should be crying," Helen said. "I should be in shock at the loss of my husband, but I'm not."

It will come later, Helen. It's too soon.

Helen gave a twisted smile. "Do you know what I feel, Jack? Nothing. The shot awoke me, and I looked at William's dead body, and I felt nothing. We hadn't been husband and wife for some time, you know. Not in a physical manner."

"You don't have to tell me, Helen."

"Oh, but I do. I have to tell somebody, and you're my oldest and closest friend."

Helen faced him. "What I said before when William lay sick. About you getting promotion over his dead body? I didn't mean it, Jack. I was in pain and wanted to hurt somebody back. I am sorry."

"There's no need to apologise, Helen," Jack said. "You never need to apologise to me. We know each other too well."

"Do you know something, Jack?" Helen swirled the brandy in her glass, staring at the liquid as if it held the secret of existence. "Part of me is relieved."

Jack let her talk without interruption.

"I should never have married him, Jack. We both know that. William knew that I should have stayed with you."

Jack filled her glass. "I'll find more suitable accommodation for you, Helen. You can't stay in that room." A colonel's duties encompassed more than just fighting, Jack realised.

"We were never suited," Helen continued. "I always preferred you." And then she began to cry.

The surgeon tapped on the door and entered. "Sir," he glanced at Helen, "I can come back later."

Mrs Major Baxter peered over the surgeon's shoulder. "Come along, Mrs Windrush. I'll take care of you." She looked at Jack. "She'll be better with a woman, sir."

Helen shook her head. "I'll be all right, Jack." She allowed Mrs Baxter to lead her away.

"Colonel Windrush committed suicide, sir, in my opinion." The surgeon waited until Helen was out of the room.

"Take the body away, please, doctor," Jack said. He poured himself another brandy and settled back in his chair. He had barely spoken to William for the past twenty-odd years, but they were still brothers. The brandy tasted sharp on his palate. He would miss him in an odd way.

For a moment, Jack thought of his childhood, when he and William were close and ran free on the green Malvern Hills. He could hear the laughter and see the bright sun and extensive views over Worcestershire and Herefordshire. Childhood was a precious time, Jack thought, and it was a pity that people could not retain such innocence. A third brandy followed the second as Jack relived the days before he and William separated.

Damn the world and its divisions. Why do people have to struggle against each other? William and I were so close, once. And what the devil will I do with Helen?

* * *

With Ayub Khan defeated, the fighting around Kandahar ended, except for the occasional ghazi attack and stray shot at a British patrol. Even the Royal Malverns accepted such things as the norm for any frontier garrison.

On the 6th of September 1880, General Phayre's column marched in from Quetta, multiplying Kandahar's problems of supply and accommodation. With no enemy to fight, Roberts gradually reduced the garrison and ordered some regiments to march back to India. Sick with fever and worn by the intense mental strain of the last two years, Roberts accompanied MacGregor's Third Brigade, the first British troops to leave. Suffering from an enlarged liver, nausea, lack of appetite and possibly a duodenal ulcer, Roberts handed command to Phayre.

Standing on the city walls, Jack watched MacGregor's brigade march away, with the 113th Foot in the middle. Despite his new rank and responsibilities, he felt a pang as he watched his men swing past.

Major Burridge noticed Jack on the walls. "March to attention!" he ordered. "Eyes left!"

The 113th, not yet the 2nd battalion Royal Malverns, stiffened as if on parade and looked to their left. The officers drew their swords and swung them up and back down in acknowledgement while the sergeants slammed a salute.

Jack stood to attention, fighting the prickle in his eyes that threatened to unman him. For a moment, he contemplated throwing up his promotion and returning to the 113th, but he dismissed the idea.

These were my men, and the 113th was my regiment. I will always be Fighting Jack of the 113th, but destiny has guided me to the Royals. I'll carve out my future here.

The 113th passed, with every man marching erect, and Jack felt strangely lonely on the wall, with the harsh Afghan sun burning him and the Royals waiting for his commands. He watched MacGregor's brigade march away until the dust of its passage began to settle, and he knew that a section of his life had ended. He no longer belonged to the 113th.

However, when one door shut, another beckoned. In future, men would talk of Roberts' Kabul to Kandahar march, and Jack could lift his head and say, "I was there."

* * *

"Curious fellow this Colonel Jack Windrush," Captain Inkerrow lifted his voice so that Jack could hear. "He's night and day to our last commander. Quite the queer fish. He's half-black, I heard." Inkerrow gave a high-pitched laugh. "Not quite up to the standard we expect in the Royals."

On the opposite side of the room, Jack slowly swivelled to face Inkerrow. He had been dealing with such slights for many years.

"No, Inkerrow," Bryant spoke in his Eton-educated drawl. "You're right. He's not the standard we've come to expect. But that's all right. He'll raise us to his level." Bryant raised a languid eyebrow. "Not you, though, Inkerrow. I heard you have put in a transfer request to a down country regiment in the sloth belt."

"I've done no such thing," Inkerrow said.

"I have the chit on my desk," Bryant said. "I suggest you sign it today and go on leave. The Royal Malverns is no place for such as you." Lighting a cigar, Bryant lay back in his chair and closed his eyes.

It was not until November 1880 that Gladstone's government in Britain finally decided to abandon Kandahar and hand the city to Abdur Rahman. They persuaded Sher Ali to abdicate as Wali and further reduced the British garrison.

All the time, Jack trained his Royals, altering them from a regiment suitable to parade in Hyde Park to men able to fight the Afghans or anybody else. He introduced mounted infantry, taught them to move and fight in extended formation, offered prizes for marksmanship, and watched his men develop.

For the first month, the Royals complained. They thought of themselves as equal to the Guards in drill and appearance and resented these new forms of soldiering. Jack ignored the moans and pushed them all the harder until they woke tired and fought their way through the day.

"The harder you train, the easier you'll fight!" Jack told them.

Jack ditched the scarlet uniforms except for formal parades and indented for khaki.

"You are real soldiers," Jack told them, "not pipe-clayed Hyde Park strollers." He viewed their gleaming white sun helmets, obtained replacements for parade, and ordered that the men dye the old helmets khaki.

"The Afghans like nothing better than a soldier in scarlet, with a white belt and helmet to give him a perfect target. Get them dyed!"

When the men looked sulky, Jack substituted white and khaki sun helmets for the more normal targets at musketry drill.

He allowed each man five shots and showed them the tattered remains of the white helmets.

"Imagine your head inside that," he said.

The following morning, every helmet was khaki.

When the Royals mastered the basics, Jack moved on to more advanced soldiering. He showed the men how to seek cover and fire from behind rocks and trees, how to fight by platoons and sections and, finally, as individuals, each man covering his companion.

Simultaneously with training the men, Jack worked on the officers. They were excellent at display and parade ground soldiering but fell far short of Jack's requirements as fighting leaders.

"You officers lack aggression and tactical skills." Jack had called them into an empty chamber to address them en masse. "I will give you the basic rules that, from this day on, the Royal Malverns will follow when on campaign."

Jack noticed that Bryant and Baxter looked attentive, with Sarsens producing a small black notebook.

"Pay attention, for my rules are the results of decades of experience.

Rule number one: get there fastest with the most men.

Rule number two: shoot first, shoot last, and shoot to kill.

Rule number three: mystify, mislead, and surprise the enemy.

Rule number four: never leave the enemy a minute to gather himself but descend on him with all the force we have and pursue him until he is destroyed."

Jack watched the faces of his officers. Some looked shocked at his ruthlessness.

"There is more," Jack said. "Casualties, losses and cost matter less than victory. We must consider them in any battle plan we make, but if we give any single factor undue weight, the plan will probably fail. A few casualties in victory may save hundreds in defeat."

Jack waited for comments. He knew that his approach was

radically different from that of his brother. He also knew that the regiment's sole battle experience at Kandahar would have opened a few eyes.

"When we are better trained." Jack decided to sweeten the pills he was forcing down well-bred throats, "we will be the best regiment in the British army. We already excel on the parade ground. We will also excel in battle."

"When will all this training be complete?" Sarsens asked.

"Never," Jack said. "There is no such thing as a perfect soldier or a fully trained regiment, but we'll be damned close before we're finished. If we have to fight the Afghans again, we'll be ready for them."

"I thought the war was finished," Sarsens said.

"We thought that before," Jack reminded, "and then they murdered our ambassador and massacred the Guides."

Sarsens took a deep breath. "Yes, sir."

Jack pushed them through the winter months, whatever the weather. He remembered General Hook's words about a coming expedition and wanted his Royals to be equal, if not better than, the 113th.

At least once a day, Jack visited Helen. She was silent for the first few days, then became emotional as reality hit her. Jack allowed her to rant, letting her anger escape.

"They killed my son, and now they've killed my husband," Helen said. "Oh, I know that soldiers risk death every day." She shook her head and took a deep breath. "It's hard, Jack, to lose your son and your husband in such a short time."

"I can only imagine." Jack sat beside her, a sponge to soak up her grief and anger.

"With William's younger brother also dead," Helen said, "I've only a daughter left, and you."

"I'll always be here if you need me," Jack told her. His youngest brother Adam had died some years before. Jack was now the last of his father's issue, and his son David was the last male Windrush.

Helen hugged a glass of brandy like an old friend. "Jack. You followed the Pashtunwali code with *melmastia* when you helped that Pashtun woman."

Jack nodded. "Zufash," he said.

"I want you to make me a promise." Helen's gaze did not stray from Jack's eyes. She was tight-lipped, with deep grooves around her mouth.

"If I can," Jack said.

"You can." Helen's expression was as cold as anything Jack had ever seen.

"What is it?"

"As you're keen on Pashtunwali, I want you to use their code of *badal*."

Helen had not tended her hair that day. It was a tangled mess on her bare head, while she had not changed her clothes for at least three days. The mourning black made her appear even older.

Jack did not hesitate. "Zamar Khan?" He closed his eyes and saw Zamar Khan firing his rifle again and Crimea crumpling to the ground.

"Crimea was your blood, Jack. He was your nephew. Don't let your feud with William take away your blood duty. If you can adopt Pashtun ways and offer *melmastia* to a stranger, then you can use *badal* for your nephew." She gripped Jack's arms in hands like claws. "If you can't do it for Crimea's sake, Jack, do it for mine!"

Jack remembered Helen as she had been at the durbar only a few months previously. That Helen was still there, beneath the tangled hair and soiled clothes. "I will, Helen," Jack promised.

"Here!" Helen released Jack and nearly ran to the desk. "I gave this to William years ago." She produced a leather-covered Bible. "I never felt safe with all these heathen religions, and I wanted him to have some spiritual protection. Swear on the Bible, Jack. Swear that you'll avenge my son!"

"I can't swear a death oath on the Bible!" Although Jack was not a particularly religious man, he found the notion disturbing.

"Swear, Jack!" Helen grabbed his left hand and thrust it in between the pages of the Book. "An eye for an eye, Jack, blood for blood! *Badal* is no different!"

"I swear to honour my pledge to you," Jack said. He knew the words were insufficiently robust. *Damn it, man, Helen needs your support. Do it, man; the Lord will understand.*

"I swear by this book, and by the Pashtunwali code, that if I meet Zamar Khan again, I will kill him."

Helen was watching. Jack saw her face alter as though Jack had already done the deed. "Thank you, Jack." She retrieved the Bible and hugged it close as if she were holding her baby son once more.

A shaft of sunlight entered the tall, pointed window and caught Helen's arm as she held the Book. The shadow fell on the far wall, at right angles to the tall pole of a lamp, so for a moment, a cross wavered there. Then Helen moved, and the image was gone.

A cold shiver ran from the base of Jack's spine to the nape of his neck. *Dear God, forgive me. If I kill Zamar Khan now, I will be an assassin and not a soldier, and if I don't kill him, I'll have broken my oath to Helen.*

Helen replaced the Bible where it belonged and glimpsed herself in the small shaving mirror William had on his desk. She paused, staring.

"Dear Lord, Jack. Is that me? Is that what I look like now?"

"That's you," Jack confirmed.

When Helen faced him, her shoulders had straightened slightly. "Well, we'd better do something about my appearance, hadn't we? We can't allow a memsahib to look like something the cat refused to drag in."

"No, we can't," Jack agreed. He would have been happier if Helen's eyes had altered, but, despite her words, they were as expressionless as granite.

CHAPTER TWENTY-FOUR

One by one, the regiments marched from Afghanistan until only the Royal Malverns remained in Kandahar, and eventually, they also left. Jack stood at the citadel's gate, listening to the men as they passed.

"Why are we leaving?" Private Hanley was twenty years old, with a sunburned face and broad shoulders. "We beat them, didn't we?"

"Yes, we beat them," Private Brotheridge spoke with the authority of a man two years older.

"Bobs beat them at Kandahar and Kabul and Peiwar Kotal and other places."

"Yes, he did." Brotheridge shifted his Martini to a more comfortable place against his shoulder.

"So why are we leaving?' Hanley persisted.

"The politicians say so."

"Why? We won, didn't we?" Hanley looked over his shoulder at the frowning walls of Kandahar. "We beat them hollow."

"I dunno why we're leaving. Ask the politicians." Brotheridge shifted his rifle again.

"Bugger the politicians. What do they know about anything?"

"Bugger all, and not much of that," Brotheridge explained. "A politician is a man who doesn't have the skill to get a decent job or the guts to join the army."

There's a lot of truth in that, Jack thought.

RSM Deblin intervened. "Why did you join the army, Hanley?"

"'Cause I had no job, Major." Hanley jumped at being addressed directly by such an imposing person as the RSM.

"You joined to fight the queen's enemies, didn't you?" Deblin marched alongside.

"Well…" Hanley hesitated between telling the truth and contradicting the RSM.

"Right then, that's why you joined. You fought the queen's enemies, and now what are you doing?'

"Dunno, Major." Hanley's face flushed a deeper hue of red.

"You're marching away, Hanley, that's what you're doing.' Deblin said.

"Yes, Major."

"You're marching, not being carried on the flat of your back, so you faced the queen's enemies and won. Now shut your mouth, face your front and try to look like a soldier."

Jack pushed on. He understood the men's frustration. In any action where they had a chance of success, they had emerged victorious. The men in the ranks had let nobody down. Any fault lay with the vacillating politicians and some poor leadership.

He watched the column, his regiment, march out of Kandahar on the road to Quetta and then India.

The war was over, and now the British had to win the peace.

The baggage train followed behind the fighting men. There were wagons, carts, camels, horses, and mules, with officers' wives and men's wives, camp followers, and assorted people whose functions Jack could only guess.

The journey to Peshawar took longer than Jack had imagined,

but he did not push the Royals, and they arrived fitter than they had set out. Jack settled them into their barracks, attended to the hundred and one details that befell the lot of a regimental colonel and looked up as the surgeon walked into his new office.

"Ah, doctor, what can I do for you?"

"Venereal disease," the surgeon said.

"What about it?" Jack knew that sexually transmitted disease was one of the curses of any British regiment in India.

"It's not a problem we had in Kandahar, with the Pashtuns' close hold on the women there, but Peshawar will be a different story." The surgeon glared at Jack as if he were personally responsible for every foul disease in the regiment. "I want you to create a clean brothel for the men."

British other ranks could enjoy life in India, with their new status as a soldier sahib, and servants to perform the menial tasks, but some stations were renowned for boredom. If the men were fortunate, there might be some sport, but often the facilities only comprised a canteen that served adulterated drink and poor-quality food. Tedium pressed down upon them, but prostitutes provided some relief.

"Men need sex." The surgeon was brutally frank. "They'll find a woman somehow, and with their lack of pay, it will be a sand-harlot rotten with disease."

"I'll look into it," Jack promised. *How the deuce do I organise a regimental brothel? I never read about that in any military manual.*

"Sir!" Donnelly tapped on the door, entered, and came to attention. "Telegram for you."

"Thank you." Jack scanned the flimsy slip of paper.

I will be with you shortly. Hook.

"Thank you, Donnelly," Jack said. *What now? Is there no respite for a poor benighted colonel?*

Hook had St John by his side when he walked into Jack's office. "Don't stand up, Windrush. Just pour me a brandy, and the same for St John."

Jack did so, adding a third glass for himself.

"You were with Cavagnari in Kabul," Hook began.

"I was," Jack acknowledged cautiously.

"And you survived."

"More by luck than judgement," Jack said.

Hook smiled. "You survived Maiwand, too. Your men call you Fighting Jack, I hear. Maybe you should be Lucky Jack, to walk away from a brace of disasters."

"Or Unlucky Jack, to blunder into them in the first place," Jack murmured. He sipped at his brandy with the sound of the busy city around them and the faint hum of a *punkah* above, keeping the air mobile.

"Do you know the Yusufzai or the Afridis?" St John asked.

"I know of the Yusufzai, and I have had dealings with the Afridis," Jack said.

St John smiled. "Don't look so nervous, Windrush. We know your capabilities. We haven't created your reputation to throw it away. I happen to know both tribes well. There are some fine men amongst them, but overall, the Pashtun is a lazy individual and careless to a degree."

"They are also honourable by their lights, brave, religious and tenacious," Jack countered. "I have more respect for the Pashtuns than for most people I have encountered."

Hook handed each man a cheroot. "Have a smoke."

"What's the to-do, General?" St John was perfectly at ease. "I know as little of my purpose here as Windrush."

"The Khyber Pass and the Amir are the to do," Hook replied at once. "With Warburton on sick leave in England, you two gentlemen are probably the army's greatest experts on the Pashtuns."

Jack raised his eyebrows, aware that General Hook's flattery usually preceded a dangerous mission. He inhaled smoke, held it for a calming ten seconds, and then exhaled slowly.

"What do you want me to do, sir?"

Hook held Jack's gaze. "It's the same mission, Windrush. I want you to persuade Batoor Khan to support both the Amir and the British. You know that the Khyber is nominally under our control, but the local tribes, the Afridis and Shinwaris, only pay us lip service." His smile was entirely without humour. "To say nothing of the Shilmani and Zakha Khel."

"As I said before, sir, Batoor Khan is a law unto himself. He won't align himself to any particular faction, British or Afghan, unless it suits him."

"Then make it suit him." Hook's eyes hardened. "Make any damned promise you like, Windrush, but we must keep the Khyber open. We've agreed that Abdur Rahman Khan is the Amir, and he's already under pressure from Ayub Khan. If we lose Rahman, we'll need another blasted Afghan War to restore the situation, and Gladstone won't countenance that. The Russians will increase their influence, and we're back to square one."

"So, we need to keep the Khyber open in case we have to bolster Rahman?" Jack grasped the essence of the plan. "Batoor is only a tool in this great game, and I'm a lever to work the tool."

"We're all only tools, Windrush," Hook said.

"Am I going alone, sir?" Jack asked.

"The Khyber is a trouble spot, Windrush. Despite your enhanced reputation, you'd last about a day. We'd find what's left of you, naked and mutilated, outside our outpost at Landi Kotal." Hook shook his head. "No, Windrush. Until we can persuade the tribes that peace is the best policy, we'll have to move in force. I'm sending a brigade into the Khyber to show the flag and as cover for your mission."

"The last time we sent a single brigade into Pashtun territory, we ended up with Maiwand, sir."

Hook watched as the *punkah* dissipated the smoke from his cheroot. "I have chosen a brigadier with more fighting experience than Burrows, Windrush." He lifted his voice. "Come in, Brigadier!"

The door opened, and Arthur Elliot walked in.

"Arthur!" Jack was on his feet immediately with his hand extended. Elliot had been junior to Jack in Crimea and through the Mutiny. Since then, Elliot had achieved more rapid promotion and now wore the rank of a brigadier. He and Jack were old friends.

"That's brigadier, sir, to you, Jack." Elliot gripped Jack's hand. "Congratulations on your promotion."

"Thank you, brigadier, sir, and your Honour," Jack said.

"I understand that you two know each other," St John observed dryly.

"Never seen him before in my life," Elliot responded. "Although I once knew a thrusting lieutenant with the same name back in the fifties."

"When you've finished pawing each other," Hook said, "we can get down to business." He unrolled a map of the Khyber and laid it on the desk. "Now, Brigadier, here is what I want you to do…"

With Elliot in charge, Jack knew the column would be well organised and prepared. Elliot had the Royal Malverns, 113th foot and a battalion of Sikhs for infantry, with three troops of Guides cavalry. Jack had emulated Roberts in recommending a battery of screw guns rather than wheeled artillery and suggested reducing the camp followers to a minimum.

"We'll leave the details to you," Hook said. "Remember, Windrush, we want Batoor Khan onside."

"I'll do what I can, sir," Jack promised.

* * *

Jack found the British cantonments at Peshawar spacious compared to the citadel at Kandahar, with broad, rose-tree lined streets and large mulberry trees at regular intervals.

"This place has developed since I was here last," Jack said.

"The bungalows are very civilised," Elliot agreed. "I'd show you my *burra*-bungalow, but you'd be jealous." They walked side-by-side for a few moments. "I was sorry to hear about young Crimea," Elliot broached the subject, "and your brother."

"Helen took Crimea's death badly," Jack said.

Elliot nodded. "I am not surprised. Where is she now?"

"She has a bungalow in the cantonment."

Elliot was quiet for a few moments. "I'd like to speak to her if I may. I always had a liking for Helen."

"You don't need my permission, Arthur," Jack said.

Elliot nodded. "I thought I'd check."

The European station included some bazaars, where Jack saw men of the 113th glowering at a group of privates from the Royals.

"Peacocks in khaki," Crozier stepped forward. "Out without their ma!"

"Maybe we'd best remind them what real soldiers are like." Todd removed his belt and coiled it around his fist, buckle foremost like a knuckle duster.

Private Kerswell of the Royals lifted his chin. "You'd better find some first when you're not butchering babies!" He stamped his feet on the ground. "Come and feel my fives, you ranting bastard!"

Hanley and Brotheridge backed Kerswell up, standing four-square to face their rivals.

Jack walked between them before they began to brawl. "Have you men no duty to attend?" He put an edge in his voice as Elliot joined him, two senior officers preventing a brawl by privates. "You're letting your regiments down by this behaviour!"

Both groups stiffened to attention and saluted.

"Be about your business," Jack ordered and watched them move away, with Todd glancing over his shoulder for a final glower at Kerswell.

"This expedition is intended to bind the two battalions together," Jack said. "That will take a miracle."

Elliot smiled. "They'll get used to each other. I don't expect any fighting from the Pashtuns, except the odd sniper or two. We'll march up the Khyber, show the flag, persuade your old chum Batoor with a bag of gold sovereigns, and march back. Zar, Zan, or Zamin always works with the Pashtun."

"Batoor is not easily swayed," Jack said. He ensured his antagonistic soldiers were out of sight before continuing his exploration.

"I'm sure you'll find a way," Elliot said. "Hooky and St John have great faith in your abilities."

Jack took a deep breath. "I've enough on my hands moulding the Royals." He told Elliot how the regiment's morale had slumped.

"You have experience in training the 113th and the West Indians in Africa," Elliot said. "That's another reason Hook and Roberts chose you, Jack. They have their eye on you."

The old city of Peshawar had not changed much. The local authorities considered it so dangerous that they kept it closed to Europeans unless they obtained a pass. Even then, armed police escorted the visitor to wherever he wished to go.

"People used to call Port Royal the wickedest city on earth," Elliot said. "I'd wager that Peshawar beats it hands down. Half the *badmashes* and *loosewallahs* of the Frontier end up here, together with men running from blood feuds."

"All the glories of Empire," Jack murmured. He looked westward towards the mountains of Afghanistan. *I am not looking forward to returning there again.*

"If you'll excuse me," Elliot said. "I have arrangements to make." They shook hands, and he strode away.

That evening, after he had inspected his men, Jack wandered around the bungalows, nodding to the *chuprassis*, the doorkeepers who guarded the houses against the inevitable *loosewallah*s. The thieves in India, Jack thought, could steal the food from a man's fork between the plate and his mouth.

With no particular direction in mind, Jack was surprised to

find himself outside Helen's bungalow. He saw her shadow at the window, silhouetted by a lantern.

Should I say good evening?

As Jack contemplated stepping forward, he saw a second figure in the house, taller than Helen.

She has a man with her. Who?

The figures shifted, so the lantern light fell on both, and Jack saw it was Elliot at Helen's side. They seemed to be talking, and then Helen drew the blind, and Jack saw nothing at all.

Good man, Arthur, Jack said and walked away.

* * *

The Bugles sounded "fall in" at four the following morning, and the brigade assembled on the maidan. Jack inspected his men. The Royal Malverns looked like soldiers now, with their khaki uniforms travel-stained and their faces set and sun-browned.

"Pack up your kits, boys," Jack ordered, "load your tents on the camels." He watched their bearing, noting with pleasure that they tried to race the Sikhs and 113th at loading.

That's the way, Royals. Strive to be the best at everything.

As the column began its march, Jack noted a lone figure standing at the edge of the maidan. Dressed in her mourning black, Helen looked so forlorn that Jack fought the temptation to rush up to her.

What is she thinking? Is she looking for her son amongst the tall young subalterns? Or does she still see William at the head of the Royals?

As the regiment passed her, Helen lifted a hand. Jack acknowledged with a salute, and for a moment, looked directly into Helen's face. She shouted something, with the single word lost in the crunch of thousands of feet. Then Jack passed, and Helen stood there alone, a solitary woman shrouded in sorrow, watching men marching to war. Jack knew that Helen had shouted, *"badal."*

* * *

As so often in India, the column kicked up fine dust, so the men were soon coughing.

"Watch the breeches of your *bundooks*!" RSM Deblin shouted. "Cover them, or the dust will get in the works, and some great hairy Paythan will rise up with his sword and slice you up before you can fire!"

Jack watched the men check their rifles, with the more cautious having wrapped cloth around the breech. Experience had taught them to look after their weapons.

After a few miles, the column passed the old border, a small station with half a dozen mud huts and a small fort baking under the sun. A company of armed police watched the column pass.

"Is this Afghanistan or India?" Baxter asked.

"I believe it's still Afghan territory," Jack replied, "but under our control."

As they passed the frontier, the 113th cheered, while the Sikhs and Royals marched in silence, with the Guides looking warily about them.

We're back, Jack told himself. *Hopefully, only for a short time.*

The road was no better on the Afghan side of the border. The men kicked at loose stones, commented on the lack of trees or signs of life, and shifted the rifles on their shoulders. Flies rose from the expected bodies of camels or bullocks that had perished on the path, while the vultures remained, feasting as they ignored the passing soldiers.

"I hate these things," Baxter said.

"That's all right, Baxter," Bryant said, puffing at a cigar, "they'll quite enjoy you."

Jack said nothing, appreciating the grim humour.

The brigade camped at the entrance to the Khyber Pass, where the gaunt Jamrud Fort provided security and a reminder of the fragility of Empire. "Hari Singh Nalwa built this place in

1836." Jack had researched the area. "This was the limit of the Sikh Empire, and then we defeated the Sikhs."

"Nothing lasts forever," Baxter said. "Not even empires."

Jack surveyed the hostile land to the west. "Not even empires. Maybe not even ours. I heard that Colonel Warburton wants to raise a regiment here, the Khyber Jezailchis, and garrison the fort."

Elliot dismounted and stretched his legs. "Is that not how the Romans policed their Empire? They raised local units and eventually relied more on auxiliaries and mercenaries than on Roman soldiers?"

Jack listened to the Royals as they prepared to camp. The mixture of English, Welsh and Irish accents was reassuring, with Elliot diplomatically placing the Sikhs between the Royals and the 113th. "Maybe we'll go down the same road."

The brigade settled down for the night, with the resident garrison indicating the best campsites. Jack found a perch on the fort's battlements and looked westward. It was four miles to the entrance of the Khyber and then fifty miles of dangerous road, overlooked by Pashtun strongholds.

The Khyber is Batoor's home territory, the land of the Afridis. How can I persuade Batoor to side with us? He's seen us close up and knows our strengths and weaknesses. What leverage can I use? Zar, zan, and zamin? Women, gold, and land? I can't offer him land, and he already has at least two wives. That leaves gold. How much?

Jack sighed and continued to look west as the sun slid behind the mountains, and the British bugles sounded for the last time that day.

CHAPTER TWENTY-FIVE

After Jamrud, the brigade column entered an area of stones. The rocks underfoot and on either side reflected the sun's heat until the men felt as like they were walking through a furnace. Remembering the torments of the march to Maiwand, Jack loosened his revolver in its holster. He waited for the ghazis to strike while the British were reeling.

"Do you expect trouble, sir?" Bryant had noticed Jack's movement.

"No more than usual, Bryant," Jack said.

As a break in the monotony of rock, the men could look at the occasional grave of man or animal or look at the vultures that circled overhead.

"These damned birds know that when armies march, food follows," Baxter said.

"We give them plenty," Jack agreed.

An hour into the march, the path descended sharply into the bed of a river. Jack guessed that the river would be a torrent in winter, but now it was shallow, with bitter cold water that lapped around the men's ankles. Most of the pack animals took the opportunity to drink, slowing down the column.

"Royals!" Jack shouted. "One company at a time, go

upstream of the column and fill your water bottles. One section guarding the next."

Jack felt the atmosphere tighten when they approached the two hills that marked the entrance to the Khyber. He saw the heliograph on the right-hand hill winking a message back towards India, perhaps informing distant Simla of their arrival, and then he was ushering his men along.

"Double the flank guards," Jack ordered as they entered the Khyber. "Every man march with his rifle loaded. Company commanders! Ensure nobody falls behind. I want no stragglers in the Khyber. NCOs, inform your officers the instant you see anything unusual!"

The Khyber closed in, dark and forbidding. The road bordered the riverbed, sometimes fording the river, with bare, ugly hills on either side. Jack saw no people, although he was sure the Afridis were present, silently watching this new British invasion of Pashtun land.

"Watch the hills," he murmured to Baxter. "Look for signs of movement, the glint of sunlight on metal, anything that shouldn't be there." He knew the Royal Malverns had been in Afghanistan for some months, but they had avoided battle. They were Johnny Raws in terms of Frontier experience, maiden soldiers in this stark land.

After another hour, with the column breaking the watchful silence of the hills, the road eased to the left. Elliot remained in front, pushing his horse up the flank of a ragged mountain.

"This section is known as Mackeson's Road," Jack said. He felt the back of his neck prickle as if somebody was aiming a jezail at that spot.

A dozen Guides cavalry rode in front, their turbans bright against the drab rocks and their heads constantly turning to inspect their surroundings. Jack watched the jemadar call to his men, the sound of his voice faint in the pass.

Thank God for the Guides.

"Baxter! Get the men ready to form into extended order!"

"Sir?" Baxter looked over his shoulder.

"Do it, man!" Jack knew the Guides had seen something.

He heard the first shot as a distant pop, more like a champagne cork than a weapon, but the Guides instantly scattered to seek cover.

"Extended order, Royal Malverns!" Jack roared. "Number One Company, take the left flank! Number Two, take the right! The others form a firing line!" He heard similar orders the length of the column as the Sikhs and 113th moved. In the Khyber, only a fool took chances.

Another pop sounded, and then an irregular fusillade. The Guides' jemadar issued an order, and his men dismounted and began to fire back.

At the head of the column, Major Burridge of the 113th sent a company to reinforce the Guides, the men like tiny khaki-clad marionettes, nearly invisible against the dun background. Jack watched his Royals take their positions as they pushed aside their excitement and fear, and their training took control.

"Sir?" Sarsens asked, "Shall we help the 113th?"

"Stand fast," Jack growled. "The 113th won't thank us for interfering."

The 113th company pushed further up the hill, moving effortlessly from cover to cover. The unseen assailants fired another volley, with the sound echoing from the surrounding mountains. Nobody fell, and nobody returned fire until the Pashtuns fired a third volley. This time, the 113th fired a volley that flushed out half a dozen warriors.

"There they are," Baxter said.

The 113th followed the Pashtun to the summit of the hill and settled there without firing again.

Well done, 113th. Let them come to you.

After a few moments, the Pashtun fired again, with the return volley hammering the ground around the muzzle smoke. Meanwhile, the Guides began a flanking movement, running up the hillside, jinking, covering each other, and never allowing the enemy time to aim.

"Watch the Guides!" Jack ordered. "Learn from the best."

The musketry eased into the distance as the combined fire of the 113th and Guides pushed the attackers from rock to rock, with the gun smoke drifting and the commands of officers and NCOs hoarse echoes. At length, the tribesmen ascended a prominent knoll, set up a tremendous yell, waved a black flag and vanished.

"*Shabash* the 113th," Jack said quietly. "*Shabash* the Guides."

The skirmish had seen one Guide killed and one man of the 113th wounded. It had been a minor Khyber incident, not important enough to be recorded except as a footnote in a regimental history, yet sufficient to put a Punjab family into mourning. Elliot posted more men on the flanks and pushed on.

"Did we kill any of them?" Baxter asked.

Jack shook his head. "I don't know. The Afghans usually carry their casualties away, so we'll never find out."

The column continued, with the flanking companies and Guides even more cautious than before the skirmish. Jack noted that Baxter and Sarsens started at every sound, both riding with a hand on their revolvers.

"Baxter!" Jack reined up at the major's side. "Try to look relaxed."

"This is a terrible place," Baxter said. "I feel as if even the hills are watching me."

"I know," Jack agreed. "But don't let the men see you are tense. Our nervousness will transmit to them, and they'll shoot at shadows. We can't have that."

Baxter licked dry lips. "Yes, sir."

Bryant took a pull from a silver hip flask and patted the neck of his horse. "It's rather like being a fag at Eton, sir. You don't know when somebody will attack you next."

Jack grinned. "Use that experience, Bryant."

The column plodded on, with the road rising steadily along

the side of the hill for the next two until it reached a windy plateau. The men looked around them, adjusted the weight of their Martinis and grumbled.

"We're on top of the world," Hanley said.

Brotheridge grunted. "Or the arse end of creation. I always thought Birmingham was the worst place in the world to live. Now I know better."

Jack rotated the flanking companies when they crossed the plateau and descended into a savage ravine. Another cold river rattled over its rocky bed, as different from the Severn or the Wye as London was from Malvern. An old fort stood guard here, beside a fertile oasis of trees and grass.

"An hour's halt," Elliot ordered as the animals enjoyed the grazing and the men lay down to rest.

Jack patrolled the Royals, talking to officers and men.

"How are they, Deblin?"

The RSM pondered for a moment before he replied. "They're not bad, sir. Some still believe that a soldier's job is to look pretty and stand guard, but an encounter or two with the Paythans will put them right."

"Are they as good as the 113th?"

"Not yet, sir." Deblin had retained his old loyalty.

Jack smiled and walked on. Despite the potential dangers of their position, many of the men were asleep. Jack nodded; as well as courage and endurance, the British soldier had two abilities. They could always find something alcoholic and could sleep under any conditions.

From the fort, the men had to wade knee-deep in the bitterly cold river for a few hundred yards, and then the road thrust on to Ali Masjid and another halt.

Jack shivered as he looked at the fortress. Dominating the pass from its 5000 feet high hill, Ali Masjid was one of the major strong points defending Afghanistan. Back in 1879, Sir Samuel Browne had captured Ali Masjid after an artillery bombardment and encircling movement.

Well done, Sir Sam, Jack said as his men stared upwards at the battered walls. The British flag flew defiantly above the fort, and a careworn captain descended to speak to Elliot.

"How far are you going, sir?" The captain was about thirty, with the eyes of a man twice his age.

"We're visiting Batoor Khan of the Rahmut Khel," Elliot said.

The captain frowned. "There's trouble up that way," he said. "A tribal feud."

Jack pushed forward. "What's happening?"

"I'm not sure yet, sir," the captain said. "I've only heard rumours, but my patrols have heard gunfire, and they picked up a couple of dead bodies in the pass."

Elliot grunted. "Thank you, Captain. They'll probably snipe at us, but I don't expect any serious trouble."

The Muslim members of the Guides prayed at the shrine of Ali ibn Abi Talib, Mohammed's cousin, while their Sikh colleagues watched, and the British soldiers played cards or dozed. The 113th and Royals watched each other from a wary distance, exchanging the occasional insult.

"How are the lads, Burridge?" Jack handed over a cheroot.

"Thank you, sir. They're accepting things," Burridge said. "They'd prefer to be in India and wonder why they're here."

Jack grunted. "These Afghan troubles never end. I think the Frontier will smoulder until the tribes drop Pashtunwali, and I don't see that happening." He eyed the hills, wondering how many hostile eyes were watching, wondering if he could persuade Batoor to become a British ally and hoping that Helen recovered.

Elliot gave the order to leave, and the column jolted into life once more. As they left Ali Masjid, Jack saw a group of Afghan horsemen high on the slopes above.

"Sir!" Sarsens pointed to the horsemen.

"I see them, Sarsens," Jack said. "They're watching us."

"Shall I go and chase them away, sir?"

Jack shook his head. "They're doing no harm. If they attack, then we'll react. Take a message to Major Bryant. He's commanding the flank guards. Give him my compliments, inform him of the Afghans and ask him not to make any offensive moves but to retaliate if they attack."

"Yes, sir!" Sarsens wheeled his horse around.

"Oh, and Sarsens," Jack called him back.

"Sir?"

"Inform Bryant that the horsemen are Afridis. They might be Batoor's men, so we want to keep them friendly."

Jack watched Sarsens ride away. As a lieutenant, Sarsens should walk alongside his men, but Jack had requisitioned him as the battalion galloper. He knew Sarsens' nerves had not recovered from Maiwand and hoped to build up his confidence by constant activity.

A string of camels walked sedately towards them, with the camel driver glancing curiously as the British soldiers and half a dozen men carrying jezails and Khyber knives as an escort.

"*Salaam Alaikum,*" the camel driver said as he drew level with Jack.

"*Salaam Alaikum,*" Jack replied. He remembered passing a string of camels on his first trip to visit Batoor, twelve years previously. Rulers may alter, Amirs come and go, but time stood still in this part of the world.

"May you never tire," the camel driver said.

"May you never see poverty."

The camels passed on, ageless as if the egos of Empire builders did not matter. Jack wondered if one or more of the three Magi had passed this way, two thousand years previously. *Was Gaspar not from India? If so, he may have come through the Khyber Pass. He would not be alone, then, but part of a kafilah, much like the one we just passed.*

The pass narrowed further, with grim rocks overhanging them on both sides, so the sound of their footsteps echoed all around. An occasional armed man stood or sat, cradling a jezzail or rifle. None acknowledged their greetings but watched them, silent with menace. The trail led upwards for mile after sinister mile to the summit of the pass at Landi Kotal, where Jack kicked his horse forward to speak to Elliot.

"This is where we leave the Khyber," Jack said.

To the south, the hills of Tirah rose in menacing beauty, while a valley probed northward to the Inzar Kandao Pass. Jack checked his surroundings. He could not see the Afridi horsemen, but he knew they were watching him.

"I know," Elliot said with a sudden smile. "I'm not sure where British-controlled territory ends here, and Afghan territory begins. The map is less than helpful."

Jack met Elliot's smile. "I don't that the British or the Afghans control this area, sir. The Pashtuns own all this land."

Elliot nodded to his column toiling up the pass. "When we're here, Jack, we're in control." He glanced around. "This is as good a place as any to spend the night. There is water and some grazing for the horses."

Centuries of labour had carved terraced fields out of the bare hillsides, with an occasional village crouching beneath the inevitable watchtower. The area had an atmosphere of grim resilience, wary rather than malicious as if the hills were ready to strike if opposed.

Elliot doubled the usual number of pickets and ordered the men to camp. The tents rose in ordered ranks, each regiment separate from its neighbour.

Bugles sounded their message, and the army routine continued, as it did from Canada to Ceylon, Scotland to Jamaica.

"We've lost a dozen tents!" Jack heard the shout from the 113th's lines. "Some thieving *loosewallah* has run off with two of our camels!"

Jack gestured to the Royals' quartermaster. "How many extra tents did we bring?"

"Fifteen, sir." The quartermaster looked puzzled.

"Take a section and lend a dozen to the 113th, with our compliments," Jack said.

The quartermaster stiffened. "That will upset the books, sir!"

"I know," Jack agreed. "Bring them to me for adjustment later. Get these tents to the 113th. *Jildi,* man!"

"Yes, sir." The quartermaster stifled his indignation at handing over priceless equipment to a rival regiment.

"Take Privates Kerswell, Hanley and Brotheridge of One Company to help carry them," Jack added.

Bryant was listening and smiling. "Extending the olive branch, sir?"

"Exactly so, Bryant."

Donnelly stood at the entrance to Jack's tent, sniffing the air like a pointer dog. "Can you smell that, sir?"

"Smell what, Donnelly?"

"Trouble, sir," Donnelly said. "Something's in the wind."

Jack frowned. When a man who had grown up in barracks scented trouble, it was time to be wary. "What sort of trouble, Donnelly?"

"I don't know, sir." Donnelly shook his head.

"Sleep with your rifle handy," Jack advised.

"I always do, sir, when I'm out here."

Despite Donnelly's warning, Jack slept soundly that night. He woke with a jerk, aware that something was wrong.

"You are going to die, Colonel Windrush!" the voice came from outside the camp, shouting in Pashto. "Colonel Windrush! Can you hear me?"

Jack lifted his revolver and left the tent. He peered into the dark, seeing nothing except the guard lights around the camp.

"I hear it, sir." Sarsens emerged from his tent in his underwear and carrying a pistol.

"I see you've learned to carry a weapon out here," Jack said.

"Yes, sir." Sarsens stared around. "What's that fellow saying, sir?"

"He's saying that I'm going to die," Jack said.

"Shall I take a patrol out?" Sarsens asked.

Jack shook his head. "He'll have an ambush waiting for us. Sit tight."

"Colonel Windrush!" the voice came again, high-pitched now. "You won't live to see England again, Colonel Windrush!" It ended in the laughter of half a dozen men.

"Go back, Colonel Windrush. Go back to your wife. We'll kill all the Royal Malverns!"

"They're after us, sir," Sarsens said.

"Shall I fire, sir?" Donnelly hefted his rifle.

"No!" Jack said shortly. He saw RSM Deblin and a squad of men standing at attention with their rifles at the ready.

"Give the word, sir, and I'll go after them," Deblin said.

"No. Don't let them unsettle us. Get the men back to bed, RSM." Jack raised his voice. "Everybody get back to bed except the sentries."

Jack waited until the camp settled down. The laughter came again and a parting shout.

"Go home, Colonel Windrush. You will die in the Khyber."

* * *

The following morning, Elliot led them into the Torkrud Valley, where isolated villages sheltered behind mud-and-stone walls within a patchwork of fields. A watchtower dominated each settlement, with armed guards watching the British column march past.

"*Salaam Alaikum!*" Jack shouted to the closest watchman.

The man neither replied nor acknowledged.

The valley was narrow and twisting, with groups of pine trees adding variety to the scenery and a growing number of Pashtuns following the column.

"These lads don't look friendly," Baxter indicated the Pashtun warriors.

"They can't do much against an entire brigade," Jack said

although he agreed. If Batoor supported the British, he should have sent a delegation of welcome before now.

If Batoor decides to oppose us, we'll have to fight our way out against one of the wiliest warriors I've ever met. Despite his earlier warnings to Baxter and Sarsens, Jack touched the butt of his revolver. The valley suddenly seemed oppressive, with the heights frowning down on him and the Afridi horsemen menacing as they gathered on either side of the column.

Did Batoor send these men to intimidate me last night? Has he switched sides? Or is he merely looking after his best interests?

With the column marching slowly, they reached Batoor's village of Torkrud an hour before the sun set.

"Here we are," Elliot said. "All safe and sound. We've shown the flag through the Khyber, and now, Colonel Jack, it all depends on you."

After last night's threats and marching through an unfriendly valley, I don't feel confident of success.

CHAPTER TWENTY-SIX

Batoor's village was more extensive than Jack had remembered, with two towers thrusting upwards from loopholed walls and armed guards on the arched doorway. More armed men peered at the British from the towers, with some levelling jezails or Sniders.

Jack and Elliot reined up a hundred yards outside the gate as a company of mounted Afridis came out to investigate. The leading rider was broad-shouldered, with the end of his turban wrapped over the lower half of his face, so only his eyes showed.

"*Salaam Alaikum.* Pray tell Batoor Khan that Brigadier General Arthur Elliot and Colonel Jack Windrush have come to speak to him." Jack shouted.

"Colonel Jack Windrush?" The leading rider unwrapped his turban and grinned at Jack. "My men have been following your column since Ali Masjid. We knew it was Colonel Windrush but thought it was your brother!" Batoor leaned over and gripped Jack's arm. "Colonel, is it? I am glad the British finally promoted you! And Elliot is a general now!"

"You thought I was William?" Jack said.

Batoor touched the silver-and-ivory hilt of his sword. "I was unsure whether to kill you or not."

Jack glanced at the menacing horsemen. "Is that why you sent your warriors?"

Batoor laughed as though at a great joke. "That's right, Windrush. I've already sent men to warn away Colonel Windrush as a favour to you, my friend!"

"They failed," Jack said dryly.

"So I see, praise be to Allah the all-merciful." Batoor laughed again. "Come into my home and welcome, Windrush and General Elliot. My home is open to you, and your men are free to camp in the valley of the Rahmut Khel." He shouted orders to his men, who turned and rode away, some into Torkrud and others scattering over the valley.

As they entered Torkrud, Jack saw the head of a man on the end of a stake. He looked closer, wondered if it was one of the men who had threatened him the previous evening, and said nothing. Batoor did not accept failure from his warriors.

When the guards at the arched gateway realised that their malik was friendly with the visitors, they smiled. Jack returned the smiles and greetings.

"*Salaam Alaikum*!"

The interior of Torkrud village was no different from a hundred other Pashtun settlements Jack had visited. Houses stood within their private walls, children played in small groups, and animals wandered freely. Batoor had expanded his home and the number of his wives, so their quarters occupied a larger space within its enclosing wall.

"Welcome, my friends," Batoor said.

Melmastia, Jack thought.

The courtyard was more elaborate than on Jack's previous visit, with a fountain playing in the centre and a covered area with Persian and Afghan carpets on the ground.

Batoor summoned servants who brought fruits and bowls of scented water, with a bubbling hookah and a meal of grilled lamb and mantu dumplings under a sea of yoghurt.

"You are my guests," Batoor said as Elliot hesitated. "You are as safe here as you would be at home in Empress Victoria's Great Britain. Maybe safer here, now that William Gladstone is the Prime Minister."

Elliot glanced at Jack as Batoor revealed his knowledge of British politics. "I wonder how many people in Britain could name the Amir of Afghanistan," he murmured.

Once they had eaten, Batoor revealed his curiosity.

"You are always welcome, Windrush. You did not need to bring an army with you. And you, General Elliot, are a friend of Windrush's. Unless you plan to attack the Rahmut Khel, you are also welcome."

Elliot smiled, smoked at the hookah, and stifled his cough. "As a friend of Her Majesty, you will also be welcome at any British base, Batoor Khan."

Jack saw Batoor's expression alter. "Am I a friend of Her Majesty?"

"I certainly hope so," Elliot said.

Batoor listened as Elliot extolled the benefits of friendship with the queen-empress, from security when any of the Rahmut Khel ventured into British territory to trade and free medical attention.

Batoor smoked his hookah, stroked his beard, touched his pearl earring, and said nothing.

Elliot sensed that his negotiations had stalled. "And of course," he said, "there is the gold."

Batoor's face altered slightly. "The gold?"

"Yes, indeed. All the true friends of Her Majesty are entitled to treasure. If the Rahmut Khel agree to keep this section of the Khyber Pass open to trade and travellers and promises not to attack any British merchant or soldier, we will pay an annual subsidy."

Jack watched a shadow pass across Batoor's face. "There is more," Batoor said.

"More?" Elliot asked.

"With the British, there is always something more," Batoor said.

Elliot glanced at Jack before he spoke. "We wish you to support Amir Rahman Khan," he said.

"I know you once wished to be Amir," Jack said quietly, "but now we hope you will be his ally along the Khyber."

Batoor leaned back, surveying his guests. "If I were to accept your subsidy and your offer, I would be tied to the British cause."

"You would be assured of our support," Elliot said smoothly.

"A tribe is attacking me at present," Batoor touched the hilt of his sword. "They have killed my men, stolen away my women and animals and claim some of my lands. Will the British send a punitive expedition against this tribe?"

Jack saw Elliot's expression alter. The British had resolved not to interfere with tribal affairs unless the dispute or raiding spilt into British India. "We cannot do that," Elliot said.

"Not even for a loyal friend of the Queen-Empress?" Batoor asked with a hint of irony.

"We can only interfere if the trouble impinges across the Border or if a tribe attacks British troops."

Batoor tugged at his pearl earring. "Then I wish you farewell, General Elliot. You and your men are safe in my land."

"*Melmastia*," Jack said.

Batoor nodded.

"The second rule of Pashtunwali," Jack murmured. He looked up as a thought struck him. "As *badal* is the first."

Elliot looked at him, frowning.

"Tell me, Batoor, which tribe is attacking you?"

"The Nazar Khel," Batoor held Jack's gaze as if transmitting a silent message.

"I thought the Nazal Khel were well to the south, around Kandahar." Jack had expected the reply. For some reason, he had a vision of Armaghan sitting at Batoor's side, smiling at him.

"They are, but a branch is here. If you recall, Windrush, I have been at feud with them for some years."

"Aye, but you can look after your own," Jack said.

"I could," Batoor said. "After your General Roberts defeated Ayub Khan, Babrakzai Khan and Hyder Ali returned home, with Zamar Khan's lashkar as reinforcements."

"Home?" Jack felt his anger rise at Zamar Khan's name.

"Home to the Bolak Valley, over that range of hills," Batoor indicated the ridge behind Jack. "With Zamar Khan's warriors, the Nazar Khel outnumber me by two to one."

"Zamar Khan killed my nephew," Jack said softly. "He was one of Ayub Khan's supporters."

"*Badal*," Batoor said.

"*Badal*," Jack agreed. He thought of his promise to Helen and again saw Crimea falling slowly with Zamar Khan smiling as he lowered his rifle.

"The British army doesn't follow Pashtunwali," Elliot reminded.

"No," Jack agreed, "but Zamar Khan is one of our principal enemies, and Batoor is a staunch friend. If Zamar and his allies were to overcome Batoor, the Nazar Khel could block the Khyber and cut us off from the Amir in Kabul."

Jack leaned back, waiting for Elliot to make his decision. It was a heavy responsibility, judging whether to lead a British brigade to help in what was essentially a tribal feud. On the one hand, intervention here might trigger a resumption of the war with Afghanistan. On the other, doing nothing could lead to losing a valuable ally and the main route to Kabul.

"You two put me in a quandary," Elliot said.

Jack felt a stab of sympathy for Elliot. *What would I do if I were him? I'd keep my word to Helen.*

Jack shivered. "Sir," he said. "Maybe we don't have to attack the Nazar Khel. Zamar Khan is the problem, not the entire clan. I could lead a small force to kill or capture him."

"No!" Elliot immediately rejected Jack's idea. "The British army does not assassinate individuals."

"It would save more bloodshed," Jack argued.

"No." Elliot mustered a smile. "What would I tell Mary? That I sat tight with an entire brigade while her husband fought with a handful of men? It's out of the question, Jack."

"How many men can you raise, Batoor?" Jack asked.

"Not as many as I could last summer," Batoor admitted. "I lost many in the war."

Elliot began to pace the courtyard, back and forward, as he pondered the problem. "Damn it, Jack, you've put me in a pickle."

Jack nodded. "You can ask Simla, sir," Jack said.

"I'll have to." Elliot came to a decision. "Thank God for the heliograph! Batoor, we'll have your answer before long. Sit tight and keep your men alert."

When they returned to the British camp, Elliot spent a full creative hour writing the signal to headquarters. "There you are, Jack. That's the best I can do. Send that, and it's in God's hands, or Simla's whoever is more important."

"Simla's in this case," Jack murmured.

Jack took a dozen Guides cavalry and a section of the Royals, with a score of Rahmut Khel horsemen to clear the way. He led his signallers to a prominent hill at the foot of the Torkrud valley.

"Establish a signal station up there, boys, and heliograph the garrison at Ali Masjid." From Ali Masjid, the signal would flash from point to point until it reached the British headquarters at Simla.

"Trouble with the Rahmut Khel. Zamar Khan and the Nazar Khel threatening Batoor Khan. Batoor requesting British support. Please advise. Elliot."

It was a short signal that contained the essence of the situation. Hopefully, the powers-that-be in Simla knew that Zamar

Khan and the Nazar Khel had fought beside Ayub Khan at Maiwand.

"Now we wait for the reply." Jack looked around him, with the Khyber Pass like God's sword slash through the wild hills. Out here, it was difficult to think of the soft green slopes of Herefordshire and days spent fishing the slow, cool rivers. Mary seemed far away, and the sound of a coachman's horn or the conviviality of an English inn was a different world.

"Somebody's watching us, sir," Private Cooper, his chief signaller, warned.

Jack brought his mind back to the present. Cooper indicated the slopes on the opposite side of the valley.

"Over there, sir."

Jack focussed his binoculars. "You have good eyes, Cooper." He saw movement on the slopes, then gradually, the shapes became clearer. A column of men, Pashtun warriors, were slowly advancing beneath the skyline up Batoor's valley. Above the column, a small group watched the signallers and their escort.

"Trouble," Jack said. "I'll wager any money these lads are Nazar Khel."

"Maybe so, sir," Cooper said.

Jack saw the column moving steadily up the valley, men on foot on the lower slopes and horsemen above. *We might not have time to wait for Simla's reply.* Jack shouted to the Rahmut Khel riders to identify the moving men.

"Nazar Khel!" the Rahmut men replied at once.

"Inform Batoor!" Jack ordered.

As more of the Nazar Khel headed up the valley, Jack ordered his men to pack up. "If we stay here, the Nazar Khel will cut us off. We'll have to warn the Brigadier."

Jack's evacuation of the signalling position was faster than his arrival as he gathered his men and headed back up the valley. The slope on the far side now seemed alive with men as the Nazar Khel moved up, joining another lashkar that surged over the crest of the ridge further up.

"We're in the middle of a full tribal war." Jack hurried his handful of men up to Torkrud.

"Sir!" Donnelly walked backwards behind Jack with his rifle held ready.

The Nazar Khel had come in force. Thousands of Pashtun warriors filled the slopes, with banners above and the dying sun gleaming on rifle barrels, sword points and steel helmets.

"Glad you're back, Jack," Elliot said calmly. "Take over your regiment, will you? Major Baxter is a trifle agitated."

"Yes, sir."

"Did you get a reply from Simla?"

"Not yet, sir. I thought it best to return here rather than have the Nazar Khel surround us."

Elliot nodded. "This is like old times, Jack. All we need is General Havelock."

"Yes, sir, but you're the general now."

With the Rahmut Khel manning Torkrud's walls, and the Nazar Khel on the slopes opposite, Elliot ordered his brigade into a defensive formation.

This position is like Maiwand all over again. An outnumbered British brigade on the defensive, with a large Afghan army opposite us.

Jack checked his men. He placed them two deep, with the front rank kneeling and the rear rank standing, watching the Nazar Khel across the valley. Elliot had drawn up the brigade in a square, with the artillery at the corners facing the Nazar Khel and the Guides' cavalry and baggage in the centre.

"Now we wait," Elliot said. "If the Nazar Khel attack us, we can retaliate, but until they do, we sit tight."

Zamar Khan had all the patience of his race. As the sun set, his men lit campfires and made no moves to attack the British or Torkrud.

"Don't have pickets outside the lines." Elliot puffed on a cheroot as he watched the flickering campfires. "Keep the men together, with one man in four awake."

Jack agreed. Zamar Khan could have parties of men waiting

to pick off any small British pickets. He did not sleep that night as he patrolled inside the perimeter of the Royals, peering out at the campfires, and wondering what Zamar Khan planned.

"They're very quiet." Major Bryant joined Jack.

"Surprisingly so." Jack had expected the Pashtuns to fire a few shots at the British out of sheer devilment or test the defences. Nothing happened. The Nazar Khel kept perfect discipline.

Once again, Jack was impressed by the ability of British soldiers to sleep under any circumstance. He stepped over sleeping bodies as he walked inside the lines, talking to the men on duty.

"All right, Cooper?"

"Quiet as the grave, sir," Cooper replied. "I'd like to have got Simla's reply, though."

"So would I, Cooper, so would I."

Brotheridge and Hanley stood side by side, staring at the ridge opposite. Both straightened to attention when Jack appeared.

"Stand easy, men," Jack said. "Any sign of life out there?"

"Only the fires, sir," Hanley said.

"Keep alert," Jack said, "and sing out if you see or hear anything at all unusual. It's better to wake the entire camp for a false alarm than to have the Pashtun sneak up on us."

"We will do, sir," Brotheridge spoke for them both.

RSM Deblin was also on patrol, with his khaki uniform immaculate and a Martini under his arm. "Good evening, sir."

"Good evening, RSM. Anything to report?"

"No, sir. It's as quiet as Sunday morning in Ledbury." Deblin remained at attention.

"Very good. Carry on, RSM."

"Yes, sir!" Deblin saluted and marched on, a reassuring presence in the night.

Elliot roused the men an hour before dawn, ensured they were fed and toured the defences. Pashtun *dholak* drums began to throb as the sky lightened and the Nazar Khel's camp awoke. A score of banners lifted to the sky, dim in the half-light, although Jack knew they were green or black.

"What will this day bring, Jack?" Elliot asked. "War or peace?"

"Or neither," Jack said. "The Pashtun are the most amazingly patient people. Zamar Khan could keep his people camped on the hillside for days purely to taunt us into action, then blame British aggression for starting the war again."

"We could withdraw and return to Ali Masjid, or even Peshawar," Elliot said, "which would give them no excuse to attack us."

Jack shook his head. "Aye, maybe so, but that would leave Batoor alone. Whatever happened then, he would never trust the British again, while all of Afghanistan would think we ran away."

Elliot lit two cheroots and passed one to Jack. "We sit tight and see what happens."

Jack looked over to Torkrud, where sentinels paced the walls. He saw Batoor on top of the closest tower, viewing the Nazar Khel.

An hour after dawn, a group of horsemen rode towards the British camp from the Nazar Khel's camp.

"Here we go," Elliot said.

"We'd best go toward them, sir," Jack said. "Meet them halfway so they can't see our defences, although I'd guess they already have a good idea of our numbers and dispositions."

"The crisis is coming to a climax," Elliot murmured, thrusting a cheroot into his mouth. "Come along, Jack, and we'll meet these fellows."

Jack felt a surge of hatred as he thought of Zamar Khan shooting Crimea. *No, I cannot let my personal feelings interfere with my duty.* "As you say, sir." He touched the hilt of the Khyber knife he wore instead of a sabre and headed towards the enemy.

CHAPTER TWENTY-SEVEN

Calling to Colonel Christopher of the Sikhs to join them, Elliot and Jack rode out, with half a dozen Guides cavalry as an escort. The Nazar Khel warriors had halted a quarter of a mile from the British camp and waited on top of some rising ground, enabling them to look down on the approaching British. Two banners floated above the Pashtuns, one green with Persian script in gold and the other black with white writing.

"The middle fellow," Jack murmured to Elliot. "That's Zamar Khan. The tall man at his side, with the eagle's beak of a nose, is Babrakzai Khan. I don't know the others."

Elliot grunted. "We'll see what they want."

"*Salaam Alaikum*," Jack greeted the Pashtuns, examining them minutely. They were dressed like noblemen, and Zamar carried Jack's old Wilkinson Sword sabre at his belt as a trophy of war.

"*Salaam Alaikum*," Zamar replied. Noticing the direction of Jack's gaze, he touched the hilt of the sabre.

"May you never tire," Jack said, tapping the Khyber knife at his belt in return.

"May you never see poverty," Zamar responded.

With the formalities completed, Zamar spoke directly to Elliot, with Jack translating. "The Nazar Khel have come to this valley on private business with the Rahmut Khel. We have not harmed the British since peace was declared."

"I am glad to hear that the Nazar Khel is peacefully disposed towards the British," Elliot said. "I will be equally glad when he takes his warriors back to their home."

"We are in dispute with Batoor Khan," Zamar said. "Our honour is at stake." He faced Jack directly. "Colonel Windrush understands the concept of honour."

"I do." Jack wondered how Zamar had learned of his promotion.

"Then you know that we must observe *badal*," Zamar said.

Jack nodded. "You know I understand Pashtunwali, and *melmastia* can sometimes supersede *badal*. We are Batoor Khan's guests, and as such, we shall fight to defend him." He glanced at Elliot, whose grasp of Pashtu and Pashtunwali was not as comprehensive.

"What did you say?" Elliot asked and nodded when Jack explained. "Yes, follow that through, Jack. We'll try and scare him away."

"Zamar Khan," Jack said, translating into English as he spoke, "we stand shoulder-to-shoulder with Batoor Khan, through *melmastia* and friendship. Any attack on the Rahmut Khel is an attack on us."

Zamar Khan spoke to Babrakzai Khan, who had been a silent spectator, and the two men wheeled their horses and galloped away. Their escort followed a moment later, shouting wild slogans as they rode.

"Now the die is cast," Jack said. "Either we've called their bluff, and they'll return to their own valley, or they'll attack us as well as Batoor."

"We'll sit tight," Elliot said. "I'm not leaving the valley until I know what the Nazar Khel intend."

Twice that day, Jack contemplated riding across to Torkrud to speak to Batoor, but he thought the Khan of the Rahmut Khel had sufficient worries.

"I could lead a party down to the signalling hill, sir," Jack volunteered.

"Not yet," Elliot said. "We'd be tempting Zamar Khan into attacking us. Sit tight."

"As you wish, sir." Jack returned to the Royals. "Right, boys. We're not lounging about another day, enjoying the sunshine. We're gathering rocks today."

"Rocks?" Private Hanley asked.

"That's what the officer said!" Deblin roared. "The colonel wants rocks, so you'll collect rocks!"

Jack sent the men out, two companies at a time, with one company gathering rocks and the other acting as escort. A third company used the stones to build sangars – small, drystone defensive sites – and the others dug trenches. By lunchtime, the Royals had created a rudimentary fortress, which the Sikhs and 113th hastened to emulate.

"That's looking better," Jack said and had his men pace out distances in front of their sangars, placing in stakes every fifty yards.

"These stakes are our range markers," Jack explained. "If the Nazar Khel attack, we'll know the range and adjust our sights accordingly."

In mid-afternoon, Jack sent out working parties to clear any vegetation and trees that might cover an attacker. He gave a hand for a few moments, working in his shirtsleeves as an example to his men.

"Sir." Sarsens puffed up. "The enemy is moving, sir."

"They're only the enemy if they attack us, Sarsens," Jack said.

"Yes, sir." Sarsens pointed across the valley. "The Nazar Khel are leaving their positions, sir."

Jack lifted his binoculars. The Nazar Khel were marching back over the ridge, company by company, heading for the kotal to return to the Bolak valley. The infantry moved first, and then the cavalry as a rearguard. At last, as the evening died, a final group of horsemen stood at the summit of the kotal with a green banner. They stood on the skyline as if they intended the British and Rahmut Khel to see them, and then they disappeared over the far side.

"And that is that," Baxter said. "We scared them away, sir."

"Maybe," Jack said.

That was too easy. I've never known Pashtuns to give up like that.

"What do you think, Jack?" Elliot asked.

"I think I'd like to put a strong picket on the kotal, sir," Jack said. "With a heliograph and limelight to let us know what's happening."

"Company strength, I'd say," Elliot said.

"Yes, sir, and maybe another company halfway down the pass as a reserve."

Elliot nodded. "We'll have a company of the 113th at the head of the kotal and two companies of Sikhs at that dry *nullah* further down."

"And my men?" Jack asked.

"Sorry, Jack. The 113th and the Sikhs are more experienced. I'm keeping the Royals in camp for now."

"They won't get experience sitting behind a row of sangars!" Jack protested.

"And I won't jeopardise my brigade by having untried men posted in a precarious position. That was one of the mistakes Burrows made at Maiwand. I'm sorry, Jack, but that's an order."

Jack bit back his retort. He knew Elliot was correct. The 113th was well trained and experienced in Afghan warfare, while his Royals had only been on the fringes. The Royals were paying for the caution of their previous colonel.

Jack watched as the chosen companies marched out an hour before dusk. Captain Singer of the 113th paused to throw Jack a salute, which he returned with a smile.

"Aren't we involved, sir?" Baxter asked.

"Not this time, Baxter. The brigadier wants us to mind the shop."

"We're good enough to fight now, sir." Baxter understood immediately.

"I know," Jack said. "We'll get our chance, Baxter, don't you fret."

The night was cold, with a northerly wind biting through the thin khaki uniforms. After not sleeping the previous night, Jack slumped on his charpoy as Donnelly took away his tunic to brush and boots to clean.

"Major Baxter will look after the regiment, sir," Donnelly said. "You get some sleep. You look done in."

"Thank you, Donnelly." Jack lay on his side with a hundred ideas for the Royals tumbling through his mind and the wind plucking at the canvas of his tent. He dreamed of Crimea crumpling to the ground and Helen's tormented face as she forced him to promise revenge, and then the noise woke him.

"What's happening?" Jack groped for his boots and tunic. The dark was intense, yet he heard the sounds.

That's gunfire. Where? Who?

"Donnelly! Major Baxter! Bryant! What's happening?" Jack sat up, found his boots, and began to pull them on, swearing. "Where is everyone?"

"I'm here, sir!" Donnelly appeared at the tent flap with a lantern in his hand. "The regiment's all right. The firing is over at Torkrud, sir."

"The devil! Did the Nazar Khel get past our pickets?"

"I don't know, sir. I only heard the firing and saw the muzzle flares at Torkrud." Donnelly stepped aside smartly as Jack rushed outside.

"Stand to! Bugler! Sound the stand to!" Jack peered around in the dark. "Get some light on, for God's sake!"

"Sir!" RSM Deblin came to attention. "There is musketry at Torkrud, sir. None at the kotal picket and none in our lines."

Trust the RSM to know what's happening.

"Thank you, RSM. Stand the men to, call in all our standing

pickets, and arrange an early breakfast. If we have to fight, I don't want the men fighting on an empty stomach."

"Very good, sir!" Deblin saluted again and strode away, bawling orders.

Baxter hurried up with his tunic lopsided and without his sun helmet. "Shall I send the men to the fighting line, sir?"

"Yes, do that," Jack said and watched the initial confusion turn to an organised regiment again as discipline took over.

The firing continued, now intermittent, now furious, with muzzle flares lighting up the darkness around Torkrud. An occasional stray bullet whined overhead. Jack focussed his binoculars on the kotal, looking for signs of a struggle there. The glare of limelight came instead.

"Cooper!" Jack bawled. "Where is Cooper?"

"I see it, sir!" Cooper arrived. "It's a message from the kotal, sir." He intoned the words as the Morse code blinked through the night. "All quiet here. Trouble at Torkrud."

"All quiet there? Zamar Khan must have another way to enter the valley." Jack looked around. "RSM! Have the men had their breakfasts yet?"

"Yes, sir," Deblin said. "They are eating at the firing line."

"Baxter!" Jack shouted. "I want Number One Company kitted out and ready to march. Each man with seventy rounds of ammunition and a full water bottle. No excess kit."

"Very good, sir!" Baxter looked harassed in the growing light.

"Sarsens!" Jack beckoned the young lieutenant to him. "Find the general, give him my compliments and inform him that Number One Company of the Royals is ready to help Batoor Khan." Both men ducked as a shot whined overhead. Jack watched as Sarsens hurried away.

The Royals waited behind the sangars, rifles loaded, waiting for whatever Zamar Khan threw at them. Jack checked his watch. Ten past five. It would be dawn soon. He wished he had grabbed some breakfast himself.

"Here we are, sir." Donnelly appeared at his side. "A hunk of bread and cheese, sir. It's not much."

"But very welcome," Jack said.

"And a mug of tea, sir. I put in plenty of sugar for energy."

"You're a lifesaver, Donnelly."

Jack heard the hammer of hooves and saw a troop of Guides trot towards Torkrud. He toured his regiment, checking the men were in position.

"What if the Paythans come?" Hanley asked.

"Then we shoot the buggers," Brotheridge told him.

"What if there's no officer to give permission? You remember how the last colonel never let us fire without permission?"

"This colonel is different."

Jack paused behind the two men, interested in their opinions.

"So why has he the same name?"

"They're brothers. Shut up and face your front!"

Jack stepped on, peering into the half-dark, waiting for a sudden rush of tribesmen and listening to the crackle of musketry from Torkrud.

"Sir!" Sarsens hurried up. "General Elliot says could you send Number One Company out, sir, liaise with the Guides and see what's happening at Torkrud. The general says that on no account are the Royals to take offensive action, but if the Nazar Khel attack, they may retaliate."

"Thank you, Sarsens," Jack said. "Tell Major Baxter, with my compliments, that I am accompanying Number One Company, and he will take charge of the battalion."

"Yes, sir." Sarsens disappeared again.

I should remain with the regiment, but I cannot delegate such a critical mission to a junior officer. Jack found excuses for accompanying Number One Company.

Captain Smith of Number One Company looked up as Jack joined him. "Sir?"

"We're liaising with the Guides," Jack said. "How's your Pashtu?"

"Basic, sir," Smith admitted.

"Urdu?"

"Only a smattering, sir."

"Come on, then." Jack led them between two sangars and towards Torkrud. Immediately they left the defensive perimeter, the atmosphere changed. Jack could feel the tension in the air.

Smith was a quiet man in his late thirties but seemed capable. He kept his men together, with sections in advance and on each flank, and moved steadily forward.

Jack heard the hooves before the Guides appeared, a dozen bearded men on tall horses looming through the gloom.

"Risaldar!" Jack shouted as the officer halted his men. "What's happening out there?"

"The Nazar Khel have attacked Torkrud, sahib." The risaldar was calm. "They must have come over the ridge by another pass. The Rahmut Khel gave way on the eastern wall, and the Nazar Khel gained a foothold. The fighting is continuing within the village."

"Thank you, risaldar," Jack said. "Please take that information to the general and inform him that I am assessing the situation."

"Yes, sahib." The risaldar hesitated for a second. "Are you the new Colonel Windrush sahib?"

"I am," Jack agreed.

The risaldar saluted with a grin and led his men away. The night seemed lonelier without the Guides for company.

The firing was intense around Torkrud, with men swarming around the walls.

"We are British soldiers!" Jack roared. "We are the Royal Malverns!"

The fading dark allowed Jack to assess the situation. The Rahmut Khel held both towers and much of Torkrud's defending wall, but gunfire and yelling inside told of fierce fighting inside the village.

"What do we do, sir?" Smith asked.

"We halt the men here," Jack said. "Form a defensive

perimeter."

"Are we at war with the Nazar Khel, sir?"

"God knows," Jack replied. "If they attack us, return fire and get back to the camp."

Number One Company formed a rough square, with men kneeling or standing, rifles ready. Jack took a deep breath and checked his revolver. *We're doing no good out here. Either I enter Torkrud, or we return.*

"Captain Smith," Jack said. "I'm going inside Torkrud. If I am not back within the hour, take your company back to camp."

"Very good, sir." Smith did not appear perturbed about Jack's possible demise.

When Jack stepped outside Number One Company's perimeter, he found Donnelly at his back. "What the devil are you doing here, Donnelly?"

"Following you, sir. Mrs Colonel Windrush ordered me to look after you."

Jack sighed. "I remember. Come along then, Donnelly." He knew that approaching a Pashtun fort in the middle of a battle was foolhardy, but he could think of no other way to gather accurate intelligence.

"Windrush!" the booming voice came from the tower above. "I see you!"

Jack halted. "Is that you, Batoor?"

"Who else would it be?" As always, Batoor Khan seemed larger than life. He stood on top of the tower, pulwar in hand, grinning down at Jack. "What are you doing, scurrying around my home?"

"You seem to have some uninvited guests," Jack shouted.

"Not for long," Batoor replied. "Have you come to help us repel them?"

Before Jack replied, he heard an outbreak of gunfire close behind him.

"That's Number One Company," Donnelly said. "They're under attack."

CHAPTER TWENTY-EIGHT

"My men are fighting," Jack shouted to Batoor.

"As are mine!" Batoor lifted a hand in farewell as Jack ran back to Smith's company. He heard the wild shouts above the controlled volley fire of British infantry.

"Allah Akbar! Din! Din!"

"Ghazis." Donnelly pointed to the flicker of white robes. "They've rushed the company."

Jack nodded. Even if Zamar Khan ordered his men not to attack the British, the religious fanatics would grab the opportunity to kill the kaffirs.

Number One Company seemed in no immediate danger. The ghazis were charging one side of the square, pulwars raised and shields covering their bowed heads, and the Royals shot them with precision.

Jack waited until the ghazi's charge lapped away and ran to the square. "Open up, there!"

"Welcome back, sir." Smith was reloading his revolver, thrusting brass cartridges into the chambers. "These fellows saw us and decided to charge. I had to fire back, sir."

"You did right," Jack said. "Now withdraw to the camp, keeping the square intact."

It was a manoeuvre Jack had practised during the winter, with the men moving together as one unit. However, practising with an audience of small boys and moving under fire were two different things.

With their initial assault repulsed, the ghazis had resorted to firing at the square.

"Give them a volley." Smith ignored the shots that buzzed past his head. Jack nodded as one wall of the square dissolved in smoke and flame, with the men reloading as calmly as veterans.

The British marched slowly back to the camp, alternatively firing and moving, with the ghazis threatening from a distance without attempting another charge.

It was full daylight when Number One Company arrived at the camp, with one man slightly wounded. By that time, the Nizar Khel had advanced in force and surrounded Torkrud.

"That's your pups blooded," Elliot said calmly. "Zamar Khan's set the ball rolling, so we can retaliate now."

Jack reloaded his revolver. "Captain Smith did well," he said. "The Nazar Khel are inside Torkrud, but Batoor seems confident about throwing them out again."

Elliot raised his voice. "Gunners! The Nazar Khel attacked our men. Show them our response!"

The artillery had been waiting for the command, for Elliot hardly finished speaking when two guns crashed out, with the shells exploding amid the Nizar Khel.

"Signal to the lads on the kotal to return to camp," Elliot continued. "The rest of us will sit tight until we see what Zamar Khan intends."

"Here they come, now," Jack said as the Nazar Khel changed the direction of their attack. Rather than face Torkrud's walls, they charged at the British camp in a screaming horde.

"Ready, Royals!" Jack ushered Number One Company to their places in the sangars and watched them closely. The Royals still lacked the laconic professionalism of the 113th, but they stood to their posts like soldiers and waited for the Pashtuns to come closer.

"Use the range markers, boys," Jack said. "When they reach five hundred yards, fire."

The Pashtun rushed on, and despite the danger, Jack felt a twinge of admiration for these brave men charging an encampment of trained British soldiers. As the Nazar Khel reached the first of the markers, Jack gave the order.

"At five hundred yards! Fire!"

The first volley thundered out, accompanied by gushing smoke and muzzle flares. The leading Pashtun ranks staggered, but pressure from the rear pushed them on. Some men held up banners, brave invocations to Allah in flowing Persian script.

At 450 yards, Jack shouted again, "Fire!" and a second volley crashed out, felling a score of men. The rest, undaunted, continued, with their faces now visible.

"If they kill me," Hanley said, "you take my kit, Brothers."

Brotheridge worked the underlever of his Martini and thumbed in a cartridge. "And if they get me, take mine, Hanley."

Both men waited for Jack's order before they fired, with the Martinis kicking back viciously. They worked the underlever, thumbed in another Boxer brass cartridge, and returned the rifles to their shoulders, pressing their cheeks against the cool wooden stocks.

"Fire!" Jack shouted again.

Each volley took a more significant toll on the attackers, but the Nazar Khel were much closer now, faces twisted in hatred and naked swords waiting to gut the kaffirs.

"They're getting too close!" a man said, twisting to see behind him. He met Jack's glare and hastily returned to his position.

"The closer they get, the more we kill!" his backmarker said, shoving a cartridge into the breech of his Martini.

"Raise your barrel, Borway!" Jack lifted the muzzle of one of the rear rank men. "You'll take Private Walters' ear off if you fire like that!"

He waited until Borway complied and ordered, "Fire!"

At two hundred yards, the Nazar Khel attack faltered, with more men dropping to the Royals' bullets.

"Fire!" Jack shouted again as the charge ended, and men turned to flee.

"They're running!" Brotheridge jeered. "Come and fight, you cowards!"

"Reload, Royals," Jack said, "and stand fast."

Gunsmoke drifted over the camp as Jack checked his men for casualties. One man held his leg, torn by a stray bullet.

"How many did we kill?" Baxter asked.

"I don't know." Jack disagreed with keeping an account of the enemy's dead as if war was a sport and the tally a game bag. He felt suddenly weary, as he often did after an action.

The reports began to come in as officer after officer came to him. Jack dealt with them all, ordering ammunition for Number Three Company, ensuring the surgeon cared for the wounded man, and advised that somebody trained Private Borway how to fire without endangering his front rank man.

"Colonel Windrush!" Elliot shouted. "Rest your men and replenish their ammunition and water. We leave in two hours."

"Yes, sir!" While Jack had been looking after his regiment, the Nazar Khel had withdrawn. While most moved up the Torkrud valley, a strong stream headed for the kotal, still displaying their banners.

"They're on the run," Baxter said.

"Their heads are still high," Jack said. "We've repelled an unorganised attack on a prepared position, that's all."

"We can't afford to leave Zamar Khan with any power here." Elliot arrived to explain his position. "I intend to follow him to his lair and show him what it means to attack a British camp."

"I'll see if we can get some of Batoor's men to guide us, sir," Jack said.

"No." Elliot shook his head. "I don't want to rely on local help. I want to show that the British army is more than capable of settling matters itself. I'm taking the whole column, colonel, and nobody else."

Elliot's use of the term 'colonel' informed Jack that it was a formal order. "As you wish, sir," Jack said.

* * *

They moved two hours before dusk, with Elliot giving strict instructions for nobody to speak above a whisper or strike a match.

"And no bugle calls; we'll take them by surprise," Elliot decided. "Hit them when and where they least expect it."

From their camp, the British advanced up the kotal. The Royals took the van, with the Sikhs in the centre. The artillery and a minimum of baggage came next, while the 113th acted as the rearguard. The path up the kotal was narrow and slippery, with the men marching in single file and many of the officers leading their horses. Although Jack knew that Tinker was eminently capable of climbing the pass while carrying him, he also dismounted to join the bulk of his regiment.

Create an image. Follow the example of Sir Garnet Wolseley and Bobs.

When they reached the summit of the pass, Elliot left a signalling party with a twenty-man escort.

"I want to keep in touch as much as possible," he explained.

"I agree, sir," Jack said.

"Guides, scout in front," Elliot ordered and waited for the remainder of the column to form eight abreast before marching across a star-lit plateau. Jack had never visited this part of the country and looked around, trying to memorise the landmarks as they walked and stumbled on.

Twice, the risaldar of the Guides returned to make a quiet report to Elliot, and once, they stopped to investigate a crumpled body. The man had been a warrior and lay face down beside the path. The Snider remained strapped across his back and the *peshkabz* dagger at his hip, suggesting he had died alone. No Pashtun would leave such valuable possessions to rust in the hills. Jack passed the Snider to the Sikhs, who used such weapons, thrust the dagger under his belt and walked on.

The night was easing when the column reached the far end of the plateau, where Elliot left another signalling party with a thirty-man escort.

"We're thinning out our column rather a lot," Elliot said, "but it's necessary."

When the column struggled down the opposite side of the kotal, they found themselves at a riverbank. The water rushed by, cold, broad, and fast, slicing through the Bolak valley.

"We'll stop here," Elliot decided. "Two hours' halt for the men to grab some sleep."

Jack nodded, posted pickets from Number Two Company, and lay on the hard ground. With the responsibilities of command heavy in his mind, he lay restlessly, barely dozed and was up long before the allotted two hours was complete.

"Here we are, sir." Donnelly handed over a ration biscuit and a mug of hot coffee. "I used flat stones to shield the fire, sir, and there's a bit of a mist that hid the smoke."

"Thank you, Donnelly." Jack sipped at the coffee, savouring the heat. He lifted a hand to Baxter and ordered that he feed the men before the march resumed.

Elliot consulted his watch, nodded, and the column moved again. The 113th took the van, the Royals the centre and the Sikhs acted as rearguard and baggage guard. Dawn found them following the fast river, with rocky hills on both sides, some with the dark holes of caves cut in the sides.

"Man-made or natural?" Baxter asked.

"Probably a mixture of both," Jack replied.

"I wonder who lives there, sir."

"It could be holy men or wandering shepherds," Jack hazarded.

"Or ghazis waiting to attack us."

Jack grunted. "In Afghanistan, that is always possible."

The Bolak valley was empty, without even a shepherd on the hills. Jack felt that some giant had drawn a giant broom to sweep away all trace of human or domesticated animal habitation. Only the jackals remained, loping behind the column to scavenge for scraps, and the vultures, circling above.

As they marched, the men had to break formation to avoid large rocks that the river had dragged when in spate. They cursed as they slithered on loose stones while the wind carried cold rain that seemed to penetrate their tunics. Jack examined his Royals, comparing them with the gloriously uniformed creatures they had once been. Now they were weather-battered and as ragged as any other British regiment on the campaign.

"Sahib." the Guides' risaldar reined up beside Elliot. "A village is ahead, sahib. We reconnoitred and found it was empty, except for some stores of grain."

"Thank you, Risaldar," Elliot said. "The Nazar Khel must know we are coming. We'll halt there for a while and feed the horses."

As the Guides continued their ceaseless patrolling and the infantry posted strong pickets on the surrounding hills, the bulk of the column settled down. Jack saw a hundred campfires as men boiled water for a meal of meat and potatoes cooked in their dixies.

"The boys looked quite relaxed." Jack accepted one of Baxter's cheroots.

"They look happier here than they did in Kandahar," Baxter said.

Jack exhaled a dribble of blue smoke. "They haven't been tested in battle yet. That is the true measure of a soldier."

Baxter forced a smile while avoiding Jack's eye.

The Guides' risaldar returned an hour later and again spoke to Elliot, who indicated that Jack should join him.

"We're about to have visitors," Elliot said. "I want you to translate for me, word for word and with no comments."

"Yes, sir." Jack already guessed who the visitors were.

"Zamar Khan and Hyder Ali," Elliot said.

"Only two? I wonder where Babrakzai Khan is."

"Watching us, no doubt," Elliot said.

"No doubt, sir," Jack agreed.

Badal! I promised Helen Badal! Jack closed his eyes, seeing Zamar Khan press the trigger and Crimea crumple to the ground. He fingered the *pesh-kabz* at his belt. It was a dagger designed explicitly for thrusting, and Jack imagined himself ramming it into Zamar Khan's chest, twisting the blade and watching the malik of the Nazar Khel die at his feet.

"Are you all right, Jack?"

"I'm all right." Jack removed his hand from the dagger hilt and mounted Tinker.

The Guides acted as an escort for the Nazar Khel delegation, with Zamar Khan riding in the centre under a green banner and Hyder Ali slightly behind him.

Jack sat on Tinker to Elliot's left, with Major Burridge and Captain Sinclair of the Guides on the right. The remainder of the Guides stood nearby, partly as a show of respect to the visitors and partly as a security measure.

After the usual introductions, Zamar Khan asked politely why Elliot had shot at his men and now invaded the Bolak valley with an army.

"Your men attacked mine," Elliot said, "and they attacked Batoor Khan, who is our ally. The British always help their friends."

Zamar Khan shook his head in denial. "My men did not attack yours, Elliot sahib. The men who attacked were ghazis, who are a law to themselves. Nobody can control the ghazis when they see an unbeliever, a kaffir."

Elliot smiled. "In that case, Zamar Khan, you should not have included them in your army. There is also the matter of the livestock your men stole from the Rahmut Khel. Batoor Khan estimates you owe him a thousand rupees for the sheep."

Zamar spread his arms wide. "I do not have such a sum, Elliot sahib. I am just a poor farmer from Helmand, visiting my cousin in the Bolak valley."

"Sir!" Donnelly ran up to Jack and saluted.

"Not now, Donnelly!"

"It's important, sir!"

Jack swore. He knew that Donnelly would not interrupt him for anything trivial, so he pulled his horse away and withdrew a few steps. "What's the matter, Donnelly, and it had better be important!"

"Sir, Cooper the signaller says he's got a heliograph message. Babrakzai Khan and the Nazar Khel are attacking Torkrud again."

Jack stiffened. "Are they, by God? They keep us talking here while they go behind our back. Thank you, Donnelly."

Elliot frowned as Jack returned. "What the dickens?"

Jack explained what had happened.

"The dirty blighters! No wonder the valley was empty." Elliot smiled at Zamar Khan. "It seems that I was mistaken, Zamar. I thought you were a man I could trust, and all the while, you have planned to attack my ally."

Zamar shouted a command, and a hundred horsemen rose from a *nullah* behind him, drew their pulwars and charged at the small British party. The Guides dashed forward to intervene, and the two forces clashed with the clatter of swords and bang of carbines. However, the odds were too much even for the Guides, and the Nazar Khel horsemen pushed them aside.

"Elliot!" Jack grabbed Elliot's bridle and pulled him away as Hyder Ali slashed at him with his pulwar. The blade missed Elliot but caught his horse, which screamed but kept moving.

"Would you, you bastard!" Jack drew his Khyber knife and

thrust, but the blade was shorter than his sabre and missed by an inch.

Zamar Khan swung at Jack, his face twisted, and Jack swerved away, parried with his knife, and thrust in his spurs.

"Come on, Elliot!"

An elderly Pashtun unhorsed Major Burridge, who sprawled on the ground until Sinclair of the Sikhs put out a hand.

"Up you come, Burridge!"

Burridge grabbed Sinclair's hand and swung himself up behind the saddle.

Jack hauled Donnelly onto Tinker, and they staggered back, with a company of Sikhs running towards them. When the Sikhs halted to fire a volley, the Nazar Khel horsemen wheeled around and fled, with Sikh bullets whizzing around them.

"*Shabash* the Sikhs!" Jack roared as he reached the British lines.

"They would have assassinated all the leadership at a stroke," Elliot said. "What a devious, underhanded, clever man Zamar Khan is. He would do well at Westminster."

The Nazar Khel had withdrawn, leaving the Bolak valley empty. Bare rocks and patches of scrubby grass wilted under the rising sun.

"What now, sir?" Burridge asked.

Jack took a deep breath. *I should have killed Zamar Khan. I let you down, Helen.*

CHAPTER TWENTY-NINE

Elliot barely hesitated. "We promised Batoor Khan our help, and by God, we'll keep our word. Colonel Windrush, take two mountain guns, three companies of the Royals and three of the 113th. Advance up this valley and destroy anything that fights back."

"Yes, sir," Jack said. "I'll take Number One, Two and Three companies of each regiment."

"Major Burridge, you will bring the rest of the 113th with me. Major Baxter, you will command the remainder of the Royals and also accompany me. Colonel Sinclair, I'll need you and all your Sikhs." Elliot looked around. "I'm taking all the Guides and the remaining four screw guns. We'll force march to Torkrud."

"We might not get there in time," Baxter warned.

"Then we must waste not a minute," Elliot said. "Windrush, organise your men."

* * *

Jack began his march up the Bolak valley with a composite force of 480 infantry and two screw guns. He did not know how many of the Nazar Khel opposed him or the precise geography of the valley but was aware of how dangerous Zamar Khan could be.

Without cavalry, Jack could either advance cautiously or try a bold approach. He looked at his men. After years with the 113th, he knew them well, but the Royals were still a little hesitant.

"Captain Singer." Jack made his decision. "Take Number One Company of the 113th as the advance guard, skirmish ahead."

"Yes, sir." Singer shouted orders.

"Lieutenant Sarsens, I want you to patrol the right flank with Number One Company of the Royals."

With his dispositions made, and the river guarding his left flank, Jack pushed along the valley. He drove his men hard, searching for Zamar Khan's cavalry, keeping patrols around the main column, securing every ambush point before moving. They found two small villages, both abandoned, with food cooking on the fires and several fowls running around.

"Look here, lads!" Private Hanley shouted as they entered the second village. "This house is full of walnuts."

Usually, Jack took a firm line on looting, but he turned a Nelsonian eye after Zamar Khan's duplicity. When they left the village, many of the men carried haversacks bulging with walnuts. Others had newly slaughtered fowls hanging from their belts.

Jack ordered the towers and outer walls of the villages destroyed to prevent the Nazar Khel from holding them against the British.

"They'll know we're coming now," Bryant said as the smoke coiled skywards.

"I suspect they already know everything about us," Jack replied.

The next settlement was also deserted, except for an old woman who looked astonished to see strangers. When she pleaded for alms, half a dozen soldiers immediately gave her handfuls of walnuts, and one young man laid his chicken at her feet.

"That's probably more food than she's seen all month," Captain Singer said.

"Maybe so." Jack stared ahead, where the valley stretched between seemingly endless heights. "I feel that Zamar Khan is trying to draw us into a trap."

"Sir!" Sarsens ran to Jack and saluted with more energy than precision. "There's a large village ahead, sir, and it appears to be fully garrisoned."

"Thank you, Sarsens." Jack rode to a slight rise and focussed his binoculars. The village sat on a rocky hillock behind small fields. Two tall towers glowered over the valley, while a loopholed mud wall acted as protection, with the usual green and black banners hanging limp in the clear air. As Jack scanned the walls, he saw scores of men waiting and the flash of late afternoon sunlight on metal.

"Halt the men here and place in a defensive position, Bryant." Jack tried to appear calm, although his heart rate had begun to accelerate. "I'll ride forward and see what's to-do."

"Take an escort, sir," Singer advised.

"Not this time," Jack said and kicked in his heels. He felt surprisingly lonely as he crossed the open space between his men and the walled village. He had heard that a boxer in the ring was the loneliest person in the world, but at that moment, he'd willingly have swapped places.

Nonsense! Jack told himself. *I'm a lieutenant colonel with a regiment to command. It's the highest position I've ever held.*

"*Salaam alaikum!*" Jack shouted when he was thirty yards away. A dozen men crowded the top of the tower, with another score ranged along the wall. Nobody replied by word or gesture.

"I have come to speak to Zamar Khan," Jack said.

One of the warriors lifted a jezail to his shoulder and aimed it at Jack, with the long barrel steady in his grip.

"Tell him that Colonel Jack Windrush wishes to speak to him." Jack tried to ignore the jezail. "Tell him that unless he responds within half an hour, I will bombard and capture his fort and raze his valley."

That was a bold statement for a man commanding fewer than five hundred infantrymen and two small screw guns.

When the jezail man shifted his weapon slightly, Jack decided he had spent sufficient time negotiating. "Twenty-eight minutes," he said, wheeling round his horse. Jack felt even more vulnerable with his back to the fort but refused to move at more than a walk. He heard the resounding thud of the jezail and braced himself for the agony of a bullet, but the shot was wide, burrowing into the ground two feet from Tinker's hooves.

That was a warning shot to speed me on my way. Jack glanced at his watch and moved on.

Singer greeted him anxiously. "They fired at you, sir," he said.

"They missed." Jack tried to sound laconic. "I gave them thirty minutes to reply. I want the guns aimed at the tower and the men in a square. Zaman Khan will attack as soon as we begin to fire."

As before, Jack had the men build simple sangars, which kept them occupied as the minutes ticked away.

"Sir," Singer pointed above where the vultures were gathering, waiting for fresh meat.

"I see them," Jack said. He faced Lieutenant Symington of the artillery. "Are you ready to fire?"

"Ready, sir."

Jack checked his watch. Five minutes to go and no sign from the village. Either Zamar Khan was utterly confident of his strength, or he enjoyed playing brinkmanship.

"Common shell," Symington said. "Aim for the centre of the tower." He checked each gun, adjusting the sights of the second.

"Two minutes." Jack held the watch in his hand as the minute hand slowly closed on the appointed time.

"Ready, lads," Symington whispered, rechecking the guns. Jack noticed dark sweat patches beneath the man's arms and in the small of his back. More vultures circled above. Kerswell of the Royals swore as he dropped a rock, with the resulting clatter seeming to resound across the valley. RSM Deblin glowered at him without speaking.

When the minute hand marked the thirty-minute deadline, Jack closed the watch case and placed it inside his tunic. "Fire."

Both guns roared together, and Jack saw the orange flower of the shell bursts at the base of the tower.

"Keep firing," Jack said. "We'll pound them for an hour or so."

"We only have fifty rounds common shell, four star shells, and thirty shrapnel," Symington warned.

Jack nodded, aware he might need the guns if Zamar Khan attacked his position. "Very well. Use fourteen rounds common."

He watched as the shellfire hammered the tower, with pieces of masonry flying in the air with each round. After ten minutes, the officer sounded the cease-fire, and quiet descended on the valley. The gun smoke drifted over the British position, acrid, biting at noses and eyes.

Jack lifted his binoculars. There was no sign from the village, no eruption of screaming ghazis or wild charge of cavalry. "I'm going forward," he said. "Take over here, Bryant."

"I'll come with you, sir," Donnelly said. "I don't trust these people."

Jack's men waited with the officers ordering them to continue building defences. Smoke from the screw guns drifted across the valley as the dust settled on the village. The Pashtuns remained quiet, without even a marksman trying his luck.

The shellfire had virtually destroyed the tower and the surrounding walls, tearing holes that a horse could ride through. The top half of a man lay on the ground, shredded below the waist, and other equally gruesome fragments lay scattered among the debris.

"I can't see any movement," Jack said.

"There, sir." Donnelly indicated a gap at the foot of the wall. "It's a woman."

Again? Does Zamar Khan always abandon his women?

For a moment, Jack thought the woman in the burka was Zufash, but she was much older and spoke in a croaking voice when Jack asked who she was.

"They left me here to die," the woman said. "They told me the feringhees will cut my throat."

"Not today, grandmother," Jack said. "Where have all the men gone?"

"Away. They've gone away," the woman said.

"Watch her," Jack said to Donnelly. "I'll check inside the village."

As he suspected, the village was empty. This time, even the fowls had left. "We'll sleep here tonight," Jack decided. "It's more secure than the open valley."

Jack posted pickets on the walls, alternating the Royals and 113th, so the rival regiments grew accustomed to one another. The moon rose, cold and stark, casting shadows onto the houses below as jackals prowled around. Darkness magnified the surge of the nearby river, so the sound seemed to dominate the valley.

What is best to do? Jack asked himself that night. *Do I lead my men onwards into this valley, with the possibility of an overwhelming attack as at Maiwand? Or should I withdraw and allow Zamar Khan to escape?*

Even at night, the hills seemed oppressive, as though they leered at the British presence and resented the feringhees in their country. *That's nonsense;* Jack shook away the fancy. *These mountains were here for thousands of years before the Pashtuns. They are only lumps of rock, inanimate, without feelings.*

"It's eerie here." Hanley gripped his Martini tightly, peering over the wall. "I don't know what's worse, having a thousand screaming Afghans charging at you or when you can't see anybody."

Brotheridge grunted. "It's worse when you can't see anybody because you know they're there, watching and waiting."

Jack agreed. He preferred to see his enemy. The Pashtun were masters at psychological warfare; they had the patience of Job, able to wait for days to take a single shot at a British soldier. Jack knew they were out there, beyond the shadows, waiting their chance, playing the cat and fiddle with British nerves, using the land and the night as weapons.

By God! I can play that trick as well as Zamar Khan. I drilled the mantra into the Royals' officers: mystify, mislead, and surprise the enemy. I will not sit back and allow Zamar Khan to take the initiative.

"RSM Deblin!" Jack only touched Deblin's shoulder before the man awoke. Jack half expected the RSM to sleep at attention, wearing his dress uniform and his boots polished to a sheen.

"Sir?" Deblin blinked himself awake.

"Wake the men, RSM! But keep them quiet. We're on the march."

"Yes, sir." Deblin was too good a soldier to ask questions. He rose at once.

The officers were less amenable, with only Sarsens alert on Jack's touch. *You've grown up, son. You've got potential if Afghanistan doesn't kill you, as it has killed so many of our best men.*

Grumbling under their breath, unshaven and bad-tempered, the infantry formed up within the village. Above them, the sentries continued their endless pacing until Jack called them down.

"We're moving out," Jack told the assembled men. "Follow me and don't speak. No pipes, no lights and no noise." He led them out the second gate and up the valley, hearing the tramp of boots behind him. For once, he did not post an advance guard. He kept his men together and marched on.

I don't know what I'm looking for, but I know that Zamar has something planned.

After ten minutes, the men were back into the routine of marching, following the gleam of moonlight on the river, listening to the maniacal call of jackals and the hoot of night-hunting birds.

"Halt!" Jack held up his hand, and the column shuffled to a halt, with a few muttered curses as men banged into each other in the dark. "Wait here." He walked forward, careful of each footstep, listening intently. He was unsure what was wrong, aware it was more instinct than sound that made him wary.

No, it wasn't instinct. It was experience. I saw something ahead. What was it?

The jackal called again, sending a chill down Jack's spine. A cloud passed over the moon, blotting out what light there was, and Jack sunk to a crouch.

Light. I saw moonlight reflecting on something. It was not a wet rock, so there's something ahead.

Jack took another step, placing his foot carefully on the ground. He knew Donnelly was behind him.

A slant of wind shifted the cloud, allowing a sliver of moon to appear. Jack studied the valley ahead, looking for anything out of the ordinary.

There it is again, a definite gleam of moonlight on metal. Jack halted, listening again. He heard the soft slither of feet on the ground, the rustle of clothing and the rattle of a loose pebble.

Stopping, Jack moved back, with Donnelly at his side, rifle ready. A shaft of moonlight caught Donnelly's face, showing the high cheekbones and square, determined chin. Jack gestured backwards, and they returned to the British position, still wary, expecting an attack.

"Form a firing line," Jack whispered when he returned to his men. "Quietly as you can! Four men deep, with flanking companies facing at right angles."

The training paid off as his composite force formed a rough horseshoe, moving in the shifting dark. Men obeyed without question, trusting their comrades, putting their faith in their officers and Jack.

They waited, kneeling or standing, hands clutching their

Martinis, listening to the gurgle of the river as the chill Khyber wind cut at their faces. Jack ordered two gaps in the line and placed his screw guns there. "One round, star shell," he said.

Jack pulled his revolver from its holster. He was certain he had heard a Pashtun lashkar approaching, but every passing moment increased his doubt. He counted to fifty, looking ahead, feeling his mouth dry.

"Artillery," Jack murmured. "Number One gun, fire!"

The gunners had been waiting for the order. The roar of the gun shattered the silence, and two seconds later, the star shell exploded in the air, five hundred yards in front of the British position.

"Dear God!" Singer said.

"*Az Barae Khoda,*" – "for God's sake," Jack echoed.

Pashtuns filled the valley a few hundred yards ahead of the British position. Jack could not calculate the numbers in the dark as the star shells illuminated a mass of startled men.

"Fire!" Jack shouted. "Five hundred yards range! Fire!"

The first British volley was slightly ragged as men recovered from their surprise and blinked in the sudden light. The second volley was better aimed and more precise, and then the infantry settled down to controlled firing, loading, and firing again.

The Nazar Khel surged forward. Taken by surprise, Zamar Khan had no opportunity to organise them, so they charged without formation, depending on numbers and ferocity to break the British line. Their yelling rose high in the air, filling the Bolak valley, echoing from the rugged mountains on either side.

"Keep your rifles down!" Deblin snarled. "You can't miss if you shoot ahead!"

Staggered by the initial volleys, the Nazar Khel recovered and charged again until Symington ordered case shot. Two volleys of one hundred and eight bullets created carnage in the advancing ranks and, followed by steady volleys, broke the Pashtun charge.

"Bayonets!" Jack ordered and heard the evil snick as

hundreds of men fitted the eighteen-inch-long triangular bayonets into their sockets. The bayonets had no other function than to kill. They could not be used as knives to cut firewood or for any other useful purpose.

"Remain in formation," Jack ordered, "slow march forward." In daylight, he could have unleashed his men to complete the defeat of the Nazar Khel. In the dark, in territory the enemy knew, such a move would be unwise.

When he neared the Nazar Khel casualties, Jack warned his men to be careful. "Even wounded Pashtuns can be dangerous. Each man look after his neighbour, and if an injured man attacks, don't hesitate to kill him." It was an ugly thing to say, but that was the reality of war out here. Soldiers had to cast aside the supposed traditional values of fair play and compassion when dealing with people who would sneer at such concepts.

They moved slowly forward, stepping across the dead and badly wounded. Twice, Jack heard curses and shots and knew men were heeding his advice.

"Sarsens!"

"Sir!" The lieutenant was breathing heavily, perhaps reliving the horror of Maiwand, as if any battle, win or lose, did not provide sufficient horror for anybody's lifetime.

"Scout ahead. The enemy may be forming up again."

Jack did not expect Zamar Khan to give up after only one reverse. The words of Jack's military mantra pounded in Jack's head.

Never leave your enemy a moment to gather himself again, but fall on him, pursue him to his utter destruction.

"Increase the speed, boys!" Jack ordered. The moon was invisible now, hidden behind the mountains as it continued its circuit of the Earth. Jack checked his watch. Four in the morning. It would be dawn in two hours.

The first sign of renewed resistance came from a scatter of long-range shots.

I thought it was too quiet.

CHAPTER THIRTY

"Extended order! Volley fire by sections! Target the muzzle flashes!" Jack gave rapid orders, ensuring that a dozen Martinis hammered every enemy that fired. He continued the advance, expecting the Nazar Khan resistance to stiffen as he moved up the valley.

When a score of shots came from a specific location, Jack ordered the guns into action and blanketed the area with common shell and then a couple of volleys of musketry.

By dawn, Jack had advanced to the head of the valley, where a village stood on a small knoll. When the artillery fired a star shell, Jack saw a dozen flags flying above the walls and a single squat tower.

"Artillery, give them four rounds," Jack ordered.

"We're running low on ammunition," Symington warned.

Jack nodded. "Keep six common and two case shot in reserve for emergencies."

He watched the shells explode, with the resulting rising cloud of smoke and dust, and then the Pashtun attacked. They came from the hill slopes on the right, erupting from behind rocks and *nullahs*, the white-robed ghazis in a solid mass and tribesmen spread out under their green or black banners.

"There's thousands of them!" Hanley shouted.

Jack agreed. He estimated two thousand warriors were charging at his less-than-five hundred men. Zamar Khan must have mustered every available warrior he had in this last throw of his dice.

"Artillery," Jack said. "Pick your targets!" He knew the artillery officer did not need his advice.

By now, the men of both Jack's regiments were veterans. They fired coolly, sending volley after volley into the screaming, charging mass.

"The bastard's jammed!" Brotheridge and Hanley were at the extreme right of the Royals' ranks, with men of the 113th on their left. Brotheridge swore at his Martini and stepped back to clear the jam, leaving Hanley without a rear-rank man.

As Brotheridge struggled with his rifle, O'Hara, the private of the 113th on his right, experienced an identical jam. The musketry eased, temporarily weakening that section of the line. Simultaneously, a mullah lifted his green flag and led a charge of ghazis.

"*Allah il Allah!*" The ghazis ran on, ignoring their casualties, and crashed into the vulnerable section of the British line, slashing with their pulwars at the desperately struggling British soldiers.

Jack saw the line bulge inward as men resorted to bayonets, rifle butts, fists, and boots to try and hold the charge. A ghazi slammed his shield into Brotheridge, knocking him down, and lifted his sword to finish the job. Brotheridge sprawled on the ground, dazed, unable to defend himself.

"Brothers!" Hanley shouted as he parried the groin stroke of a ghazi with his rifle. He twisted around, as concerned for his companion as he was for himself.

Jack aimed his revolver, shooting the nearest ghazi. He saw the man fall, then turned towards Hanley. Crozier of the 113th was there first, thrusting out his rifle to block the ghazi's blow, then turning the bayonet and slicing. The point of the blade ripped through the ghazi's robes, opening up a long wound in the man's side.

"*Allah Akbar*!" the ghazi yelled, ignoring the blood that poured from his injury. He recovered his sword and lunged at Crozier, screaming. By that time, Brotheridge had risen from the ground. He jumped on the ghazi's back, grabbed his beard and hauled back his head. Crozier poised his bayonet, jammed it into the ghazi's stomach, twisted the blade and dragged it out.

Brotheridge and Crozier glared at each other, panting.

RSM Deblin lifted Hanley's rifle, cleared the jam, and handed it back. "Get back into line, Brotheridge. We've not won this battle yet!"

Beside Crozier, Todd blocked the upward thrust of a Khyber knife and swung the butt of his rifle into the ghazi's jaw while Kerswell leaned across and shot the man.

"You lads of the 113th need the Royals!" Kerswell said.

Todd spat on the ground, glaring, and slashed his bayonet across the throat of the next Ghazi.

"Bloody peacocks!"

"Bloody Baby Butchers," Kerswell rejoined.

Jack fired automatically, shooting at the ghazis who had penetrated the line. Private Barton lay dead with his head split open, and Jenks of the 113th was reeling back, covered in blood. Jack grabbed Barton's rifle, fired into the mass, and stepped into his place.

"Close up, lads! RSM Deblin! Make sure there are no more ghazis behind the line!" He lifted Barton's haversack, grabbed a handful of cartridges, and reloaded, surprised that his hands were steady.

Donnelly was at his side, firing and loading with the calm professionalism of a lifelong soldier as men of the Royals and 113th rushed back into line.

"Push them back!" Jack knew it was not a colonel's job to stand in the firing line and glanced about him. The initial rush of ghazis had eased, and the line had stabilised. Jack stepped back, retaining hold of the rifle. He noticed that the Royals and the 113th were mixed at this point, standing shoulder to shoulder against a common enemy. Todd knelt, with Kerswell as his rear-rank-man.

"Dooley bearers! Look after Jenks! Don't stop firing!"

The British fired another volley, which slammed into the Nizar Khel.

That was the crisis of the battle. Never leave your enemy a moment to gather himself again, but fall on him, pursue him to his utter destruction.

"Advance!" Jack ordered. "Push them back!"

That charge of the ghazis was the Nizar Khel's last surge. Now they began to withdraw, but Jack was determined to end the campaign. "Fire!" he yelled, keeping pace with his men. "Fire and advance!"

Jack followed the Nazar Khel, with the artillery pounding any sizeable group and the infantry using musketry and bayonet against individuals who fled or tried to fight.

When one group ran to the riverbank and crammed into rafts, the artillery waited until the rafts were well onto the river before firing their last case shot, followed by common shell. Jack watched as one raft overturned, and the case shot turned the other into a floating abattoir. Warriors struggled in the fierce current, drowning before the eyes of the British soldiers.

Most of the Nazar Khel engaged in a running retreat, waiting behind makeshift sangars and isolated rocks to fire at Jack's men. When the Nazar Khel held a strongpoint, the Royals feinted a frontal attack while the 113th came in from the flanks to winkle out them out. The result was hand-to-hand butchery, and the Nazar Khel survivors fled to their next defensive position. Twice Pashtun cavalry formed, but the narrowness of the valley was not in their favour, and Symington's artillery scattered them. When Zamar Khan organised a more formidable resistance in a mud-walled enclosure, the screw-guns dropped shells within the walls, and Jack sent his men forward under cover of the bombardment.

"That's our last shell, sir," Symington reported.

"Thank you, Symington." Jack shielded his concern, feeling relief as the Nazar Khel broke, running across the hillsides without looking back.

"Sir." Singer was out of breath and streaked with powder smoke, "permission to chase them, sir?"

Until that point, Jack had held his men under tight control, so they advanced as a disciplined unit. Now that the enemy had scattered, he saw no reason to allow any to escape.

"Granted," Jack raised his voice. "Number One Company of the Royals, remain to guard the guns. Cooper, you and the signallers, remain with me. The rest, general advance!" He saw the disappointment cross the faces of Number One Company as the remainder surged forward to hunt down the enemy. "It's all right, boys, we're taking over the village. You'll have whatever food you can find."

And whatever loot you can pick up, but that's unofficial.

Leaving Bryant and the infantry to mop up the remnants of Zamar Khan's army, Jack retraced his steps to the village. The artillerymen treated their guns like children, fussing over them and cleaning them with cloths and oil while Number One Company explored.

"The Paythans might have left some women behind," Kerswell said hopefully.

"Nah," an anonymous voice said. "They heard you was coming and hid up in the caves."

"Cooper!" Jack ordered, "Send a message that we have defeated Zamar Khan and scattered his army.

"Very good, sir." Cooper immediately began work, flashing the signal to the posts Jack had left further down the valley. He reported to Jack fifteen minutes later. "A signal from General Elliot, sir. He's relieved Torkrud and pushed out the enemy, and

Babrakzai Khan is dead." He saluted belatedly, "and Simla has granted permission for our attack."

"Well, that's a relief." Jack had forgotten about Simla. "Go and find a comfortable billet for you and your men, Cooper."

"Yes, sir. Thank you, sir." Cooper saluted again and withdrew.

Jack checked his revolver, found it empty and sighed. He had fired all his cartridges. *Thank goodness the fighting is over.* He suddenly felt incredibly weary. He had not slept properly for days and had fought skirmishes and battles throughout the Afghan war. He leaned against a compound wall and closed his eyes.

Dear God, I hope this is the last campaign of this war. I don't have the strength for another.

"Sir?" Donnelly was at his side at once. "Are you all right, sir?"

"Yes." Jack opened his eyes. "Find us a decent billet, will you, Donnelly? We'll rest here for a bit before we return to Torkrud." *I can rely on Bryant to finish off the Nazar Khel.*

"Yes, sir." Donnelly hurried away with his rifle over his shoulder. Stocky rather than tall, he looked every inch a typical British soldier, adaptable, foul-mouthed when with his peers, callous against the enemy yet capable of surprising kindness. Jack watched Donnelly disappear around a corner and closed his eyes.

Sleep. I need sleep.

"Colonel Jack Windrush."

Jack opened his eyes.

Zamar Khan stood before him with his head on one side. His turban was ripped, and blood soaked his left arm.

"Zamar Khan," Jack dragged himself back to full consciousness.

"Who are you, Colonel Windrush," Zamar Khan asked. "You granted *melmastia* to my daughter yet defeated my armies. You showed notions of Pashtun honour while fighting for the British. Where does your loyalty lie?"

"I've been asked that before." Jack was not sure if he were dreaming or awake, talking so openly to a professed enemy. He knew that Zamar Khan was an honourable man by his code.

Where does my loyalty lie? Am I Indian or British? I have blood from both, and although my culture is entirely British, I understand the Pashtun way of life. Even if I accept myself as British, do I belong to the Royal Malverns or the 113th? Helen or Mary? Good God, do I even have to ask that?

Jack realised that Zamar Khan was staring at him with his head still to one side and a quizzical expression on his face.

"You saved my daughter, Colonel Windrush," Zamar Khan said, "but one of my sons died at Maiwand and another in our battle this morning, along with Hyder Ali, my cousin."

Jack knew what that meant. "You killed my nephew after Maiwand," he said. "He was the last man standing outside the enclosure."

Zamar Khan smiled. "He was a brave man. It was an honour to kill him."

"I have sworn to kill you, Zamar," Jack said. "*Badal.*"

"And I must kill you for the same reason," Zamar Khan sighed. "In other circumstances, Colonel Windrush, we might have been friends." He drew Jack's Wilkinson Sword sabre from its scabbard and stepped back.

Jack expected the sudden rush and had his Khyber knife ready to parry. Zamar had the advantage of a longer blade, but Jack knew the Pashtun's wounded left arm must weaken him. The sabre hissed down, and Jack blocked, with the power of Zamar's blow forcing him back.

Zamar attacked again, using the length of the sabre to keep Jack moving, dodging the controlled, deadly swings.

Twice Jack lunged forward, only for Zamar to match his move with a quick withdrawal and a sudden thrust forward. They fought in silence except for an occasional grunt or gasp.

Jack circled left, forcing Zamar to guard his weakened left arm, watching the Pashtun's eyes as much as his hands and feet.

I've fought more skilled men, but none so brave. Judging by the amount of blood Zamar is losing, he should have collapsed long ago.

Jack began to back away, forcing Zamar to use more energy in following, quickening the rate of his heart, pumping more blood from his wound.

"Sir!" Donnelly stood at the side of a house with his Martini poised. "Move to your right, and I'll peg him!"

Both Jack and Zamar ignored the interruption. A moment later, Zamar stumbled as the loss of blood took effect. Jack rushed forward, only for Zamar to flick up the point of his sword, catching Jack on his forearm.

"*Badal!*" Jack shouted and thrust his Khyber knife deep into Zamar's stomach, ripping upwards in a stroke he knew was fatal.

Zamar fell without a word. As the Pashtun malik lay at Jack's feet, Jack could only see Helen's eyes, implacable because of Crimea's death.

"Rest easy, Zamar Khan," Jack said, retrieved his old sabre, and collapsed.

CHAPTER THIRTY-ONE

They sat in Batoor's courtyard in Torkrud, with the pleasant tinkle of the fountain a musical background.

Batoor passed over the hookah. "We've done well, Windrush. My enemies are defeated, and you revealed yourself to be a true Pashtun beneath your British façade." Batoor grinned and touched his pearl earring. "All you need is Durrani blood, and you can try for the throne."

"Jack Windrush, Amir of Afghanistan?" Jack shook his head. "I can't see it, Batoor. What would Mary think?"

Batoor bit into a peach. "Mary would find you half a dozen young wives so she could order them around and live a life of indolence and luxury."

Jack laughed. "I can't see Mary doing that. It's a nice idea, though." He used the hookah for a moment, then lay back and became more serious. "Will your neighbours turn against you for helping the British?"

Batoor shook his head. "I wasn't helping the kaffirs. They were helping me, and one of them was following Pashtunwali." He finished his peach and tossed the stone to a servant. "As a Muslim malik, I am titled as a king, but am only first among equals. I will sweep the unbelieving pork-eating feringhees into the sea if I get the chance, but as I temporarily needed their help, I had to treat with them."

"I see." Jack trusted Batoor more than any man except Elliot, but he understood his point of view. "I'll remember that the next time there's trouble along the Khyber."

Batoor threw a massive arm around Jack, "and I got another wife as well as gold from the British."

"Zar, zan, and zamin," Jack murmured. "Gold, women or land."

"That is so, Windrush. You haven't seen my new wife, have you?" Batoor clapped his hands to summon a servant. "Bring my new wife," he ordered.

Jack knew that Batoor was treating him as a family member by introducing him to his wife. He had only minutes to wait before a woman glided towards him, shrouded head to foot in a black burka.

"Here she is," Batoor said. "Allah has granted me the most beautiful woman in creation."

"I am sure she will be," Jack said.

"This man, Jack Windrush, is a friend," Batoor announced, "so close a friend that he is family. You may reveal yourself to him."

The woman threw off the burka and smiled at Jack. From the top of the *shal* that covered her head to the sandals on her feet, she was, as Batoor claimed, beautiful. Her Pashtu clothes of *partug* trousers, a long-sleeved dress with a *waskat* with beaded panels at the shoulders and a full *kamiz* skirt were bright with colour.

"*Salaam alaikum,*" Jack said.

"*Wa-Alaikum-Salaam,* Windrush sahib," the woman said in a very familiar voice. "I told you there was a man I wanted."

"Zufash!" Jack said.

"I am she," Zufash said.

Jack stared at the woman he had escorted with Roberts' column. "I thought you were Zamar Khan's daughter," he said.

"I am Zamar Khan's daughter." Zufash held Jack's gaze. "You killed my father."

"I did." Jack wondered if Zufash would demand that Batoor sought *badal*. The last thing he wanted was Batoor as an enemy.

Zufash nodded. "It is fitting. He killed many men, and you killed him for *badal*. It is our way."

Jack felt relief surge through him. "I am glad you found the man you wanted."

Zufash smiled and withdrew, leaving Jack confused but relieved.

Batoor watched Jack through smiling eyes. "As I said, Windrush, I temporarily needed British help, so I had to treat with them."

"You're a devious man, Batoor Khan," Jack said. He rose. "I'd better be on my way now. My regiment is lacking its colonel, and my escort is growing restless." He nodded to the troop of the Guides that waited at the gate of Batoor's courtyard.

"God go with you, Windrush," Batoor said.

"And may Allah keep you safe, Batoor," Jack responded.

* * *

As Jack left the Khyber and headed for Peshawar and, eventually, Gondabad, he turned back to face Afghanistan. The Guides reined in around him, watching with some curiosity as Jack swept off his sun-helmet and made a low bow to the dark mountainous country where he had spent the past two-and-a-half years.

"Farewell, Afghanistan," he said. "I hope never to see you again."

Yet, for all the horrors he had undergone and the loss of his half-brother and nephew, Jack knew he was taking something of Afghanistan with him. He would never forget Afghanistan's stark beauty and the bravery and honour of its people. *I am leaving a good friend behind in Batoor, and I may never see him again.*

"Come on, lads," Jack said. "Take me home."

* * *

The regiments stood on parade at the maidan at Gondabad. On the right in deference to their seniority in the army list was the Royal Malverns, wearing their glorious scarlet with the blue facings. Each officer and man displayed their medals and the sun-helmets a pristine white under the Indian sun. On the left, the 113th Foot formed up, also in scarlet, but although they would bear comparison with nearly any other line regiment, they could not compete with the perfection of the Royals.

Lieutenant-colonel Jack Windrush sat on his horse in front of the Royals, with newly promoted Lieutenant-colonel Charles Burridge looking proud but slightly awkward in front of the 113th Foot.

Facing both regiments, Major-general Arthur Elliot sat erect on his grey Arab, failing to hide his smile.

"I am here to make two announcements," Elliot said. "The first concerns Lieutenant-colonel Jack Baird Windrush, late of the 113th Foot and now commanding the Royal Malverns."

Jack felt a prickle of apprehension. He did not know why Elliot had called this parade, which had necessitated a great deal of brushing, cleaning, and polishing for two regiments recently returned from an arduous campaign.

"Lieutenant-colonel Jack Windrush, please step forward!"

Jack still rode Tinker, the Kabul pony that had served him so well on Robert's march from Kabul to Kandahar. It looked small beside Elliot's magnificent grey, but Jack refused to part with an animal for which he felt so much affection.

"Lieutenant-colonel Windrush," Elliot began in ringing tones. "For conspicuous bravery during the withdrawal after the action at Maiwand, you are awarded the Victoria Cross. When the overwhelming forces of Ayub Khan were pressing hard on the British rearguard, you took charge of a group of the 66th Foot and then with a gun of the Royal Horse Artillery. On both occasions, you displayed bravery to encourage the men and delay the enemy's advance, allowing General Burrow's force the opportunity to reach safety in Kandahar."

Elliot lifted a small box and displayed the bronze Maltese cross with its red ribbon. The obverse had a standing lion and the motto, *For Valour*.

Jack stood still as Elliot pinned the medal to his chest. "Well done, Jack. It's about time the country recognised what you've done for them."

"Thank you, sir," Jack said. He noticed a ragged looking man with two camels at the edge of the maidan. When Armaghan lifted a hand in salutation, Jack remembered his words.

"I see a pile of bloodied khaki bodies leading to a cross."

Jack started. The horror of Maiwand had gained him the Victoria Cross. Armaghan's vision had been correct, although not in the fashion Jack had expected. When Jack looked again, Armaghan was leaving, with his two camels swaying away from the maidan.

"Three cheers for the colonel!" RSM Deblin shouted, and the men responded, with a few of the more eager throwing their gleaming white sun-helmets in the air.

Is this what it feels like to be popular? Jack glanced down at the bronze cross at his breast. The Victoria Cross was the highest award any British soldier could gain. Formed from the metal of Russian cannon captured at Sebastopol in the Crimean War, only the bravest men earned them for acts of desperate courage.

I am not the bravest of men, Jack told himself. *I don't deserve this medal.*

Elliot waited for silence.

"My second purpose concerns every man in both battalions assembled here," Elliot said. "You may have heard of the Childers Reforms." He explained about the plans to link battalions, tie them to a geographical area, and remove the old-style numbered regiments that had served the army so well.

The men listened with various degrees of attention until Elliot raised his voice. "As from this day, the Royals and the 113th Foot will become the first and second battalion of the Royal Malverns."

Jack anticipated the murmur from the ranks and waited for an outburst of anger. British soldiers valued their traditions and disliked change. Men who had joined the 113th expected to serve with that regiment until they left, they did not expect the army to pitchfork them into a rival unit. On the other hand, men who had joined the Royal Malverns did not wish to be linked with a lowly regiment with less than forty years of existence.

Instead, both regiments began to cheer. Jack felt the relief creeping over him. Their joint actions in Afghanistan had created a bond of unity, such as the Gordon Highlanders and Gurkhas shared. He glanced sideways and met Burridge's eyes and smiled.

I am the colonel of the Royal Malverns, my family regiment, linked with the 113th, a unit where I have spent most of my military career. I have achieved my aim after thirty years of service.

Major-general Elliot saluted, dismounted, and walked towards the officers' mess, leaving Jack with one more ordeal to face. General Hook wished to see him at noon.

"Major Baxter," Jack said, adjusting the old sword at his waist. "Take over the regiment, please." He noticed Helen watching from the veranda of a bungalow and was not surprised when Elliot stopped to talk to her.

* * *

General Hook sighed and drew on his cheroot. "You got rid of Zamar Khan, I hear, Windrush."

"That's right, sir."

"You do know that he wasn't particularly interested in fighting the British. He supported Ayub Khan to take over as

Amir rather than Abdur Rahman, but like many Pashtun maliks, he was a pragmatist. He supported the strongest side."

"Yes, sir. Jack tried to unravel Afghan politics in his head. Then why attack Batoor, who was Abdur Rahman's man?"

"Family honour," Hook said. "Babrakzai is – was – Zamar's cousin and was feuding with Batoor. Zamar supported his family. Then, of course, after Roberts defeated Ayub at Kandahar, Batoor kidnapped Zamar's his daughter for his next wife."

"Batoor kidnapped her? Zufash seemed willing to me."

"Oh, she was a willing victim," Hook said. He swirled the brandy in his glass. "Shall I start at the beginning?"

"Please do." Jack felt his head spin with the ramifications of Afghan power politics and Pashtun family honour.

Hook smiled. "Before you were involved, Zamar Khan arranged that Babrakzai was to be Zufash's husband, but Zufash preferred Batoor and fled before they consummated the marriage."

"Zufash mentioned a threat to mutilate her," Jack murmured.

"There was no such threat. Zufash was lying to gain your sympathy. She escaped from Babrakzai, but rather than run to Batoor, she ended up near Kabul. You helped escort her to Zamar, who brought her back to Babrakzai Khan. That was the real reason for the feud with Batoor. He sent a party to recover her."

"Zar, zan, and zamin," Jack said again. "We think that we're so important out here, but we're only an irritation to the old, old traditions."

Hook smiled. "Precisely, Windrush. Sir Frederick Roberts once gave me his opinion on Afghanistan, and I think he was correct."

"What did he say, sir?"

"He said, and I quote, 'We have nothing to fear from Afghanistan, and the best thing to do is to leave it as much as possible to itself'."

"That's good advice, sir," Jack said. "Let the Afghans sort out their problems without our interference."

Hook gave Jack a hard look over the rim of his glass. "Anyway, Windrush, it all worked out the way we hoped."

"Did it, sir?"

"It did," Hook said. "We have a strong Amir in Afghanistan who will not allow the Russians to interfere, and we control the Khyber Pass, the main thoroughfare to Kabul. We needed a powerful ally in that part of the world to keep the Khyber open, and by helping Batoor with Zufash and some military aid, we got Batoor Khan." Hook sounded pleased with himself. "Also, we have a soldier that the Pashtun respect."

"Colonel Warburton," Jack said. "He knows more about the Pashtun than any soldier in the British army."

"Warburton is more a political agent and a diplomat. We wanted a fighting soldier." Hook pointed at Jack. "That's you. When the next trouble with the Pashtuns blows up – and it will – we will send you to negotiate. A man who uses Pashtunwali and who has a reputation for military efficiency could turn the scales."

"What happened to Kandahar," Jack asked. "I thought we wanted to hold onto Kandahar."

Hook shook his head. "Bluff and counter bluff, my boy. We used Kandahar as a sweetie for the Amir. If he did as we wished, we would allow him control. By defeating his enemies, Ayub Khan and Zamar Khan, we showed Rahmed Khan our good faith, and then we handed him Kandahar to complete his kingdom." [1] Hook's smile was the smirk of a hunting leopard. "Everything went according to plan. There was a small blip with that Maiwand fiasco, but we turned that to our advantage by creating a national hero of Bobs Roberts and a local hero with your good self."

"Did you need a national hero?"

"Undoubtedly, my naïve soldier. The British army is divided into factions. The African faction, or Wolseley Ring, has Sir

Garnet Wolseley, known as our only general. Now the Indian faction has Bobs, our other general, hero of the Kabul to Kandahar march. And we have you."

"It's all very cynical," Jack said.

"Life, and politics, is a cynical game, Windrush. Out here, all the manoeuvring with Russia is one great game, and we are all pawns." Hook lifted his glass. "Cheer up, my boy, you entered this war as a major and came out as a lieutenant-colonel with a Victoria Cross and an enhanced reputation. You should be grateful."

Jack thought of the dead men at Maiwand, the heroic sacrifice of the 66th Foot, and Crimea's gallant death. He relived Roberts' unsupported march and Zamar Khan's men fighting their desperate retreat against Martini Henrys and case shot.

I am grateful I survived. That's all anybody can ask in any war. Look to your front, trust the man at your back and pray to your God.

* * *

It had been a long time since Jack was home. He could hardly believe he was back where he belonged. They sat in their bungalow at Gondabad with the sounds and smells of India creeping in the open windows as Mary looked at him across the table. "I don't care that you are now Lieutenant-colonel Windrush VC with all the prestige in the world. To me, you'll always be Captain Jack."

"That'll do me," Jack said. "That will do me."

ABOUT THE AUTHOR

Born in Edinburgh, Scotland and educated at the University of Dundee, Malcolm Archibald writes in a variety of genres, from academic history to folklore, historical fiction to fantasy. He won the Dundee International Book Prize with 'Whales for the Wizard' in 2005.

Happily married for 35 years, Malcolm has three grown children and lives in darkest Moray in northern Scotland, close by a 13th century abbey and with buzzards and deer more common than people.

★ ★ ★

To learn more about Malcolm Archibald and discover more Next Chapter authors, visit our website at www.nextchapter.pub.

NOTES

Chapter 8

1. An Afghan source (Sirdar M. A K Effendi) gives Ayub Khan's numbers as high as 25,000, which may be an exaggeration.

Chapter 10

1. The final stand of eleven men, two lieutenants and nine privates of the 66th Foot and Bombay sepoys excited the admiration of the Afghans. The defenders charged out of the compound, faced their enemy and died fighting. Even the ghazis were scared to approach, so the Afghans shot the British down. Ayub Khan's men were so impressed by the bravery of the British soldiers that they built a monument in their honour.
2. Bobbie was the dog of Lance sergeant Peter Kelly. Bobbie (or Bobby) survived the action at Maiwand and returned home to Britain. Queen Victoria later presented him with the Afghanistan Medal. Bobby was not the only animal honours, for Victoria also awarded Roberts' horse with the Afghanistan Medal, with four clasps.
3. An Afghan shell blew open the RHA treasure chest during the retreat. I altered this incident to include Jack.

Chapter 20

1. For this action, Major George White was awarded the Victoria Cross.
2. The Battle of Kandahar was the British final victory and the last battle of the Second Afghan War. The British killed an estimated 1,200 Afghans, losing forty dead and 228 wounded. Roberts also captured all of Ayub Khan's artillery, including the two guns the Afghans captured at Maiwand.
3. Although Roberts won various victories in Afghanistan, his uncontested march from Kabul to Kandahar brought him public fame. He became one of two well-known British generals, the other being Sir Garnet Wolseley. Both were from Ireland, and they were intense rivals.
4. Ayub Khan was not responsible for Maclaine's death. Ayub left the camp about eleven, giving instructions not to kill Maclaine and the other prisoners. Either the guard or some other person disobeyed the order.

NOTES

Chapter 21

1.

Chapter 31

1. Ayub Khan was not yet finished. In July 1881, he raised another army, defeated an Afghan government army and captured Kandahar. Abdur Rahman called up 12,000 regular Afghan regulars, plus some tribal lashkars and defeated Ayub. Some units of Ayub's army deserted to the Amir, which possibly affected the outcome. Ayub Khan fled to Persia (now Iran), where he threatened more trouble until 1888, when the British granted him political asylum in India.